I0761628

SUPERFAN

ALSO BY JENNY TINGHUI ZHANG

Four Treasures of the Sky

SUPERFAN

JENNY
TINGHUI
ZHANG

This is a work of fiction. All the characters, organizations, and events portrayed in this novel are either products of the author's imagination or used fictitiously.

Printed in the United States of America. For information, address Flatiron Books, 120 Broadway, New York, NY 10271. EU Representative: Macmillan Publishers Ireland Ltd, 1st Floor, The Liffey Trust Centre, 117–126 Sheriff Street Upper, Dublin 1, DO1 YC43.

www.flatironbooks.com

Designed by Leah Carlson-Stanisic

Library of Congress Cataloging-in-Publication Data

Names: Zhang, Jenny Tinghui, author.
Title: Superfan : a novel / Jenny Tinghui Zhang.
Description: First edition. | New York, NY : Flatiron Books, 2026.
Identifiers: LCCN 2025021321 | ISBN 9781250369666 (hardcover) | ISBN 9781250452689 (international, sold outside the U.S. subject to rights availability) | ISBN 9781250369673 (ebook)
Subjects: LCSH: Fans (Persons)—Fiction | Boy bands—Fiction | LCGFT: Fiction | Novels
Classification: LCC PS3626.H364 S87 2026
LC record available at https://lccn.loc.gov/2025021321

First U.S. Edition: 2026

First International Edition: 2026

10 9 8 7 6 5 4 3 2 1

For those who live with love

I'll follow you until you love me

—"paparazzi,"
lady gaga

I love my fans . . . and my what

—"idol," bts

How foolish men are! To see nothing but beauty in what is clearly evil! And how benighted to dismiss as absurd what is clearly well intended!

—pu songling
(translated by john minford)

2014

MINNIE

The boys are there, waiting for her. They have always been waiting for her.

She is browsing the front page of a video sharing site when she sees them: draped in white, frozen, yet exploding. *ASIAN BOY BAND STUNS AT LOCAL MUSIC FESTIVAL,* the title of the video says. Normally, she would ignore a declaration like this, preferring to decide for herself the things that stun her, but their faces—which are undeniably lovely—give her pause. Two million views. Uploaded ten days ago. She cannot fathom the numbers and she cannot fathom the boys. Between *Josh Tries to Eat Everything at Whataburger* and this, she chooses this.

The music begins. The four of them leap forward, stage lights rolling off their bodies as if unable to latch on. The video was recorded on a cell phone, the picture peppered with grain, but the boys remain clean. Their hair is the color of acorn, honey, liquid silver, and midnight; their bodies are sheathed in white fabric. She can feel them through the laptop screen, count all the pixels that come together to form their sublime faces. She imagines, too, the pulsing tangle of pixels beneath their clothes, the ones that make up their blood, their muscles, their precious bones. The boys are tall and lanky, the kind of model bodies that are 90 percent legs and the rest pure charisma. Glossy boys, unstoppable boys.

It starts like this, then. With a video of boys.

The boys are singing and dancing, gliding and spinning, and glowing, really *glowing,* and she is glowing with them, because between her and them, there is no longer a laptop screen. There is no audience, no band, no crew in the wings. Not the concept of distance, not even air. There is only them and all the things she wants, which is to be with them, to love them and for them to love her.

The performance ends. The crowd screams their approval, the sound a white-hot current that shoots back and forth between her ears. The boys bow for the final time, each face softened with a smile. They press their palms to their lips and wave.

The screen fades to black and she is left staring at her own stunned face.

She replays the video four times more, watching one boy at a time. She tracks his dance, his song, the shimmer of his face as he struts up and down the stage. She follows these faultless boys, these irresistible boys, these boys with voices pitched to an octave of angels, and she feels herself falling and rising at the same time.

I have no idea who these boys are, one comment below the video says, *but I'm in love with them.*

HALO'S POWER!!! reads another. *MURDER ME KING!*

I'm drowning in so much bliss.

Why are their bodies built like that? Are they telling me to die?

And on and on, for one thousand more.

A new hunger blooms, the desire to know every single thing about these boys until she brims with them. She opens a tab and types the band's name into the search bar. A column of results greets her: fan-made websites; web-encyclopedia entries; message boards; blog rings; video compilations. All created in the past few days by fans like her (can she call herself a fan already? It feels that way). She skims through the results, and then, knowing that she may very well never come back from whatever lies ahead, clicks the first one.

She consumes. Until the light drains from her dorm room and the only source left is the glare of the laptop, illuminating her slack face. Until a whine in her stomach reminds her that she has not eaten in hours. The dining hall is surely closed, but it no longer matters, because the boys are here now and she can eat her fill with them. Every interview she reads brings them closer. Every video she watches makes them more hers. When she goes to sleep that night, she is surrounded by the boys, their faces warm and handsome, their hands all holding her, rubbing her, passing off some of their magic onto her so that she, too, might shine the way they do.

In class the next day, she cannot concentrate. The professor asks her to read a poem out loud, Borges, and she does so, but the words fatten and blur into spongy macaroni. *You are invulnerable*, she recites. *Didn't they deliver (those forces that control your destiny) the certainty of dust?* Beyond the words, she imagines a screen on which play images of the boys, their necks taut and pearled with sweat. *Lovely*, the professor intones. She is inclined to agree.

The sound of the carillon bells releases her back to them. She shoots through campus to her dorm and climbs into bed with her laptop on her thighs, searching for more information. What she knows so far: There is Minwoo, the responsible leader; Denim, the affable all-American; Jelly, the ethereal dancer; and Halo, the aloof and mysterious bad boy. The four of them, together, make HOURglass.

Those are my boys, she thinks as she listens to them sing to her. She has never done drugs before—she has not had the chance—but she *has* known what it is to love: a detective book series, a gorgeous actor, the soft spot behind her first dog's ears. Those had been her obsessions, briefly, but they wither next to the imperative of the boys. She imagines this must be what they mean when they call it taking a "hit." But there is nothing dangerous about it, nothing nefarious. The boys stand on every side of her, radiating love, and she feels it course through her own body, plumping her up, making her skin smooth, her lashes long, her lips pink, until she is the most beautiful version of herself, one everyone can love, one even she, herself, can love.

WE ARE YOURS, AND YOU ARE? the boys ask in one video. *OURS*, the crowd shouts back. A call and response that is almost holy. It is not clear to her who belongs to whom, but this is the way it is supposed to be: They belong to each other.

When the day is over, she knows what Minwoo's favorite fruit is (pineapple), where Denim went to high school (a private performing arts academy in California), the qualities Jelly looks for in his soulmate (someone who can cook), and what scares Halo the most (ghosts). The boys feel like a place where she can live a while, perhaps forever. They could be her friends, her brothers, her lovers. In fact, she thinks, they are all those things combined.

In the hallway, a door opens and she hears the laughter of two girls who occupy the room next to hers. One of them has just returned from a study date and recounts the titillating details to the other. Their conversation forces her to reenter the atmosphere. She remembers just how far away she is from the boys—they in Los Angeles, she in Austin. They up so high in the sky, she tangled in her comforter. It is a heavy realization, an unwelcome disruption of the happiness she has cultivated for the past forty-eight hours. She rises to lock her door, even though no one ever comes to her room, and returns to bed, where she watches videos of the boys until she falls asleep.

EASON

They are on in five when the tremors come. His left hand succumbs first, then his right, until both hands vibrate a violent magic. To anyone watching, it would seem that he is casting a spell, but they would be wrong. The spell has been cast by something outside himself.

He clenches his hands into fists, but nausea is not far behind. The nearest trash can is back in the green room, which feels worlds away from where he is now, so he dives behind a handcart full of stage lights and retches there, wincing as milky bile splashes on the floor. The smell of it rises, hot and sour.

"Dude, come on," a stagehand groans, but there is no time for him to clean the mess or apologize. His makeup is ruined and there is residue on his shirt cuff. As if on cue, a stylist appears beside him, swiping gloss on his lips and patting down his cheeks. She presses something hard into his left hand. Looking down, he finds a breath mint.

2 MINS, the display monitor signals.

The curtain is lifting, floating upward like a ghoul, as the announcer takes the stage once more. "You're in for a treat," he hears her tell the crowd. He pops the mint.

Nearby, his bandmates run through their last-minute rituals—for Minwoo, it is a prayer, and for Colt, three knocks on wood. Julian cranks his head left and right, then jumps in place. For Eason, there is no pre-show ritual, because this is the first performance of his life. Instead, he remembers a trick his sister once taught him as a remedy for nerves: Take a deep breath in, form an infinitesimal hole with your lips, then push the exhale through. *It's called an embouchure*, she told him. *That's how brass players get their sound.* He does this now, closing his eyes and feeding the air in his body through the opening between his lips.

It works. He opens his eyes and sees the four of them anew: Minwoo is *Minwoo* and Colt is *Denim* and Julian is *Jelly* and he—he is *Halo*. The tremors are gone, as is the nausea. The four of them stand in the dark, beacons newly lit to burn into the night.

Out they go, to a pavilion with a sweeping, domed roof and stone steps leading out onto a dew-struck lawn. The audience is there, waiting for him. Perhaps they have always been waiting for him. He looks out at the bodies spilling over the grassy field. When he was young, he always wondered what celebrities felt in front of a crowd such as this. Now, gazing into a mirror of two thousand reflecting his own wild hope, he finally has some idea: the *need* for them to love him. This is all he can think when the music begins and the beeps inside his in-ears cue him to his starting position. In this moment, nothing matters more.

The first song ends. Time is precious—they only have eight minutes to capture the audience's hearts and make enough of an impression that they might become lifelong superfans. As the second song cues in, he feels himself relaxing, his body settling into the playful movements of the choreography. Eight eight-counts of footwork, then a body roll before unleashing the bubblegum charm of the chorus. A few women in the front row go nuts for it, reaching for him with outstretched hands. "I LOVE YOU!" they shriek. But they do not know him enough to love him, not yet. There is still so much he has to earn. He sends them a wink, a reflex from his training, and they scream even louder, their voices verging on a shatter.

Then it is all over. Eight minutes goes by too quickly, he thinks, dazed. The display monitor facing them flashes *GOODBYE* in warning. The four of them scatter around the stage, waving at the audience until their wrists go soft. *Thank you*, he mouths to a group of girls bobbing up and down against the barricade. Their faces are a cross-pollination of stage lights, lit in purple, lemon, baby blue, and gold. They look beautiful, he thinks. Like flowers opening in the face of a splendid sun.

Everything will change. He knows this with unshakable certainty as they run off the stage. Minwoo is beaming, Colt is whooping, and Julian returns the high fives that every stagehand throws at them. *HOURGLASS! HOURGLASS!* the audience chants behind them. A name they did not know eight minutes ago, but will now remember forever. The backstage area, which once felt suffocating, now expands with possibility. As he stands there with his bandmates, the four of them panting and spent, he realizes why. *They* are the splendid sun.

POST #28

I discovered the most wonderful thing today.

I was looking for something to watch during my lunch break. I like to watch shows when I eat, because it makes me feel like I'm with friends and not alone. I usually stick with sitcoms, but I just finished the one I was watching and felt burned out from fake laughter.

That's when they found me. I don't know how, but I came across a video of four boys. They were singing and dancing like any other boy band, but they were not like any other boy band. They were the most beautiful things I have ever seen. I couldn't look away. And all of a sudden, I felt the joy of just living life. Like life was worthwhile, because these boys existed in that same life.

Where did they come from? How did they get here? I look around at everything I have ever loved and it all pales in comparison to them. I only wish they had been in my life longer, so that I might have had a longer time to be happy.

MINNIE

Her name is Minnie, short for nothing. Like most Chinese kids who immigrated to the States in their single-digit years, Minnie had no say in what her English name would be. She did not know any English back then, so why would she have a preference? Besides, she already had a name, 亮心, one that she was proud of because she thought it described her well: someone who had a bright and clear heart, where that brightness was not a marker of her intellect, but evidence of the way she went about the world, with hope and earnest curiosity.

It was with this same bright heart that she answered *Disney World* when her parents asked what she most wanted to do when she arrived in America. Because every kid knew what Disney World was, even if they did not speak English.

That had been a mistake. From then on, she was Minnie. Her parents had bestowed the name upon her as if it were an invaluable gift. But as the plane descended into the Denver International Airport, she knew that this new English name was inferior to the one she already had—that it was trying to diminish and replace her, and even without knowing all the things it meant, she knew that she did not like it.

By the end of her first week of school, Minnie was aware of all the connotations of her new name, too. None of them felt right. She was not miniature, as her name suggested, but taller than most kids her age, her legs shooting out like bamboo from the jeans in the children's, then juniors, and eventually women's clothing sections. Nor was she a cartoon mouse. But in their new home of Colorado Springs, she had suddenly become conditioned to be quiet like a mouse. Her white classmates, initially curious about the newcomer from China (a word they never said normally, instead elongating the syllables so that it sounded like *hyena*), were certain she possessed some otherworldly power that she would eventually reveal to them, a mystical mixture of martial arts that involved karate, flying, and dragons. They were disappointed. Instead, this girl from Hyena was simply a weirdo with halting English and slatted eyes. They made fun of her, and once they got tired of that, they did something worse: They ignored her. She took these abuses, and each time, she felt her voice getting smaller even as she continued to grow taller, the distance between her and everyone else increasing not just in height, but in those delicate ways so felt by young girls.

How is our big poet? her Lao Lao and Lao Ye would ask when they called. *Tell us again the story of the dog who wanted to grow up.* Her grandparents remembered her as she had left them in China: a storyteller. While the other kids played chase during breaktime, she had held court by the monkey bars, regaling the smaller ones with made-up tales of wolves in the woods, cats that could fly, a dog traveling the world in a quest to be great. She learned something powerful during those early years: Respect and redemption could be achieved with something as simple as a story, as having the space to be able to speak.

But this was no longer the case in America. In America, her mouth was full from all the things she wanted to say, but they were dammed in by a language she could not grasp. Was the wolf *in* or *on* or *at* the woods? Did the cat fly *through* or *with* the sky? The dog who wanted to be great—there was no English idiom to describe the vastness of his desire.

By the time Minnie got to high school, she was at the top of her class in English. But she had stopped trying to speak and her stories did not return. In class discussions, where participation was mandatory, her classmates filled the quiet with meaningless phrases like, "to piggyback off of . . ." or "going off of that . . . ," and Minnie could only nod. Her classmates parroted each other, whereas she prided herself on her deep and intricate interpretations of the texts they read—but it was all lost on her peers. Once, during a discussion of *Pride and Prejudice*, she wondered out loud if there was a difference between being alone and being lonely. The discussion faltered—no one seemed to want to piggyback or go off of what she had to say. That was okay, though. Minnie was off to college with a major in English Literature at the University of Texas in Austin, and she could not wait for all the things she could say then.

"I keep thinking," her mother mused when they moved Minnie into the dorm. "When you move out next year, you won't be the same as you are now."

"And all for the better," her father said. He did not like the sheet of dust on the window blinds, nor the mealy texture of the walls. "This time next year, she'll be a scholar."

She watched them drive away, realizing that this was the first time she would truly be alone. When the U-Haul finally disappeared, she turned to face her dorm, clutching her laundry bag and meal card to her chest.

This was what she had been waiting for her whole life. In all the movies she had seen, in all the books she read, college was where it was supposed to happen. Here was where she would find lifelong friends. Here was where she would blossom into the winning personality she was sure she possessed. Here was where she would meet the love of her life. Here, most importantly, was where she could reclaim her bright heart. It was all beginning now, and the promise of her new life filled her up with such joy that she hardly registered the tinge of sadness at the thought of her parents returning to their home in Colorado Springs, the house now quieter and emptier. But that was fine. It was even necessary. Some things have to die in order for others to flourish. And that was what this was—in place of her childhood, an invitation to flourish.

The Honors Quad is a cluster of four buildings—Littlefield, Andrews, Blanton, and Carothers—located on the north side of campus. These are the nicer dorms for cheap, its residents like to gloat as they point to the sun-soaked courtyard, which the four buildings share. Unlike the rich kids whose parents paid for posher dorms like San Jac and Duren, everyone in the Quad was there because they were in an honors program, thus earning their residence through talent and intellect.

Minnie lives in the Honors Quad, although this, much like her name, is a mistake; due to a confusion of first initials and last names, she found herself placed on the second floor of Carothers dormitory despite the fact that she is not an honors student. An additional administrative error made her the only resident on the floor without a roommate. It was a blessing, she decided in the beginning; the room was small, and with a roommate, there would barely be enough acreage to stretch out her arms without imposing on space that did not belong to her. But as the days went on and she heard laughter pealing out from beneath the doors surrounding hers, she began to suspect that she was missing out on something crucial.

It's impossible to live here and be bored, the resident assistant told them on their first day. *There's always something going on.* This was true: There were so many clubs to join and meetups to meet up, and all of it was displayed in kaleidoscopic color on the bulletin board located on the first floor of each dorm.

And yet she was bored. The postings were always the same: athletic club tryouts, study groups for courses she would never take, meetups for a religion called the Flying Spaghetti Monster. Nothing that ever said: *me.*

What did: Books. Writing. Sunsets. The esoteric quotes about life, love, and sensibility that she collected on Tumblr. Cozy bookstores on a gloomy day. The word "petrichor." Wisteria, or the color of it.

And now, the boys.

Tonight, after she returns from class, she glances at the bulletin board as she does every night. No new colors, which means no new postings. She will try again tomorrow.

On the second floor, she finds ten girls in pajamas sitting outside her door. Some she recognizes from rooms along the hall, but a few must have come from other dorms in the Quad. She wonders when the girls in her hall had time to make friends in other buildings, it being only the second week of classes.

The girls' heads snap up when they hear her approach. For a delirious moment, she lets herself believe that they are here for her. But then, one by one, their heads fall and return to each other and she remembers: She is a stranger to them.

"So no cover?"

"Obviously."

"It is a truth universally acknowledged that freshmen get in to everything for free because we're young and hot."

"My sister used to live at the Co-op. She says their parties are insane."

"Okay, we're in."

"Group trip?"

"Group trip!"

The girls collapse against each other and stay that way, giggling. It is not weird or awkward; they already know each other well enough to welcome the pressure of each body. She finds herself staring at them with a dumb grin on her face, as if she were a part of their laughter, too. But then one of the girls looks back up at her, and she catches herself.

"Um, sorry. This is my door."

What she wants to say instead: Hi. I'd like to go to this party with you all, too.

The girls exchange raised eyebrows and a few of them snicker. Others pull faces of exaggerated embarrassment. One by one, they rise, their pajamas levitating with them.

"Oh my god, we're the worst."

"We must be so annoying."

"I feel like we're already drunk."

Before she has a chance to tell them that actually, it's fine, they can stay outside her door for as long as they want and can she join, they saunter down the hallway and repark themselves at the very end, in front of a new door, their laughter bouncing back to her and disappearing before she can grab hold.

EASON

Overnight sensation. That was what the news pundits, late-night hosts, and internet journalists called them. The day after the festival, someone had uploaded a recording of their eight-minute set to a video sharing site. By the end of the week, Eason had seen his face so much that he no longer recognized himself, as if he were a word that had been spoken too much and now sounded wrong. *Who are the boys of HOURglass?* Everyone wanted to know. They watched as their social media followers ballooned from 2,000 to 400,000 and their publicists went into overdrive fielding requests for interviews. An up-and-coming actress mentioned them on the red carpet. A singing competition on primetime asked if they might like to perform for boy band week. The record label said yes. So, ten days after the music festival, they found themselves back in the practice room.

"Your shoulders are wrong," the choreographer, a small coil of a man, tells him during today's practice. "Relax, please. It's ta-TA-ta, not ta-ta-TA." He shows Eason the difference, stabbing the air with each shoulder like a pike.

Eason adjusts. The others are wet clay, their bodies primed for shaping and reshaping, but he has always been the outlier. He started with nothing. To make up for it, the record label paid for over one thousand hours of private dance lessons before he was deemed somewhat decent. Dancing, he came to realize, was nothing more than following counts and memorizing movements, a simple game of mimicry, and with that knowledge, he was able to keep up. It was difficult, but not impossible. His instructor had seen something in him that could be manipulated into talent: His hardness, which he had been cultivating since he left home, could translate into power. That was how he made up for his weaknesses, by always pushing himself to mirror an explosion. If he couldn't be perfect, then at least he would be earth-shattering.

Today, his reliance on power is falling apart. The song in question is a lament to an ex-lover, a slow drip of R&B and electronica. Rather than energy and excess, this choreography asks that they isolate one body part at a time while pulling back the rest, as if resisting the dance but for one wrist, one hip, one toe. The song is about waiting so long for something, only to realize you had it the whole time. The song is about love. In that way, they must express an endless yearning—the kind of desire that could run a city dry—all in the rise and fall of a shoulder, the turn on a heel, the step ball change.

"It should look easy," the choreographer tells Eason. "But you're making it look like work."

"Maybe *I'm* not the problem," he snaps back.

"You're too tense," Julian says. He takes the bottom of Eason's shirt between his fingers and shakes it back and forth. In the mirror, Eason's torso ripples as if made of snakes. "Relax the parts of your body that you don't need." There was that word again: *relax*. From the choreographer's mouth, it was a taunt, but from Julian's, it was an answer.

By the time practice ends, their bodies, each its own furnace, have fogged up the windows, blurring Sunset Boulevard into a slide of gray watercolor. Colt jogs to the mirrors, pulling out a Ziploc baggie of sea salt from his duffel. He sprinkles a few grains into his water bottle and gulps it all down, the shiny bulb of his throat bouncing gratefully with each swallow. Minwoo limps over to join him, each step accompanied by a wince. A motorcycle accident as a teenager left him with short stamina and aches meant for someone triple his age. But this, their manager Brooks was always reminding him, was no excuse. "You're the leader," Brooks would say. "You have to lead."

Eason remains in front of the mirror, practicing the shoulder isolation from before. He knows the choreographer is right: He had indeed been doing the movement wrong. It was the lingering pain in his shoulder that prevented him from getting a full rotation, but he had never told anyone about the pain, just as he never told anyone where his tremors came from. He would not be seen as weak, or worse—defective.

Julian stays, too, practicing the move with him. "Try bringing your chest forward. Then you can cheat the rotation."

Julian moves the way the sun does in the early hours of morning, so easy in its ascent that you would not notice the world has flipped from darkness to light until you are surrounded by it, part of that light, too. Some people are born with bodies meant for work, Eason's mother used to say, and some are meant for comfort. Some are meant to suffer. If he were to believe her, then Julian's body was meant to be on a stage, twisting and spinning and propelling, his body the greatest proof that perhaps they were all built for a purpose, and that when it was right, it was perfect.

Eason tries again, leaning his chest forward as Julian instructed. His shoulder comes around obediently, the familiar pinch more bearable than before.

"You've got it. Let's drill it in."

Square up. Core tight. They do it ten times more. Julian puts the music back on and they run it from the top, then another five. Eason does as Julian says, following the baton of his voice, a strange vernacular that only dancers seem to know: *di-no-saur, ba-ba-ba, zhuzh-zhuzh-zha, and-wash-your-hair-out.* This is the way it has always been. In their nine months of training together, it was Julian who stayed behind after practice, leading him through the movements again and again, a teacher he never asked for, but needed all the same. *Stop thinking so hard. Your body already knows the words, now speak in full sentences.*

"See," Julian says, finally stilling. "Easy."

Eason squares his hips and wrings his shoulders once more for insurance. This time, his reflection follows without protest. Julian claps out the tempo and the studio fills with his voice, then the voices of Minwoo and Colt, chiming in: *ta-TA-ta, plant-a-tree, ba-ba-ba, and-cry-your-heart-out.* That's it, Eason, they tell him when he is finished. You killed it.

◦ ◦ ◦

The singing competition tapes at eight in the morning, so they are in hair and makeup by four. The makeup artist tells him to close his eyes and he obeys, letting her swipe black shadow across his lids. When he opens them again, the hollows of his cheeks are more pronounced and his eyes are ringed in smoke. He wonders why they have made him look like a dead thing. In the chair next to him, an assistant holds Colt, who has fallen asleep, up by the temples, so that his makeup artist can finish applying contour. The room is hot with hairspray and rollers and the sweat of the stylists, who flit between the four of them like moths. Their hushed frenzy only adds to the twist inside his belly—the music festival had been nerve-racking, but this will be their first appearance on national TV. There is the performance to think of, but there is another consideration: that he will finally be seen, not just by everybody but by *her*, and is he ready for that?

At least, he thinks, eyes passing over Minwoo, Colt, and Julian, *I will not be alone.*

Out on the soundstage, the four of them click into formation: Minwoo at the front, Colt behind, Julian following, and Eason at the rear. When Minwoo finishes the first verse, he turns and saunters to the back of the line, letting Colt take the front for the pre-chorus. The cameramen circle him, filling their lenses with his baby blues. Then the chorus hits and Colt moves away. Julian slides into place. Two giant cameras attached to cranes lurch forward. Julian finishes, spins out and glides past, leaving Eason exposed.

The giant cameras on cranes see him now. They pick up his scent, a tangle of mania and acidic nerves, and they descend. The studio lights burn his face as he dances for his life, the shoulder movement finally perfected. The audience goes crazy for him, but he stays locked on the cameras. One of them comes up to his left side, a black hole in his periphery, and he wills himself not to notice it, to keep going, keep pushing, but when he cannot stand it anymore, he dares to peer at it, through it, shooting past the lens to the other side, where he can see himself as everyone else will, as *she* will, and god does he look skinny, god does he look raw, god does he look mad. His lips are mouthing the lyrics and his body is on stage, but inside he is all tremor and he knows, he *knows* that when she sees him later on her flickering screen, she will also see the truth: that he is still that scared little boy, same as he ever was.

MINNIE

September's humidity gives way to the tantrums of October, bringing with it a false fall. In the morning, clouds the color of concrete hang low in the sky, threatening rain, but the sun always returns by the afternoon, snatching away any hopes of cooler weather. Another day spent baking, Minnie thinks. Her professors call this year "a scorcher" and then laugh in a disturbed way when they remember that they have been saying the same thing every year. She misses the fall in Colorado, how the leaves would have turned to their sunset colors by now, the air snapping with the first promise of cold. In Texas, there is no such thing as fall. There is no such thing as winter either, she learns from those who grew up here. There is just an interminable summer that does not relent. Summer exists in January, in March, in October. Summer is never-ending. For this reason, Minnie begins to hate the idea of summer.

Inside an unused classroom in the old anthropology building, Minnie sits in a circle of desks, waiting for instruction. It is a recruitment meeting for a zine, led by a senior named Anna Peng. Minnie saw the flyer pinned to the dorm bulletin board earlier that week, and the sight sent a shock through her: *NEW ZINE LOOKING FOR ARTISTS && WRITERS <<ON THE FRINGES>>. FIRST MEETING WEDNESDAY @@ 7:00PM.* She dismissed it at first—she was not even sure what a zine was. But as she went about her day, the loud, cheeky fuchsia of the flyer refused to leave her mind. Of all things, she paired it with the boys, who had stepped on stage at that music festival and set the world alight. *We are yours and you are ours*, they were always telling her. To be their fan—and deserving of being called their fan—was to demonstrate the same courage they did. At least, that was the unspoken agreement between her and them: When the boys did hard things, they made it easier for her to do hard things, too, as if they were an elixir she could drink to make herself stronger.

Anna Peng is skinny and angular, and carries herself with the defiance of someone who has constantly been told to "tone it down." At the top of the hour, she walks to the center of the desk circle with a ruler held erect. "You should know this isn't *The Daily Texan*," she tells them, ruler bouncing with each word. The tops of her ears are pierced with safety pins that stick out in points, making her look like an elf. "If you came here because you want to report on what the rotary club is doing for charity, then you should probably leave."

Minnie looks around. There are five of them, herself included. No one moves.

"Cool. Then we all agree to fight the good fight together."

Anna is a double design and philosophy major in her final year. The zine is her magnum opus, a mixed-media thesis exploring the intersection of publication design, storytelling, and technology, and she has grand visions of breaking some invisible boundary that Minnie has yet to understand. "Zine culture was a major form of protest and community in the '90s," she tells them. "But people say zines are dead. I beg to differ."

Introductions come next. They take turns calling out their names and majors and what their theme song would be if a movie were made about their lives. A husky-voiced junior named Kate goes first, followed by Harrison, a freshman in the same design program as Anna. Minnie tries to concentrate on their responses, but she feels her heart quicken as her turn nears. After the sophomore next to her introduces himself as Akash and lists N.E.R.D.'s "Hypnotize U" as his theme song, the room goes silent, waiting for her.

"My name is Minnie," she stammers. "I'm an English major, and my theme song would be—"

"It's hard to hear you," Harrison, the other freshman, says. "Did you say Mindy?"

She repeats herself. Alone, her voice sounds flat and distant, as if passing through a body that is not hers.

"Is that short for something?" Harrison wants to know.

Anna spins to face him with the ruler. "What we're not going to do is ask people to justify themselves. Minnie told us her name is Minnie, so that's what we'll call her."

They spend the rest of the meeting discussing Anna's vision for the inaugural issue, which will coincide with Lunar New Year in February. The words *mixed-media*, *subversive*, and *irreverent* dive in and out of Minnie's consciousness like small birds. She wants to catch one. She wants to understand what this all means.

"When people read our zine," Anna tells them, "I want them to feel like something has changed. Do you understand?" The group nods, their faces resolute.

The meeting comes to an end. Minnie stays in her seat. No, she does not understand. It would be better to back out now. She looks to Anna, who is furiously typing on her laptop, and rises from her desk. "Thanks for this," she says, "but I think I committed too soon. I'm so busy this semester, I won't have time to work on much else."

"Really?" Anna's brows knit at her laptop. "That's disappointing."

"So, um, I'm going to head out. If that's okay."

"I mean, I can't stop you," Anna says. "But you'll need to reassign your piece to someone else. Them's the rules." She looks up and her eyes meet Minnie's, in what Minnie recognizes as a challenge.

She turns. Harrison is putting together a mood board for the cover and Kate is already deep in research. Akash, the boy who sat next to her, is unraveling his headphones, a steno pad perched on his lap. Which is worse: bearing her discomfort or disrupting one of their lives and risking their annoyance?

"Never mind," she murmurs, turning back around. "I think I can manage."

Anna smirks and returns to her laptop. "Your first draft is due in December."

On Tuesdays and Thursdays, Minnie's classes end at 4:15 in the afternoon. She walks from the English building to the dining hall at

Kinsolving, a fifteen-minute trek across what the university calls "the Forty Acres," so named for the original campus, which measured exactly forty acres. In the West Mall, a tree-lined plaza crowded with student clubs offering sign-up sheets and homemade cupcakes, she squeezes along a narrow walkway, ducking and dodging so that she does not walk headfirst into the onslaught of pedestrians, bicycles, scooters, and skateboards moving against her. But this is also her favorite part, where she can see the entirety of campus distilled into this small pocket of bodies as they rush to and from class. Whoever they may be, they are all equalized here in this walkway. She watches the frat boys with their Croakies and Sperry shoes, the sorority girls with their huge T-shirts and running shorts, the business students clicking along in their business heels, the art kids with their portfolios and skinny jeans, the student athletes who loom tall and godlike over everyone else. And, her. She does not yet know to which group she belongs, and every time she walks through the West Mall, she wonders who other people think she is.

Minnie eats dinner at 4:30 P.M., which is exactly when dinner service begins. She likes eating at this time because the dining hall is quiet and empty, and she can sit in a booth against the wall, which shields her from looking like someone who has no friends. She spreads out all her books and makes a great show of eating absentmindedly while doing homework. Eating alone is not so pathetic when you have things to do.

Because the truth is that college is going horribly. After the failed encounter with the girls in her hall and the icy glare of Anna Peng, Minnie is ready to stop trying. It was not always like this; in those first few days, she felt the thrilling possibility of expanding herself, but she also felt the weight of that possibility. She had to choose friends wisely if this was to define the rest of her collegiate life. And so, as others in her dorm made plans to eat or study together, she sat back, watching and waiting for the people who would feel called to her. She wanted something deep and lifelong and pure. But every time she tried to forge such a friendship, she found herself lacking in some way, having missed a crucial moment of entry that would have unlocked the whole equation. When she replayed these interactions later, she felt deep shame. It was as if she could see beyond herself, see the potential that she had to be funny, easygoing, personable, cool—a Minnie with a vibrant inner world that was reflected in her outer world. But in practice, she could never behave beyond her actual self, the one who was afraid of mistakes, who was uncertain and overthinking and too slow to act. By the time October arrived, Minnie realized that everyone had already formed their friend groups. She had waited too long.

College will be the best time of your life, she remembers hearing from teachers, counselors, her own parents. Even from herself. College was the time when you discovered who you were and became the person you were supposed to be. But it was all a lie. College is nothing more than shitty dining hall food and dorms that smell like mold. She hates having to share a bathroom with forty-two others, hates her neighbors for never being there, hates her neighbors when they are there, hates the girl down the hall who sings opera in the shower. She hates everyone for having such a wonderful and easy time. Most of all, she hates herself for hating everything so much.

There is one thing she does not hate.

At midnight, the boys' new single releases on all music platforms. Minnie plugs in her earphones and closes her eyes. The music is upbeat, with a dance club vibe and a killer hook, but the message is sad. *When you don't have anybody / And you want somebody / Can I be somebody / The one you love? / But when I am that somebody / Why does it feel like falling? / Why does it feel like / You'd rather have nothing at all?*

They were made for me, she thinks. How else would they know exactly what I feel?

She listens for the rest of the night—it makes her feel warm and held, and somehow, pink. That is the color she sees when the song plays, a pinkness that pours out from the song and funnels into her. *It's so lonely being lonely, baby*, the boys lament, and she agrees. Somewhere on this campus, the frat boys are crushing beers and the business kids are calculating bottom lines and down the hall, that girl is still singing opera in the shower. And she is here, receiving a signal from the boys through her earphones, one that has traversed distance and time, all so they can tell her: Your loneliness can be good—it can even be great.

POST #76

Have you ever imagined what the boys would be like as boyfriends?

Imagine Minwoo, the perfect man to take home to your parents. Your mother adores him and your father respects him. Imagine Minwoo pulling out your chair and keeping a blanket in his car so you never get cold. He always holds the door for you, and the ten others behind you. Can you blame them for walking through? He's too handsome to not take advantage of.

Imagine Denim and the life of adventure you would lead. He cracks jokes nonstop and compliments your smile when you laugh. Imagine him playing little pranks on you and the punchline always ending with a kiss.

Imagine being with an angel. Or, imagine being with Jelly. Imagine his softness, his sweetness, his silken hair and the feeling of running your hands through it. He takes you out dancing. He buys you roses. He makes you feel so precious you won't remember a time when you felt any other way.

Imagine the one I want most: Halo. He is intense and turbulent and possessive, but all in the name of loving you. The sky could be on fire, but in Halo's arms, everything is okay. Imagine him protecting you. Imagine him dying for you.

EASON

They arrive at the radio station in Burbank to the welcome of fifty fans. Eason counts them all, then counts them again. There are kids, teens, adults in their twenties and thirties. A few who look older than his mother, maybe even his grandmother—if he had known her.

Two months have passed since the music festival, which was more than enough time for the news cycle to move on. A war escalates, a volcano erupts, an eighteen-year-old named Michael Brown is killed by police. Surely, the world would lose interest in their little band. Or so he thought.

At the sight of the black SUVs, the crowd dissolves into screams. Up fly the homemade signs, full mast, declarations in sparkling pink, lavender, and cherry red: JELLY IS MY HUSBAND! FILIPINOS 4 HOURGLASS! I GOT MINWOOED! Bracelets strung with letters spelling out his bandmates' stage names dangle from their wrists. His own stage name, *Halo*, is there, too, and he cannot help but think, this is what will remain of me when I'm gone.

The SUV in front stops and Brooks disembarks with the bodyguards, former pro wrestlers, now on BabyGold Records's payroll for the protection of their most precious jewels. The four of them separate the crowd and a pathway emerges, the back entrance of the radio station now clear. Brooks surveys the work, then gestures to Eason's car.

His hand rattles against the door, the tremors returning. He has only ever seen the fans from the stage, separated by a barricade or security personnel. Seeing them this close opens a new vulnerability: There is no hiding here. As if he knows, Julian reaches over and opens the door for him.

Eason steps out. Earlier that morning, a stylist coiffed his hair, then spun him around to face the mirror, proclaiming him a star, a killer, the kind of man who could command an army with just the twitch of his finger. The stylist was right—when they see him, the fans become hysterical. He takes a few steps and they surge against the outstretched arms of the bodyguards. Brooks grabs him, pulls him to the back door, urging him to get inside, it's too crazy out here, get inside.

He is the first one through. Julian topples in behind him, his sunglasses askew—one of the fan's flailing arms had slammed into his head as he passed by. Then Colt, who looks astonished but pleased, and finally Minwoo, eyes calm and steadfast, but given away by his hands, which clutch his bag as if it were a rope tethering him from free fall.

"I feel," Colt says, "like a Beatle."

Minwoo runs his fingers through his hair, a nervous habit. "I guess we're not nobodies anymore."

The station intern, a mousy twentysomething, guides them to the green room. A gift basket waits on the coffee table, and Colt rifles through the iridescent packaging of crackers and chips and chocolate granola bars before shoving the basket away. Together, they hear the voice of their trainer: *Every bite must be answered for. Calories in, calories out.*

"You okay?" Julian asks Eason. "I stepped on you. Back there."

"I didn't even feel it. How's your eye?"

Julian removes his sunglasses, revealing a grass-blade scratch above his eyebrow. Eason wants to blow it off, send it spiraling away from Julian's otherwise pristine skin. "Could be better."

Brooks appears, his eyes raking Julian's face to inspect the damage. "Little psychos," he says. "Good thing it's radio."

"They were just excited," Eason says, suddenly protective. "They weren't trying to hurt us."

Brooks swings to Eason. "That's funny. You seem to think your opinion matters."

On the couch, Colt clasps his hands behind his head and leans back, taking in the autographs that previous guests scribbled across the ceiling. "Do you think we'll have riders one day? I heard JLo has one that says you have to spray any room she walks into with her own perfume. Otherwise, she's not performing."

"She's JLo," Brooks says. "She's irreplaceable. You're not—not yet."

The day's mandate: a coveted appearance on LA's most-listened-to radio program to promote their upcoming tour, a six-month, forty-eight city marathon. Ten minutes, uninterrupted. It is just enough time to showcase their charisma, followed by a live performance—a one-two punch to feed current fans and capture new ones. The radio host, an edgy, gotcha character named DJ Quicksand, is what Brooks calls a "kingmaker."

The station intern pops her head in to let them know that they will be on shortly. Brooks holds the door open, giving each of them a high five and a slap on the ass as they pass through. "Kill 'em, get 'em, crush 'em, eat 'em."

DJ Quicksand greets them with fist bumps. He looks like a proper punk, with pale skin, inky hair, and cigarette-thin jeans, but his age shows in his sagging face. Somewhere in his sixties, Eason guesses. He reads the wrinkles around the DJ's neck as if counting the rings of a tree.

"The boys of HOURglass." The DJ takes his time with their name, passing it through his teeth. "Isn't this a treat."

Thirty seconds, the red countdown on the wall reads. Eason feels his stomach turn. On stage, he can rely on muscle memory to take over, the kind of divine automation that absolves him of choice, like riding in a car that someone else is driving. Here, in a live interview, all he has to show for himself is just that: himself.

"Welcome back to HOT95.5, you're listening to *The Show* with DJ Quicksand. And boy do we have a treat for you today: We've got an up-and-coming band called HOURglass here in the studio with us."

He presses a button on the switchboard before him. A horn blares for comedic effect. When it ends, the four of them clap, because no one else in the studio claps for them. Colt lets out a whistle that droops, then dies.

"Now, you've been together for about a year and you've just started performing here and there. But this is your first radio show. I have to say, guys"—DJ Quicksand brings a hand dramatically to his chest—"I'm honored."

"So are we," Minwoo says with a practiced laugh. "It's—"

"I called you a band," the DJ says, "but what you really are is a *boy* band and we don't get many boy bands on this show. Maybe because they're actually girls. But if you're here, then you must have some balls." He grins at them, the first of many landmines.

Minwoo grins back. "We're just here to have some fun."

"Oh, we'll have fun," the DJ says. "Now, my producer tells me you're East meets West: You've got the heart of Western boy bands and the training of Korean pop. I've heard of K-pop and let me tell you, I can't stand it. But you guys aren't just K-pop. You're American pop, which is better I guess. But I see three Asian dudes here and I gotta ask the question on everyone's mind: Are your parents disappointed you didn't become doctors?"

Eason glances at Julian. A stone pulses in his cheek, but his face remains placid.

"None of our parents are like that," Minwoo says, still in his good-natured tone. "They're all very supportive."

"How sweet," the DJ says. "My producer also told me you guys still live together." He turns to Colt, leaning in as if the two of them might share a secret. "For you, my guy: What's it like? Do you get sick of eating rice?"

Colt has no answer but to laugh. "Oh man," he says, shaking his head. "You're going to get me in trouble."

The DJ turns his attention to Julian. "Now I know *you* don't eat rice. You're smaller than my ex-wife's brain." A pause here as he presses down a button on the soundboard, which releases the sound of a woman moaning. "What's your secret—Keto? Paleo? Lipo?" He lets out a syrupy burp.

Julian feigns nonchalance. Feigns, Eason knows, because Julian hates comments about his body. "There's no secret. We eat healthy and exercise like anyone else."

Once, after a four-hour dance practice, Brooks forbade them from drinking water due to a photoshoot the next day, giving them ice chips to suck on instead. Dehydration would make their muscles pop, their veins engorge. Eason spent the night with a mouth full of sand.

The DJ turns to Eason, eyes hungry for a show. It is clear to him now: They have not been asked here out of kindness, but to be made fools of. So far, none of them have relented, but it is Eason's turn and he has never been strong like Minwoo, charming like Colt, or slippery like Julian. He feels the skin over his bones sucking in as if someone is squeezing all the air out of him. *I am well trained*, he reminds himself.

"So you're the last one?" the DJ says, scanning him. "I'm having a hard time keeping track. It's not easy telling you guys apart."

As Halo, he is aloof, untouched. As Eason, he is furious.

The DJ smirks. "You look like you want to fight me. Is that what you want, brother? To fight?"

I could do it, Eason thinks. Could launch across the table and spiral my fist into the bastard's throat. The instinct for blood is in him, it has always been in him. He remembers Brooks's imperative as they left the green room: Kill, get, crush, eat.

His bandmates shift in their seats. The air has changed, pulled taut at each end. Minwoo is still smiling, but his fists are clenched. Outside, Brooks is mouthing something and waving his hands in a frenzied circle. Eason feels a light staccato on his thigh, just above the knee. Julian's fingers, tapping three times. *I know*, they say. *Relax*, they say.

The anger retreats, submerging itself again. Not today. Not now. He remembers the signs outside, the ones that saw him as Halo, not Eason. He is here as Halo of HOURglass, and as Halo he will remain. "I'm a lover," he tells the DJ, shrugging. "I'm not a fighter."

The DJ sits back, disappointed. "Well folks, there you have it. You've been listening to *The Show* with DJ Quicksand and the boy band HOURglass, and they're every bit the angels you'd expect them to be. Catch them on tour starting this month and see for yourself."

They transition to the in-studio performance. Stripped to only their bare voices, Eason worries that the imperfection of their vocals will be obvious, but this is where Minwoo carries them, his resonant tenor masking Eason's tendency to be flat in pitch, Colt's poor breath control, Julian's weak falsetto. Separate, they are acceptable. Together, they are magnificent.

"You got off easy this time, boys," the DJ tells them afterward with a wink. "Come back when your LP drops and we'll give everyone a show."

"We'd be happy to," Minwoo says.

"Next time will be different," the DJ says. "I don't really believe in angels, do you?" He is looking at Eason.

"Nailed it," Brooks tells them as they file out of the studio. "Online search activity went up at the start of the segment and spiked during the performance. Sold out the Cedar Rapids date, too. The label is going to be happy." He pulls Eason aside. "The 'I'm a lover' thing was genius. I could just hear the fangirls creaming themselves."

Eason winces. Brooks always talks like that—like the audience is a formless mass of horny teenagers. He opens his mouth in a retort, but catches Minwoo's glare. *We're doing so well*, it says. *Do you have to ruin it?*

Outside the radio station, news of their presence has spread. Brooks opens the door to a chorus of howls. The four bodyguards barrel through, forming a barricade. Eason walks forward, the glare of the afternoon sun following him like a curse. He spots a green-haired girl, the face on her shirt winking as she jumps up and down. His face. "Halo, Halo, Halo!" she shrieks. The order from Brooks was to go straight to the car. Give the fans too much and that is what they expect forever. Normally, he would listen. But today, especially after the DJ and Brooks's lewd comment, Eason feels a tug of rebelliousness. Rather than walking to the SUV, he veers right, to the girl.

Brooks calls from behind him. He ignores it. Their fans are here, have raced the sun to stand outside some radio station without food or water or shade, all so they could catch a glimpse of HOURglass. Of him. If he is to deserve that kind of love, then he must give some of it back. "Hello," he says to the girl. "What's your name?"

In his periphery, Eason senses cameras recording, footage that will be offered, later, as proof—*he was this close, I swear to god, I could touch him, I could smell him, I could feel him.* He will not acknowledge them, though. In this moment, he and this girl who loves him enough to be here, even without knowing who he really is, are the only people who matter. Looking at her brimming face, he feels warmth and, inexplicably, sadness. "I like your shirt," he says.

The girl's pupils quiver, two small planets experiencing a seismic shift. Then, without warning, she stumbles forward and falls into Eason's chest. He wraps his arm around her out of instinct, counts the insistent drumming of her heart in her chest. Behind her, a middle-aged woman emerges, having shoved her way forward. "I'm obsessed with you," she crows, waving a gelatinous-looking object in Eason's face. "Will you sign my vibrator?"

Eason's first instinct is to curse at her, but then he sees the face on the shirt she wears. His face. She is his fan, just as much as the girl, who is now crying in his arms. Before he can act, a colossal arm swings out from above and rips the vibrator from the woman's hand. The impact sends her flying back into the crowd. A bodyguard appears and pulls the crying girl away from Eason, throwing her to the ground. "Stop," Eason tries to tell them, but the damage is done. "I'm sorry," he says to the confused crowd, hoping they will understand that this was not his doing—he did not know, he had not asked for this.

Someone pulls him back. "Time to go." Julian. Eason protests, moving to find the girl, but Julian's hand is firm on his arm. "It's already done," he says. He guides Eason to the car, where Brooks is fuming. "Inside," he says through his teeth. "*Now.*"

This time, Eason has no fight left. He climbs in and collapses against the seat. Outside, the fans are chanting his name, but he no longer hears them. He is only thinking of the girl's heartbeat, quick and desperate like that of a rabbit's.

"Drive," Brooks tells the chauffeur. The car inches forward into the gathering swell and the mass of bodies splits as they cleave through, then closes behind the car like a suture. Free. They drive for five blocks before turning into a quiet alley, where the car holding Minwoo and Colt has been waiting.

"What—were—you—thinking?"

Eason begins to respond, but Brooks does not afford him the chance. "I tell you to go to the car, you go to the car. You listen to *me*, not them. That's how this works."

"Hey," Julian says. "Take it easy—"

"Shut the fuck up," Brooks says. He turns back to Eason. "Do you know why we have these rules in place, hotshot? Do you? The girl—what if she was bait? What if you get too close and the crowd loses control and someone gets hurt? Boom: instant lawsuit."

Eason looks down, refusing to believe it. "They've been out there for hours."

A bark of a laugh from Brooks. "Let me tell you something. This—all of this—it doesn't work if you go off and do your own thing. *We* have a formula. It. Works. You want to be the biggest superstars in the world? We're here to do that for you. But only if you listen. What happens if you get sued? The media would demolish you, and they'd take the others down, too. You know how they work. You know they love you, until they don't."

No, he had not thought about the group, only himself. He looks sideways at Julian, who is staring into his lap. What if something had indeed happened? Would he be able to bear the responsibility for destroying another dream? Hadn't he promised himself to never bear such a thing again?

"You're right. I'm sorry."

The car is on the 101 now, crawling back to the training annex, where four hours of dance practice await. The sun is finally out, lifting the pall of the morning into forced cheer, and it is raining, too, a meager, inconsequential spray, but the driver clicks on the windshield wipers and they cry like whelps as they drag back and forth against the glass. Eason stares out the window. His hands are shaking again, but he makes no effort to quiet them. He is thinking of the windshield wiper in his old car, the one he wishes he had fixed. This is what he deserves, to be restless, an edge that never quite dulled. Whenever he tries to run away from himself, there he is again: the same Eason who never does seem to know any better. Always at the expense of others. It makes him burn.

MINNIE

For their first date, Nate picks her up in a two-door 2001 Jeep Cherokee. She knows this not because she cares about Jeeps, but because this is how he says thanks when she tells him she likes his car. Most cars look the same to her, and she cannot say she has ever really *liked* one. But this one belongs to Nate, and for that, she decides she does like it.

The sun is setting on the city and they are hurtling straight into it. Nate lowers the visor and squints against the light. Minnie, who has only seen him in the harsh fluorescence of the campus bookstore, takes this opportunity to inspect his hair, the slope of his nose, the thrilling stubble from cheekbone to jaw. In their brief texts, she discovered that he was in his fifth year, a super senior. It was a momentous realization at the time, but now, sitting in Nate's car furnished with possessions that reflect his adulthood (Zippo lighter, leather seat covers, dash cam), she remembers that she is eighteen to his twenty-three and notes all that she must catch up to.

Nate sets the radio to 103.5 BOB FM and the car fills with indie alternative. Somewhere down Enfield Road, "Lisztomania" by Phoenix comes on. The song reminds Minnie of the first time she learned to drive. It was her father who taught her, in their 1998 SAAB that she drove in bursts across the parking lot of her high school. When this song played, her father asked if the band was singing, "like a rhino, like a rhino," which made her laugh so hard she nearly ran into the football field.

She smiles at the memory and turns to tell Nate, wanting to reveal something of herself, but he is already switching the station over to the local news.

"They're so overrated," he says, making a sharp left into the parking lot of their destination, an outdoor coffee shop overlooking Lake Austin called Mozart's. In the distance, Minnie sees storm clouds the color of a bruise. "Don't you think?"

"Oh," she says, waving away the memory of her and her father. "I guess so."

"I knew I could count on you for good taste."

She met Nate a week earlier, at the campus bookstore while picking up books for her World Literature class. There, waiting in a line of half-asleep students, she watched as a tawny-haired boy with broad shoulders swung a bag of books onto the counter and called out her name.

She walked to him, admiring the muscular width of his neck and the parts of his torso that strained against his T-shirt. His body said jock, but his occupation revealed that there must be something more. In her head, she began to write the story of who he was: an athlete with a profound personality and deep love for literature.

"You have a unique name," he told her when she reached the counter. "I've never met a Minnie before." He glanced down at the books on her list and made a face of mock disgust, but it somehow made him look even more alluring. "I remember reading *Jude the Obscure* when I was a freshman. I hated it."

She asked him why, not out of flirtation, but genuine curiosity. "Everything that can go wrong, does go wrong for poor old Jude," he told her while ringing up the rest of her books. "It's a tragedy, but some people see it as satire. I see it as a really reductive take on humanity. I'm Nate, by the way."

"Minnie," she said, then felt herself flush, for he already knew her name. But Nate just smiled, looking endeared by the red tipping her ears. Out of all the students who had been up to the counter, she had stood here longest.

"It's nice to meet you, Minnie the Obscure."

"You, too," she managed to say back. "I'll be thinking about you when I read it. Not about you, I mean. About what you said. I—sorry. That came out weird." She flushed again and he laughed.

"It's okay if you want to think about me, too."

She left the bookstore that day feeling as if she were a seed sunned and watered and on the verge of its shoot. She had never wanted anything more than to spend time with Nate and talk about books.

In the morning, a message appeared on her phone from an unknown number. *Hope this isn't weird, but it's Nate from the bookstore. I found your number on the receipt. Can I take you out on a date sometime?*

From their texts, she learned that Nate was pursuing a double major in physics and English Honors, yet another quality that made him endlessly desirable. He could talk kinematics and discuss the Weinberg-Witten theorem, then turn around and quote a Philip Larkin poem. He was averse to social media, preferring real conversations to the vapid unreality of the internet (she quickly agreed, then scoured her own profiles, wondering whether the many pictures of flowers she posted were childish). On top of that, he was a member of the recreational water polo team, a fact that Minnie returned to in the nights leading up to their date. She imagined his glossy half-naked body in the pool, the single rivulet of water running down the length of his marbled back. The image made her squeeze her thighs together, and a pleasant sensation would ripple through her abdomen, the tide of her desires intensifying as Nate's body swam through hers.

Rain descends in reproachful pellets by the time they reach the front of the line at Mozart's. Nate pays for the drinks (mint tea for Minnie, a flat white for him) while she searches for a seat. It is nearly fall break and the coffee shop is overrun with students plucking away at their laptops. In the seats next to them lie backpacks thrown as placeholders for friends on the way. Minnie finds the remaining option, a wooden picnic table on the far side of the deck. Half of it sits under an awning. The other half is already soaked from the rain.

She waits for Nate on the dry half, arranging and rearranging herself. Today, she is wearing skinny jeans tucked in to old cowboy boots and a magenta cardigan from Urban Outfitters. Sale rack, 60 percent off. How did she want Nate to find her? She could pretend to be engrossed in a riveting conversation on her phone, showing him that she was sociable. She could pull out her book of Rimbaud poems, showing him that she was a deep thinker. She could stare wistfully at the rain as it scattered across the lake, showing him that she had a hidden side, one she would only allow him to see in the most intimate of moments.

In the end, she does not have time to settle on anything before Nate arrives with the drinks. The rain, now slanted by the wind, falls with increasing fury. A few droplets splatter rudely on Nate's corduroys. He hesitates, and she sees him assess the scene: her wet face, the now-drenched table. It is not the romantic, whimsical first date she had in mind.

"Sorry," she says, feeling responsible for the weather. She wonders if he regrets asking her out. But Nate shrugs and inserts one foot into the space next to her, then another. His body, big and alive, descends. Elbow touches elbow. Knee grazes knee. In the warmest part of her, desire swells.

"You smell nice," she tells him. He reminds her of winter in Colorado—pine and sandalwood and crackling fire. The long yawn of stars at night, flour sprinkled across the sky, and she, tucked into a sleeping bag on the living room floor, listening to her father's stories of his school years.

Nate shakes water from his hair and a few drops catch her cheek. He turns to her. The scant distance between them is both wondrous and terrifying. "Hold that thought," he murmurs. "You have something on your face."

Panic, then embarrassment, floods her. But Nate reaches out and his thumb paints along her jawbone, then her left cheek. A trail of heat follows in its wake.

"It's just the rain," he says, voice as soft as a song. "What do I smell like?"

She dares herself to hold his gaze. "Winter."

"I've never had a girl tell me that before," he says, but he looks pleased.

The conversation begins with an easy topic: school. Minnie tells him about her interest in books and writing, how she eventually wants to apply for the Honors Program in English, like him. She asks Nate about prerequisites, which professors to heed, and whether the senior thesis really is as awful as everyone says. "But of course," she says, beaming at him, "no one has it as hard as you, with a double major in physics and all."

Nate takes a sip of his flat white. "It's not hard. You just have to write your thesis about something no one else has written about. What are you interested in? Who do you like to read?"

"Nabokov," she says, pronouncing his name with the emphasis on the *bo*, as she practiced. "Fitzgerald. The Brontë sisters."

"Those are high school level, aren't they?"

From the awning, a big, fat raindrop lands on her hand.

Nate sees the change on her face. "I didn't mean it like that," he says quickly. "I just thought—well, most people read those books in high school and their tastes develop from there. But if you like Nabokov, you should check out David Foster Wallace. Remind me to give you a copy."

The date moves on. Nate talks about the invasion of Crimea and questions the effectiveness of President Obama's economic sanctions against Russia, which she is unfamiliar with. He references *Silicon Valley*, a show that she has never seen. He pontificates on the benefits of single-gear bikes versus fixed-gear, what he called "fixies," to which Minnie responds, "I didn't know there were so many kinds of bikes."

"What do you like to do for fun?" he asks her. "Do you play any sports?"

She thinks of HOURglass, and Nate, the coffee shop, and the rain are all gone. In their place, a rolling tape of the boys in their best moments, images which now feel as familiar to her as her own memories—Minwoo's steady gaze, Denim's laugh, the swanlike curve of Jelly's neck. Halo, in all his handsome glory.

"There's a band I really like." She imagines telling Nate how all the colors in her world have been turned up to their brightest hues now that she knows the boys exist in the same universe as her, but stops there. It is too soon. "I can't play any sports," she says instead. "I'm not very coordinated."

"That's a shame. You're quite tall for an Asian girl. I mean that as a compliment."

The hour passes. She could stay there with him forever, she realizes, but the rain has other plans and soon, her once-magenta cardigan is so wet it looks oil black. Nate helps extricate her from the picnic table and the two of them run side by side across the street to his Jeep, laughing as they hold his jacket overhead as if gliding through the air with it.

"Was it awful?" she asks when they reach his car, loosened by the absurdity of the situation, which feels like something out of a movie. "Was this the worst first date of your life?"

"Far from the worst," he grins, shaking off the water from his jacket. "But definitely the wettest."

Never, her mother once told her, put anyone on a pedestal. But she cannot help herself. For the first time since coming to college, she feels like she is close to being the version of herself at full potential. Nate is everything she wants, everything she believes she needs in order to move into that next stage of life, one synonymous with happiness. Here is a man who knows who he is, and as a result, makes it easy for her to know the same. All she has to do is follow.

On the car ride home, Nate turns the heater up and she snuggles into the serape he hands her from the back seat. He does not ask for it back when they reach her dorm, which makes her warmer than anything the artificial heat of the car could provide. At the entrance, she holds herself up to all of him, wanting to take in his face at this proximity one final time. Stragglers from the dining hall trudge past in sandals and sweatshirts, their ordinariness accentuating the magic of him, of her. In this moment, Minnie thinks, she looks like someone who matters. She gazes into Nate's brown eyes and she glows.

He swings down to kiss her on the cheek. She feels her flesh sink under the pressure of his lips. It is a chaste kiss—but there is promise in it, too. When she returns to her room, she waits twenty minutes to send him a goodnight text and then she hugs herself, spinning.

EASON

MONTH ONE.

He was eighteen, working a shift at the wing place off Westheimer when the order came in: two hundred wings, downtown Houston. The drivers fought for it, anticipating a fat tip. In the end, Eason won—he was the only one who did not drive a sedan. They secured twenty boxes of wings to the back of his Tacoma and he drove off with a tail full of soy garlic and gochujang, the jealous glares of the delivery boys flashing in his rearview mirror.

The address led him to a Four Seasons, which led him to a ballroom on the second floor. On the door, a sign screamed QUIET! AUDITIONS IN PROGRESS. He walked in to see a scrawny B-Boy spinning on his head like an upside-down top. Eason unloaded the wings box by box, waiting for someone to give him his tip. But none of the people in the room noticed him. Audition after audition, Eason stood waiting by the wings as they soaked through their boxes. When forty minutes passed, he stalked over to the judges' table, receipt in hand. He would get that tip.

A week later, his phone rang with an unknown number. It was one of the assistants from the audition. The judges were interested, she said. They wanted to see him again.

"But I wasn't there to audition," Eason told her.

"It's called BabyGold Records. Look us up and then see if you still want to say no."

One quick search took him to the official website. Sleek banner, big steel letters:

BabyGold Records
is looking for the next
Global Superstars
Think you've got what it takes to be a pop idol?

The company, he learned, was a record label, helmed by a man who called himself The Duke. In the past five years, The Duke had been responsible for turning out some of the buzziest musical acts currently dominating the charts, including a three-time Grammy Award–winning diva and a jazz vocalist who recently penned his own Broadway musical. Now, he was setting his sights on taking BabyGold Records even further by adapting the Korean pop music machine to Western tastes. Same formula, just different boys.

We've seen the success of the K-pop model in its home country, he was quoted saying in a *Rolling Stone* interview. *When it comes to creating fan engagement and loyalty, no one has been able to do it better than them—and we see the fruits of that labor in their revenues year-over-year. But it's not a secret science. It's about changing our strategy from the top-down and saying, we're going to make the bond between the artist and the fan so strong that the fans feel like they really know the artist and they're a part of it, too. If we combine the passion of homegrown American boy bands with South Korea's training model and marketing strategy, we will be unbeatable.*

Eason remembered the boy bands of his youth: men with bodies dripping with cool, but faces that made them totally boyfriendable. He was vaguely familiar, too, with K-pop idols, the ones who danced like princes and possessed facial features that looked as if they had been plucked from a well-tended garden. Neither kind of man, he thought, really existed on this Earth, nor could he replicate them—he was too unrefined, too rough. All the ugliness of who he believed himself to be showed clearly on his body, from his feral gait to his downcast eyes. He had trouble keeping weight on and always looked like he was ready for a fight. There was no way the record label actually wanted someone like him.

He called the assistant back. “If this is a charity case thing, I’m not interested. I can’t even sing.”

She laughed in a way that made him feel as if he were something to be pitied. “We’re not looking for singers. We’re looking for potential. The label wants someone who can do a bad boy concept. Cold and detached, the kind of guy your mother warned you about.”

“That’s not me.”

“You interrupted them in the middle of auditions just to get your tip. Everyone who comes in cares too much and it shows, but you didn’t care at all. Out of all the people they’ve auditioned, they’ve never seen anyone with so little to lose.”

He said nothing. They were not wrong about that part.

“What are your dreams?” the assistant continued. “Whatever they are, it doesn’t matter, because The Duke is going to make them come true. I’m going to send you the audition info, okay? It’s up to you.”

She hung up before Eason could ask any more questions.

What are your dreams? He had a few answers. Then, hating himself for the delusion of it all, he imagined what that would mean. He would become an Eason who was more than a high school dropout, more than a kid working three jobs just to make rent, and certainly more than his past, until the old Eason was nothing more than a mistake, and he could emerge as someone new. Someone clean.

Three weeks after the second audition, he got off the red-eye to find a black car waiting for him at LAX. The air in Los Angeles was different from Houston—fast and nervous and charged by the lofty dreams of everyone who had ever landed in this city, hoping to be something. The car stuttered down La Cienega, the sky crowded with telephone lines and advertisements for plastic surgery and liposuction.

“Soak it in, kid,” the driver said, watching him in the rearview mirror. “Right now’s the best this city’s ever gonna look to you. It gets uglier the longer you live here.”

The car dropped him off at the training annex on Sunset Boulevard. It was a flat-roofed, white stucco building between a modeling agency and a dental reconstruction clinic. His sister, Faye, liked to joke that it was impossible to take a serious picture in LA—there was always a palm tree in the background, ruining the shot. This building had three along its walkway, their trunks lanky and too long, their fronds overgrown, reminding him of goofy interlopers in need of praise. Inside, a pinched-face woman took his name and photo in exchange for a badge on a lanyard, which he looped around his neck. He rode the elevator up to the dance studio on the third floor.

They were waiting for him. There was the manager Brooks and his new bandmates, Minwoo, Colt, and Julian (although he would not feel comfortable calling them his bandmates for quite some time). In the corner stood a man with yellow hair, long enough to reach his shoulders. He did not greet Eason or introduce himself, but simply watched. This, he knew, must be The Duke. He looked different from what Eason had imagined; not at all imposing nor polished nor expensive, for that matter. Instead, his faded T-shirt, loose linen pants, and thong sandals reminded Eason of an alumni who spoke at his high school about traveling to Kenya to spread the word of God.

Brooks introduced Eason to his bandmates. "These next nine months of training are make-or-break," he told them. He was a head shorter than Eason, with a thick neck and thick fingers, and his face was constantly red, either due to sunburn or the temper that they would come to know in the following months.

Minwoo was the oldest. Back in Seoul, he had been on the path to being the youngest professional opera singer in the world before a bad surgery on his vocal cords following a motorcycle accident took his voice away. He dropped out of conservatory shortly afterward, convinced the dream was over. In swooped The Duke's scouts, who gave Minwoo the opportunity of a lifetime, where it would not matter how technically brilliant or vocally gifted he was. What mattered was how much he wanted it, and Minwoo still wanted everything very much. With the help of vocal trainers and rehabilitation specialists, he spent the next year building his vocals back up, although he would never sing opera again. Minwoo was on his way to being the founding member of HOURglass, and he took on that responsibility with a gravity and seriousness that Eason could see even on that first day.

Colt was the second oldest and, noticeably, the only white person in the band. According to market research conducted by BabyGold Records, an all-Asian boy band would not make it in the States, even if the goal was to follow in the steps of K-pop. The country was ready for a lot, but it was not quite ready for *that*. So they found Colt, an objectively handsome, all-American boy with startling blue eyes. He had the kind of face that recalled the Hollister and Abercrombie models of the early 2000s and the body of someone who looked like they smelled good.

Julian was a trained ballet dancer turned competitive figure skater. By the time he was twelve, he had already won gold at Junior Nationals, the first skater of Vietnamese descent to do so. By eighteen, he was retired. He was not tall, but he was thin, and that thinness made him seem taller. When he stepped forward to shake Eason's hand, his arm shot out like an arrow released from a bow, its precision and focus already communicating the years of training that resided in his body.

"And Eason's our ace, picked from a national audition of thousands," Brooks announced. That was when Eason remembered his place: He was not chosen for talent or skill. He was here to play a character. That was what he would let them all believe, at least. They did not need to know the rest.

Throughout it all, The Duke kept watch. He was not ugly, but still somewhat uncomfortable to look at, for he had a tight face and its features slanted up and back, as if he had been hurtling into the wind for a long time. But his eyes were vivid and sharp, and they followed the four of them as they moved across the studio. His indecipherable stare reminded Eason of his mother, and for that reason, he decided The Duke was dangerous in a way he did not yet know how to explain. Even after he turned to leave the studio, Eason could feel him watching. And, months later, when HOURglass finally began to come together and it no longer took Eason a week to learn choreography or keep the beat or memorize lyrics, he could still feel The Duke's gaze on him, those crystalline eyes tracing his every move.

MONTH TWO.

They lived in a two-bed, one-bath in Koreatown. It was important, Brooks told them, to become a team as quickly as possible. When you think, move, and feel as one, you become unstoppable.

It was a small apartment. There was a slice of kitchen immediately to the left of the front door and no dishwasher, although out of the four of them, only Colt had relied on one before. They had just enough room to fit some barstools at the counter and a love seat against the wall. Eventually, Minwoo found a coffee table off Craigslist and Colt insisted on a blender to feed his green smoothie habit. The record label would be paying for everything anyway, although Eason wondered about the part of the contract that said the four of them would not be paid until they recouped all expenses after they officially debuted. It was standard, the in-house entertainment lawyer assured them. They would not see any money in the first few years, but once they hit it big (which they would, it was promised), there would be more money than they could spend. Plus, they were not in this for the money, were they?

The apartment faced the back of a grocery store. Every morning, they heard garbage trucks rolling through the alleyway and the workers clowning around during their smoke break. Minwoo and Colt claimed the larger bedroom because it was quieter and they were both light sleepers. Julian and Eason took the second bedroom, which was no bigger than a utility closet. Inside, they stuffed two futons and a rack for their clothes. They had a window that looked out onto the street and that was the one nice thing about getting this smaller room—at least they had the sun. Every morning at five, Minwoo's alarm sounded through the apartment in a waterfall of chimes, and Eason would hear him padding to the kitchen to throw on some porridge, or the static of a cereal bag as it dislodged sugarless kernels into a bowl. That was what they ate most days: porridge or cereal. *We'll eat when we've made it*, Minwoo promised. *We'll eat when we're dead*, Colt would joke.

Eason liked sharing a room with Julian. The two of them kept the same schedule, returning to the apartment late at night after practice. Sometimes, they stayed in the dance studio and slept there, because the fifty-minute drive was not worth it. Julian was deliberate without being forceful, something that must have carried over from his figure skating days, and looked Eason in the eye when he spoke. He was only a year older than Eason, but he reminded Eason of his sister Faye, who was four years older but always treated him like an equal. The private instructor taught Eason how to learn and mimic choreography, but it was Julian who gave him the language to become a dancer. He taught Eason how to look at himself in the mirror, something Eason had resisted ever since he left home.

The vocal training came later. He was not a good singer, but his voice was deep and earthen, a sound he was surprised to discover he possessed. BabyGold Records was not worried about whether they could sing well, though. They had Minwoo for all the difficult runs and big belts, while the rest of them were to serve as garnish. "We can cover anything with a backing track," Brooks assured them. "Most live performances are pre-recorded these days, anyway." What mattered was giving the performance of a lifetime. Still, Eason always wondered if people who could actually sing, who knew about the nuances of technique and breathing, winced when they heard his voice.

The four of them lived, breathed, and trained as one. Soon, Eason knew their bodies better than his own. He knew that the subdued musk was Minwoo's sweat and the sour fruit was Colt's. He knew that three hours and forty minutes was when Julian began to fade. He knew the weight and length and density of each of their bodies, because he also knew what was required for him to lift them overhead or dive through their legs. In becoming a part of this group, he had to forget everything and put himself at the supreme mercy of others. It was easy for him—he had no pride to shed, no self to hold on to. He wanted to forget himself, and that was what becoming a part of HOURglass was: the chance to give up everything that haunted him, if even for a moment.

MONTH EIGHT.

They could call themselves dancers, they could call themselves singers. Models, actors, comedians, entertainers—they could do it all. Every morning began with vocal lessons, followed by dance training, then a session with the physical trainer. They adhered to a spartan diet, because salt begot bloat, and what they wanted to be was cut and lean. Lean was formidable. Lean meant you were in control. They learned to count the days by their diet cycle and tell time by which parts of their body hurt the most. In the afternoons, they trained with the acting and modeling coaches, who taught them how to pose in front of a camera. The thing about being an idol, Eason began to understand, was that there was no such thing as normal, which was just another word for human, which was just another word for ugly.

At a certain point, he looked around and realized that they were no longer the same boys as before. Minwoo was a confident diplomat during mock interviews, Colt excelled at improvisation, and Julian lost the remaining baby fat on his cheeks, transforming from cute to arresting overnight. And Eason, the role that he was meant to play, that of the cold, savage bad boy? He settled into it as well, perhaps too easily. The stylists draped him in black and dyed his hair to midnight, spiking the ends until they were sharp enough to draw blood. He felt himself calcifying into this new persona, at once dangerous and alluring. "The fans will eat that shit up," Brooks said when he asked if people would think him rude. "They'll tell themselves—I can *change* him." So, he let himself harden, let himself darken, and for once it felt right, because maybe now, he could find a place for the pain to go.

MONTH NINE.

They were back in the dance studio. The final assessment. The Duke was there, accompanied by two assistants and a cluster of business suits from the BabyGold Records board. Eight songs back-to-back, and then it was over. Minwoo fell to the floor. Colt and Julian went to help him up. Eason did not move, both because he could not and because he was sure that if he moved, he would lose this chance forever.

The Duke said nothing at first. Then, he walked to them, thong sandals quietly slapping the floor. It was his quickness that unnerved Eason most; he moved as if he had never known an obstacle.

He stopped an arm's length away. At this distance, Eason could see the splatter of freckles across his cheeks. He looked both ancient and newly born.

"What do you want?"

Minwoo was the first to answer. "To be the best in the world."

"To be huge," Colt said, breathing hard.

"To touch people."

Eason was the last. "To be loved."

The Duke nodded. Then, he smiled for the first time. "HOURglass at last."

One of the assistants brought cake and champagne. The cake they had one bite of (they were still on a diet), but the champagne they downed whole. Eason felt it dissolve within him, relieving his muscles, his sinew, his exhausted bones. They had made it, together. Everything was going to change.

He raised his glass with the others, his three new brothers, and they said it together, the mantra that would later sound back at them from hundreds, one day thousands of fans, starting with a music festival in seven weeks' time:

We are yours and you are ours.

"To HOURglass," The Duke said.

"To HOURglass," they repeated.

MONTH ZERO.

His mother is on the line and she wants to know when he will be coming home. I need you, she tells him. It's not good to be away for so long.

I'm not going home, he says. What he does not tell her is that he will never go home again. Not after what happened. Not if he can help it.

POST #352

DEATH to that DJ for how he treated the boys

what did they do to deserve this????

i havent stopped crying

DEATH to their record label for not protecting them better they should have stopped it our poor sweet boys oh god

my heart hurts when Ii think about how bad they must have felt they worked so hard only for this old sack to treat them like shit

he needs to die in a fire JUST DIE

MINNIE

The university is quiet over fall break, a sigh of four days in the middle of October. With half the student population gone, Minnie finds herself enjoying campus for the first time. She studies in the architecture library, a massive cream-colored building designed in the style of the Spanish-Mediterranean Revival. Inside, chandeliers drip from sloped ceilings and hover over long rows of wooden tables with feet that look like talons. She likes it here, finds the vastness of the space comforting. Occasionally, someone at a neighboring table will cough or shift their chair back, and the sound, rather than startling her, comes as a welcome interruption, a reminder that there are indeed others who are here alone, like her. During mealtimes, she walks to the dining hall with a lighter step. She eats whenever she wants and sits wherever she wants, because there are no groups of friends laughing at other tables, no one to wonder why she is eating alone. In the Six-Pack, so named for the six same-sized buildings that face each other on the south side of campus, Minnie lounges under one of the many oak trees lining the lawn that leads to 21st Street. She reads Camus for her literature class and Calvino for pleasure, per Nate's recommendation. And campus, for all its quietude, finally feels like it belongs to her.

In the evenings, Nate picks her up in his Jeep and they go about the divine business of dating. Because they must be dating for all the time they spend together, although she is too afraid to ask for confirmation. Thursday is a night swim at Barton Springs, but Minnie never learned how, so she sits on the ledge of the cold pool and watches Nate glide through the water, marveling at how a person can be both strong and light. On Friday, they attend a special showing at the Dobie Theatre on campus, where they pay two dollars each for entry into a horror flick from the seventies about a sentient, murderous car. On Saturday, they eat dinner at a halal place down the street from his house. Nate spends most of their date eyeing the TV above Minnie's head, where a soccer game between England and France is taking place. Minnie turns around in her chair to watch as well, but cannot understand why Nate finds such excitement in a game where the players so rarely score.

Being with Nate, she quickly realizes, is a welcome lesson in adulthood. He is different from the popular boys of her high school, puffed-up jocks who wore disinterest and nonchalance like proud badges. Instead, Nate has a confident knowledge about everything. Minnie is keenly aware that, in order to be with Nate, to deserve Nate, she must match him in his maturity, which is why, now on their fifth date, she proudly tells him that she is writing for a zine.

"A zine, huh?" They are sitting on a blanket at Zilker Park, a large, flat field in the center of the city. Turkey sandwiches and jalapeño chips spill out of the picnic basket between them.

"How's it going so far?" Nate wants to know.

"It's okay," Minnie says. She tells him about the first meeting. "I've never written anything like this before and I'm not sure where to start, so I've been reading other zines for research."

Nate contemplates this. "That's nice, but I wouldn't spend too much time on it, Min. Zines aren't where people go for real literature. If you want to be taken seriously, you need to submit to something like *The New Yorker*."

Minnie bites into her sandwich. Nate recently published a short story in the university's literary journal to great fanfare. It was about a homeless man who pushed a stroller around every day, although no one knew what was inside. Soon, all the residents of the neighborhood began taking bets on what might be inside the stroller—some said it was a baby, others a small dog. At the end, it was revealed that the man had been pushing an empty stroller the whole time. Minnie read the story in one sitting, treating each sentence as a window into Nate's genius. She admired his style, which was tight and economical and somewhat brusque, whereas her own writing had once been called "overly romantic" by a high school teacher and "sappy" by a few peers.

"You're so right," she tells him, grateful. "I thought your new story was amazing. I could definitely see it in *The New Yorker.*"

"You think?" Nate leans back on his palms. "Maybe I'll send it in."

She leans back, too. Ahead, the downtown skyline sits over the trees like a small crown. One building in particular she finds strange and beautiful, its roof not flat like the others, but sharp and pointed, a cluster of stalagmites reaching for another galaxy. That, Nate tells her, is the Frost tower. Appropriately so, she thinks, for it looks as if made of frost. This she voices to Nate, who snorts and tells her that the building is named for Frost Bank. And as she takes in the tornado of dogs playing, the frisbees arcing overhead, the shouts of a soccer scrimmage, the chaotic dubstep of a fitness class, the giggles of a group of friends all sprawled on their bellies, sharing cake, and the contented hum of trees as they sway in the wind, leaves flittering like small bells, she thinks that this is the first time she can appreciate Austin as her new home.

The sound of a typewriter breaks the spell: Nate, receiving a text on his phone. He reads the message and types something back, then grins. She follows his gaze, wanting to see the source of the grin, but he flips his phone over. "My roommate has an extra ticket for the Octopus Project show tonight. Do you mind if we call our date early?"

She tells Nate yes, it is absolutely fine. Is this the hallmark of a good girlfriend—*potential girlfriend!* she has to keep reminding herself—one who is absolutely fine? She stands. Back in the basket the sandwiches and chips go. Nate rolls up the blanket. The sky is mauve and the trees around them have darkened at the trunks, but the topmost branches are still gold, clinging to the fading sunlight. Downtown, buildings light up one by one. It would have been so romantic, she thinks, to stay here with him. He had not kissed her beyond the one to her cheek after their first date, and she hoped that tonight would be a touchstone; that he would finally kiss her on the lips—the first kiss of her life.

When they arrive back at the dorm, Minnie recognizes three girls from her hall standing on the steps. They form a tight triangle, each body its wall. These girls she knows; popular and lovely, the kind of girls who never go anywhere alone. Tonight, they are in their pajamas, a pack of smokes and a lime-green lighter between them. Smoking is not allowed within five hundred feet of any university building, but one of the girls, Minnie heard, is dating the resident assistant. As Nate pulls up, his headlights cast a spotlight on their sacrosanct triangle and the girls stare back insolently, not bothering to hide the cigarillos dangling from between their manicured fingers.

"We're having a house party next Friday," he tells Minnie, throwing the girls a desultory glance. "It's a send-off for my roommate before his study abroad. Tell me you'll come?"

She nods. He rewards her with another chaste kiss on the cheek.

The three girls stare as she exits Nate's car. "Was that your boyfriend?" one of them asks. She sounds astonished. And, Minnie notices, envious. She nods, even though she knows it is not yet true.

The second girl takes a long drag from her cigarillo and blows it out the side of her mouth. The smoke makes her look like a beautiful kettle. "He's so hot." She takes another puff and greedily eyes the spot Nate's car just vacated. "He's the TA for my Foundations of Mechanics class. How do you know him?"

All three girls are staring at her now.

"We met at the bookstore."

"Are you kidding me?" says the third girl, who is wearing Tinkerbell pajama bottoms. "That sounds like something that would happen in a movie."

The rest of them agree. "I'm Jillian," the first girl says, stepping closer to Minnie and extending her hand. "I live at the end of the hall."

"I know," she says. Jillian had been the one leading the group of girls who sat in front of Minnie's door all those weeks ago. She takes Jillian's hand. Her palm is soft the way avocados are when they have hit that delicate window of ripeness. "I'm Minnie."

"Cute name," Tinkerbell says.

"We do a study group every Thursday night in the Joynes Library," Jillian tells her. "You're welcome to join."

"Maybe you can bring your boyfriend, too," the second girl says. She throws her cigarillo on the ground, stomping it out with her Ugg boot.

Jillian gives the girl an annoyed look. Minnie understands that she must be the leader of the group. "Seriously," Jillian says, coming closer. Her breath smells like blueberries and tobacco. "We'd love to have you both."

Inside the dorm, Minnie takes the stairs three at a time. When she is finally alone in her room, she presses her face into her pillow and lets out a small scream.

So this is how it happens. This is how it all falls into place.

From her laptop, she plays the boys' EP, letting it fill the room at full volume. *I'll be a better man for you,* Minwoo croons, *one who can give you the sun and the moon.* Her life is finally beginning to accelerate because the boys made it so—she had found them, loved them, and now they are rewarding her for it. Everything they touch turns into gold, she thinks. Me, too. I'm turning into gold.

EASON

Tour begins. Now, Brooks says, it's really showtime. Eason marks down the list of cities on a map and when he connects them, it looks like he has drawn a jagged fang across the country.

The tour blazes through forty-eight cities, a mix of opening sets, festival circuits, and solo shows. It has been nearly three months since that first performance at the music festival, and everyone is hungry for it. Up-and-coming they may be, but their fanbase has grown; half the shows sell out, so the record label adds twelve more. This must be it, Eason thinks as they land in Boston for their first stop: making it.

He imagined it would be glamorous, all catered meals and free-flowing champagne. The life of a rock star, the way he had seen it depicted in the movies. But what tour really is: Fly the red-eye; arrive in the dark; stumble into an unmarked SUV that takes them straight to the hotel; try to get some sleep, even though he never can the first night at a new place (he read somewhere that the brain coded strange new surroundings as an emergency and just how many first days, how many first nights inside strange hotels in strange cities, how many times had his brain decided that it was all an emergency?);

In the morning, pray that there are no aches in the body, that the joints are greased, that the neck is neither stiff nor sore, that he can *move*; skip breakfast; power through back-to-back stage rehearsals, which means no time to see the city, for the day must be spent checking their synchronicity and practicing the one transition they cannot seem to get right; eat an early, light dinner at the hotel, a choice between salad and grilled chicken or salad and grilled fish; say no to salt, yes to water, then a cocktail of vitamins, a humidifier, more water;

The hours before the show, try not to shit himself, even though anytime he thinks about what's coming, his stomach drops like a trapdoor and he has to run for the bathroom; go over the setlist again, then forget everything; ask Julian which foot steps out first in the song after the intro; ask Colt if they all sing the chorus for the encore or if they come in one by one; find Minwoo and hope that their leader will steady him, because every time, he feels like his throat is going to fall out of his ass;

The hour of the show, it's push-ups and downward dogs and jogging in place; it's slamming down lozenges and warming up vocal cords for that out-of-range E# in "Need You Bad"; it's a button breaking on his jacket and the stylists losing their heads as they try to find a replacement; it's the backup dancers forming a prayer circle and asking the Lord to bless this night; it's Brooks lingering in every corner reminding them that they have to be impeccable, because a mistake on stage is a mistake forever; it's the four of them, Minwoo and Colt and Julian and Eason, avoiding each other's eyes, because seeing the fear in those eyes would be enough to make anyone say, *Nope, I'm out, this is crazy, no way*, until the last moments before the lights come on and they are ushered backstage, when they can finally look at each other, assured and confident, not at all the terrified boys from that first day of practice, and Minwoo puts his hand in and the rest follow, chanting: *HOURglass 'til we die*; it's the four of them, together, facing this battle head-on, as a team, as one.

After the show, they are too excited to sit, even though their bodies are spent. They whirl around the craft services table and dangle off the sofa. The costumes their stylists created for them are salty from the effort of their dance. They will have to be steamed and repaired in the morning.

"Did you hear them singing along to 'Love Crush'—"

"That was the most in sync we've ever been—"

"The stage looked incredible—"

"I can't believe we sold out another show—"

The others recall the thunderous chants of the fans, the dance moves that made the crowd go crazy. What *he* remembers is the cold terror of those first few seconds on stage, when everyone could finally see him. Colt once described it as feeling naked, but naked would be a blessing—what he feels is closer to no skin and no bones, as if he is sludge waiting for its container, waiting for a directive to render him into being and thus necessary.

In that moment, he hears every particle of the Earth's soil falling into place beneath him, a tectonic manipulation at which he is the center. And then the screams of the fans engulf him, pleading with him to let them in. He remembers the blur that their phone lights make as they wave at him. He remembers the opening notes of the first song. His body detaches from his brain. In order to transform into Halo, he must leave himself first.

He remembers the wet, medicinal spray of the fog machine, the heat of the pyrotechnics, and the fireworks, the dazzling fireworks. He remembers tasting sweat, a satisfying brine that trickles through his lips while he gyrates around the stage. He remembers the rolls on the back of a bodyguard's neck as he tries to stop the fans from collapsing the barricade that separates them from the stage. And he remembers, more than anything, how much they love him.

It is a blinding love. A love that wraps around him and says, *You can be anything you want, you can do anything you want, because of this love.* Their faces blend together—pained, glistening, the features all stretched out, the mouths open in a long moan, the eyes both vacant and sharp. Hair, everywhere. Hands, grabbing for something they will never be able to hold. But the key is making them think they can. So Eason reaches out, extends his hand. They strain to touch him. They will never wash their hands again if they do. But he always pulls away at the last second.

Their love is strong. It has force. It is enough to propel him through ninety minutes of choreography and song, a fuel that will never be mined or captured. It is a constant, regenerating thing. Their love scares him sometimes, but on nights like these, he can only beg for more.

◦ ◦ ◦

After the initial excitement following their concert in Philadelphia, the fifth stop of tour, Minwoo, Colt, Julian, and Eason are quiet. The fans have a name for it: Post-Concert Depression, a state where the great cloudburst of dopamine they experience during the concert finally catches up to them. As they leave the venue, they are also leaving the fantasy. What the fans do not know is that their idols feel it, too.

What they crave is more fans, more chants, more love, but the evening is over and the city prepares to sleep. As the four of them follow the twisting hallways that lead them out to the private garage, Eason thinks it cruel. Only a few hours ago, they had been larger than life. Now, they are nothing more than human.

In the garage, a quarry of black SUVs waits to take them back to the hotel. Eason follows Julian to their car, one they have shared since their training days, but a manager steps between them, pushing a cell phone into his hand. Eason accepts it, waving Julian forward.

"Hello?"

He knows it is her before she speaks. Knows because of the absence of her voice, that terrible silence that hung around their townhome all those months, lingering the way a cold fog does from night well into morning. Knows because he sees her without having to hear her, the hair in a low bun, the hands rivered by veins. Knows, because happiness has never been a long enough promise. Then she speaks his name and all he can do is—*no.* A wave of terror spreads across his chest—the same shameful terror from years ago—and suddenly, he feels gills form on the sides of his neck. He remembers that he must breathe, breathe the way they tell you to *breathe, just breathe*, but the gills are too big and too open and now all he can do is breathe and it is too much air, too much sensation, he wants to close the gills, cut them off, he would rather suffocate now than breathe anymore and he hates himself for it—is he not stronger now, bigger? How can he still be that same kid that hid in the bathroom, under the dining room table, in the closets?

"Wrong number," he chokes out. His hands are shaking again, and he has to pin the phone hard against his temple to make it stop. *Embou-*

chure, Faye would say. He forces his lips into a small hole and pushes the air out through it. The gills close.

His mother laughs. The same hard, fearless laugh she had before his father went away and something else came to stay in his place. Eason feels himself relenting, keening for that sound—the last thing he recalls of love. But then he remembers everything that came at the cost of that laugh, and the terror returns. He tears the phone from his temple and throws it to the ground.

The manager gapes at him.

"Sorry." He squats down to pool the broken glass together, but leaves the shards there. "Why would you let this through?"

"I'm just the messenger," the manager says. The rest of the crew is watching them now. "They said she was your mo—"

"Well she isn't," he snaps. "Next time, vet these things before you give them to me, okay?"

"A few shows and he thinks he's a rock star," one of the stagehands whispers loudly.

Eason ignores it. The makeup artists are piling into their cars, the stylists are folding the costumes into the trunks, the managers are doing final checks, and a bodyguard hovers behind him, waiting. Julian, in the car, waiting. Minwoo and Colt reviewing concert footage in theirs. He is surrounded by people, so why does he feel so alone?

The women of our family, his mother told him and Faye, *have always been the ones to answer for the sins of your great-great-grandfather.* She called it a curse.

His great-great-grandfather was not a kind man. His wife endured him, but at night she prayed the child inside her belly would not grow up to be like its father. One day, a girl appeared at their door. She was a lover from his youth, did he remember her? He was not a kind man. The girl, heartbroken, drowned herself in the lake behind his home. Inexplicable tragedies followed: His wife died in childbirth; his sister's house burned down; his niece disappeared in the woods and was found frozen in the morning; his daughter, Eason's grandmother, suffered from nosebleeds and passed before Eason was born. The last remaining member of the line—Eason's mother—lived her life carefully, cleanly, determined the curse would not touch her. For her troubles she was awarded a devoted husband and two children whom she named after Hong Kong superstars; such gilded names would shield them from the curse, too.

Eason grew up in Sugar Land, a city twenty miles south of Houston, in a starter townhome with a tongue-red door and faux balconies caging the windows. The house did not have a front yard, but a patch of grass on which grew one shrub, and there was nothing special about this shrub, nothing that made it any different from the other shrubs in the neighborhood. In fact, without the number on their door, it was often hard for Eason to know which house was theirs. The backyard was not much of a looker either: square, flat, and yellowed by continuous summer droughts. A yard full of potential, the realtor who sold it to them promised. His father wanted to gut the whole thing and replace the dying grass with gravel, erect a patio, maybe even a gazebo, but his mother refused. She wanted peach trees. Not just one or two, but rows and rows of them. *Peach wood will protect us*, she said. When the peaches ripened, they could wear the pits around their necks to keep the curse at bay.

And so, in lieu of the gravel and patio and gazebo, the backyard was torn up, the land tousled and turned over. Landscapers came to give their estimates—sanctioned robbery, his father called it. But Eason's mother would not hear anything else. Evil spirits fear the peach tree and hold it in awe, she reminded them. The landscapers dug the earth full of holes and when they finally left, small bombs of soil ran up and down the backyard, each holding a peach sapling as slight as a bone.

The divorce came when Eason was twelve, but his father moved out months before. He was going to live with Rachel, a woman from work. *Some things you can't change, so it's you who has to change*, he told Eason the night before he left. By then, Eason was not listening anymore. He never wanted to hear anything his father had to say to him ever again.

After his father left, the house grew quiet. His mother was still there, but she shut herself in her room and may as well have left, too. His father did not take much, just a single suitcase of clothes, but as the days passed, it became clear that he had departed with something crucial from each of them. From Eason, it was whatever boyishness he had left. From his mother, it was her mind. But Faye—Faye gained. She was tall for sixteen, taking after their father's side of the family. In her freshman year, she made the track team and quickly ascended to varsity, conquering the 400m and 800m races in just one season. She grew her hair out long, then cut it short, then grew it out long again in the span of a year. She was living well for all three of them, and maybe they needed that from her, to see that there was a way to go on.

Then, five months after the day she locked herself away, their mother emerged from her room. Her body had shrunk, desiccated to vertebrae and rib cage and spindles where once her fingers grew, but her head remained big and untouched, as if whatever anguish she underwent had decided to spare this part of her. But why? Eason tried not to think about what it could mean; he was just glad to have his mother back. He and Faye both were.

It was simple, she told them: All of their sorrow, her husband's affair and his leaving, was due to the curse. She consulted a suanming xiansheng, a Chinese fortune teller who had expertise in the art of dissolving ghosts and curses. The suanming xiansheng inspected the pictures that his mother sent over, taking in the flat bones of her face and the wilt of her torso. He read the lines of her palm, calculated the pillars of her birth time. He asked about the layout of her home. *The ills that have befallen your family are the machinations of a demon*, he concluded, *the vengeful spirit of your ancestor's scorned lover*. Living in the bones of girls and women, she turned them to madness and destruction as penance for her heartbreak.

His mother wanted to know if there was a way to destroy the demon once and for all. The suanming xiansheng told her there was. But it would not be easy. He charged $200 USD for forty minutes of consultation.

Faye did not believe in the curse, Eason did not know what was true, but their mother—their mother believed with all her being. How else could you explain all the tragedy that had befallen their family? How else could a loving husband leave his wife? That was why her head was so vibrant and fierce while the rest of her body continued to fade away; she was being well fed on the promise of an answer. At the suanming xiansheng's urging, she followed a slew of remedies that he prescribed at a rate of $250 USD per session. They were mild at first: burn incense and *ketou* every day. Place rooster figurines around the house to keep bad spirits away. Add three drops of a special oil to morning meals, a concoction reserved for only the most critical of clients.

It's not working, their mother complained. *I feel the demon growing stronger with each passing day.*

The demon is clever in its trickery and unbearably cruel in its punishments, the suanming xiansheng agreed. It's a green-faced monster with teeth like a saw. The pain that your ancestor dealt upon the poor girl who loved him, the demon now vows to deal upon you. That is why it has chosen to live inside your daughter, painting itself with her skin. Rid her of the poison inside and you will rid yourselves of the demon for the rest of your lifetimes.

For $300 USD, they moved on to more drastic measures. Skunk vine, the suanming xiansheng assured her, is proven to drive evil spirits out. Gone was the shrub from the front yard; in its place, skunk vines so ordinary it was hard to believe they possessed any sort of power beyond their flat arrow leaves, that dull wash of green. But how quickly they grew. They crawled out of their plots, up along the walls of the townhome, and when they had nowhere else to go, his mother brought them inside. The vines choked the banisters and dripped off the countertops, overtaking the floors with the speed of something supernatural. Soon, the whole house was covered, and no matter how carefully Eason moved, the vine would find a way to touch him so that he trembled as he walked through the house, hating the contact of the leaves and their sulfuric smell that seeped into his skin.

There were other things, too, things his mother did to Faye that scared him more than the skunk vine or the figurines. By then, he knew the truth: The demon *was* real, but Faye was not the one whom it had chosen. No, the demon lived in his mother, had crawled inside her bones and possessed her. That was what he began calling them: possessions. Easier to believe that their mother had been taken by an evil spirit and contorted into something unrecognizable than to admit the reality. Easier to claim a divide between her and the demon and cling to the echoes of her old self that were still in there, their *real* mother, who did not tear through the house with a switch made out of the wood from her peach trees, than to accept that this was all of her. Sometimes, it was calm and she was loving, and Eason would feel that swell of adoration return. But then a darkness would come over her and it would start again. Their mother was a small woman, a feather of a woman, but she could grow into a huge and powerful thing, someone neither of her children could recognize, but they did still love her, and that was the most terrifying part—that this person you loved more than anything in the world could also cause you so much terror.

On the way out of the garage, Julian asks him about the call.

"It was no one," Eason says. "Wrong number."

Julian peers at him. "You smashed the phone because of a wrong number?"

They know each other too well. Spend nearly a year memorizing the shapes a body makes, and you will start to notice its cracks, too.

The car slows at a stoplight. Julian watches him, thinking. Then, he leans forward to whisper something to the driver.

The car starts moving again. Eason follows the buildings as they pass by, lights from offices and shops blurring together into long streaks. It reminds him of a screensaver on the family computer, which shot the viewer through a perpetual night sky, all the stars flattened into lines of yellow and white from the velocity of travel. It was not so bad, letting the universe swallow you whole, he had thought then. It still would not be so bad, he thinks now.

The car turns onto a street busy with the glow of neon signs. Women stalk down the sidewalk in bodysuits and heels, their blown-out hair bouncing behind them. From the nightclubs, loud, throttling music plays.

Julian exits the car. He hands the driver a hundred-dollar bill for his discretion and instructs him to pick them up in three hours. Eason stumbles out after him. He watches the car go and when he turns, Julian has already disappeared into one of the clubs.

Inside, the ceilings are low, the floor purpled with lights that shoot in different directions like oil dropped in a hot pan. The crowd, too, cannot be wholly captured; there are cold-shouldered goths, tight-jeaned hipsters, sparkle-pony girls with rhinestones on their cheekbones. Julian leans over the bar and asks something of the bartender, a pretty girl wearing a red corset and fishnet gloves. The music here is neither pop nor hip-hop, but something rhythmic and squirming, as if searching for an opening in the flesh to slither through.

"Tequila," Julian yells, sliding a shot glass over. Eason reaches for his sunglasses, remembering the threat of hidden cameras and watchful eyes. They are far from being household names—Brooks is constantly reminding them of that—but they also stand out in a crowd. Idols are bred to have that pull.

Julian leaves his face open, unfazed. "No one will recognize us here," he says. He puts the shot glass to his lips and throws his head back. Behind him, the pretty bartender is watching, her eyes following the arc his head makes against the lights. Eason throws his back, too. The tequila burns its way down, draining into his abdomen.

The bartender has two rum and Cokes waiting on the counter. "On the house," she says, flashing Julian a hopeful smile. He does not seem to notice, looking instead to the dance floor on the lower level of the club. Eason already feels the effects of the alcohol as it creeps through him, his head growing lighter, limbs floating upward as if he is on a plane just after takeoff, climbing the open sky.

Julian grabs his arm and pulls him to the stairs leading down to the dance floor.

"Aren't you tired of dancing?" Eason has to shout.

"You mean what we do on stage? That's not dancing."

The dance floor is a crowd. Eason sucks his arms in to avoid the bodies pressed around him, but it is like flicking off one fly only to attract ten more. From every direction, limbs slick with sweat rub against him, and he spins and spins, dodging their touch, until he looks up and finds himself in the middle of the dance floor, surrounded by strangers. He wants to get out but he does not know how. Someone grazes the small of his back and he jerks around to glare at them. It is a man who looks to be in his fifties, the violet lights deepening the grooves that time has carved into his face. "Are you the demon?" Eason asks him dumbly, but the man rolls away, replaced by a woman with the same lines around her eyes as his mother, wearing pigtails and a tutu and a smile that stretches beyond the realm of her face. "You're the demon," he tells her, and she leans forward, rising on her sneakered toes, and plants a kiss on his cheek. "You bet I am, handsome!" she caws, and then she is gone, too, and now a group of five emerge, encircling him, their heads crowned by blinking fairy lights, elves or faes or stupid fucking jesters, it does not matter, because they are the demon split into five, and he roars at them before ripping himself from their outstretched arms, a human bazooka through the crowd, until he finds himself in front of Julian again.

"There you are," Julian says, holding him steady by the shoulders.

"Sorry," he hears himself say. He sounds drunk.

Julian is not bothered by it. He begins to move to the music, still that strange rhythmic beat with no melody. This time, Julian does not dance as he does on stage. Here, under the artificial fog and strobing lights, he becomes a more compact, threatening version of himself.

It is difficult to dance to this kind of music—there is no predictability, no instruction. It simply beats on and on. Eason looks around at the rest of the dance floor, and no longer do they look like the demon. They move in the way that Julian is moving now, succumbing to the music and the freedom of vanishing within it. Everyone is here, Eason realizes, to rid themselves of something.

Knowing this, he also knows now what to do. His body already yearns for the riddance of many things: His guilt. His regret. His mother and the demon that twisted her. He feels the solid reminder of his existence as the bass hits him again and again. He welcomes it. Hit harder, he urges. Harder. He wants to be filled up and cut down until he is nothing but a slab off which all light is broken and refracted. As the music swells, he closes his eyes, melting into the bodies that writhe around him, and gives in.

POST #588

I keep seeing people speculating about whether or not the boys have girlfriends and I'm just like HELLO?? Are you DUMB??

I'm not saying the boys aren't allowed to have girlfriends. I'm just saying there's NO WAY it could work with their busy lifestyles. Remember Denim's *Day in the Life* video? His schedule was packed with dance practice, album recording, a music video shoot, and press junkets. And that was just ONE DAY. They barely have time to eat and sleep. How would they be able to keep a girlfriend? Be real, I'm begging you.

And even if they did have time to date, what girl out there would actually be deserving of any of our boys? How do we know a girl isn't just chasing fame? I, for one, wouldn't trust ANY girl who gets her claws on the boys. It would make more sense for the boys to just date each other.

Plus, the boys have stated MULTIPLE times they aren't looking to date right now. They're fulfilled by touring and meeting the fans. That's us, in case you forgot. For them, WE are enough.

MINNIE

The walk to Nate's house is pleasant. It is the first below-seventy night of fall and college students are out in droves, laughing and falling over one another. Minnie walks alone. Down Guadalupe, she dodges drunken frat boys, who shout out, "Konnichiwa, baby!" She bristles at this, but as the frat boys high-five and laugh to each other, she also feels a small glimmer of gratitude—at least she was worth noticing.

Nate lives on Pearl, a street in West Campus saddled with craftsman homes built in the seventies. This is the side of town where the party houses and historic fraternities lay claim, their fenced yards perpetually glittering with empty beer cans, but Nate's street sits at the edge of the neighborhood, closer to the hardware store and thrift shops lining Guadalupe. Quieter here, more mature. *I could live in a place like this*, she thinks as she nears his house. She hears voices drifting from the front porch. This will be her first party.

Nate told her to use the side door, so she walks up the driveway, the uneven gravel causing her to stumble. She is glad it is dark. She wonders if her eyeliner is smudging. This is one of the things she hates about herself—her fat, oily eyelids never seem to wear makeup the way others' do, the liner always devolving within an hour and tattooing the flesh beneath her eyes with a faint black bruise. As she reaches the side door to the house, she wipes at her face, reassuring herself that she is pretty, that she looks put-together.

Inside, she meets a thrum of bodies awash in booming bass and multicolored liquor. A group is gathered around the kitchen island, cheering. For a moment, Minnie panics, fearing that she will have to make her way through the entire house to find Nate, but then she sees him: Nate is at the head of the kitchen island, drinking from a red Solo cup and looking completely cool. He smiles happily at his friends, eyes crinkling. Then, he sees Minnie.

"Make some space," he commands, tunneling through the group, to her. He grabs Minnie's hand and leads her to the kitchen. "Everyone"—their heads turn obediently—"this is Min."

The group gazes back at her. What began as interest quickly wanes to polite acknowledgment as they take in the anxious youth of her. A few girls give her smiles, but only one side of their mouths lift. They wear tank tops and jeans, a stark departure from Minnie's own floral shift dress, which now feels tacky in comparison—she is a costume; they are themselves. The girls scan her, but not out of competition; rather, irritation, as if she were a little sister who had snuck into the back seat. *Who's this Asian chick?* their gazes say. *What's Nate doing with her?*

Nate hands her a red cup filled with beer. "They're about to play flip cup. Do you want to join?"

She does not want to make a fool of herself in front of Nate's friends. But she also wants to be close to Nate, to look cool for Nate. He knows this, too—she can tell by the way he already expects her to say *yes*.

The rules are simple: Chug the drink in the cup, then flip the cup so that it lands face down. They will play in a relay, five per team, running up and down the line. Minnie will begin and end the game.

"No pressure," a man on the other side of her says. "I'm Clark, by the way. Nate's roommate."

His eyes are blue or green—she cannot be sure, for they are partially hidden behind the glare of his glasses. She remembers Nate mentioning that his roommate majored in geology, and that this party was a send-off for his study abroad trip to Argentina. She shakes Clark's hand, which is wet with drink, but she does not mind. He is the only one to offer her this kindness, and for that, she decides he is an ally.

"You're up, Min," Nate tells her. To keep the teams even, he takes the place of referee.

Minnie stares at her cup. Drink, set it down, flip the cup. Nate brandishes three fingers and begins counting down. *Don't let them think you don't deserve to be here*, she tells herself. *Swallow, even if it hurts.*

"Go!"

The group erupts into hollers and cheers, their trash talk breaking down whatever polite comradery existed only moments before. She hears "YOU SUCK" and "CHOKE" and someone somewhere is definitely chanting "FISH!" but she absorbs none of it. She sees only the bottom of the cup as she throws its contents in her mouth. The beer slams against the back of her throat, the impact so violent it makes her want to throw up, but she cannot embarrass Nate now. She forces herself to swallow.

"Oh shit!"

"She's a chugger!"

Minnie sets the cup down, and, without thinking, flips it over. It lands, face down. The group roars their approval before turning their attention to Clark, who is next in line. He, too, is successful. So are the two people after him. Her team is ahead, but only just.

At the end of the line, the order reverses. She watches as the cups flip and land one by one, each time getting closer to where she stands. And then it is her turn again, the beginning and the end. She chugs her beer, which Nate refilled for her, now hardened to its sting. She sets her cup back down over the ledge of the kitchen island. She can feel Nate's eyes on her, and the sharp eyes of the girls, all of whom, she is certain, desire him, too.

She places her middle finger underneath the cup. She feels its weight, imperceptible, and the smooth texture of the red-painted plastic. She thinks of pressing down on a piano key, of sliding a sheet of paper from a drawer. Of the pressure she uses to dot cream around her eyes.

With a touch that could be called chaste, she flips her cup.

There is no time to register the victory, for it is Nate who grabs her first. "You did it!" he shouts, at her and everyone. "Yes, yes, yes!"

The team takes her from him, pulling her into a hug. Her nose slams against a shoulder, the smell of wet bread engulfing her, but she does not turn away. Then she is being passed around to her teammates, each one yanking her in for their own version of a clobbering hug, until she goes limp and smiles, because this—surely this—is what college is really all about.

At the end of the kitchen island Nate waits, gazing at her with the same awe she so easily gave him.

"Hey," she says.

"Hey." He gives her a lopsided grin. "You did great."

The earlier uncertainties of the evening are forgotten. Behind them, her teammates chant each of the team member's names, hers included. "Where'd you find this one, Nate?" someone shouts. "She's a keeper."

"You should go to your team," Nate says, looking awkward for the first time all evening.

"I should," Minnie says. "But I'd rather dance with you."

Fed perhaps by the victory, perhaps by the alcohol, a warm glow of confidence builds in her chest and radiates through her bones. She hums with it. She thinks of the boys of HOURglass, the swagger that ripples across their skin. Tonight, she will take some of that for herself. Nate sees the change in her. He seems to like it. He shrugs his shoulders in mock defeat as Minnie leads them to the living room, where Daft Punk transitions to Outkast.

Minnie has never been a dancer, but she has studied for this moment, replaying countless videos of the boys dancing. She twists her hips the way she has seen Jelly do. She runs her fingers up and down her body, touching herself, when really, all she wants is for Nate to touch her. But Nate is all pumping chest and stomping feet. He has no particular rhythm, darting and jerking as if every beat shocks him with electricity. It is difficult to dance with Nate in this way, difficult when he is not mirroring her, but moving to his own time.

When the song ends, Minnie is out of breath. A cold spoonful of sweat deposits between her breasts, making her bra damp and uncomfortable. Her head rings from the loud music and alcohol. When a new group arrives at the party, catching Nate's attention, Minnie excuses herself, promising that she will be back.

In the bathroom, she breathes from her mouth to avoid its smell.

The room feels inexplicably wet; all of the towels have already been used so many times that they hang heavy and soggy on the rack. She tries not to look into the trash can or the toilet, convincing herself that the dark liquid at the bottom of the bowl is rust and nothing else. The sink has a rim of razored hair around it, and the mirror is splattered with white flecks, which Minnie deduces must be toothpaste.

She assesses herself. Her cheeks are flushed from dancing and alcohol, but in a way that makes her feel vibrant, more attractive. Her eyeliner has indeed smudged beneath her eyes, but rather than making her look foolish, it adds a reckless allure to her face. Perhaps it is this face that will finally earn her a real kiss from Nate.

Someone knocks on the door. Minnie finishes patting herself, then tosses the toilet paper in the trash can. She ruffles her hair to give it volume, smiles at herself in the mirror, and exits.

In the living room, "Sex on Fire" by Kings of Leon blasts from the speakers while everyone screams out the blistered words of the chorus. Someone zooms past her and drapes a red feather boa over her shoulders. Another person crashes into her mid-spin, spilling his drink on the carpet.

Nate is in the center of the crowd, but his body is not thrashing about to the song, nor is he bellowing out the lyrics like everyone else. He is still, chin to his chest. His hips are the only thing that moves. Pressed against them is a thin woman with short, white-blond hair—a newcomer to the party. She has her back to Nate as she grinds into his pelvis, eyes closed, lips parted. As the song reaches its chorus, the woman turns to Nate, holds his face, and begins kissing him.

Minnie backs away, letting the other bodies swallow her. The red feather boa is scratchy around her neck. She wants to cry.

"Hey." She turns. Clark the roommate is there. He sees what she sees. "Let's get you a drink."

Minnie can tell that he feels sorry for her, which makes her want to cry even more. The warm glow vanishes as quickly as it came, leaving behind the pit of a stone fruit in its wake. She wishes the boys were really here, that their beautiful faces and love—love for her—would be enough to light up all the ugly corners of this party and blind everyone who had caused her hurt this evening—the haughty girls, Nate, the thin woman with white-blond hair. But no. Out of everyone here, she is most to blame, for daring to believe that she could be someone deserving of Nate's time.

Clark steers her back to the kitchen island, which is strewn with empty cups. He places two shots of clear liquid down in front of Minnie. She takes one, and, with the image of Nate and the white-blond woman on the dance floor flashing violence, empties it into her mouth.

She doubles over, choking.

Clark laughs so hard it looks like he, not Minnie, might now be the one to cry. "Sorry," he says. "I just wanted to see if you could take it."

"What *was* that?"

"Everclear. You needed a wake-me-up."

The unpleasant feeling starts to dim, replaced by a new coat of the same courage she tasted earlier that evening. The more she gives in to it, the faster it hits. *I like this*, she thinks. She feels loose, like every valve in her circulatory system has opened and blood is gushing through, filling her with heat. Clark takes her in, watching as she sinks into this altered state. He looks amazed by her.

"Do you know who's dancing with Nate?"

"Kristín. She's studying abroad from Iceland."

"Are they—"

"Together?" Clark looks over to the pair, still glued in their slow grind. "Well, yes and no."

Minnie nods, not sure how she should receive this information. It is all so confusing, these invisible boundaries of what a relationship is and is not. "I thought maybe we—"

"You and Nate?" Clark chuckles. "He does this a lot. Goes out with freshmen, keeps them on speed dial, because it can never be anything serious. *And* because you all treat him like a god. But really, he's in love with Kristín. Everyone else is just a placeholder."

Clark is not trying to make her feel bad. In fact, he is being merciful by telling her the truth. Still, what he says hurts—not so much the what, but what it means: that Minnie is not special after all. In reality, she is just a freshman, a fish, a little girl.

Clark watches her. “Hey. You shouldn’t be wasting your time with someone like Nate. You could be with anyone you wanted.”

“That’s not true,” she says, looking down.

“Trust me.” He lifts her chin with two fingers, willing her to look back up at him. “I think you’re really cool.”

Minnie knows what he is saying. She is grateful to him for saying it. Nate, with his boy-crush face and athletic frame, is the one she wants. But at least Clark is here with her now, and interested in looking at her, talking to her, keeping her company.

On another night, if she were not so humiliated, she might give Clark a smile. She might even give him her number. But tonight, when she is fully aware of how close and far away Nate is, how the woman who came between them was there all along, she just wants to crawl back into bed and watch videos of the boys on her laptop.

“Have one more drink with me,” Clark says.

She will not let Nate see his power over her. She will stay here, cool and unaffected, for just a moment more. Clark pours more Everclear in her cup and soon, she is no longer thinking of Nate and Kristín, but of how nice Clark is, and how many similarities they have despite the difference of their majors. She is not sure if it is the alcohol or the evening itself, but Clark begins to look handsome to her, even as he strokes her face, touches her neck, pulls her in closer to him.

At some point in the evening, she allows him to lead her onto the dance floor. Clark is only a little taller than her, so it is difficult to line up her face against his shoulder. Her cheekbones hurt from the awkward placement, but she endures it, telling herself that at least she is dancing with someone who likes her. Clark holds one hand to the small of her back, so close to her butt that she cannot be sure if he is actually touching it or not. The other hand holds hers. They sway and turn in circles. Minnie thinks that they must look like a teapot and giggles at the idea, stumbling against him.

“Whoa,” he whispers. “Easy there.”

She is, she realizes, extremely drunk. So drunk that she is no longer sure if she is spinning or the dance floor is. She clings to Clark, whose smell reminds her of the body spray that fogged out from the boys' locker room in middle school. But on Clark, the scent is okay. Could she date a guy like him? He holds her with delicacy, the way one might a baby chick, but there is a tremble to his touch, too, as if he is afraid that she might run away.

"I'm really drunk."

He stops dancing and peers at her. It would be so easy to go to sleep right now, she thinks. In fact, that is all she wants to do.

"I'm sleepy," she tells him.

"Okay. Let's get you cooled off."

She clutches him as he takes them through the crowd, to the bathroom. Inside, the white ceiling light hits her and she yelps. "This is so embarrassing."

He eases her down against the edge of the bathtub, then steps back to assess her. "I just realized you've been wearing a boa this whole time."

"Someone gave it to me. God, I'm *so* drunk." Then, without understanding the impulse, she throws her face into the bathtub, spraying vomit everywhere.

Clark has a wet towel in hand. Minnie takes it, the beginnings of a headache cresting on her skull.

"Thank you." Her throat burns. "I think I should go home." She wipes her mouth with the towel, recoiling at the musty smell. "Can you help me up?"

She raises her hand, waiting for Clark to take it. Instead, he turns and locks the door.

Minnie gazes up at him. This is the first time she has seen Clark's full face in the light and now she can finally see his eyes. Green. It is these eyes, which remind her of a snake, that introduce a new sensation in her. He is a man who looks much older than he is. And, he is a man who wants something from her, a want both so unfamiliar and recognizable that it rouses her from her stupor.

"I'm going to go now," she says, firmer this time. Without the alcohol clouding her head, everything in the bathroom comes into sharp relief—the mildewed towels hanging from the door, the soap scum around the faucet. Looking at these things makes her salivate. The bile rises in her throat once more. She wants to be in her bed. She wants to brush her teeth. She wants the boys.

"Clark," she says, "let me out."

When Minnie leaves the party twenty minutes later, she does not say goodbye to anyone, especially not Nate. Not that she would have had a chance to; he and Kristín are nowhere to be found, although everyone, including Minnie, hears the moans coming from upstairs. She walks alone to the end of the driveway, past the drunken conversation coming from the porch.

"Bye, fish!" someone yells at her. She pulls out her phone—it reads 3:42 A.M.

The October night is not cold, but her skin is clammy from everything that has come before this. Her mother would chide her for walking into the wind after sweating so much. She clutches the red feather boa and wraps it tighter around her neck and shoulders, trying to create a scarf for herself, but finds that half its feathers are ripped out. The other half, she remembers, are strewn across the bathroom floor.

EASON

By the middle of November, they've put on twelve shows in eight cities, running down the East Coast from New York City to DC, then jutting inward for the chilly bluster of Chicago. The performance improves with each show until it is close to sublime, and Brooks has nothing left to threaten but "break a leg" and "kill 'em dead." Reviewing the concert footage, Eason thinks that this is what a professional band looks like after hundreds of shows, not four boys on their first year of the job. He can barely recognize them when he watches the videos, maturity and confidence now sewn into their skin. Most of all, he can barely recognize himself, no longer a tangle of anger and shame that tears around the stage as he did in those early days, but someone who has control of himself, who can capture and release the emotions within and feed them back to the audience. Each time, he vows, he will do better. And each time, he does do better, because there is no greater reward than what the fans can give him in return.

When it comes time to say goodnight to them, he finds it increasingly difficult to leave the stage. He looks out into the sea of cell phone lights and wishes that he could remember what this feels like forever. The sound of his stage name in their mouths, the way they will scream it until they are hoarse. How faultless he is, in their eyes. By the time the four of them return to the dressing room, he is already longing for the stage again, torn from it as he was, because those ninety minutes are not enough.

"That's how addicts talk," Colt says when Eason expresses this out loud. "Should we be worried?"

Minwoo tells Colt not to joke about that sort of thing and gives Eason an encouraging pat on the back. "It's good. It's how we should all feel."

Eason shrugs. He does not need anyone thinking there is something wrong with him. He glances at Julian, hoping for a smirk or under-the-breath comment to diffuse the awkwardness, but his friend just watches him, concern on his face.

This show in Chicago concludes the first leg of their tour, with the South and West Coast still to come. For now, they have a week of rest before their next two shows in Charlotte. It is the first reprieve from back-to-back performances in weeks, which, Minwoo decides, deserves a celebration, so the four of them grab a private room at a KBBQ restaurant along South China Place in Chinatown. They order pork belly and soju and skilletfuls of corn cheese, all agreeing to forget their tour diets for one night. Eason stuffs his mouth with beef dumplings and a ream of fish cakes. He slurps the ramen up like a dog at a water bowl, not minding when the errant noodles slap against his cheeks. Every shot of sodium makes him gleeful. Tomorrow, they will pay for their transgressions, but there are ways to take care of that.

"I can't wait to move out of the apartment," Colt says. He is red-faced from the food and the drinking—they all are. "They have to put us in a nicer place, right? Now that we're blowing up?"

Julian flips pork belly on the grill. "It's not like we'll be there much anyway."

"Still. It's nice to have your own space. I want a big yard. Lots of trees, so the paparazzi and stalkers can't find me."

Easy for him to say, Eason thinks. Colt's parents could bail him out of his debt to the record label in the blink of an eye. He tries not to think of how much his own debt must be by now.

"It's embarrassing," Colt continues. "We're on our way to being the hottest band in the country, but we're still sharing one bathroom. Imagine if the fans knew. They'd freak out."

"Some things they don't need to know," Julian says.

"Well maybe they should. I bet we could leak it and get them to put pressure on the label to move us to a better place."

"You want to use them?" Eason says, nostrils flaring. "They're not weapons."

Colt rolls his eyes at Eason. "Stop being so precious. I'm not saying we would use them. I'm just saying—well, our fans want the best for us, right?"

Julian reaches across the table, picking up a nest of ramen with his chopsticks. "Let's drop it. Look, Eason's hands are shaking."

Eason shoots back the rest of his soju. Colt talks about the fans the same way Brooks does—as if they are brainless, ready to follow the four of them to the ends of the earth, no questions asked. But what hardships, other than strenuous hours in the practice room, has Colt endured? Of course he thinks it is easy to receive love—he has never been in a position to question whether or not he deserves such a thing. Love, to him, is a given.

"You're both wrong." This time, it is Minwoo, who has been watching the conversation quietly.

"What are you talking about?"

Minwoo jabs a finger in Colt's direction, his head swaying. Eason looks down at his shot glass—it is empty, and he cannot recall how many times they have refilled it for him. "You're talking like we have any sort of power over the fans when that's not true. There wouldn't even be an HOURglass without them."

Julian puts down his chopsticks. "We're here because we've worked really hard. Give yourself some credit."

Minwoo refills and empties his glass, the blush of alcohol burning through his carefully applied foundation. "The fans made us, and they can break us. From now on, everything we do has to be for them." He slams a closed fist down on the table. "I already lost everything once. I'm not losing it again!"

"We get it," Colt says, looking alarmed. He moves Minwoo's glass away. "It's okay. We get it."

"I think that's enough for tonight," Julian says, standing. "I'll go pay."

"I'll do it," Colt says. "Eason, watch him, will you?" He and Julian both exit the room.

Minwoo's head slumps down, chin hitting his chest. It is rare to see him in this state, the coat of an upright captain shed. Minwoo, who must have woken up after his surgery and felt, long before he was told, the destruction of his vocal cords by a surgeon who downed two bottles of wine before breakfast. Minwoo, who would have borne that anguish alone in his hospital bed, holding in a scream. For the first time, Eason sees the unfathomable responsibility that rests on Minwoo's shoulders, not just as the founding member of HOURglass and its leader, but as a man who has been offered a second chance at a dream. He reaches out to clasp Minwoo's hand.

"You get it, right?" Minwoo mutters, rocking himself back and forth. "We can't end up like those girls."

Only a few months ago, another K-pop-inspired girl group from a rival record label hoping to beat BabyGold Records to the Western market had been slated to storm the scene. They were called IN X BLOOM, designed to fill the girl-next-door niche that had been recently vacated by a pop star arrested for drunk driving. The market was ripe for IN X BLOOM's wholesome image to conquer North America, and then the world. Just days before their debut, an anonymous source leaked one of the girl's blogs, a forgotten relic from her middle school years of nearly a decade ago. The blog was seemingly innocuous, filled with poems about her crush and complaints over homework. In fact, the blog could have been an additional lever in cementing IN X BLOOM's narrative as Your Relatable Girlfriends Who Also Happened To Be Pop Stars.

It could have been, but for three posts: one, making fun of a bigger girl at school; two, calling all people over 135 pounds "whales"; and three, expressing that she would never, in a million years, ever let herself get fat, and if she did, then she would simply kill herself.

The fans were furious. They launched a petition to have IN X BLOOM disbanded before their first-ever live performance, a venture that gained nearly seventy thousand signatures. They spammed every news article, video, and mention of the band, urging networks, sponsors, and brands to cut ties. In the end, it worked. The guilty member issued a tear-ridden apology—*I was twelve*, she said, *I didn't know any better. I no longer hold those hurtful views and they do not represent my heart*. But the fans did not believe her. *Even I knew better when I was twelve*, one commenter said. *You're only sorry because you got caught*, spat another. *If I were you, I'd just kill myself.* They called her phone, sent threats to her apartment. The harassment got so bad that the member had to be checked into a facility for debilitating anxiety. IN X BLOOM's debut was delayed, then eventually canceled.

When they heard the news, the four of them kept saying how glad they were that it did not happen to them. But for Eason, a new fear arose: The secrets that he kept—it was imperative that they stay hidden. If something as minor as IN X BLOOM's transgression could lead to the implosion of a life, then he was more at risk than they would ever know.

"Idols," Minwoo repeats to Eason now. "That's who we are. That's who we have to be."

"I know," Eason tells him, even though he is not sure how much he believes it yet. "I know."

"I don't even have friends outside of you guys. All my friends back home stopped talking to me. They moved on with their lives, they've got jobs and degrees now. They think I'm crazy. I mean, it *is* crazy if you think about it. So many groups have tried and failed before us. All that training we did. Not seeing our families for nearly a year. Not being able to date or even have friends that are girls. It's crazy. But for me, it's worth it. For Colt and Julian, too. But what about you?"

"What do you mean?"

"You never talk about your *why*. You didn't always want to do this, did you? So why do you stay?"

He wonders if he should tell Minwoo the truth. Wonders how many words it would take to sum up the sadness of his existence, and would this room of burnt meat and scorched fat and wounded, wounded air be able to contain it all. But before he has a chance to answer, Minwoo buries his head in his hands, the alcohol making the choice for both of them.

"I don't want them to see me like this. Why'd you let me drink so much?"

"I'm sorry," Eason says. Then, without really thinking about it, he reaches out and plucks a strand of hair from Minwoo's head.

"Ow!"

"There," Eason tells him, examining the strand. "Now you aren't drunk anymore."

Minwoo stares at him, his expression shuttling between shock and anger. Eason wonders if Minwoo will strike him. But then he laughs, rubbing the spot. "I do feel better. What was that?"

A silly game, one he and Faye used to play. Demon hunting, they called it. Faye would pretend to be the demon and chase after Eason. The only way to defeat it was to pluck a hair from the head of the possessed. He did not know why. It was just some rule that Faye made up.

"Eason?" Julian and Colt have returned, their faces apprehensive.

"Just a dumb superstition," Eason tells Minwoo. He stands, giving the others a small nod to let them know that the storm has passed. "Ready to go?"

"If you're so scared of the demon," Faye said, "try being it for once."

He told her that did not make any sense. The demon only possessed girls. That was what their mother and the suanming xiansheng said.

"You don't know that," Faye said, shaking her head. Her long black hair swung behind her like a pendulum. "Just try. It'll make you feel less scared. I promise."

They were in the backyard. The summer was at its height, a blazing stretch of triple-digit afternoons that made the hair on their heads burn. Their mother had sent them outside to water the peach trees, which had begun dropping their leaves from thirst.

He lay down on the earth, the way he had seen Faye do whenever they played this game. Small rocks shifted under him, kneading his skin. He did not hate it.

"Oh, fearsome demon," Faye called out in a singsong voice. "Are you there?"

He sprung up, his back straight and rigid like Nosferatu. "Wo laiiiiiiiii le," he croaked.

Faye looked like she was trying to hide a laugh. "Oh no," she cried, backing away from him. "It's really you."

He was on his feet. He imagined himself a dead and decaying thing, all the skin dripping off his bones, bones which housed a century of rage. "Youuuu wiiiiiiill paaaaaaay," he gurgled. He took a stiff step toward his sister, but caught the end of his shoelace and toppled to the ground. Faye began laughing, and soon, he was laughing, too. He felt a prickling sensation on his scalp and looked up to see her holding a strand of his hair, black and straight as a needle. "Got you."

"You look awful," Colt tells Eason the next morning at the elevators. "How much cheese was in that corn, Minwoo? Eason's blown up like a pufferfish."

"It's just mozzarella." Minwoo's voice is hoarse from his own hangover. "It shouldn't make you bloat." He inspects Eason's face. "Have you been crying? I thought I was the only one who cries when they drink."

Julian interrupts the inquisition. "We're going to be late." He waves his phone. "The managers just called—they're downstairs."

It is good timing. Minwoo, always one to be punctual, forgets about Eason's face and rushes into the elevator. Colt follows, already interested in whether they can get an IV drip on the way to the airport.

Downstairs, the managers are nowhere to be found. "What happened?" Minwoo asks Julian. "I thought you said they were here."

"Oh," Julian says. "Maybe I misheard."

Colt lets out an annoyed sigh. "You're still drunk. If I don't get a coffee, I'm going to kill myself."

But when the two of them walk away, Julian turns to Eason and gives him a small nod. Eason looks down at his watch—they are twenty minutes early for their call time. "Thanks," he says. "I owe you."

"No, you don't. I'm just returning the favor."

It's true, Eason thinks. How many times over the past year has he woken up to the sound of Julian retching in the bathroom, followed by the final flush afterward? How many times has he smelled the rancid air that followed him out? He never asked Julian about it, only rolled over in his bed, pretending to have been asleep the whole time.

"I just had a bad dream."

Julian nods again. "Good thing you woke up."

MINNIE

Minnie will not be going back home to Colorado Springs for Thanksgiving. "I have too much work to do," she tells her mother over the phone. "I'll see you and Dad over winter break."

It is a lie, the part about having too much work. Actually, her classes have been manageable this semester. The advantages of being a first-year English major, she thinks wryly.

Her mother is disappointed, but understanding, which makes Minnie feel worse. "Your dad and I are always thinking of you," she tells Minnie. "We wonder if you are getting enough to eat, if you are taking care of your body. If you are happy and enjoying time with your new friends."

"I am," Minnie says, crawling to the edge of the bed, away from her phone. As if distance will make the lie better, or true. She hears a voice in the hallway exclaim "Have a good break!" followed by jaunty footsteps and the purr of luggage rolling along carpet. Minnie listens for the body that holds such happiness, tracing its path as it descends the stairs and emerges onto the sidewalk below her window, where it joins the other happy bodies waiting at the curb, their conversations overlapping as they bid each other goodbye. She slams the window shut. The voices go away and the dorm is finally quiet, save for the fuzz of her mother on speakerphone.

"It's such a shame for you to be on campus all alone. Will you be okay?"

"I won't be alone. Someone invited me to a Friendsgiving."

Earlier that morning, she received an email from Anna Peng inviting all staff members of the zine to an anti-Thanksgiving potluck. Akash declined; he would be going home for the holiday, but Harrison and

Kate responded yes. Minnie wrote back thanking Anna for the invite, but saying she was busy. *Sorry to hear that*, Anna responded almost immediately. *How's the writing coming along?*

Great! Minnie sent back, but that was a lie, too. She had not even started.

"Just a *someone*?" Her mother wants to know. "Does this someone have a name? Is he handsome?"

She digs her nails into her knees. "It's not like that."

"Well, we love you," her mother says too gently, too dearly. It is the way they have always ended their conversations—neither could leave until the other said it back. Lately, it has been hard for Minnie to say it back. She still loves her parents, of course, but it feels like that love has been tainted by something she cannot explain.

"I love you, too," she manages. The words, a scab in her mouth.

After the party, Minnie did not hear from Nate again. Every time she opened their conversation and began typing, her mind flashed to his slow grind with Kristín on the dance floor. What had Clark called her? A placeholder. The word clung to her no matter how hard she tried to fling it off, as if she had unknowingly walked through a cobweb, and as the weeks passed without any word from Nate, she felt it become more and more true.

She willed herself not to think about Clark and what happened in the bathroom, but it was a losing game. He had not touched her during the encounter, except at the beginning, after he unzipped his pants and she had looked away in horror. He had reached out with the ease of someone reaching for a familiar mug from the shelf, and grabbed her by her cheeks, yanking her head back around so that she could do nothing but look at him. No, he had not touched her but for this moment—anyone observing the situation would say that all he did was touch himself. And yet. He had touched her, had he not? Had he not?

It was this question, and the shame of not knowing the answer, that occupied her. He had drilled a hole in her head and pooled himself in, so that every silence, every lapse, belonged to him. He was there when she completed her homework, hovering over the words of her American poetry anthology; he was there at the crosswalk, watching her scurry head down and folding in to herself; and he was there in her mother's voice, so that the words Minnie heard were not tender, but false. In the shower, Minnie would rake at her skin until small pipettes of red soaked through and then, only then, would she feel that perhaps she had shed a layer of Clark somehow. But the skin always grew back. In the morning, there he was again.

Her only respite lay with the boys. When she was with them, she could forget that Clark happened to her. Minwoo, Denim, Jelly, and Halo—they were her armor, repelling the misery and shame that pooled around her. *Lean on us, Minnie*, they said with their smooth voices and gentle eyes. *Because we are yours and you are ours.*

On Thanksgiving Day, Minnie disappears into a big-hooded coat, even though the weather is temperate, and quickly walks to Kinsolving for dry turkey and chalky mashed potatoes. For dessert, she lets herself have pumpkin pie with a sad squirt of Reddi-wip. Without its students, campus is quiet once more, but this time, she does not feel the cozy belonging that permeated the place during fall break. Instead, she sees stains along the sidewalk and skeletons in place of trees. The ugly sand color that paints each building. Campus becomes another pounding reminder of the thing that happened to her, done by a man who also calls such a campus home.

When she exits the dining hall and turns for the dorm, the wind picks up, blowing dirt in her face. There, in her big stupid coat and with a belly full of lifeless food, she thinks of what her mother would say if she could see just how alone her daughter is now, and she cries.

Back in the safety of her room, it is Halo who waits for her. "—wanted to say a quick hi before bed," he murmurs as she logs on to the live-streaming website. His hair is soft and fluffed, a sign that he must be fresh from a shower. When he moves to adjust the camera, the collar of his bathrobe unfurls, revealing the pale triangle of his bare chest. Minnie brings the laptop closer.

He is not noble like Minwoo, or boisterous like Denim. He does not have the delicacy of Jelly. No, he is imperfect and hard, a knife of a person, but this is why she loves him most. She loves him for his silence, his discernment, for that hard-set jaw and the muscle that pulses against it like a small fist. She loves him because she can see through him. Like Halo, she protects herself by closing herself away. Like Halo, there is more to her than meets the eye. It is his need for secrecy that makes him beautiful to her, for she recognizes it in herself.

"Tell me what's on your mind," Halo says, looking directly into the camera, at her. "I want to hear it all."

He pauses to read the messages, which flood into the live chat box below the video screen. Minnie watches them flash by, visible for a millisecond before being buried by new messages. *I don't know how to explain it but I feel at peace watching you*, says one. *Why eat food when you're the five-course meal????* demands another. *HALO I LOVE YOU!!!*; *te amo te amo te amo*; *I would let you kill me*; *I AM ON THE GROUND, IN TEARS, RIPPING AT MY HAIR, PULLING MY TEETH OUT, THROWING UP, SLIDING DOWN THE WALLS, SOBBING.*

She closes the live chat. She knows that she is not the only one who loves the boys; the six thousand other viewers on this livestream alone are enough to remind her of that. Still, she does not like seeing the evidence. The boys make her feel like she is the only one that exists, and this is the way she likes to keep it—a hidden universe where the love they share is theirs and theirs alone.

"You're all so colorful," Halo says, sitting back. He swallows, throat rippling. A moan escapes her at the sight of his neck, a rope of muscles that leads down to his broad shoulders, his strong back. Without thinking, her fingers flutter across the keyboard, transcribing the chant in her head: *If you were the sun and I were the clouds, I would cover you forever to keep your beauty for me.*

Halo's eyes flit across the screen. "Oh?" he says. "But then the sky would be so dark."

Her fingers freeze above the keys. In the deluge of comments, he had seen hers.

"Lately I have been thinking about secrets," Halo continues, looking off. "The kind of secrets that could eat you up inside. The kind that you can't tell a single soul."

He brings his face close to the camera now, staring straight at Minnie. "But you don't have to hide from me. We're that close, aren't we? I want you to tell me your secrets. I want to know them all."

The word *secrets* rings against her. She pictures Nate's house, remembers the overripe sweetness of spilled beer, the thump of the bass, and then, without wanting to, remembers the dark hallway leading to the bathroom, where the door is still locked. She reaches out a hand to open it, but before she can, the word *secrets* rings again, and she is back to this video of Halo. It is safe here, at the altar of his kindness.

"Will you trust me?" Halo is saying. "Will you let me keep your secrets for you?"

Minnie opens the chat box again. *I'm still scared of the dark*, one comment reads; *I think my husband is cheating on me*; *I'm having an affair*; *Everyone thinks I go to work but really I just sit in my car and cry*; *I've been unemployed for 5 months*; *I hate chocolate but I never say anything because people will think I'm weird.*

I was at a party Minnie begins typing. But the next few words stop her. It is too painful to write, too real. Bruises heal if you leave them be. And that is what this is: a bruise. Clark has already left for Argentina, and with him taken the shadow he cast over her. All she has to do is hold on until this bruise inside of her fades. There is nothing wrong with me, she promises to herself. Nothing broken. She deletes her message and tries again. *I'm lonely.*

"Lonely?" Halo says, his eyes vibrating as they try to catch the messages zooming by. "Lonely is no good."

Minnie's breath stops—again, he had chosen her message out of thousands. There is no mistaking this destiny now, the one that led him to her, her to him. She leans forward, jamming her finger on the volume button so as not to miss his next words.

"But that's why HOURglass is here. That's why I'm here. If you're lonely, lean on me and I'll make sure you won't be lonely anymore." He gives the camera a rare smile. "It works both ways, you know. I was lonely and now I have all of you. Okay, who's next?"

Minnie replays the video on her phone as she falls asleep, placing it under her pillow so that it sounds like Halo is lying next to her in bed, his voice a whisper that feathers her ear. She falls asleep to it, and when she dreams, she does not see the locked bathroom door, but light, pouring into all the tightest, darkest parts of her, until she awakens not from the sun, but from how bright she feels inside, like she is made of nothing but the light that Halo has bestowed upon her.

POST #861

TITLE: A Love Like That Someday

RELATIONSHIP: Halo/Jelly; Minwoo/Halo; Colt/OC

STATUS: WIP

RATING: NC-17

TROPES: Alternate Universe, Jealous!Minwoo, Love Triangle, Heavy Angst, The Record Label is Evil, Genetic Experimentation, Suicidal Jelly, Bottom!Jelly, Halo Saves The Day, Betrayal, Slow Burn, That Sweet Sweet Aftercare

WARNINGS: Some torture and non-con stuff, proceed at your own risk

SUMMARY: The year is 2080 and humans are dying at a faster rate than ever. The only ones who can afford to live past thirty are those with money and power, or a special gene that only .01% of the population possesses. When Jelly, who is now living in isolation as an addict, learns that he carries the gene—and that the evil overlords of BabyGold Records will do anything to extract it from him—it's up to Halo, a fighter in the Resistance, to get the band back together and bring Jelly to safety. As the four of them flee for the Resistance Headquarters in the land formerly known as Quebec, Halo begins developing feelings for his ward. Can he keep his mind on the mission? Or will his love for his bandmate compromise everything they have worked for—and destroy the world as they know it?

EXCERPT: Jelly is covered in blood and ash, but his gorgeous face is still recognizable through the grime. Halo brushes a silver lock of hair from his forehead and pours some water from the canteen onto his cracked lips. Jelly moans. His fever makes his skin like fire to touch. Halo leans over and places a hand on Jelly's glistening forehead. Hot. So very hot. He knows he should move his hand away now, but he cannot bring himself to do it. The feeling of Jelly's skin on his is electrifying. He looks down at his friend again. He never noticed before how handsome he was, even in the throes of pain. His eyes travel down to Jelly's lips. They had always been plump during the days when they were still performing, but now, in Jelly's feverish state, they look even more flushed . . . and enticing. Halo leans down, bringing himself closer to Jelly's face. This is crazy. This is insane. They are being bombed left and right, but here he is with a sick and injured Jelly in his arms, and all he can think about is kissing him . . .

EASON

After Chicago comes Charlotte and after Charlotte, Atlanta. They slingshot down for the bouncy drawl of New Orleans, then draw a zigzag through Florida. The tour stops are based on demand, not proximity, so sometimes it feels like a mere walk between cities, other times a flight across the length of the country. The cities blend together, an endless reel of hotel rooms. In place of landmarks, he catalogues the pine cleaner that lingers in the tub, the dryer warmth of the sheets. If only the fans knew—the best part of being a star was getting to shine for them. Everything else dulls in comparison.

At dawn, they arrive in Nashville, the twenty-fifth stop of the tour. A crowd of twenty waits for them in the lobby of their hotel, a Four Seasons, and when they arrive, the group rushes forward, running straight into the meaty chests of the bodyguards. Eason recognizes them. They have been following the band ever since Newark, where they stood sentry at baggage claim. He had given them a wave then, thinking them fans like any others, but they did not react in the way of normal fans. Instead, they held up their cameras in unison and zapped him with flashes, each one as intrusive as it was blinding. It made him think of the cows he had seen in those long drives across Texas ranchland, but this time he was the cattle and they wielded the prod.

From there, this group followed them to every city of the tour and soon, they were no longer an anomaly, but a certainty: They would be there at the airport, waiting for HOURglass's arrival, and again at the hotel lobby, silent and watchful. How they acquired the information of the band's whereabouts and lodging, Eason did not know, but he was learning that in the world of celebrity and fame, anyone could be paid off in exchange for information. Brooks called them Remoras, because they were like suckerfish, attaching to creatures larger than themselves.

Minwoo had protested this name. "They're still our fans."

"These are not your fans," Brooks said, his expression darkening. "They're something else."

But who they were and what they wanted, he could not tell them. The Remoras watched and waited at their stations, ever faithful, but they did not ask of the band anything. All they wanted, it seemed, was access. Eason did not know what they did with the many pictures and videos they captured—they never appeared in the gossip magazines or celebrity news sites or even social media as far as he could tell—but they had to be doing something with them, for what else could all their time, all the money spent on flights and information and passage, serve? That was what made him uneasy about the Remoras—they were looking for something, documenting and poking and witnessing, as if building a collage of all their lives, and for Eason there was nothing more terrifying. If they could pay their way to uncovering confidential travel itineraries, what was stopping them from also digging up the most damning parts of his past?

As he passes through the lobby, he peers out from under his ballcap. Without meaning to, he makes eye contact with one of the Remoras, a girl in cat ears and rimless spectacles. She is pale, but her eyes are lined with a chunky black pencil that makes them look sunken in. The girl's gaze chills him; there is nothing inherently violent about her, but her quiet, unmoving presence feels like a menace all the same. He remembers reading a headline about a singer who took a picture of herself and posted it online, only to have a stranger who called himself a fan outside her home hours later; the man had zoomed in on the singer's eye and recognized the buildings and skyline reflected in her iris.

At the elevators, Brooks funnels them inside and jams the door-close button with the heel of his palm. The four of them watch the floors increase one by one, too tired to speak. Ever since the appearance of the Remoras, the managers had begun booking their rooms on separate floors, making it more difficult for anyone to find all of them at the same time. A twisted sort of insurance, Eason had thought, against what? Exposure? Kidnapping? He was too afraid to ask.

Floor seven. Minwoo exits with a yawn. Twelve. Colt signals goodbye. Fifteen. Julian. Eighteen comes quickly. Eason gives Brooks a nod and steps out into the hallway, the carpet swallowing his sneakers like hungry underbrush.

He pads down the length of the corridor, unnerved by its silence. Once, his parents tried to take him and Faye up to Palo Duro Canyon, but the trip was cut short by an EF-3 tornado warning and they had to turn back somewhere around Lubbock, thinking it better to outrun the storm than to seek shelter and deal with the consequences. A stupid, utterly human arrogance. He still remembers how the whole thing felt so exciting to him at the time, the prospect of speeding down the interstate with a storm at his tail no different from a game of schoolyard tag. But when they pulled over for gas and he rolled down the window and stuck his hand out, he was surprised to feel nothing at all—no wind, no weight, no *sound*, as if someone had pulled the plug on the world and it had gone dead, even though he could see it right there. It was not fun anymore, and he screamed at his parents to go, go, go. He never liked the quiet after that, and when his mother's possessions began and that deathly stillness would come over her, he was reminded of that day at the gas station, when he finally understood that something terrible was going to descend upon them if they did not run away.

At the door, he slides the keycard against the sensor. Yet another city. Yet another hotel. How is it that he could travel so far, only to see so little? He leans against the wood, too tired to push it open, letting the leaden slant of his body do the work.

Someone is there, already inside. Just over the threshold, someone waits with a scowling face and gaunt cheeks. It is a Remora, it has gotten through at last and now it is here, waiting to tear him apart, to sink him, to—

He takes a step back and stumbles over his luggage. The Remora stumbles, too.

Eason freezes. Then, he raises his left hand and waves it in front of him.

The Remora waves back.

"Idiot," he says. It is not a Remora or even an intruder. He is looking at a full-length mirror. It is just himself.

He edges into the room and sits down on the carpet in the entryway, unable to shake the feeling. They are not expected back downstairs for four hours, but he has no chance of sleeping now. He pulls out his laptop and powers it up.

The camera light flickers green, signaling that he is live. "Hello," he says, peering at his own face. Under the yellow lighting of the hotel room, the shadows under his eyes stretch down, making him look like a sad clown. He quickly selects a filter from the special effects menu to brighten his face to an artificial vigor. "Hello," he says again. "I've missed you."

He watches as the counter in the corner, signifying the number of people now watching him, rises with each second. He breathes in and it is at six hundred. He breathes out and it has reached one thousand.

What's wrong baby? someone writes. *You look tired.*

I've never needed a person more in my life.

Can you say "I love you" in Portuguese?

When will you come home?

He catches their comments as they flicker by, trying to picture the face behind each one. It is a one-way mirror—they can always see him, but never he them—all three thousand of them now. The livestreams were another practice The Duke adapted from the world of K-pop: Every video bridged the distance between idol and fan. Minwoo called it awkward and Colt detested the way his face looked when flipped by the front-facing camera. Julian found it a waste of time. But for Eason, the livestream felt like a place where the exploding world of his stardom suddenly shrank to this singular, local terminal in which he and those who watch him could reside.

"Do I look tired?" he says, giving them a small smile. "It's because we just got in for our show tonight."

I'm seeing you tonight.

Get some sleep baby.

Can you say hello to your French fans?

Come home

"*Bonjour*," he says. "Maybe we'll be lucky enough to do a concert in France one day. What should I do first when we visit?"

Eiffel tower picnic with wine (avec moi)

Come home

Walk the Seine, it is so lovely in the autumn

Come home

Do you like art Halo? We have the best museums!!!

COME HOME.

"Whoever is telling me to 'come home' in the chat," he says, frowning, "I don't understand what you mean. I'm already home. I'm here with you."

COME HOME.

COME HOME.

COME HOME.

"That's enough," he says. "If you don't stop, I'm just going to leave."

COME HOME.

COME HOME.

COME HOME.

YOU'LL REGRET DOING THIS TO YOUR LAO MA.

The laptop slams shut. He hurls it from him and the treacherous thing hits the leg of an ottoman with a crack. Steam or smoke or his own warped imagination puffs out. He tries to stand, but his legs are long gone, and his mind is not far behind. His head slams into the carpet and he lies there, chest to chest with it, the same sick powder-blue as the carpet in their townhome back in Sugar Land. He would know that color anywhere, for he had once spent an entire afternoon staring at it, nose an inch away as he hid under the dining table, until he knew it so well he could count the fibers of every tuft. Above him, from somewhere horrible, his mother, with a sequined black dress in one hand and scissors in the other, screaming at Faye, determined to catch her, for the dress had been a gift from their father but the dress no longer fit and it must have been Faye who stretched it out, must have been the weight of the demon inside her that made it so ugly and shapeless now, and it didn't matter that Faye had never seen the dress before, didn't matter that it was their mother who had lost too much flesh from her bones. She cut through the dress with her scissors, each slice as loud as a guillotine. The fabric fell to the floor around Eason and glittered like black snow. He wanted to pluck a hair from his mother's head the way he would from Faye when they played the demon hunting game, but this was no longer a game and it was not funny anymore. He could hear Faye imploring. *Mama, it wasn't me. Give it to me, I can fix it.* Her sharp gasp as one of the blades caught against her palm and the silence that followed, the townhome, the powder-blue carpet, and Eason yet again listening, solemn and still, for the raggedness of his mother's breath, the hitch and the realization, the hateful, *Look what you made me do, you little bitch.*

His throat swells. He croaks out in protest, the sound dreadful and, at the same time, deserved. *I am going to die right here,* he thinks. *I am going to die and no one will know except for her—*

"Eason?"

He opens his eyes.

"It's me."

His vision sharpens, the details of the room coming back into view. In the floor-length mirror, he catches his reflection again. A thin kid, bony at the wrists. Eyes that look red, even from far away. He does not remember when he got so hollow. He does not remember when it hurt this bad.

"Eason, open up."

The last thing he wants is for Julian to come in, to see him like this—surely his friend will be able to sense it, how the air in the room is all wrong, but Eason knows Julian and knows that he will not go away. Life returns to his legs. He stands, takes a shaking breath in, and unlocks the door.

"I couldn't sleep," Julian says, walking in. He looks around the room, at the untouched bed. "I guess you couldn't either?"

Eason shrugs. His mind is still seared by his mother's messages. Right now, she would be sitting in the kitchen, blinds drawn to keep the house cool. November in Texas, but indistinguishable from a summer day. The seasons can change, but the leaves will not brown, and if they do, it is from the rot within, nothing else. His mother is no different. She is rotting, too, and everything trapped in that house rots with her. Not him, he had thought. *He* had left. Faye, too. He was so close to being clean.

But he had been wrong. With one phone call, she restored the worst parts of him. He is yellow, brown, blackish-blue. The rot is inside him, too.

"What a weird life," Julian is saying. He waves around at the room, the velvet chaise lounge and ridiculous arched canopy bed. "Sometimes I feel guilty when I talk to my friends from home. *'I stare at spreadsheets all day and then I go home and my girlfriend yells at me because she thinks we don't go on enough dates.'* Can you imagine?"

"No."

Julian sits down on the chaise. "Do you ever think about what we would be doing if we weren't here right now?"

"I don't know," Eason lies. He does know: He would still be a twenty-one-year-old high school dropout, picking up odd jobs until he could get as far away from Texas as possible. And then what? There was nothing else for him in that life but the promise to eventually die.

"Sometimes I wonder if I would have gone back to skating. Un-retire myself, you know? But then I remember I've already missed my chance. It's all fifteen- and sixteen-year-olds now."

He smiles as he says this, but Eason hears the catch in Julian's throat. Julian never spoke much about his skating days, which others chalked up to humility. But once, Eason had searched Julian's name and found his biography on an online skating database. Listed there were titles he had won, competitions where he medaled. There were so many that they looked like the horizon of a city, every column of accomplishments stacked into a skyscraper. He watched, too, the video compilations put together by Julian's fans, hours of footage that showed Julian cutting through the ice, launching into twists, leaps, and dizzying spins. With every finished routine, he would collapse on the ice and weep into his hands. Not because he was disappointed with his performance, or even spent by it, Eason came to learn, but because he had just experienced a happiness that could never be quantified or replicated. It was there, on his face as he skated, and it was there in his hands that he offered up to the stands, open-palmed, as if to say, *I give myself back to you*. Listening to Julian now, he realizes what he had never asked his friend, but always somehow knew: The decision to retire from skating must have not been his own.

"Maybe you would be a skating coach. Or a choreographer."

"Maybe," Julian says. His eyes drift to the floor. "What happened to your laptop?"

"Nothing," Eason says, quickly collecting it. Not quick enough to hide the fresh dent at the top. "I was doing a livestream and I dropped it." He laughs, hoping Julian will join him.

"I thought I heard you. Earlier, from the hallway. You sounded ill."

"It was nothing," Eason says. Julian would always be there to finish Eason's breath for him. Right now, however, he wishes for anything but. "I'm just tired." He feigns a yawn, hoping that Julian will get the message.

"It's more than that, though," Julian says. He stares at Eason and his eyes feel like hot stones on bare skin. "You've been off ever since you got that phone call in Philadelphia."

"I said I'm fine." He looks at the clock—they still have an hour before call time. "I'm pretty beat. I think I'll try to get some sleep."

"You're hiding something."

The rot inside him spreads. "What about you, Jules? Have you eaten today?"

He regrets the words immediately. Julian looks back at him with surprise and, he can see, hurt. "Okay," Julian says. He stands and walks to the door, but does not open it. "You know all of *this* won't make it go away, right?"

"What are you talking about?"

"Hiding behind HOURglass and thinking it'll make everything better. I thought I could do it too with skating. Trust me, it won't hold."

He is dangerously close to the center of it all. Eason hears the horn, the rain. His own horror, hoarse and useless.

"I just need to sleep."

"Fine," Julian says. He opens the door and walks through, but does not let it close just yet. Their concert is in twelve hours—how will they maintain the illusion of carefree cool when all Eason wants to do is slam the door on Julian's face and scream until his throat bleeds? He imagines apologizing to Julian and telling him everything, but before he can speak, Julian releases the door and disappears down the hallway.

MINNIE

It is called The Heaven.

She finds them on the third page of the search results. What she is looking for are pictures of Halo with which to adorn her walls, but what she discovers instead are Jelly and Halo, their lips fused in a kiss. It is a false image, she knows—whoever made it must have chosen separate photos of Jelly and Halo and stitched them together. Still, she cannot help but feel stirred by it.

The image leads her to a message board called The Heaven, which blinks back at her in nebula blue and white, the same colors so often worn by the boys. *This is a safe haven for anyone who supports the love between Jelly and Halo*, reads the board's manifesto. Below is a video, titled *A DEFINITIVE GUIDE TO JELLY x HALO (HELLY)*.

Helly describes the relationship between Jelly and Halo, two members of the popular boy band HOURglass, the video, using a computer-generated voice, narrates. *In this video, we'll explore the history of Helly's relationship.*

They were roommates first, friends and bandmates next, lovers ever after, the video claims. As proof, it presents a clip from the boys' first live performance at the music festival. This time, the video is zoomed in and slowed, so that the boys' faces fill up her screen. Minnie has watched this video many times, but this is the first time she sees what the video wants her to see: Halo, gazing at Jelly with adoration; Halo, letting his pinky graze Jelly's as they stand next to each other; Jelly, embracing everyone but lingering in Halo's arms the longest; Jelly, glancing over to Halo as he sings, the words "loving you" no longer just a lyric, but a declaration.

Another video, titled *HIDDEN IN PLAIN SIGHT*, offers an analysis of an old video Jelly and Halo appeared in together—a livestream recorded in a hotel room. Look how comfortable they are, the video declares. Listen to how softly Halo speaks to Jelly. There was a purple mark on Jelly's neck that day which had been the subject of Halo's teasing. According to the analysis, the mark was not an allergic reaction, as Jelly insisted, but a love bite, one that had been delivered from Halo's hallowed lips, and that was why he could not stop teasing Jelly about it. Halo wants to claim what is his, the analysis concludes. This is his way of telling others: Jelly is mine.

There are more videos. A forty-two-minute analysis of Jelly and Halo at the airport. Look how Halo always walks near Jelly, it says. Look how he protects his lover. Other videos zoom in on pictures of them during interviews, breaking down with mathematical precision the angles of their arms and legs. Look how they are sitting, how their bodies cannot help but be pulled toward one another.

We are not crazy or delusional, the manifesto concludes. *We have consulted with relationship experts, body language experts, couples therapists, and astrologists who have confirmed our findings* (*please note that we do not know Jelly and Halo's birth times—if you do, let us know!*).

The rational part of her knows that this is a fantasy. Anyone could be close without being in love. But the more she watches these videos, the more she begins to wonder. The more she wants to believe. And if she lets herself believe, what then? The boys did not speak of their love lives—*We're in a relationship with our fans*, they answered when asked. Even so, long has she prepared herself for some terrible future in which news came of Halo (or any of the boys, for that matter) dating some undeserving woman. But if Halo was dating Jelly? It would not be something that hurt or made her feel worthless and left behind, but something to be celebrated. If Jelly and Halo were indeed in love, then she could take part in that love, for had they not always told her, *We are yours and you are ours*?

She joins the message board and creates a username for herself. The automated pop-up tells her she is member 6,811. She navigates to the NEW MEMBERS section and scrolls through the introductions. *I thought I was crazy*, one post reads, *but I'm so glad I found this community*. Another post begins, *You'd have to be blind to not see how much they love each other.* Another: *I'm a 65-year-old woman so believe me when I say, I've seen it all. This is what love looks like.*

Minnie clicks CREATE NEW POST and begins to type. *Hi everyone,* she writes. *I'm MinnieTheGreat and I'm a freshman in college. I've been a huge fan of HOURglass since the beginning, but only recently started falling down the Jelly-Halo rabbit hole. There's just something about them that makes me so happy.*

POST. Almost immediately, a red jewel appears in the right corner of her screen. She hovers her mouse over it. *Jello_sitc replied to your post,* the little pop-up that appears says. She refreshes the page.

Jello_sitc: Hi MinnieTheGreat! Welcome to the board ^_^

The red jewel appears again before she can respond.

angelhalo: So nice to meet you. There's something about them that makes me happy too.
HannahIsOurs18: im a freshman too! what are you studying? who is your favorite in HOURglass?

She spends the rest of the afternoon replying to new comments. Each time she clicks POST, another red jewel appears in the right corner of her screen. The comments continue streaming in, until her post has garnered eighty-two replies. She tells them about how she is studying English, how she was raised in Colorado Springs but is now attending college in Austin. She tells them that Halo is her favorite and shares typed-out squeals with another commenter over how sexy he looks in black. By the time she goes to bed, her post has accrued 321 comments. Many of these conversations, she is surprised to discover, have nothing to do with the boys.

HannahIsOurs18: i go to school at a&m. how do you like austin?
MinnieTheGreat: it's okay i guess. i don't have a lot of friends at school.

HannahIsOurs18: i dont either. there arent a lot of people who look like me here. im usually the only black girl in my classes.
MinnieTheGreat: i'm sorry :(i felt like that in colorado springs, i was usually the only asian person . . . anywhere
HannahIsOurs18: "it's so lonely . . ."
MinnieTheGreat: "being lonely, BABIEEEEEE!"
HannahIsOurs18: hahaha :D at least well always have the boys!
MinnieTheGreat: :D
MinnieTheGreat: it's not that i don't want friends . . . i just feel like i have a hard time making them.
HannahIsOurs18: are you me? im the same way
HannahIsOurs18: but im not giving up hope! you shouldnt either
HannahIsOurs18: also . . . we both just made a new friend, starting today :)

That evening, Minnie stands before the mirror, examining herself. One month has passed since Jillian's invitation to the study group, one month for her to gather the courage to finally attend. What, she wants to know, does one wear to a study group? She rifles through her closet, tossing on skater dresses, skirts, oversize button-downs. She needs Jillian and her friends to see the best of her.

In the end, she slips into skinny jeans and a black V-neck. She walks downstairs and out the back door of Carothers, gingerly stepping through the damp courtyard so as not to stain her sneakers. The honors library is a modest little cove on the bottom floor of Carothers with two seminar rooms and collections for browsing. Inside, the steady flow of air conditioning blows past her, making the untucked strands of her hair float.

Jillian and her two friends sit at a wooden table next to the window. The fluorescent lights are somehow brighter above them, illuminating each girl as if she is awash in her own spotlight. They are pretty in the way that people are when they have nothing to fear.

Jillian notices Minnie first. Confusion flickers across her face before she remembers. "Oh, wow, hey! You finally made it!"

"Where's your hot boyfriend?" the second girl says. Today, she has traded in her Ugg boots for sandals. Minnie pretends not to hear her.

"Sit here," Jillian says, moving her book bag from a chair. Minnie obeys. Last time, she had ridden the high of the girls' fascination with her. It gave her a sense of power. Today, however, Jillian's friends are not staring at her with wonder, but hesitation.

"We're glad you finally came," Jillian says. "You didn't meet us at our best last time."

She was alluding to the smoking. Minnie tells them not to worry.

"It doesn't matter," the second girl says, rolling her eyes at Jillian. "It's not like Dan cares anyway."

"Dan the RA, right?" Minnie says. "Are you dating?"

It is an earnest question, an attempt to connect on some common ground with them, but the three girls shriek with laughter, all submerging themselves below the table in enviable synchronicity. Minnie smiles awkwardly. She knows that she is on the outside of their shared history.

Jillian is the first one to resurface. "Alice and Dan had a thing."

"It was like one time," the girl called Alice says, lip curling.

"If four weeks is one time, sure," the third girl says. "I'm Courtney, by the way."

The girls, Minnie learns, are studying for a History of Modern Philosophy class. They are part of a track called Dean's Scholars, which feeds them specialized classes taught by the best professors at the university, typically only accessible to graduate students. *Prized racehorses*, Minnie cannot help thinking. Next to them, she feels completely ordinary.

"I'm an English major," she tells them, "but I'm hoping to apply for English Honors."

"What do you *do* in English, anyway?" Alice wants to know. She has big eyes with long, dark lashes. She is objectively beautiful, Minnie thinks. They all are.

"We read books and write essays analyzing those books."

"Must be nice," Courtney says.

"Sounds like a laugh," Alice agrees drily.

"I'm also a part of a zine," Minnie hurries on. What she does not say: that she still has not begun writing, even as the deadline approaches.

"Do you mean magazine?" Courtney asks.

"Sort of." She remembers Anna's little speech at the first meeting. "Zines were a major form of protest and community in the '90s."

"So, like a hobby?" Alice says. "I wish I had time for a hobby."

"Don't be rude," Jillian says. She turns to Minnie. "I think it's cool that you're doing something because you love it and not because it's a guarantee, you know?"

"Thanks," Minnie says. She is seized suddenly by a fervent desire to be Jillian's friend, her best friend. What would such a friendship look like? Her and Jillian, studying together at the library. Her and Jillian, going out to the bars and walking each other home. Her and Jillian, taking annual trips to Paris, eventually living in apartments next to each other, their gardens growing into one.

The hour passes quickly. Alice looks up from her notebook and chews her pen, staring at Minnie. "So, is your boyfriend joining us or what?"

"Oh," Minnie says. "I'm not sure if I would call him my boyfriend anymore."

Courtney looks up, too. "What happened? You can tell us."

"It was nothing, really," Minnie says. She imagines telling these girls about her humiliation at Nate's party and wonders if she can go a little further, back into that bathroom with Clark, back on that floor, but shuts the thought out quickly. Something about the girls' eyes—the spark of curiosity that held glee, not sympathy—warns her off. "It just wasn't a good fit."

"That sucks," Alice says. Not for the loss of the relationship, Minnie realizes, but for the loss of a good story.

"Relationships are hard," Jillian agrees, which seems to signal the end of the topic.

The rest of the study session passes quietly. Jillian and her friends share notes on a man named Heidegger while Minnie pretends to read the assigned chapters for her Eighteenth-Century Literature class.

Pretends, because she cannot concentrate on the book, not when the girls are in front of her and she just within their orbit. They are fashionable and witty, but their true power lies in their cohesion as a group. No matter what happens, they will always have each other. With that knowledge, they are free to be brash or coy or soft or whatever they want to be, for the walls of their selfhood will always be reinforced by the existence of each other. How nice, she thinks, to call another person home.

At nine, Jillian shuts her laptop and stretches, her arms extending above like a ballerina. Alice and Courtney follow suit. Minnie shuts her book as well and looks between the three of them. Once again, the air feels so different from the night she encountered them in front of the dorm, different, even, from earlier in the evening. They regard her from a distance now, as if they had never asked her to join them at all.

"This was really nice," she tells them, hoping to win back whatever was lost. "Thanks for inviting me."

"You're welcome," Jillian says. She smiles, but her lips stay closed. "Hopefully we weren't too annoying."

"Not at all," Minnie says. "If I studied with you guys every week, I'd probably graduate early." She waits, hoping they will take the cue and invite her to join them for next week.

But they begin packing up their bags. Alice complains that she is hungry, and the other two agree that they should get something to eat. They do not invite Minnie to join, nor does she expect them to. The message is clear: Her time with them is over.

The walk up to her room is slow, every step laden with remorse. She should have done better with the girls. She should have kept Nate's attention. Why is it so hard, when it seems to be so easy for everyone else?

Back in her room, she sinks into her pillows and reaches for her laptop. There is a new post on the front page of The Heaven, made an hour ago, titled *MOVIE NIGHT!* She clicks to open it. Every week, the post explains, members vote on a movie to watch together. Tonight's showing is *Fear*, a thriller starring a young Mark Wahlberg and Reese

Witherspoon. In the movie, Mark Wahlberg plays a handsome sociopath named David who becomes obsessed with Reese Witherspoon's character, Nicole, a teenager from a well-to-do family. When Minnie joins to watch, David and Nicole are on a date at a carnival, seated on a roller coaster. The ride begins. Nicole takes David's hand and puts it in between her legs, and when the roller coaster reaches its peak, she throws her head back in ecstasy as the song "Wild Horses" heralds her orgasm.

Ladybeth42: Who hasn't been fingered on a rollercoaster?
HALOISMYHUSBAND: GET IT NICOLE!!!!!
HannahIsOurs18: this isnt a movie its ~*~ cinema ~*~

The comments make Minnie laugh. She continues watching, occasionally refreshing the post to read through the others' reactions. When, near the end of the movie, David reveals his bare chest, on which he has tattooed the declaration NICOLE 4 EVA, the post explodes with banter.

Javertinthestars: That is the worst tattoo I've ever seen in my life
HannahIsOurs18: NO 4 EVA
Jelly_sitc: Why am I kind of attracted to this?
MinnieTheGreat: this is hilarious. run, nicole, run!
Ladybeth42: So glad you joined, MinnieTheGreat. =)

She knows the reality: These are strangers, far flung across the world, and yet. Never has a group of people felt closer to her. This is the beginning of their shared history, and it is no different, no less valuable, than the one shared by Jillian and her two friends. In fact, Minnie thinks as she continues reading through the comments, this is real friendship, too. It no longer matters that the study group had been such a failure, nor that she had lost Nate to Kristín—she has everything she needs right here. Now, wherever she walks, they will walk, too.

POST #1142

You know the perfect bite of cake? Just enough sponge and just enough sweet. Or when the day is the right temperature and everything you're wearing is just enough? Or when you wake up without an alarm clock or loud noises from the street or someone screaming at you—it's just you waking up because it's time? That's what Jelly and Halo remind me of. They were meant for each other, the way they were meant for me.

EASON

In the middle of the night, a rapping brings him to his door. He finds Brooks on the other side, looking like a dog that has lost its owner.

"Put on some clothes," he tells Eason. "Get out here, quick." He has never seen Brooks so spooked.

In the elevator, they shoot upward, through the old bones of the hotel, to the penthouse suite. They find him in the living room, spread catlike across the long sofa, gazing imperiously at the Nashville skyline. Still those same linen clothes, the hair longer, yellower, now knotted at the base of his head in a noose. The Duke is not a tall man, nor a built man, but he stands and the city shrinks behind him.

"Good," he says. "You're here."

Eason is not sure what to do. Shake hands? Say hello? He glances at the clock hanging in the kitchen—the heavy bronze hands point to 4:27 A.M. "Where is everyone?" he asks finally. He has only just noticed that he is alone.

"They'll come. I want to speak to you first. Just you."

"Oh," Brooks says. He claps his hands together, looking awkward. "Let me know if you need—"

"We won't."

They wait for Brooks to leave, which he does slowly. Stay, Eason wants to call out. The high-rise suite, the mysterious CEO, the ominous glow of the electric fireplace, logs alight in hyper-tangerine—it is all too cliché to fear, and yet fear it he does.

"You're wondering why I'm here."

"Yes."

The Duke smiles. His teeth are too big for his lips and so white they look like they hurt. "I'm here," he says, "because you're here. And you're only here because of me. Isn't it funny, how that works?"

Eason says nothing. He does not see the humor.

"I won't make you wait. I'm many things, but not cruel. Earlier today, I received a call from the editor-in-chief at *Pop Impulse*. His team received a tip for a story and he wanted a comment from me. Do you know what I'm talking about?"

Eason shakes his head. His hands are at it again, trembling like leaves in a howling wind. He digs them under his thighs, but it is too late—The Duke has already spotted their betrayal.

"I ask my artists to tell me all their secrets. Not to shame them, but to protect them if those secrets ever got out. In exchange for fame, money, adoration, I ask you to be honest with me. But you couldn't even do that."

He throws a black folder across the coffee table. Eason stares down at it. He knows, without having to open it, what waits for him inside: A little box in the corner, three paragraphs, on page nine. How pathetic, running so hard only to return to where he started.

"No one knows about this," he sputters. His mind is racing, but none of the thoughts catch. "This was the only thing written about it and you would never know it was me unless you knew my legal Chinese name and the only people who know that are my moth—" he stops.

COME HOME, the comments in the livestream said. *YOU'LL REGRET DOING THIS TO YOUR LAO MA.*

"It was her," he says.

"I don't care who it was," The Duke says. Now, there is venom. "Do you understand the danger you've put the label in? The band? What I care about is how we're going to stop this from getting out."

"I'll do anything," Eason says without thinking. But it is true. He is a kid hiding behind the door, helpless and small.

The Duke places another folder on the coffee table. This one is white. "I can protect you," he says. "But only if you listen to me. Can you do that?"

Eason nods.

"Good. Then do exactly as I say."

◦ ◦ ◦

By the time the others arrive, the sun has begun flooding through the windows. In the light of a new day, it is easy to believe his conversation with The Duke was not real, that this was simply one of his many dreams. But with the press of a button, The Duke brings the shades down. The room darkens again.

"What's going on?" Minwoo asks. He looks at The Duke, then Eason.

"Sit," The Duke says, motioning to the sofa, which is curved like a blade. "Can I get you anything? Coffee? Tea? Green juice?"

"I'll take some—" Colt says, but Minwoo slaps his knee.

The Duke raises an eyebrow, amused. "Ever the leader."

Julian takes a seat next to Eason. "You okay?"

He feels The Duke's cold gaze on them and scoots away from Julian, hoping that the space he creates says, *Don't look here, don't hurt us, look away*. But whatever The Duke has seen is enough. He smiles then, as if he has understood something fundamental.

"When I set out to create the next big thing," he tells them now, "everyone told me I was insane. 'It'll never work,' they said. Even when I was a drummer, they told me: 'You'll never make a career out of that.' You know what I hate? It's being told I *can't* do something. When I hear *can't*, I just want to kill somebody. I'm sure you've felt the same way—otherwise you wouldn't be sitting here today. Every single one of you had to kill someone to get to where you are right now. Figuratively, of course."

Eason does not dare move.

"You were seen," he says, flicking his head toward Julian. "You and Eason. The little romp at the club in Philadelphia? The editor at *Pop Impulse* sent me about a hundred pictures their pap managed to get that night. They were even kind enough to include a few of you partaking in—ah—party favors with some nice young ladies in the bathroom."

"That's ridiculous," Minwoo says, "Julian knows better—" but The Duke holds up a hand.

"You know how this works. *Pop Impulse* are not sentimental about who they go after. What they want is clicks and attention and ads, and right now, you're poised to be the hottest band in the country. In two years, you'll probably be the biggest in the world if we play it right. You're prime for the plucking. A boy band with a drug problem? You're damaged goods. You're nothing. Think of the fans—if you have any left after this gets out."

"It's none of your business," Julian says, "what I do on my own time."

The Duke chuckles. "Everything is my business."

Julian turns to Eason, his eyes pleading for a conference, a backup, anything, but Eason will not look at him. This is the way it has to be. He thinks again to the night they learned that IN X BLOOM was destroyed. They were in the practice room when they heard the news. Just like that. Whole lives ruined in the span it took for them to dance through one song.

"They're bluffing, right?" Colt says.

The Duke pulls out a series of photographs from the white folder. He passes them around, starting with Minwoo. Eason watches as the photographs shift into focus for Minwoo, the mouth that falls agape, the shock, then betrayal, that overtakes his face. "You—"

The photographs slide from between his fingers and onto the floor, where they land face down. Colt reaches for them. He takes a look at the first one, then turns it back around, a pained expression on his face. He hands them to Eason, who takes them but does not look.

"Let me see," Julian says. His hand is outstretched, steady as always. "Eason, let me see."

Eason passes them over, unable to meet his eyes.

Julian studies the first one. There is no sign of humiliation on his face. Instead, he analyzes the photograph with the same calm removal as he did with their performances. Then, he hands the photographs back to The Duke.

"Can't we say they've been photoshopped?" Colt asks finally.

The Duke looks amused. "Once these pictures go out, you're done. All four of you. It doesn't matter what the truth is. That's not what people care about. All they need is a reason to doubt, and what Julian has done is a betrayal of every fan that has loved you and followed you. They'll start to look for other things now. They'll find fault with the rest of you, more reasons why you're not deserving. I have been in this business for a long time. I've seen it happen to even the most untouchable."

They know that he is right. Silly of them to think that they could somehow crawl out from under their own shadows.

"What do we do?" This time, it is Eason who speaks. Just as he and The Duke agreed.

The Duke laughs. He is a good actor. "Even after we tell you *don't go off doing your own thing, don't break the rules, be good boys,* you don't listen. Why should I trust you?"

"We'll listen," Eason says, his voice hard. He looks to his bandmates and repeats the words that had been given to him. "Whatever it takes. Right, guys? This is our dream. We're not letting that go."

Colt is the first to nod. "Right." He prods Minwoo, who has remained motionless, as if in a trance. Perhaps he is remembering the moment when he hit the pavement on that motorcycle, or when the nurses told him that he would never sing again. Once more, Eason feels the slow pour of guilt.

Minwoo stirs. "Right."

They all look to Julian. He is staring out the window, but the shades block the view, so he is simply staring at a black screen. Eason leans over, his voice a whisper the others cannot hear. "Jules. We've come too far."

He reminds himself of Faye, he thinks. Feeding reassurances and lies in the face of the incomprehensible. He understands her better now. He will say anything to keep Julian on the team, to keep HOURglass alive.

Julian meets his eyes then. There is a shade there of the kid that Eason first knew, back when they could finally collapse in the dance studio after practice, when they no longer had to put on a brave face for the hawkish eyes who watched them for their failures and weaknesses;

underneath all the poise was a Julian who was sensitive and soft and small. The same kid who stuck his fingers down his throat and buried his hunger with coke. A Julian who, for once, was asking Eason to protect him. But Eason will not give Julian the easy way out. If he wants to walk away from the team and all that they have worked for, then let him be the one to do it, he thinks. Not me.

For once, not me.

"Okay," Julian says finally. He turns to The Duke, face set. "Tell us what we need to do."

"Well," Colt says.

The four of them are in Minwoo's room. Colt, on the bed. Minwoo, the love seat in the corner. Eason sits at the desk. Julian stands just outside the room, lingering in the entry hallway. His arms are crossed, barring his chest. "I'm not doing it," he says. "It's not right."

"We already agreed—"

"No," Julian says. "We didn't even get a chance to . . . before you"—he points to Minwoo—"decided for us."

"Don't blame him," Colt says, quieter this time. The fans would not recognize him now for his solemn expression, not remotely close to the happy, lighthearted Denim they had come to know. But this is also the true version of Colt, the one Eason remembers meeting on that first day in training—just an anxious boy, a furrow of a soul. How he has grown, he thinks. How we have all grown.

Julian lets out a faint scoff, and it is this, perhaps, that causes Minwoo to spring up from his seat in the corner. Eason can tell that anger, which so rarely flusters Minwoo, is on the verge of escaping, the way a cork threatens to explode from a bottle after too much agitation. "Looks like you have something to say, Julian. Why don't you say it?"

"Let's not—" Colt says weakly, but he is overridden by Julian, whose arms uncross. He walks to the center of the room, his body a smooth bone through his white T-shirt, vibrating with emotion.

"Did you even *think* about what they're asking us to do? What you're asking me and Eason to do? Because in case you forgot, you and Colt aren't a part of this plan. It's all on us, not you. Some kind of leader you are."

Minwoo circles the center, facing Julian. He is a few inches shorter, but no less fearsome.

"Very nice." He fakes a laugh. "You're right, it *is* on you and Eason. Actually, let me be clear—it's on *you*. Because you're the one getting caught doing blow in the bathroom with some random girls. How dumb do you have to be? Do you even care about the fans?"

"You really think this is for the fans?"

"*Everything* we do is for the fans."

"That's not true!" Julian roars. "If we were doing this for them, we would tell them the truth: that we're human and we have flaws, too. But instead, we're feeding them a lie about who we are, making them believe a lie all so we can keep taking money from them. If they don't want to be our fans after this, that's fine. But the ones who stick around, *those* are our real fans, because at least they accept who we really are."

"You're a child," Minwoo says, his voice sour with pity and contempt. "You don't know how the world works."

"And you sound just like them. The Duke and Brooks."

Colt tries again. "Should we hear from Eason?"

Julian turns to him. Eason remembers how, earlier, there had been something in Julian's eyes that said—no, let's not, don't do it. Now, his eyes are saying it again: *Protect us both.*

But rather than receiving Julian's plea, Eason addresses the floor. "I don't see any other way, if we want to stop the photos from going out."

"Eason," Julian says. The disappointment in his voice sinks Eason even further.

"We'll tell them the truth one day," he says, now meeting Julian's eyes. "But right now, we're still too new. We might not survive a scandal this big. I would never agree to this if I didn't think it could work."

"I don't—" Julian says, but he falters. Eason's endorsement has to mean something.

"I promise," Eason says. It takes everything for him to keep his eyes on Julian's. He thinks of all the things at stake, all the things he stands to lose. "Trust me."

Julian's chest rises, then falls. His silence is the final confirmation.

"So it's settled then," Colt says, forcing levity back into his voice. "Minwoo, you have the last word."

Minwoo glares at Julian for a second, then the anger on his face eases. The leader returns. "This will save us."

"Okay," Colt says, more to himself than the other three. "Okay."

The conversation is over. There is no hanging around today. As they file out of Minwoo's room, Eason waits for Julian in the hallway, hoping to speak to him in private. But Julian stalks off to the elevator without looking at him.

"He'll come around," Minwoo says from behind him. They watch Julian together. "Thanks, by the way. I know he sees you like a brother. If you hadn't gone for it, I don't think he would have, either."

"Is this a big mistake?"

"If you believe that," Minwoo says, still looking after Julian, "then you'll also have to believe that this whole thing—joining BabyGold, becoming HOURglass, becoming Halo—was a mistake, too. I don't think it's a mistake. Do you?"

Would this be the moment that he would return to, many years later, when he thought of the difference between choice and inevitability? Would he retrace his path, twitching through the strip of his life like a film rewound, and always freeze here, searching for new details that he had missed, a hint of what was to come on The Duke's face, perhaps, or what he was really looking for all along: a hint of what was possible within *him*? And if he had known, would he have still gone through with it?

But he is here now, not there, and this is what he knows: One day, Julian would eventually strike out on a solo career as a star dancer. And Minwoo would make a smooth transition from being the leader of HOURglass to managing his own record label. Colt, with his good looks and affable personality, would have no trouble landing a hosting gig on a network entertainment show or a starring role in a big-budget superhero movie. What was left for Eason?

Answer: a fifteenth birthday. Faye took him on a road trip to see Big Bend, something their father had promised to do but never did. They packed the hatchback with rabbit milk candy and shrimp chips, stuffed the trunk with pillows and sleeping bags. The drive was nine hours, so Faye invited Henry, a guy she knew from the track team. Henry was nice and funny, with hair the color of oats—he had a staggering knowledge of plants and could identify any tree just by glancing at it. They spent most of the drive playing the game of asking him to name the trees that whipped past them on the road. Cedar. Oak. Texas Ash. Henry knew them all, but even if he were lying, Eason would not have faulted him for it. In Junction, the three of them slept in the parking lot of a Walmart to save money. Eason realized that he forgot his toothbrush, so Henry went inside and bought him a new one with soft bristles. "Better for your teeth," he told Eason with an easy smile.

They arrived in Marfa the next day, Henry having driven most of the way while Faye and Eason dozed in and out of sleep along I-10. First was the Chinati Foundation, a massive contemporary art museum with installations dotted across 365 acres of the haunted Chihuahuan Desert plateau. A bucket-list item for Faye, who would be going to college for art history and finance that fall. Eason did not understand the exhibits—he did not understand most art, really—but he was happy because Faye was happy. They took the self-guided walking tour of the outdoor exhibits, even though it was February and the cold wind whipped at their flimsy Texas jackets, the three of them like lost kites.

In a field bordering the Chinati property, they came across a row of fifteen slabs of concrete, each one so huge he could walk through it. He imagined each structure as a portal, and that when he stepped through, he would emerge a different version of himself from some concurrent universe. After the first portal, he was an Eason who was six inches taller. After the second portal, he was an Eason who could fly by shooting air out of his fingers. After the tenth, he was an Eason whose father never left and whose mother had never been possessed, and it was here that he collapsed on the curling grass, crying and hating himself for doing so. He wanted, so badly in that moment, to both grow up and to become a child again. Either sounded better than this limbo of not being able to do anything, of being helpless to stop whatever it was that was happening to them now. Faye and Henry ran to him, thinking at first that he had cut himself on the concrete, but when they found no blood, they sat with him, blocking him from the wind. He did not want Henry to see him cry like this—his father always told him that men did not cry—but Henry just gave him some napkins from his pocket and patted his head. "It's okay to cry, buddy," he kept saying. "See that tree over there? That one is Italian Stone Pine."

That night, they bought grilled cheese sandwiches from a food trailer and drove nine miles east to see the Marfa Lights, those mysterious orbs that appeared on the horizon southeast of town. Some said ghosts, others said aliens. Faye was convinced that it was all a tourist trap, but she wanted to see them nonetheless. At the viewing center, Henry paid for hot chocolate and they sat on the rocky ledge, sipping from their paper cups and gazing out into the dark ridge of the mountains. Eason strained his eyes to see—he did not tell the others, but a part of him wanted badly to encounter something, for at least then he could confirm that things like ghosts and aliens and demons were real. He could reason with whatever it was, ask it to leave his mother alone. But as hard as he looked, there was nothing. What he did see, or thought he saw from the corner of his eye, was Faye resting her head on Henry's shoulder. But when he turned to make sure, the two of them were looking ahead, their bodies perfectly straight and untouching. "Did you see the lights, buddy?" Henry asked him. "I'm not sure what I saw," Eason replied. He was talking to Faye, but she would not meet his gaze, even in the dark.

Just as he would not meet Julian's gaze, there with The Duke. *I'm sorry Julian*, he thinks, and then he swallows it. There is too much to lose. Leaving the past behind and becoming Halo—these things are not so different. He can only become worthy of love again because he is Halo, not Eason. And he will only be able to keep that love as Halo, not Eason. What he has now—it must be protected. This kind of happiness is something he has been searching for his entire life, and now that he has it, he wants more. He wants so much more.

MINNIE

December. The deadline for the zine arrives, and still she has nothing worthwhile to offer. Her attempts are lifeless and unconvincing, even to herself: *Life in Carothers Dorm* (too boring); *Fall Fashion in the Honors Quad* (but who is she, to comment on fashion?); *Books that Changed My Life* (and yet, following Nate's critique of her tastes, she had begun questioning everything about her literary sensibilities). It was easier to ignore the looming deadline and instead take shelter in The Heaven, where at least she could speak without judgment. And so, when the deadline arrives on the second week of the month, as the air finally decants into real chill, she is not surprised when Anna returns back to her the essay (*An Ode to Battle Hall: The Best Place to Study on Campus*) with a disappointed shake of the head, safety pin earrings swiveling with her like antennae. "Anyone could have written this. I want something only you could have written. Akash can help, you know. He's good at teasing out this kind of stuff."

Minnie meets Akash at the Dobie Mall on 21st Street, a deteriorating two-story shopping center dominated by a Princeton Review and recruiting offices for various branches of the military. In the food court, she gets a craving for Panda Express, something she would never allow herself to indulge in if Nate were present, for he always favored more authentic ethnic food. But it has been five weeks since the party, five weeks since she has heard from him, so she suggests it to Akash, whose face lights up. "Their orange chicken is legit," he says, scanning the menu. "My parents always got it over the holidays when we'd get sick of turkey."

"We would get KFC," Minnie says.

"We had that for Thanksgiving," he tells her, grinning. "Speaking of, how was yours? Anna told me you stayed in town."

"It was okay. I had a lot of homework to do."

Together, they carry their trays to a table on the outskirts of the food court. Inspecting the orange chicken and honey walnut shrimp, Minnie feels a yearning for home and her parents that scares her for how suddenly the sensation overtakes her. "After you," Akash says, and Minnie shepherds the golden medallions of chicken into her mouth, the taste divine in its oily nuttiness, carrying her back to all the holidays when she ate these very same medallions at the dinner table with her parents, how safe she felt then, how everything stretched out before her in potential and possibility, for she had not yet been touched, she was still herself.

Akash watches her. "How is your article coming along?"

Write about something that lights you on fire, Anna had told her. She had thought and thought, and when she could think no more, she returned to what had been there since the beginning: If she thought of fire, then it was the boys at the center of it all, the burning core around which she revolved. "Good." She pulls out her laptop to take notes. "I'm thinking of writing about this band called HOURglass."

He spoons some extra fried rice onto both their plates. "I've heard of them. What do you want to say?"

"I don't know." The thought terrified her as much as it excited her, the codification of her love for the boys into a concrete, permanent artifact. "I mean, there are so many things. Why I love them. How they've helped me and what they mean to me. But I'm scared that everyone will think I'm crazy or obsessed or just some silly fangirl—"

"Can anyone," Akash interrupts her gently, "who has ever loved anything say they haven't felt the way you do?"

She pauses. He is not wrong—is there a difference between the way she loves the boys and the way a sports enthusiast loves their team? Did those fans not scream and shake and cry in the face of their god?

"Let's figure it out together," Akash says, pulling her laptop over. He adjusts the angle of the screen, urges up the brightness. And then he looks at her, a look so easy that she might as well be telling him a story about himself.

"I feel," she says slowly, "like they're a part of me. Like they really know me and want the best for me."

"What do you mean?"

"They've been there for me in a way that other people haven't. And even though they're not physically *here* with me, I feel like just knowing that they exist makes it easier for me to be a better version of myself—because they're always the best version of themselves."

"That's interesting," he says, his fingers dancing across the keyboard. "Three of the members are Asian, right? Do you think it has anything to do with that?"

"I don't know. I guess I don't really understand it yet. I've never thought much about race, or maybe I've been too afraid to think about it, growing up in Colorado Springs. But I see them and there hasn't been a band as popular and big as them—and also so visibly themselves. Maybe they make me feel proud to be Asian, too. Or, maybe it's just that they make me want to be more myself. I don't know how to explain it, but I want to try."

"I get it," he says, still typing. "I think you should."

"But how?" Minnie asks, suddenly panicked by the suggestion. "I'm not qualified." Race, social issues, politics—these were things greater than her, reserved for writers like Nate, with more years of experience and knowledge. She thinks back to the conversations during their first date, when she could not speak to the world politics that he brought up. Even Jillian and her friends would be better at tackling issues like these, with their Dean's Scholars placement and philosophy courses. Her voice is still too small, too green.

Akash looks up from the laptop. "Of course you're qualified. I used to think the same thing, you know. I didn't deserve to write about things, because what do I know? But we're just as here as anyone else in this world, and what we have to say matters. I care about the Earth, so I started writing about conservation. It's enough to just care. It's a place to start. You too, Minnie. You care. So, you *are* qualified. Look."

He turns the laptop to her. On a white page, she sees her own words shining back at her, the letters black and solid and, she is surprised to say, confident. He had taken her thoughts and turned them into a map along which she is now beginning to see the lines.

"Thank you," she says. She means it.

Akash smiles. "Speaking of bands, you never told us what your song would be."

"What?"

"When we did introductions at the first meeting. You didn't get a chance to tell us your theme song in a movie."

She laughs, surprised that he remembers when even she has forgotten. "I guess I haven't thought about it since then."

He reaches into his backpack and extracts the pair of black headphones she saw so frequently around his neck. "That's okay. I thought of one for you. Do you want to hear it?"

I cannot recall, she muses as she bows her head, *the last time someone thought of me at all*. The tips of her ears crush as Akash places the headphones over them.

Looking everywhere, I see nothing but people . . .

They are calling me, but they don't know I can't stay all night long

The melody is strange, disquieting. Not the kind of music she has grown familiar with from the boys, which was safe in its pop-infused major chords. This song, with its minor key synths and translucent narrator, is upbeat but melancholy, a fragile revolution around a sorrowful axis. In its off-kilter drums and slipping vocals, it also seems to echo all the things she herself finds so difficult to say.

"I don't know if this makes sense," she tells Akash when the song ends, "but you were right. This song sounds like me. Like the way I feel."

It is the first time she has admitted this—the lonely cavern inside her—to anybody outside The Heaven.

He nods, but this time he does not ask her for an explanation. Either because he does not need it, or because he knows that simply stating this is all that she can muster for now. Whatever the reason, Minnie feels relieved and, inexplicably, lighter.

"Min?"

She looks up, turning to the source of her name. Nate stands behind her, staring from her to Akash to the plates of leftover food between them.

"Nate." She is not doing anything wrong, so why does he look so annoyed? "What are you doing here?"

"What do you mean? I always walk this way."

Akash watches them, his face changing from surprise to understanding. "Hey man." He stands and extends his hand to Nate. "I'm Akash. I'm on the writing staff with Minnie for the zine."

Nate shakes his hand, but looks past Akash, down at the table. "Is that Panda Express?"

Akash gestures to the honey walnut shrimp. "You're welcome to have some."

"No thanks." Nate's lip curls. "I don't do MSG."

Akash slings his backpack over his shoulder, unperturbed. "You can sit here if you want. I was just about to head out."

"Wait," Minnie says.

"It's okay." He takes a few steps away from the table, and already the distance between them feels like too much. "It was nice to meet you, man."

They watch him go together. Nate sits, taking a chopstick and stabbing one of the shrimp pieces with it, an unreadable expression on his face. "Why haven't I heard from you?"

But that is not fair. It is he she has not heard from since the night of the party, he who had been kissing another girl. He who had the roommate.

"I thought you and that girl—"

"Kristín's going back to Iceland," Nate says stonily.

"Oh," Minnie says. "I guess I didn't know you were seeing other people."

"You and I never said we were exclusive, did we? I don't know how many relationships you've been in, but this passive-aggressive silent treatment is incredibly immature."

He was right—they had never defined the relationship. She had only wanted it, quietly, within herself, unable to voice that desire at the risk of wanting too much. "I'm sorry," Minnie says. "This is my first relation—I mean, just, my first time being with anyone." She feels small, like a child who has been caught with her hands in the mud.

"It shows." He releases the chopstick and sits back in the chair, his eyes flitting to the open laptop screen. "Did you write this?"

"Wait," Minnie says again. She is not ready for Nate to meet the boys. Not like this, when he already questions the merits of their whatever-the-hell-ship. But he pulls the laptop over, eyes already running down the page, brows rising higher with each paragraph. When he finishes, he looks at her with a strange expression on his face.

"I had no idea you were so obsessed."

"I'm not," Minnie says, knowing she must sound defensive. "I just really like them."

"I don't know anyone our age who still likes boy bands, but I guess there are a lot of things I didn't know about you, Min."

Yes, she wants to say back. There are. Starting with your best friend, the person he really is. Would you like to hear the things he does in the bathroom of your house? But she swallows the impulse, and along with it, her anger and indignation. Nate scans the laptop again and then he looks at her as if he has changed his mind about something. Under his curious gaze, Minnie feels a flash of that same shine she remembers from their first date, when she was worthwhile and interesting.

"Let's get out of here," Nate says finally, and Minnie takes this to mean that something has been fixed. He stands, holding out his hand, and she accepts it. They walk away from the food court together. When she looks back at the table, she sees the chopstick poking up out of the shrimp. A flagless flagpole signifying an empty victory or a stunning defeat—she is not sure which.

◦ ◦ ◦

In her dorm room, Nate comes into sharp relief against the books scattered across her desk, the tumble of pillows on her bed. It is strange seeing him in the same place where she has spent so many hours with only the boys, but at the same time, she does not want him to leave. As he moves to sit atop the grass-green comforter on her bed, Nate looks innocent, absolved by the awkwardness of the situation, and, as hurt as Minnie is, she cannot help but immediately forgive him.

He kisses her, this time on the lips. A real kiss, one she had yearned for with the intensity of a prayer. In her dreams, it would all be perfect, from the outfit she was wearing to the soundtrack commemorating the occasion—but this kiss holds none of the sweetness she hoped for. Instead, she hears bass and screams and snickering laughter, and from a roaring hole inside her memory, she smells musty towels, the scent filling her nose until it feels like she might suffocate. She pushes the body on top of her away with a force that surprises her. When she opens her eyes again, she is shocked to see Nate, not Clark, sitting in front of her.

"I'm so sorry." Her hands are shaking, but she hides them under a pillow.

"It's fine," he says. "I guess I'm your first kiss."

A foreign pressure descends on her chest. She glances down and sees his hand on her breast. When Minnie was twelve, she read on a forum that she could mimic the feeling of another person by first making her hand numb, then touching herself with it. She had sat on her hand until she could no longer feel it, then rubbed herself anxiously, trying to grasp the sensation. Her hand was rubbery against the skin of her breast, and she could not derive any pleasure from it. Now, with Nate's very separate hand touching her, she thinks that the user on the forum had been just as inexperienced and stupid as she. This is not the same feeling at all, nor does it bring her ecstasy the way she thought it would. Instead, Nate's hand weighs heavy and dreadful on her chest. The room disappears, replaced by the dirty sink, the sodden towels. Her vomit, foaming in the drain of the bathtub, and again Clark is there. *Don't you dare look away.* Looming over her on the bathroom tile, just as he looms over her now, but Nate does not notice—he moans and closes his eyes, his movements growing more frenzied.

"I—I—" she hears herself say.

The hand stops. "Does it not feel good?"

"No, it's good!" she yelps, hating herself for spoiling the moment. "It's just all so new. I've—I've never done this kind of stuff before."

Nate's mouth twitches and she is relieved to see that he is smiling. "I can go slow."

She nods. The universe has given Nate back to her, and in doing so, has also given her another chance to have the kind of life she wanted for herself—one where she is desired and important, and, most of all, happy. Why couldn't she accept its offer?

"Maybe not tonight," she says, hoping this is enough of a promise for him. "Maybe we can work up to it?"

"Sure," Nate says. His hand drops to her knee, and he feathers it with his thumb. "I can't lie—it just makes me want you more."

After Nate leaves, Minnie gives her breast a hopeful squeeze. Maybe, she thinks, she just needs to get used to being touched. Maybe she needs to associate it with something already pleasurable. She opens her laptop and navigates to a video of Jelly and Halo, uploaded a week ago. It is forty seconds long, with the two of them sitting side by side on a bed and speaking to the camera. Both are wearing faces full of makeup and black suit jackets with multicolored rhinestones at the lapels.

She keeps her hand where it is. With the other hand, she presses play.

"We just got done with our concert," Jelly says, grinning, "but we have too much adrenaline to sleep."

"But we *should* be sleeping," Halo says, characteristically serious. "Jelly has forbidden me from sleeping. I want everyone to know that I'm being forced against my will."

Jelly brushes the top of Halo's head. "I do love how obedient you are. That's something you guys should know about Halo—he does everything he's told."

"Prove it."

Jelly gives the camera a wicked smirk. Then, he turns and dips his head in to Halo, whispering something beyond the realm of what the microphone can pick up.

The video ends.

A tingling spreads through her, starting just below her navel and traveling up her belly until it meets the hand on her breast. It is both hot and cool. Her body wants to move, wants to flex every muscle of its being to hold on to the sensation.

She replays the video. She watches again as Jelly smiles at Halo, teasing him. She measures the excruciating distance between Jelly's mouth and Halo's ear. How they both beam at each other, like they cannot be anything other than what they are, which is unmistakably, unequivocally, happy.

This is what I must give to Nate, Minnie reminds herself.

She closes her eyes and replays the video of Jelly and Halo again and again, until eventually, she is in the video, too, sitting all around them. Jelly gazes at Halo through her, and she feels the electricity from his gaze. She imagines what happens when the camera turns off and the filming staff leaves. When it is just the two of them and the costumes fall from their bodies, revealing smooth skin that gleams under the moon. Every breath accompanied by a shudder, every finger painting a trail of gooseflesh. The forbidden smell of them, all heat and ink and leaking fruit, somehow the same smell as a bodywash she received on her eighteenth birthday, when she felt most like an adult. What happens when the lights turn off? Do they share more than a whisper? Do they gasp at the things they discover? Do they touch—and where?

She does not open her eyes, does not feel the echoes of Nate or permit the shadow of Clark. This she is sure of—when she is here with

Jelly and Halo, darkness cannot enter. And so she fills herself with them, until the buzzing inside her crashes against the very beach of her body and her eyes finally fly open to see the popcorn ceiling looking down at her with wonder.

There is bliss there.

EASON

The morning they are to leave for Kansas City, it is a woman, not Brooks, who comes to collect him from his room.

"Brooks has been terminated," the woman tells Eason when he asks. She takes a step back into the hallway, expectant. "You'll be working with me moving forward."

The woman's name is Cecile. She comes from a bulldog PR firm fresh off successfully rehabilitating a young starlet after what many thought to be an unrecoverable scandal involving hate speech and a very bad Halloween costume. Cecile is tight and put-together in a way that Brooks never had to be, because, he was always boasting to them, his work spoke for itself; he did not need to wear suits or press his clothes to prove that. But Cecile does, even though her work clearly speaks for itself, too. Her hair, a blond so pale it is almost white, hits the nape of her neck in a clean line, and the points that protrude from her face—forehead, nose, lips—remind Eason of the points of a star. To balance this, perhaps, she wears a shapeless white dress tapered at the wrists and ankles, so that the only parts of her body that show are her bony hands and flats-clad feet. A good disguise, but not perfect; walking behind her, Eason can see that her body is spear-sharp in every corner.

He never liked Brooks, thought him combustible and greedy for power. But Brooks had also been with them since the beginning. Eason had grown accustomed to him, the man who saw them through their training days and ushered them through the door to every photoshoot, interview, and stage. There was some kind of comfort and even trust in that. But it is very clear now that he will likely never see Brooks again. A better manager would have stopped any whispers of a scandal before it started. Someone had to take the fall.

Downstairs, his bandmates are waiting with the assistants, whose eyes lower in deference when they see Cecile. News of Brooks must have traveled fast.

"Did you get some sleep?" Minwoo asks. What he is really asking Eason is if he has heard the news about Brooks, but they do not dare voice it now, not when Cecile is standing so close. Eason nods, and Minwoo chirps, "That's great!" in a pitch so forced it makes Eason wince.

A burst of light draws his attention. Its source is a young man by the elevators, an outlier from the weary businessmen and vacationing families that mill about the lobby. Eason recognizes him as a Remora, one who joined sometime after their show in Pittsburgh weeks ago. When he sees Eason, he quickly looks away and redirects the giant camera in his hands, acting as if he has been taking pictures of the hotel, but Eason can tell by his guilty expression that he has been recording everything. Cecile is already on it. She strides over to the young man, who does not have time to register her, and snatches the camera out of his hands. With her pointer finger, she jabs the buttons on the camera, then tosses it back to him. "Fucking bitch," he cries, looking down at his camera and the now-deleted videos. "That was my intellectual property!" But Cecile is walking away, already on the phone with someone more important than this young man will ever be. "You'll be hearing from my lawyer!" he yells after her, and that is when she turns and gives him a withering look that chills even Eason.

The cars arrive. Minwoo and Colt file into the first. Julian walks to the second, but Cecile stops him with a hand around the wrist.

"We need shots of you"—she points at Eason—"helping him into the car."

Eason looks from her to Julian, who wears a mortified expression. Across the street, he notices another man with a camera, but he is not a Remora and his camera is different, with a thick, long lens that looks like a telescope.

"I'm not asking. Make it look real."

Eason cedes. He places his hand on the small of Julian's back. Long muscle, a ridge of spine. It freezes under his touch. How strange, he muses, to feel statis in a body so tuned for constant movement. He keeps his hand there just long enough for the paparazzi across the street to take a series of shots.

"Are we good?" Julian snaps. "Did you get it?"

Cecile nods to the pap, who flashes her a thumbs-up.

Eason follows Julian into the car. Cecile slides the door shut, and then it is just the two of them, no driver or manager or bodyguard. Just the two of them, like it used to be.

"I hate this," Julian says. Eason has to lean over to hear him. "This isn't what I signed up for. We're performers. We're not puppets."

"We're doing this *so* we can keep performing. It's only until this all blows over."

"Is it, though?" Julian says. Outside, the managers are running from one of the cars—someone, likely a vengeful Brooks, has planted something in the trunk that now causes them to retch and hold their noses. "You don't think this is just the beginning? You don't think they'll make us do this forever?"

"Why would they?" Truthfully, Eason believed it would only last a few weeks—that was the way, The Duke had promised, these things worked. The editor at *Pop Impulse* would grow tired. A new scoop would break, as they always did. All it took was time.

"Minwoo says it's about the fans. You say it's about the team, about our dreams. But it's not. It's about money. It's about Ronald and the record label controlling our lives so he can get his."

"Who the hell is Ronald?"

"That's his real name. Stupid, right? But you heard what he said. He thinks we belong to him."

Eason feels, all of a sudden, an ugly urge to shake Julian. Here they were, trying to do everything they could to keep this band together. Why was it so hard for Julian to understand that? "I don't get what your problem is. You're the reason why we have to do this in the first place."

He is being cruel, he knows. It is he, not Julian, who is responsible for all of it, but no one else can know that, least of all Julian.

His friend looks away. "You know," he says finally, "I never told you why I retired from skating, did I?"

This is the last thing Eason wants to hear. Anything Julian says now is simply a way to soften Eason and change his mind. He wants to be angry with Julian, and rightfully so. He does not need a whole sordid history. No one has ever needed that from him, after all.

"My whole career, I wanted to get the quad axel. No one has ever been able to land it in competition. I practiced six, seven hours a day. I was getting close. But every time I tried to do it when it mattered, I'd fuck it up. My coach told me it was because I was too heavy. If you want to fly, he told me, you have to get off the ground first. So I stopped eating, and I got lighter and lighter, and all of a sudden, I felt like I could fly. It was the best feeling, Eas. Have you ever been that close to something? I was light—I was so light that you could breathe on me and I'd fall over. But I was so close to landing that jump. And every time I jumped, it felt like someone had grabbed ahold of my head and my feet and were twisting them in different directions, like I was a towel and they were just wringing me out, and my back was on fire, my bones were cracking, my head hurt all the fucking time, and I was losing fistfuls of my own hair, until one day the doctors told me that if I kept going like I was, I wouldn't live to see nineteen, much less do a single toe loop." He turns back, facing Eason. "I love HOURglass as much as any of you. But I can't give it my life. I already did that once before, and all that got me was a room of empty trophies and an eating disorder I still can't shake. And you know what's fucked up? Even after all of that, I still want to fly. I still wish I could get off the ground."

"Don't you care about the rest of us?" Eason asks quietly. "What we want?" What he means is: Don't you care about me? But how could Julian know, when Eason had never told him? He thinks back to the night at the club in Philadelphia. Should he have told Julian then? Told him that actually, the only reason why he tried so hard, why he was so desperate to maintain the illusion of Halo, was because that was the one version of himself he could not hate?

Outside, a replacement car arrives and the managers and assistants disperse, slotting in. Julian watches them disappear one by one into their vehicles, a sad expression on his face.

"Of course I care. It's *what* you want that scares me."

"It's called shipping," The Duke explained. "Fans want to believe that two people are in a romantic relationship with each other. It's very common, especially when it comes to boy bands."

"I'm aware," Julian said, but he was frowning. "It happens in figure skating, too."

The research and development division at BabyGold Records had been tracking a curious phenomenon over the past three months: A growing faction of fans believed that Halo and Jelly were in a romantic relationship with each other, but forced to keep it a secret by the record label.

On a tablet, The Duke showed them the evidence: message forums dedicated to Eason and Julian; pages upon pages of comments left on their livestreams, photos, and videos; eighty-chapter fanfictions imagining the entire arc of a love story; in-person meetups for fans to converge and do what, he did not know. There was more, like thousands of manipulated images, artwork, and videos that placed him and Julian in situations he knew the two of them had never been in before.

"This is crazy," Colt said, red at the cheeks. "We've never even talked about our sexualities publicly."

"It doesn't matter," Eason said. He flipped through the manipulated images. One, Halo kissing Jelly's spine. Another, on a chair, Jelly straddling Halo. Another, smooth flesh, light bouncing off a chest, the pink slip of a tongue. The pictures and videos and comments spoke of a relationship between him and Julian, but the truth was that there were three, not two, people involved: Halo, Jelly, and *them*. That was what this was all about. In the world of the relationship the fans had dreamed up, love could exist without threat or loss. He could not fault them for that.

Minwoo asked why The Duke was telling them this.

"*Pop Impulse* knows the photos of Julian at the club will bring them an astronomical number of readers, which means astronomical amounts of advertising money," The Duke said. "But once the public moves on from some boy band's coke scandal, they'll be back to scrapping for C-lister dating news and blurry photos of whichever ingenue's bikini photos. What we're offering is exclusive access to the story of Jelly and Halo's romance that we'll slowly tease and unveil over the next ten months. Today, it's only a small group of fans who care. By this time next year, it'll be the whole country. You want to be the biggest boy band in the world? This is how we get there."

It was never about the music, Eason realized, handing the tablet back to The Duke. It was about what they could make people believe. And what they needed was to believe in *them*.

"Why would we want to be locked into something like that with a magazine that's trying to destroy us?" Colt asked.

Minwoo understood it before the rest of them could. "They'll be reliant on us for their ad revenue. We're a guaranteed money maker, which means that, years down the road, when the coke scandal is no longer relevant, they'll *need* to be on our good side, so that we keep giving them exclusive content. If we do it this way, we get them under our control. It's good for us in the long run."

The Duke smiled in approval. "Two boy band members in love with each other? It'll be the most explosive thing to happen in pop music in a decade." He swiped through the tablet, stopping on a drawing of Halo and Jelly dressed as superheroes, their capes replaced by rainbows. "Perfect for the times."

POST #1597

Ladies and gentlemen, the ship has officially set sail.

cue horns, fireworks, symphonic orchestral music

As of today, we can safely say that Jelly and Halo are definitely dating and, most importantly, READY TO GO PUBLIC.

After months of being called the worst names in the book, we have finally been vindicated: the boys are now being so open with their relationship that even the tabloids have started taking notice. We're not the only ones who see their true love anymore. Now, the world will too.

But we shouldn't celebrate too early. Now that the public is aware, the boys need more protection than ever. There will be people trying to infiltrate their relationship. There will be haters and homophobes. Most of all, we need to monitor the evil record label, including all employees and management, and ESPECIALLY The Puke, who will try to stop their happiness by any means necessary.

Troops, it's time to batten down the hatches. We're in for a long war.

MINNIE

The semester dwindles. In the ten days of final exams leading up to winter break, campus is indistinguishable from the site of a zombie outbreak, its inhabitants wandering the Forty Acres with glazed eyes and half-open backpacks, their clothing so lived-in it becomes a second skin. For Minnie, the last ten days prove to be challenging, but not impossible; she hands in three essays for her English courses, takes one breezy multiple-choice test for US Government, and simply shows up to earn an attendance grade for her first-year seminar. Then, it is over. The zombies turn back to humans. Campus thins, and under its oak trees the walkways empty again.

There is, of course, the problem of the zine. For her second attempt, she turns in a last-minute—analysis? summary? she cannot really be sure—of the short story "Backbone" by David Foster Wallace. *The story is about a boy who is obsessed with trying to touch every part of his body with his lips. Originally published in* The New Yorker, *it eventually became part of Wallace's novel,* The Pale King. Anna reads through the article in less than a minute. Then, she hands the pages back to Minnie with a sigh. "What is this?"

"I just thought the story was interesting."

Anna rubs her temples, causing her foundation to pill into small white beads at her hairline. A few desks away, Akash shifts in his seat. Minnie wonders if he is listening. "You're telling me that this Wallace dude is what lights a fire in you?"

Minnie looks down. No, no he was not. But following the Panda Express incident, Nate had convinced her to change course, for writing about a boy band would have no literary merit, and on some level, his assessment tapped into a fear she long held: that anything she wrote about the boys would be laughed at. "Sorry. I ran out of time."

"I know you're better than this," Anna says. "Otherwise you wouldn't still be here. I just hope that *you* know you're better than this."

Back at her desk, Akash wants to know what happened.

"I lost my notes."

His eyes widen. "You didn't back them up?"

"I must have closed the window without saving."

Doubt knots his face. "That guy who came up to us—is he your boyfriend?"

"Nate?" she says. "Yes, he is. Why?"

"I'm just surprised at the way he was talking to you."

"What do you mean?"

"I mean—I thought he was being rude to you."

"I didn't think that," she says, annoyance prickling up her neck. "That's just how we talk to each other."

"Really?"

"You don't know anything about our relationship," she snaps. "And you don't know anything about me."

It works. He pulls away from her, a real wound on his face. How gallant of him, thinking he was saving a girl who did not know any better. How lame. "You're right," he says. He turns back to his work, shaking his head. "I guess I don't know you."

No, Nate was not her boyfriend. The title had still not been bequeathed, and yet, ever since the kiss in her room, she felt a shift in him that may as well have made it so. In those final ten days before break, he visited her dorm every evening to study together, but these sessions never did involve much studying; instead, his hand would somehow find its way to her knee and begin massaging small circles up her thigh. It was flattering, his attention and his desire—she could feel his body on the verge of something hot, a live wire—and yet, she was cowed by it. She wanted him, but she was terrified by the proximity of him, the physicality. "Is now good?" he wanted to know, his chest close to hers. "Maybe next time?" she would say. "Or after break?" And he would shake his head, the hand leaving, the playful grin disappearing, reminding her in disappointment: "That's almost a whole month from now."

But Minnie could breathe, at least. She just needed more time to fortify the wall that kept her memories of Clark at bay. *You want Nate*, she reminded herself. Badly. Yes, next time, she would be ready.

The night before her flight back to Colorado Springs, the two of them join the Thursday Night Social Ride, a cycling club whose members adorn their bikes with multicolored LED lights and complete a twelve-mile route that traverses campus, downtown, and the eastside. Austin is so small that the route folds in on itself three times. Nate lends her his extra bike and off they go, surrounded by hundreds of cyclists all blasting a confused symphony of EDM from their speakers. Minnie gets lost in the throng—it is claustrophobic and dizzying when everyone moves at different speeds. Cyclists pass her with murmurs of "on your left," and she has to remember not to swerve into them, because for some reason, her body wants nothing more than to pull in the direction of another human being.

Nate rides out in front, a good ten feet or so, but Minnie does not try to keep up. He once revealed that an ex-girlfriend complained that he never waited for her during these rides and how annoying it was for him, someone who wanted to shoot to the front of the pack but was forced to stay at the back. *If you don't wait for me, then you don't love me*, he had said, mimicking his ex-girlfriend's voice in a pinched whine. So, Minnie makes sure her smile is wide and carefree when Nate turns to check behind him.

At 12th Street, the path deepens into a steep descent. The group around her thins as cyclists fly forward, whooping as the wind carries them down the smooth pavement, all of their night lights streaking across her field of vision. Minnie lets them go ahead—she has no desire to speed down the hill. She watches as Nate leads the front, his legs pumping hard to keep up with the furious spin of his bike's wheels. He stands up over his seat, hovering over the handlebars, back flat, and head down. An arrow, she thinks. At the stoplight at the bottom of the hill, he throws his hips to the right, whipping the back tire out from under him, then to the left, and again, and again until the bike skids and slows—this is the way, Minnie learned, that people who ride fixed-gear bikes brake—not relying on any other mechanism but sheer belief in physics. Seeing him handle the bike so expertly only makes him more desirable. She lets herself come to a gentle stop, the last of the group, her bike saddle rubbed hot from her exertions, and from her yearning. Ahead, Nate has already begun making his ascent up the next incline.

After the ride, the group gathers at a newly opened dive bar on Cesar Chavez hocking $2 PBRs and free chili that comes light on the meat, heavy on the beans. This part of the city seems incongruous to her, dotted with new construction and kitschy restaurants boasting shared plates, all of it too shiny, too cheerful, too much of an obfuscation, as if to say, don't look at the historic houses that stand next to us, the ones with peeling paint and overgrown weeds. Don't look at our neighbors inside these houses, who are on their way to being bought up and edged out. Don't look, there's no point in looking, because one day this will all go away, and in its place will stand condos and even more shared plates and a hot yoga studio that costs $250 per month for unlimited classes and 10 percent off at the smoothie bar next door.

Inside the bar, a local indie band costumed in suspenders and fedoras takes the stage and begins to play. One of them carries an accordion, which the audience seems to find greatly validating.

"How was the ride?" Nate's friend Indigo asks. He is in his thirties, but dresses like a teenage rebel, his thin frame accentuated by a tight T-shirt with holes he cut himself.

"Like butter," Nate says, taking a swig of beer. "This was Min's first time."

"Whoa," Indigo says, swinging around to notice Minnie as if she just appeared. "This one's new. What kind of bike do you ride, Min?"

"Nate lent me his extra."

"I didn't know you had two," Indigo says, his attention snapping back to Nate instantly. "But of course you always do have an extra." This he says with a wink.

Nate gives Indigo a pointed look. "Actually, it's Clark's bike. They're about the same height."

The two of them continue talking. They do not notice the girl whose body has gone rigid, save for her legs, which begin to shake. They certainly do not notice the change that comes over her face. Not a person knows or cares but the walls of the bar, for it is them her hands reach for.

It was Clark's bike. She rode Clark's bike.

The band starts playing a jig. She does not hear them. Nor does she hear Nate and Indigo's conversation. She does not want to be here anymore, not like this. She mutters something to Nate, who waves his hand as if swatting a fly, and stumbles out, leaving the walls with her secrets.

Outside, the air is crisp, but not unbearable. Winter in Texas, what a joke. She walks down the steps, stopping when she sees her—Clark's—bike leaning against the side of the bar. Nate had not bothered to lock it up. An unfamiliar rage, sweet in its power, fills her. She grabs Clark's bike and rolls it away with her. "Bye, fish!" someone shouts from the patio.

In her hands, the bike clicks happily, like a dog eager for its walk. She mounts it and begins to pedal, but not in the direction of her dorm. Instead, she retraces the path from earlier that night, back, back, until she is at the top of the 12th Street hill, where she watched Nate whip his way down.

The bike, once a trusted companion, feels treacherous in her hands. She brakes at the top of the hill and dismounts, gazing down. It is past midnight now. The stoplight at the bottom blinks on and off, its faint red tics interrupting the otherwise silent night. Minnie straightens the bike so that its frame follows one clean line. She squeezes the handlebars, the cushioned rubber molding to her palms. Then, with one solid push, she releases the bike down the hill.

It descends in a straight line at first, its path unencumbered, but this does not last. As it reaches the halfway point, the bike begins to swerve left and right, the pedals spinning wildly, a distant whining in its chains, until finally, it keels over and tumbles down the rest of the hill, crashing just at the bottom, underneath the still-blinking stoplight.

Minnie remains at the top of the hill, making no movement to go retrieve the bike. In this part of Austin, all hills and dips and million-dollar houses on stilts, there are flood warning signs everywhere. *Turn around, don't drown!* She hopes that a storm will come soon and bring a flood so powerful that it carries the bike away, the force of the current disassembling all its parts. That the bike will be destroyed by some massive pickup truck, or maybe stolen and resold on Craigslist, or that it will bear out the rest of its wretched life here, at the bottom of this hill, rain and dew rusting its chain until it can no longer be ridden. And she hopes that when Clark returns, he will feel the pain of losing his bike so much that it will send him into a deep, unfathomable sadness, the same one ironed into the fabric of her, until he fails all of his classes and drops out of school, and is never able to find a job, nor love, nor happiness for the rest of his damn life. She turns to go home.

EASON

In the beginning, when Eason first started dancing, Julian told him to imagine a string. It runs from the top of your head through your whole body. Where it begins is above you, where it ends is deep in the earth, maybe even farther than that, who knows. It's different for each dancer. But the important thing is that it guides you. Every movement you make is only because the string wants you to go there first.

You are only you because of this string.

Make a wave with your body. No, not with your chest. Not with your hips. Remember the string? It starts there. Feel it pull your head back, exposing your throat. Feel it draw your neck out of its natural alignment. Feel it cull out of your chest a cave. The string ropes the notches of your spine into a curve. This is the beginning of a wave.

Now the string wants you to flip your hair. It pulls your head to the left and figure-eights your head to the right. Give yourself over to the string and you can move faster than you think. You'll look like a storm, or a fury of flapping wings, or a weapon spinning in the hands of its master.

You think dance is about copying movements, but you're wrong. Show me a move and I'll show you ten ways to express it. Staccato, gooey, sharp, heavy. Look, I'm raising my arm and it's weightless. Look, I'm raising my arm and it's traveling through syrup. Look, I'm raising my arm, milking it out of me.

It's too hard, Eason told him. I don't look like you when I dance.

That's because you're trying to look like me. You should be trying to look like you.

Like him: jagged bone, long torso, two skinny legs that stalked across the floor with a jerkiness that said *don't touch me* and *I'm sorry* at the same time. Each move calculated by the same ten questions that preceded everything he did: Am I allowed? Do I deserve to? What will they think of me? Do they know? Why does it still hurt? When will I forget? How could I want to forget? Where can I hide? Could things have been different? Will this ever end?

You're thinking too much.

Yes.

Stop thinking so much.

I can't.

So go back to your string. You have to understand what it's made of. Mine is the ice and my blades and "Erbarme Dich, Mein Gott." That's what makes me move the way I do. What makes you move like you?

I don't know.

Yes you do. Yes, you do.

It is easy to pretend that he and Julian are in love. Easy, when all you have to do is capitalize on an existing story. A small gesture, a mischievous smile, a stare held for far too long. From a prestigious acting coach, they receive training on the art of looking like lovers. This new tutelage recuses them from physical training, which Colt teases them over: "If I had known that this would've gotten me out of cardio, I would have volunteered to be Julian's lover." Eason entertains the jokes, because that is what this whole thing is—a joke. None of it is real. How could it be, when he had not felt compelled to love anything again after what happened? Colt had a childhood crush he still wrote to, Minwoo a girlfriend he broke up with prior to joining the band, and Julian a few paramours from his skating days. Eason never had anyone. The implications of a same-sex relationship did not bother him, for he himself did not know what he preferred, had never given it a thought or looked at another person since, man or woman, and said: I, too, could be deserving of their affection. He envied the time the others had to figure such things out. It was almost a relief to pretend to love Julian beyond brotherhood—in some ways, it was like getting lost time back.

This is what he learned:

During public appearances, gaze at the other as if you have been starving for years and they are the only one who can feed you. Touch each other easily, without needing a map or directions, as if what you are really touching is yourself.

Stay close. You are tied by something invisible, but immense. Create a new language. Ham up the inside jokes. Share a clothing item—a beanie, a jacket, perhaps even a bag—and wear it like a new limb that grows out of you. When crossing your legs, make sure your foot points to the other person—this communicates a subconscious need to always be with them.

Upload videos and pictures of yourselves together. Selfies are good, but cryptic messages are even better. Make references to love songs with lyrics that speak about forbidden love. Make the fans wonder, make them believe. Make it so obvious for them that there could only be one answer.

It takes a while, but they both get the hang of it. They have been trained well, Eason reminds himself once again, only this time, he finally understands that all that training led to one destination: compliance. When the cameras turn on, the pre-arranged movements and signals come out of them freely. It is just another piece of choreography, just another costume. He lets the string tug him along, just as Julian taught him to. But when the cameras stop recording, Julian becomes despondent. He plugs in his earphones, draws the hood of his sweatshirt up as if donning a helmet, disappears behind his sunglasses. Gone are the days when they stood in front of the mirror in the dance studio together. A silence grows, filled by the heavy imperative now placed upon the two of them: Keep everything from falling apart. Keep the band whole. Keep the lie.

"He'll get used to it," Minwoo assures Eason, even though he sounds uncertain.

Colt is worried. "What if it wasn't the right thing to do?"

But the three of them know that it was. The threat from *Pop Impulse* has been defused, the website's front page scrubbed of its celebrity fashion critiques and reality star sightings, replaced instead with staged paparazzi photos of Eason and Julian in the backs of cars, leaving concert venues together, taking quick trips to the coffee shop around the corner from whichever hotel they were staying at. Whispers of a *special bond* arise, according to "sources close to the band." Website traffic goes up, the reception overwhelmingly positive. Comment sections breach one thousand, then two, as readers speculate and dissect each new picture, analyzing the distance between them with the same careful rigor as physicists calculating the light-years between two celestial bodies. Comments that decry their perceived queerness, that call them filthy and sinful and soon to be smote down by God, are quickly smothered by large swathes of fans who come to their defense. The website fills with advertisements from credit card companies, hot tech startups, and car brands, all clamoring for the hundreds of thousands of eyes that now rake over every page. It is all happening as The Duke said it would.

"Just a little longer," Minwoo promises, but even he sounds unsure. Their EP, a little album of six songs and already months old, had recently shot up forty spots to land just outside the top ten of the Billboard 200. Pre-orders for their next album, which had only just been announced, surpassed 500,000—a first for any artist signed under BabyGold Records. If this is the reception for a few staged paparazzi photos and videos, Eason thinks, then they will be untouchable by the time the romance is fully revealed in ten months.

If he can just hold on until then.

MINNIE

She had not planned on telling Nate what happened with the bike. It would become yet another secret she kept, folded into the long list that rustled inside her. But at least this one was wholly hers—at least she had retaliated in some way. There was reclamation there, she decided. Some sort of triumph.

It does not last long. When his car arrives the next morning to take her to the airport, she can already see his displeasure from her window. "Why did you ditch last night?" he wants to know as she climbs into the car. Then, without waiting for a response, "Did you take Clark's bike?"

"No."

"Max saw you leaving with it, though. What's going on?" He sounds annoyed. His voice is hoarse, which Minnie knows to mean that he must have gone to bed very late last night.

"Nothing. How was the rest of the night?"

"You're being childish," he says sternly. "Why are you lying to me about Clark's bike?"

Because he is your friend. Because he locked me in a bathroom. Because he tried to have sex with me. Because I refused. Because he made me watch as he touched himself. Because he would not let me look away. Because, because, because.

But was it not also her fault, what happened in that bathroom? Had she not accepted Clark's offer to dance, nuzzled into the cliff of his shoulder, closed her eyes against his chest? Had she not considered, even for the briefest of moments, what it might be like to be with him? If she told Nate what happened in the bathroom, then she would also have to tell him about what led to it, and then, it was very clear that she was not free from blame.

"I'm sorry," she says. "I took the bike to go back to my dorm, but I fell on the way."

"You fell?" Nate sounds even more annoyed. "Did you have your lights on?"

"I don't remember. I must have been tipsy."

Nate lets out an impatient sigh. This kind of sigh makes her bristle, because it reminds her of just how much distance exists between her and Nate—how age, even for its scant five years, is such a vast expanse, and there are still circumstances and emotions and rites of passage that she has not experienced, that she cannot claim to have experienced—and it is enough to make Nate superior to her.

"Is the bike okay?"

"I don't know. I left it there."

"You *left it there*?"

"I—"

"I am so disappointed in you." Then, a long, punitive pause that Minnie does not know how to fill.

"Where did you crash?"

"I don't remember. I was pretty disoriented after it happened."

"Great," Nate says in a flat voice. "Now I'm going to have to tell Clark that his thousand-dollar bike is just out there somewhere and it's because you were too drunk to think about how your actions have consequences. Really great, Min. Thanks a lot."

The rest of the car ride is silent. At Departures, Nate helps her unload her carry-on luggage and gives her a limp hug before driving off. She wishes they could have spent those twenty minutes in the car reconciling—they would not see each other for nearly four weeks, after all—but she was too soft and Nate too proud. Instead, she watches his Jeep peel away, staying with it as long as she can before it is lost in the zipper of cars converging for the exit.

At home in Colorado Springs, her parents have kept her room as it was. Still the pink flowery bedspread and furry shag rug. All her magazine cutouts of Josh Hartnett and Shane West collaging the walls. *That was before I knew the boys*, she thinks. The celebrity crushes of her youth look haggard and unremarkable against their brilliance.

It feels strange to be in her room again, to sit on her bed. The last time she sat here, she was a different Minnie. She could not have predicted that she would meet Nate, could never have predicted Clark. Her parents welcome her home eagerly, gazing upon her with the same boundless love as before, but what they love is a version of their daughter who has not undergone the things she has. The innocent and blithe décor of her youth is one more reminder of just how far away she has been taken.

"Liang Liang?" Her mother, at the door. "Why are you sitting in the dark?"

"Oh, I didn't realize," Minnie says. She has been dreading time alone with her mother. Her parents called every week while she was at school, but she had always been able to parry their questions with short, vague answers. Now, she knows, there is no button for her to press that could disconnect this conversation.

Her mother takes a step inside. She is tentative in a way that she has never been before, as if she can sense the new gulf that exists between her and her daughter. She looks around the room. "All our friends redecorated when their kids left for college. Baba and I said we would keep yours the same, so that you would know you can always come home."

"That's nice," Minnie says. The less she speaks, the less danger of leaking.

Her mother walks to the bed and sits down. "It's good to have you home again."

"It feels weird."

"I thought you might say that. When I came back to your Lao Ye's house after my first year at school, I couldn't believe how small it was. I always thought our house was big, but after seeing the world, it felt like everything was so small. But I don't think that's why this feels weird to you now, am I right?"

Minnie nods. Her mother always had a way of knowing.

"One night after you started school, I had a dream about you. In this dream you were just a baby and I was holding you in my arms. I was so happy, but you kept crying because you were hungry. So I tried to feed you, but no matter how much you ate, you kept crying and crying. Until finally I couldn't feed you anymore, and then you turned into a full-grown person—the size you are now—and you cried and raged at me for not being able to feed you."

"Why are you telling me this?"

"Are you okay?" her mother says. "Are you happy?"

It is the first time someone has asked her this question, and it startles her—how simple it is, how terrifying. Here, in this dark bedroom straddling the Minnie of before and the Minnie she is now, is the opportunity to tell her mother everything that happened. She could burrow into her mother's arms again and confess, and maybe it would lead her back to the version of herself she had lost. But the shame of it all holds her back. To speak would be to give it truth, and there is still a part of her that wants to believe that what happened to her is not true.

"I am," she says instead. Her mother looks almost disappointed.

My (older) boyfriend and I had a fight, she writes in a new post on The Heaven. *It was my fault, but I don't know how to make it right. Anyone have any advice?*

She posts the message and waits. Within seconds, the red jewel appears. She refreshes the page.

HannahIsOurs18: sorry to hear that :(in my experience, its better to give each other some space . . . you can always work things out when youre both calmer

MinnieTheGreat: thanks hannah :) hope you're having a good break

HannahIsOurs18: hope yours gets better <3

The red jewel pops up again.

icanseeurhalo: These are some of my favorite Halo/Jelly vids to watch when I'm sad. I hope this helps xx

YOURSXOURS: fights are normal dear. It'll be ok, trust me
sound_of_halo: i don't have advice but i do have hugs ʕっ•ᴥ•ʔっ
Belle6Poppy: relationships aren't easy, but if you really love each other you'll find a way back to each other (this happened to me). sending you love & strength from france!

It's silly, she thinks, that it could be this easy for her mood to lift into what she dares call happiness. Is it a superficial feeling? A quick fix? Strangers on the internet, strewn across different cities and states and continents, all converging on a cry for help from someone they will never meet in real life. Bound by nothing more than their love of the boys. But is this not what makes it incredible? The boys have brought them all together.

You're the best, she writes, to everyone. *Thanks for making me feel better.*

She begins to close her laptop, but a new notification appears in the right-hand corner of her screen, not the red jewel that she has grown so accustomed to, but a green one. She clicks on it. *You have a new private chat request*, the notification reads. *Accept?*

The request comes from a user by the name of Ladybeth42. Minnie recognizes her immediately—she was one of the longest-standing members of The Heaven, both active and adored by others, and one of the few who never added embellishments to her posts, writing instead in short, full sentences. This unwavering way of writing is also what Minnie admires about Ladybeth42—it proves that she has her life together, that she is someone who wears crisp white button-downs and pleated slacks, who takes her coffee black.

Ladybeth42: Hey there. I noticed that you specified your boyfriend is older. Was there a reason for that?
MinnieTheGreat: hey! hmm i'm not sure
MinnieTheGreat: sometimes i feel like i'm too immature for him. i'm always worried he's going to get tired of me and want to be with someone his age
Ladybeth42: Has he given you any reason to think that?

MinnieTheGreat: it's just a feeling. all of his friends (especially his friends who are girls) are 23 and up. his last serious gf was his age. apparently he only messes around with freshmen because it's a temporary thing, so it makes me wonder why he's with me at all when he could be with anyone else

Ladybeth42: What's your boyfriend like?

MinnieTheGreat: a dreamboat

MinnieTheGreat: haha

Ladybeth42: Seriously.

MinnieTheGreat: well, he's smart. like, really smart. and he's involved with a lot of stuff. and i like the fact that he's older and knows who he is. i feel like he can teach me so many things

Ladybeth42: Like what?

MinnieTheGreat: like how to . . . idk . . . be? in this world. like new experiences. i've done so much i wouldn't have otherwise. we just rode bikes with a whole bunch of people the other night and i would have never done that by myself

Ladybeth42: I see.

Ladybeth42: You're being too hard on yourself. Think of the boys—they would want you to be happy, wouldn't they? They wouldn't want to see you being so down.

MinnieTheGreat: ah, you're right. i should cheer up. thank you for the pep talk!!

Ladybeth42: I'm here anytime.

Her parents want to celebrate her return with a hike the next morning. On top of Mount Muscoco, she stands at the edge of a cliff, looking down at the path they traversed hours earlier. It is a warm day for December in Colorado, but the wind still snaps, pushing her body back. She leans against it, testing its might. If it is strong enough to hold her there, or if it might release her to tumble down the mountain to join the rocks below, a fleet of ships dusted with snow. When she turns away from the cliff, she finds her father taking photos of the ridgeline. "A good view, isn't it," he says, gesturing to the world around them.

"Just like your mother." A corny joke. Her mother huffs and slaps his arm, but when she turns away, she is smiling.

At home, her parents putter, overjoyed to have another body in the house. In the mornings, her mother wakes her with ginger tea and goji berries; in the evenings, the three of them watch films after dinner. The films are always boring because they are picked by her father—they burn through *The Mothman Prophecies*, *K-19 the Widowmaker*, *Letters from Iwo Jima*, and nearly every movie Russell Crowe has ever been in. Minnie pays little attention, instead scrolling through her phone to see what the boys are up to and sometimes texting Nate, who lets more and more time pass before responding to her. He was spending the holidays in Austin—his second job at the coffee shop was short-staffed. It makes her feel panicked, imagining Nate back to a version of his life before her. Or perhaps, after her. When he takes twelve hours to respond to a text, she sends him a photo of her blowing a kiss to camera. He responds in an hour—a record.

What's this for?

Just miss you is all. What are you up to?
Can we speak on the phone?

Sorry. I've been swamped with work.
Maybe next time? Or after break?

Ladybeth42: How are you? It's been a while since you posted.
MinnieTheGreat: i'm okay. hanging out with my parents mostly
Ladybeth42: It sounds like you have a good relationship with them.
MinnieTheGreat: i guess haha. it feels like they don't really know me anymore.
Ladybeth42: That's what happens when you grow up.
MinnieTheGreat: thanks for checking in on me. it means a lot.
Ladybeth42: I take it things haven't been resolved with your boyfriend?
MinnieTheGreat: no :(
Ladybeth42: Well I have something that might cheer you up.

Ladybeth42: But you have to promise that you won't tell anyone.
MinnieTheGreat: i promise!!!

On her screen, a photograph appears. It is hazy, blurred, as if whoever took it had their hand jerked away just before capture, but even so, Minnie can make out the familiar angles of bodies she knows better than her own. The photo had been taken from an upper level of what appears to be a nightclub, dropping down into the dance floor to reveal Jelly and Halo in the middle of the throng (so unspectacular, everyone who writhes around them! So undeserving, these plain people who had no idea that kings were in their midst!). The two of them had been caught mid-dance, and there is no denying it: They were dancing *with* one another, facing each other, their lips a breath away from touching. She tightens at the picture, the intensity of their gazes so intimate that she wants to look away.

MinnieTheGreat: oh my god!!
MinnieTheGreat: is it really them?
Ladybeth42: Of course it is. You can tell it's Jelly from the silver hair.
MinnieTheGreat: and Halo's ear. I would recognize it anywhere
Ladybeth42: Exactly.
Ladybeth42: They're getting bolder with their relationship. Like they don't care what anyone else says anymore.
MinnieTheGreat: they look like they're on a date :')
MinnieTheGreat: they're dancing so close!!!
Ladybeth42: So was I right? Did it cheer you up?
MinnieTheGreat: you have no idea. thank you!!!
Ladybeth42: Just remember that this stays between us, okay?

She has so many questions for Ladybeth42. Where did this picture come from? Why did it not appear anywhere else on The Heaven, which militantly updated with any sightings of the boys within minutes? But asking such things, she senses, will only make her appear too eager, too greedy. Ladybeth42 asked her to keep a secret, so a secret she will keep.

Minnie examines the photograph again. There is something nice about keeping this kind of secret, she decides. Like her relationship with the boys, which had blown up to include the entire expanse of everyone in The Heaven, had shrunk back to just her and them again, and in doing so, had brought her even closer to them—this time, with one addition: Ladybeth42. But she does not mind it. To Ladybeth42, she is a Minnie who can be spoken to like an adult, who is worth being listened to. A Minnie who matters.

On New Year's Eve, her parents bring home sparkling apple cider. The three of them gather in the kitchen to make potstickers, a tradition they have observed since Minnie was young. Back then, they would spend all day filling the wrappers, then drive around the neighborhood delivering plates to her classmates. It was something she looked forward to every year, because for one day, she was the girl everyone wanted to see, the Dumpling Girl, and this was a feeling that she held on to and replayed in the weeks after.

This year, however, there will be no deliveries. "I'm too old for that," she tells her parents. The truth is that she cannot bear to show up at her former classmates' houses and see them as they are now—happy, fulfilled by new relationships at colleges where they must be thriving. They would take one look at her, pathetic Minnie the Dumpling Girl, and know that she has failed at what so many others found easy.

Instead, she spends the afternoon helping her parents make dumplings for just the three of them. Her mother stirs ground pork and celery and diced shiitake mushrooms into a filling and deposits a drop on each wrapper while Minnie crimps the edges. Her father heats oil in a pan and transfers the dumplings one by one. They sizzle and pop, pale skins browning as if left too long in the sun. "These are the best we've ever made," her mother declares later, as she bites into one. "It's a shame we didn't give them out."

When the clock strikes midnight, her parents share a quick kiss, then take turns hugging her. Her mother insists that they must eat some fish for prosperity in the new year. They kneel in front of a small ceramic statue of a goddess—Minnie does not know what it represents—and *ketou* several times. She is not sure if she is supposed to make a wish or a promise, but she does both.

At two in the morning, her phone lights up with a notification—not from Nate, but from the boys, who have uploaded a new video. When she presses play, they come into focus, their big, gleaming smiles cleaving the stone of her.

The boys sit at a table, four flutes of champagne in the center. They look thinner, Minnie thinks as she inspects the new shadows on Halo's face.

"We wanted to wish our fans a happy new year," Minwoo says.

"Thank you for being by our side this year," Denim says. "We promise to make you proud in the new year."

"Everything we have is because of our fans," Jelly says. "Everything I love is because of you."

"So stay by our side," Halo finishes. "And let's take this journey together. Let's make ourselves come true."

"Ourselves?" Jelly says.

Halo shakes his head as the rest of them laugh. "I meant to say *our dreams*." His voice rises above their laughter. "Oh, stop." But he looks amused all the same.

They lift their flutes and clink them together. Then, they turn to the camera. "From HOURglass to you," the boys say in unison. "Let's find joy in the new year—"

"—and make ourselves come true," Jelly adds, winking at Halo.

When the video finishes, Minnie lies back down and presses her phone to her heart. It is a new year now, and there is something undeniably powerful and instructive about that—as if the universe has decreed, regardless of where you are, that you must simply move on. She will listen, just as her own universe—the boys—urged her to.

To making myself come true.

EASON

So stay by our side and let's take this journey together. Let's make ourselves come true."

"Ourselves?"

Shit. That hadn't been in the script. "I meant to say *our dreams*," Eason stammers. But the others are laughing, Minwoo hardest of all, which signals that this is a moment to be milked. "Oh, stop."

They raise their flutes of sparkling cider. The camera zooms in on the clover of their glasses clinking together in midair. Eason's eyes float to the laptop next to the camera, where he sees twenty thousand people screaming into the live chat:

HAPPY NEW YEAR I LOVE YOU SO MUCH

MY BABIES AHHHHHHHHH

PUKING YOU ARE SO HOT

who wants to know Halo's secret?

They are supposed to say something in unison now. The video is supposed to end and they are supposed to go back to their rooms and in a few hours hurtle through the air to Salt Lake City, and not one of those twenty thousand people watching are supposed to know that the New Year's they see here is false; there are no sparklers, no confetti, hell, they even missed the ball drop and the fireworks. All of this is supposed to happen, but it does not, because once again, Eason has missed his cue.

who wants to know what Halo did?

i know

don't u want to know?????????

I'LL TELL EVERYONE WHAT HALO DID

:)

:)

:)

LIAR LIAR PANTS ON FIRE HE'S A STEALER AND A KILLER AND A BAD BOY TO HIS MOTHERRRRRRRRRRRRRRRRRRRRRRRRRR

Someone—Minwoo, maybe—pinches his back.

"From HOURglass to you," Eason chokes out, joining the other voices that have been waiting. "Let's find joy in the new year."

He thinks he hears Julian speak, something about making something come true.

Minwoo is annoyed. He wants to know if Eason read the script at all. Eason tells him sorry, it was hard to remember the words, and Colt backs him up on it and Eason almost breathes because it seems no one else has noticed and he can go back to his room.

But for Julian.

"Did you see the comments?"

"What comments?"

"Weird comments."

"Weirder than usual, you mean?"

"I mean the one that called Eason *a stealer and a killer and a bad boy to his mother.*"

No, this evening did not include fireworks, save for the ones now exploding in his head. He cannot tell them it was his mother. He cannot tell them about the skunk vine, how every day he woke to the smell of an animal dying. He cannot tell them about the storm. All these things he cannot say. But she—she could. And she would keep appearing, hounding and rooting and ripping his very skin from the bone, until—what? What was the end that she would be happy with? When all of him was exposed and he had no choice but to return to her?

But Colt snorts, rolling his eyes. "Well, yeah. Of course they said that." He jumps up and down on the balls of his feet, voice squeaking. *"He steals our hearts and kills us with his hot body and he's a bad bad boy and he's my baby.* It's nothing we haven't heard before."

"But this was different," Julian presses. "More like a threat."

"So then let's ask the bad boy," Colt says, turning to Eason. "Did you steal something else we don't know about?"

He found it on the floor of the car. He had been back there looking for his wallet when he saw the stick, peeking out from under the front seat.

He thought it was a thermometer at first, which was why he picked it up—how odd, he remembered thinking, that there would be a thermometer in the back of the car. Was someone sick? Did it belong to their mother? But when he held it between thumb and forefinger, he knew it was something else—the stick was smooth and cold and marked by two faint pastel-pink lines, and when his eyes were finally able to focus and understand what those two lines meant, he flung the stick away in horror. It was only after some time that he reached out again and shoved it in his pocket.

"—in the car, on the floor." The words were matted in his throat. He did not know why he was so upset with her, but he was. The stick terrified him—the implications and consequences even more so.

Faye asked if she could have it back.

"No."

They stood in her room in silence. Eason had envisioned a righteous confrontation where he had all the power, demanding answers from his sister and shaking from her *why* and *how* and *when* and *who*, even though he already knew who, had known ever since they took that trip to Marfa for his birthday—and perhaps that was what tore at him the most: that this all happened under his nose, under the guise of celebrating him, when really it had been a secret between Faye and Henry. The two of them had entered a private world that Eason had never been invited to join. Now, with this revelation, he would forever be on the outside of that world. He had lost his father to a woman, lost his mother to a demon and a hack fortune teller, and now, he was on the verge of losing his sister—but to what, exactly? He could not allow himself to put a name to it for the same reasons he could not bear to look at her stomach, even though he knew that it was still as flat as a plank, that there would be months to go.

He felt his eyes swelling, the brimming against his pupils and the danger it promised. When the tears finally fell, he knew that he had lost all the power he so wanted—that he never had any power to begin with. Faye placed a hand on top of his, which was still clutching the stick, and said, "I'm sorry I didn't tell you sooner. I wanted to be sure."

He asked if she was keeping it. *It*, because he could not fathom that the thing inside her could be anything more. She nodded, then pressed a finger to her lips, a reminder to them both not to disturb the closed door at the end of the hall. It was then he realized: Faye did not plan to tell their mother.

"And college?" he wanted to know. Faye had received a scholarship from Rice University in Houston, a thirty-minute drive away. Such a distance Eason could live with. He could see her on weekends, maybe even spend the night once in a while. But now a new distance, one he could not measure or traverse, was already taking root between them.

"I'm figuring it out. It'll be a little more complicated, but when has our life ever been easy?"

She was smiling. How could she look so at peace, he wondered. How was she not terrified?

"Just promise me you won't tell Mom." She looked down, where the stick was still clutched tightly in Eason's hand. For a moment, she looked as if she was going to ask for it back again, but she stopped herself.

Later, in his room, Eason studied the stick once more. If he held it up at certain angles against his desk lamp, he could almost make one of those pink lines go away. He shoved it into his desk drawer, behind the crumpled-up candy wrappers and out-of-battery calculator and all the pens that he would never use to completion, nothing more than sarcophaguses for the ink drying out in their tubes. It brought him a strange comfort, knowing that the stick was there, in his possession, and that perhaps he still had some semblance of control, even when he was about to lose it all.

POST #1933

Jelly and Halo are in danger.

It's obvious that the new blond bitch of a manager is in love with Halo. Have you seen her touch him? The way she looks at him? She follows him around like he's a kid who can't do anything by himself, instead of a grown man. She wants to be his mother and girlfriend and wife all at once. She's a vile cunt, and she's trying to steal him away from Jelly.

Meanwhile, our angels are too sweet to tell her no. Their hands are tied by the record label, which means it's up to us to protect them.

It has always been up to us.

MINNIE

The release party for the zine's inaugural issue takes place in East Austin, at a dive along a strip of bars off the intersection of 12th and Chicon. A surprising location for a party, for the strip had, until recently, been referred to as a *bad part of town*, as with most things east of the interstate that ran through Austin. But Anna was adamant about supporting a local bar with historic roots, and as Minnie's rideshare plunges down Chicon, she can't help but think that perhaps the warnings she read online were simply another way of saying, without saying: *That's where all the Black people once lived.*

Inside Bar 1812, so named for its address, old wooden planks panel the walls. A maroon carpet stretches down the length of the bar, which is no bigger than a living room. It smells wet, the way a cave does. A single disco ball hangs over the dance floor and as it spins, catching two yellow LED lights brought by Anna, drops of gold splash upon the walls, making the bar look like the inside of a waterfall.

By the time Minnie gets there, the bar is packed. She squeezes past giddy freshmen filling their plates from a self-serve buffet of egg rolls, wings, fish tacos, and oranges cut into smiling quarters. The crowd is a mix of art students and writers and friends of the staff, all people who are here because they belong to someone, but Minnie invited no one, certainly not Nate, whom she still has not seen since returning from winter break the week prior.

At the back of the room, the floor rises into a small stage, balloons dangling from the ceiling above like ripened berries. Minnie stands to the side of it, in shadow. She spots Akash cradling a drink at the bar, his eyes intent on the stage, but the expression on his face tells her that he had been looking in her direction. She retreats further.

Anna takes the stage in a black, floor-length qipao. Tonight, she has traded her safety pin earrings for long silver daggers sheathed at the lobes. "Thanks for coming," she says. "This zine is a part of my thesis project, but it's also a labor of love and we're all volunteers, so I want to first thank my amazing team. Can you please stand up if you're on staff?"

It takes a moment for Minnie to remember that she, too, is part of the team Anna is referring to. But she does not step forward into the light, where her fellow staffers are receiving applause, for none of her pieces had been accepted. Instead, Anna relegated her to organizing invoices from the printers. She had not contributed artful, heartfelt work; she had been too cowardly to even try.

"Now I have an announcement to make," Anna continues. The bar quiets again. "Last semester, I applied for a $10,000 grant for student-led initiatives in journalism and communications. I'm pleased to say that we got it." She pauses for cheers, stomping, beer bottlenecks clinking, and for once, allows herself to smile. "Which means we can start paying our staff and bringing more people on. So, if you're interested in contributing your writing or artwork to *MOON//BRIGHT//WIND*, please come talk to me . . . and have a good time tonight."

The crowd whoops again. "Are you on staff?" someone asks Minnie, but she does not stay to answer. She slips through the mingling bodies, to the bar. To Akash.

"Hey," she says, tapping him one-two-three on shoulder.

He looks around, arranging his face into false surprise. "Oh. Hey."

"I just wanted to say I'm sorry."

He studies her. For a second, it looks like he will turn back around, leaving her to wither in all her stupid shame, but then he bends down so that she can hear him over the loud bass that begins shuddering through the speakers. "I wasn't out to get you or anything, Minnie. I just wanted to make sure you were okay."

"I know." She gives him a hopeful smile. "Want to try again?"

Anna appears next to him, forehead glistening. "Wow. You came."

Minnie flinches at how hard the words sound. "I wouldn't have missed it."

"I'm just shocked because this is the first offsite you've actually shown up to. We've invited you to so many."

"I know," Minnie says again. She wants to look Anna in the eyes, the way Anna has always looked in hers, but Anna's stare is so direct that she focuses on the dagger earrings instead. "You're right—I haven't been pulling my weight. But I think I have something I really want to write about now." She glances at Akash, who gives her an encouraging nod.

Anna looks skeptical. "And I should believe you because?"

"I understand why you wouldn't," Minnie says. "But I'm not just saying this to get back in your good graces. Akash helped me with a rough draft."

"Really?" Anna swings around to Akash for confirmation. "What do you think? Should I give her one more chance?"

"Yes," he says, without missing a beat.

"I'll consider it," Anna says, but she still sounds unconvinced. "We were going to get some food after this. I can't eat anything right now, I'm too all over the place. You can come if you want. Tell me what you're working on."

The invitation is not just a friendly request, Minnie recognizes. It is a final test.

Back in her dorm, humming in the laptop on her bed, are the boys, waiting. The Heaven and all the friends it holds, waiting.

But Akash has his hand on her purse strap and he is tugging it, ringing her like a bell. For once, the boys dim. "Come on, Minnie," he is saying. "Come eat."

When the party is over, Anna chauffeurs them to a twenty-four-hour diner off Guadalupe, across campus. Minnie remembers walking past this diner the night she returned from Nate's house all those months ago, after the party. Looking inside then, she had seen groups of friends stuffed into booths, talking and laughing as if all the happiness of their lives converged there, in that moment. She had wondered, then, if she would ever get to experience such a feeling.

The waiter brings three waters and takes their orders: pancakes for

Akash, Texas scramble for Anna, a club sandwich and home fries for Minnie. She looks around and tries to take it in. Tonight, she is on the other side of the glass and for once, she is not alone. It is a realization both terrifying and exhilarating. She wonders if Akash and Anna, who are talking animatedly about the grant money, can see how untrained she is, her body still learning to settle into this new position of being with, rather than without.

The food arrives quickly. Anna takes to hers with a knife and fork, squeezing a medley of ketchup and Cholula over her hash. Minnie inspects her club sandwich—the bread is dry, the bacon almost black, but still, it looks delicious.

"So tell me about the new piece you're writing," Anna says. She unfolds her napkin and tucks it into the neck of her qipao, not caring when the table next to them snickers. Minnie feels a forceful urge to tell the table to shut up.

"Well," she says. "There's a boy band called HOURglass that I really like. I want to write about them."

"Like a biography?"

"No. Like about how much they mean to me."

Anna looks up from her plate and stares again into Minnie's eyes. This time, Minnie does not look away. The diner is brighter than the bar and she knows that all the insecurities on her face—her smudged eyeliner, her nervous, rapid blinking, the worried creases around her lips—are glaringly visible, but she is propelled by Akash's supportive nod, propelled by the boys, propelled by Ladybeth42, who had told her, *just imagine I'm there, cheering you on.*

"The real freshman experience sucks," she says. "It's a lie. It's lonely and miserable and the food is bad. But no one talks about it, and I don't know why. The only thing that has kept me going this year is this boy band. Everything I do is because I imagine they're behind me, they're standing with me, and it makes everything easier. They make me want to be better. That's what I want to write about."

She waits, fearing Anna's response. Would Anna think her pursuit childish and silly, the way Nate had?

But Anna puts down her fork and reaches across the table. Minnie feels something warm on top of her hand: it's Anna's fingers covering hers, a small stick-and-poke mahjong tile tattooed in the space between the thumb and pointer. "There you are," she says, and Minnie is shocked to see that rare smile on her face again.

"You think it's okay?"

"I think it's great, but that's not what I'm worried about." Her hand leaves Minnie's. "I'm more worried about you actually following through this time."

"I will. I promise."

Anna returns to her plate, letting out a small chuckle. "Not to be a cop," she says, "but you promised last time, too, and then you gave me a Buzzfeed article."

"We workshopped it together," Akash says. "Minnie's got this."

"Anna's right," Minnie says. Both Akash and Anna look at her in surprise. "My word doesn't really count for much anymore, does it?" She looks around the table and her eyes land on the syrup dispenser next to Akash's pancakes. "I'll drink this entire thing right now, to prove I'm serious."

"Minnie, that can't be good for you—"

"You really don't have to—"

But she does. She is tired of doing the sensible thing, of following the invisible guidelines of what *should* and *shouldn't* be. She is tired of holding herself back. She reaches across the table and takes the syrup dispenser before Akash can grab it. The top unscrews easily, releasing a perfume of artificial strawberries.

"Minnie no—"

"Wait—"

It hits her tongue first. The sensation is surprisingly comforting, a pool of slow lacquer that coats her mouth, then her throat, and slides down, down, until she feels its heavy weight enter her belly. She tilts her head back farther, remembering the flip cup game that she played at Nate's house. Clark, lurking in wait at her side. This is easy compared to that. Everything will always be easier, compared to that.

It is over in ten seconds. She sets the emptied dispenser down, her stomach very solid, as if full of rubber. The tables around them, waiters included, stare. "Damn," someone at the once-snickering table next to them mutters. And then, for some reason, they all start clapping.

"You're crazy," Anna says, shaking her head. But she looks amazed all the same. "I believe you, okay? You don't need to prove anything else to me. I believe you."

Ladybeth42: You drank the whole thing?
MinnieTheGreat: it wasn't as bad as you'd think
Ladybeth42: I'm sure your stomach hurt the next day.
MinnieTheGreat: i had to skip my first class! it was worth it
Ladybeth42: Of course it was worth it. The boys always are.
Ladybeth42: So your editor likes the pitch?
MinnieTheGreat: she loved it
Ladybeth42: I knew she would.
Ladybeth42: The boys would be so proud of you.
MinnieTheGreat: that means a lot :)
Ladybeth42: I'm going to send you a present. You've earned it.
MinnieTheGreat: what?! that's so nice!
MinnieTheGreat: you don't have to
Ladybeth42: You just had a breakthrough, so we have to celebrate.
Ladybeth42: That's what friends do for each other.

Halo's scent arrives packaged in blue and white, in a box no bigger than a card deck. Ladybeth42 said she found it in an interview, some feature on the boys for a celebrity gossip magazine. When asked what he was currently wearing, Halo had responded with a cologne called Heavenly Body.

Minnie carries the package with two hands all the way from the campus mail center back to her dorm. *To the coolest girl I know, from your friend LB*, the note along the side of the box reads. She inspects the handwriting, noticing the sharpness with which Ladybeth writes her *S*'s and the extra loops she puts into her *F*'s. Never before has she received a package from a friend. This handwriting feels precious to her, just as Ladybeth does.

It is midday and sunlight pours into the room, passing through the perfume and illuminating the warm amber liquid inside. Heavenly Body is the shape of a woman's torso, curvaceous and smooth, with bare breasts that hang off the chest like gourds. She runs her hand over the hourglass shape of it, hourglass like her HOURglass, and imagines Halo pressing down on the headless neck to release the pent-up liquid inside. *Notes of divine jasmine flower and exotic spice with hints of frankincense and myrrh.* She points the bottle at her wrist and sprays, and the liquid releases like pollen off a flower. The scent repels her at first—it is too strong, a mix of earth, ancient medicine, and sweet, rotting fruit. But she closes her eyes and draws up the image of Halo in her mind, training herself to marry the scent and the idol as one, and then she is reveling in it, swimming in it, soaring in it. It smells just like him and now, it smells just like her.

EASON

Between Kansas City and Tulsa, they detour for a photoshoot on a farm out by Fort Riley. The photographer, a newcomer who had only taken up photography two years prior, was hot property—he had been named the most important photographer in America by *Vogue* weeks before. As they sit in the back of the SUV, humming down the interstate, Eason searches for the photographer's work on his phone. The subjects of his photos are young men, often nude, although there is nothing overtly sexual about it—the photographs capture them in the middle of innocuous activities, like running through a field or airborne off a lakeside rope swing, a kind of carefree splendor that Eason finds both impossible and captivating.

In a barn-turned-studio, they meet the photographer and his assistant. The photographer is short and stringy, sporting lensless glasses and black Chuck Taylors. The assistant is young, snappy, a purse to her lips. When they arrive, the photographer is smoking a cigarette, one he keeps in his mouth, tilted at an angle, as he shakes their hands. "So you're real after all," he says, almost as if it is a detriment. "You're even more beautiful in person."

The set has been remade to look like a small field, laced with rows of what must be hundreds of sunflowers. A backdrop of blue and seashell-pink sky runs from floor to ceiling. Minwoo bends down to examine one of the flowers and is shocked to find that it is real, alive. "I didn't know sunflowers could grow indoors," he says. "Especially in the winter."

The photographer looks at his rows proudly. "Under the right conditions," he says, "the possibility of what you can grow indoors is endless."

Eason looks down at the sunflowers, past the screaming yellow petals, and into the gaping black eye of their center. He shudders, thinking of a million large and open eyes boring into him. Everywhere he turns, there are ten more, staring up at him like accusations. He feels a sudden need to hide.

"The concept is about youth and lost boyhood," the photographer is saying. He walks around the set, stopping at various places and studying the four of them against the backdrop. He gets down on his knees and peers up at them through the sunflowers, body stretched out like a cat. Then, he stands, framing them inside his fingers and thumbs, which make the shape of a square. "Everyone already knows you're on the cusp of being superstars. You can sing, you can dance, you're literally on fire. But you're also too polished. I want to show a different side of you, the rough and raw."

There will be no stylists or makeup for the shoot. The photographer tells them that what they are wearing is fine; the purple bags under their eyes will only add to the effect. "What we're going for is authenticity and movement," he says as he takes out his camera, indistinguishable from a plastic toy. He takes a few snaps. "Look alive, boys. Act natural."

After a few standard poses with their arms crossed, the photographer lowers his camera. "All right. I get that you're used to posing for the camera, but that's not what I want. I want you to play. I want you to jump! Shout! Stomp! Can you do that for me?"

They try again, this time freezing their faces in the middle of a hammy laugh. Real cornballs. The photographer does not bother to capture this attempt. Instead he stands with his brow furrowed, the dark accent of his glasses adding to the glower on his face.

"How about we pretend like we're kids again." He tosses them a football from the prop box. "Shirts versus skins."

He points to Eason and Colt. Colt has no problem whipping off his shirt, but Eason hesitates. He has never been comfortable showing people his body, the thought of baring his torso somehow equivalent to a needle sliding into his most vulnerable muscle. But Cecile, who has been observing them, steps forward, her fingers slipping under Eason's shirt easily.

He jerks away from her. "I can do it."

"Then do it."

He peels the shirt from his body and throws it at her. She catches it, unimpressed.

"It still doesn't look right," the photographer says. He turns to his assistant, who nods and scuttles to Eason. Without a word, she places her fingers around his nipples and twists.

"Ow!"

"That's better," the photographer says. *Click click click.* "Now you look *real.*"

The game is touch football. Shirts try to touch skins. Or, skins try to touch shirts. It doesn't matter, the photographer tells them. Just let it all go. Act like we're not here. Be boys again.

Eason tosses the ball to Colt, who catches it easily. Julian is a bullet running after him. He jumps on Colt's naked back, the momentum of his body causing Colt to stumble. The two topple down, engulfed by sunflowers. The photographer immediately shoots this, the clicks of his camera like small claps of applause. "That's it," he hums, moving around them and clicking. "Keep playing around."

Minwoo glances at Eason and shrugs in a way that says, "Well, what did you expect?" He takes his shirt off and joins the pile of Colt and Julian, the three of them now tangled in a wrestle of arms, legs, and necks. The artificial light, made to look like a sun, bounces off their torsos, leaving behind a sheen of sweat and pink flush. Eason feels awkward—something about the photographer's gaze, how it lingers on his body, makes him feel unclean. He joins the others, plucking a sunflower from its bed, and begins ripping off its petals, sprinkling them over his bandmates as they continue to roll around in the fake grass.

"Very nice," the photographer says. The camera continues to click. "Grab his thigh. Yes. Ruffle his hair. Good."

Soon after, the photographer wants to snap a few of just Eason and Julian. Minwoo and Colt walk off, sheathing themselves with robes. The assistant steps forward and Eason flinches, remembering the way she twisted him earlier. "Relax," she tells him, sounding annoyed. "I don't bite." She positions him and Julian against each other, back-to-back, then wordlessly holds her hand out to Julian. His shirt comes off, too.

Eason looks straight ahead. The photographer is proselytizing something about fantasy, wistfulness, dreams to come. He can feel Julian breathing against him, the steady rise and fall of his back. These photos will, no doubt, be funneled to *Pop Impulse*. With this in mind, he leans against Julian a little more, putting his weight on him, nudging the back of his head into Julian's scalp. Julian pushes back.

"That's good," the photographer murmurs as he snaps away. "Now turn and face him"—he motions to Julian—"place your forehead against the back of his head and look down, like you want to devour him."

Julian turns slowly, pressing his chest against Eason's shoulder blades. He feels the gentle pressure of Julian's forehead against the back of his head. And, he feels Julian's breaths at the base of his neck, hot with indignance at everything they have been asked to do up to this point, and everything they will be asked to do after.

"And maybe," the photographer breathes, hovering around them, "if you want to face each other now, give a little kiss—"

Julian steps away. "That's enough." He is speaking to Cecile, who looks through him, her arms crossed.

"Get back to your spot."

"No." He points at the photographer, who has arranged his face into an innocent expression. "We're done here. Right, Eason?"

Cecile turns to Eason. He wonders if The Duke told her his secret—if she knows the real reason why they have to do this. "Well?"

He looks away. "It's fine." But it is not fine, none of this has been *fine*. He hates the way his naked skin feels, like he is standing on a swaying bridge with the handrails removed, hates that everyone can see the hairs on his body rising with each pass of the fan, hates this act and the uncomfortable position the photographer, who will not stop brushing the small of his back, has put them in. But who is he, to think his hate matters? "Let's just get the shot and go."

"Remember to relax," Minwoo, who is watching, calls out.

Julian returns to his position. When the photographer brings the camera up once more, Julian dips his head so that their lips are just shy of touching. To anyone else, this would look like the image of lust and longing. But to Eason, Julian's eyes are blank, and for the first time, he is afraid of what this may mean. *Click*, *click*, *click*, the photographer continues. The flashes ignite around them.

After the photoshoot ends, he and Julian crunch through the snow back to the SUVs without speaking.

"What's with you?" Eason asks when he cannot stand it anymore.

Julian stops. Beneath him, the snow squeaks. "You're really going to pretend that you're fine with this? Or maybe you're not pretending and you really are fine with it. I don't know which is worse."

"Fine with what?"

"With being used," Julian spits. "With pretending to be something we're not. People have died for being gay, people are still fighting just to exist, and we're using it as bait. Don't you think it's wrong? Don't you think it will hurt people? All because, what? We're scared of what the fans will think of some photos of me? The person in those photos—maybe that's who I am. Maybe that's all I'll ever be. I don't know. But I can't keep selling a lie. It's not right."

"This isn't just about you," Eason says quietly. "It's about the group."

A pause. "Maybe I don't want to be a part of the group anymore."

There were so many nights, back in those early months of training, when Eason wanted to quit. It was never his body that was the problem—it was everything else. His mind was stuck, his spirit weak. It was Julian who kept him going back in those days, Julian who had taken on the role of older brother. *It'll be worth it*, he would say when the two of them were lying in bed after a fifteen-hour day, muscles torn. Eason did not know what *it* was back then—could not visualize or imagine the fans, the rush he would feel on stage, the liberation. Now, he does.

"None of us need this," Julian says. "We can make it on our own."

The others might, Eason thinks. But not me. "Minwoo was right," he says. "You can only think of yourself. You don't care about the band—

you never cared about the band. It was just a way for you to stay relevant after your failed skating career. But you know what? You're not strong enough to make it on your own."

Julian is shaking his head frantically now, pleading for Eason to stop. But he will not stop. He wants Julian to hurt the way he hurts.

"Poor Julian, still too heavy to get off the ground."

It is a curious thing, the way heart, body, and mind can hold a siege for dominance in a matter of milliseconds. In this case, as the words leave him, he knows that his mind has won out. Too late now to undo the bloodshed. Much too late, judging by the look on Julian's face.

Julian backs away. "Whatever this is"—he points between them—"it's over. We're done."

"Fine by me," Eason retorts. He turns and stalks to the SUV, a drum beating at his temples. It is not until he is back in the car, hidden behind his ballcap and headphones, that he realizes that what he told Julian was the same thing he wanted to tell Faye when he first found the stick in the car. She needed him—she and Julian both did. To think that they could go on in the world without Eason—that was what hurt the most.

MINNIE

She is halfway through a draft of her new piece for the zine when her phone sounds with a message from Nate: *You're late.*

Sorry! She writes back. *On my way.*

By the time she arrives at his house with the cake, a group has already gathered. There are some new additions this time, girls who do not look much older than her. One of them, Minnie is certain, sits behind her in first-year seminar. She watches these girls watching Nate—the way they follow his movements with wonder, mouths falling open at the brilliant things he says and then flushing prettily when he notices them. Suddenly, she feels disgust, not with them, but with herself: *Is that what I look like?*

When he sees her, Nate extricates himself from the narrow hallway where he has been holding court. He hugs her but leaves space in between, and takes her offering, a $42 red velvet from Whole Foods—his request. When she asked earlier that week what the cake was for, Nate had told her, "It's a surprise party." When she then asked what the surprise was for, he said, "It's a surprise."

It is the first time she has seen him since winter break. As the initial excitement of the New Year waned and the reality of a gray, wet February set in, communication between them continued to be sparse and unsatisfactory, but that could be solved, Minnie was certain, by simply being in the other's presence again. She had not expected that it would be at yet another party, surrounded by his friends and a new cadre of simpering girls. She inspects his face, reading for the tiny changes that might reveal what he has been up to for the past few weeks: a new wrinkle on his forehead; his scruff a little longer; tan lines around his eyes. He is the same Nate, but he also feels unfamiliar, as if a gust of wind has blown through the door, disturbing everything just enough to make it new and strange.

"Welcome back." Even his smell is different.

"Thanks. I missed you." She waits, hoping that he will return to her this vulnerability. "I feel like we didn't get to talk much while I was away," she says into his silence.

He shrugs. "It's been pretty busy for me here."

"I'm sorry about the bike," she blurts out.

He looks confused. "Oh, that. Clark is on his way from the airport right now. You can say sorry to him when he gets here."

She gapes at him. Of course. It is a surprise party, but the surprise is known to everyone except her: Clark had finished his research abroad. This party—including the cake she carried over—is a celebration of his return.

Will she have to see him often? Be friends with him? Sit at the same dinner table as him, watch as he eats his food? Laugh at his jokes? She looks down at her hands. White, thin. She can see through them.

"Hey," Nate says. He looks alarmed by the change in her. "It's not that deep, okay? I'm not mad at you anymore. Clark might be annoyed, but he's not going to call the cops on you or anything. It's fine. He got that bike off Craigslist anyway."

Minnie swallows and nods, but her vision inverts, all the colors turning against each other. She reaches out a hand and puts it on his arm to steady herself.

"Come here," Nate says. He draws her in to his body and she leans against his chest, letting him wrap himself around her. This is the kind of care and affection she has craved from him, but it does nothing to soothe her panic now; his body is lukewarm, the hairs on his forearms like hay against her skin. She needs to leave, needs to put as much distance between her and Clark as possible. But the group from the hallway that Nate vacated has spotted him, and they are on the move. She watches them draw closer, trapped in Nate's arms. Dread descends, pinning her to him. It takes twenty minutes from the airport to Nate's house, twenty-eight with traffic. Where is Clark now?

"Found you again," one of the girls says when she reaches Nate. She rests her arm on his bicep and then turns to Minnie. "He was just telling us about his short story. He said you're the one who inspired him to write it."

"What?" She looks up at Nate, searching his face.

"It's not *about* you, per se," he says, sounding almost guilty. "It came to me after I read that thing you wrote about the boy band."

His words are slow to register. The notes Akash transcribed for her that day in the food court—Nate had been inspired to write a short story about that? She unthreads her arm from his.

"He let me read some of it," another girl—the one Minnie recognizes from her first-year seminar—interjects, looking proud of herself. "It's genius. And like, it's actually so timely? We *should* be talking about how celebrities are destroying our perception of reality."

One of the men in the group turns to Minnie, a handlebar mustache in cigarette jeans and a wrinkled maroon V-neck. "Let's ask the expert, since she's right here. Can you explain what it is about this boy band that draws you to them? Like, okay, I think I kind of get it—they're young, they're hot"—he gesticulates to his lanky body in a comical way, which makes several people snort—"but is there actual talent there?"

"They're extremely talented," she says, hating how defensive she sounds. "One of the members is a trained opera singer and another used to be a competitive figure skater before joining the group. The first Vietnamese American to win gold at Junior Nationals, actually." For some reason, she pictures Anna and Akash when she says this.

But she can tell by their amused expressions that the group does not hear what she is saying—instead, her earnest defense of the boys only confirms what they already believed: that she is beyond saving. She is nothing more than another dumb girl, addled and hoodwinked by the hot boys mass-produced by the music industry to claim her dollars and her soul.

Lanky V-neck persists. "But why do you like them? I just don't understand why all these girls are going crazy for them, outside of their looks."

"Um, girl here," someone says, raising her hand. "I don't think they're that good looking. They're so artificial and they all look the same. It weirds me out. They're robots."

She wants to lunge at the girl and claw at her face until it has been ribboned to red. The intensity of this desire startles her, but it also feels good.

"They make me happy," she says, her voice rising. She can tell, from Nate's quickened breathing, that he is embarrassed, but she does not care; for the boys, she is willing to do anything—go into battle, incur the slings and arrows of these haughty hangers-on, cut off a piece of herself. "It's not really any different from having a hobby or a sport that you enjoy."

Her fourth date with Nate, eating at the halal place with a muted TV in the corner. The soccer game that he could not tear his eyes away from. When his team scored, he clapped loudly and yelled *"Yes! Yes! Yes!"* even though no one else in the restaurant was watching this game. Minnie had been somewhat embarrassed by it. But the other patrons did not seem bothered by his outbursts. They simply accepted it: A sports fan must always yell loudly for his team and make his passion known regardless of his environment. But her? Hers was a passion meant to be shamed.

Lanky V-neck raises his eyebrows. "Relax. We're just having a conversation." He turns back to Nate. "I hope you're taking notes."

The group laughs, giving each other knowing glances.

"Like I said," Nate says. "It's not about you, Min. I was just inspired by you."

"Oh, to be a muse," someone says. Again, the group laughs.

How dare they, she thinks, looking around at them. In their eighty-dollar fair-trade T-shirts and Tibetan prayer flag bandanas. Who are they to speak about the boys in this way, having never accomplished anything of value in their lives? They are laughing, but if Halo or Jelly or Minwoo or Denim were to step in here now, they would fall to their knees, begging to be noticed. Among the group, Nate laughs hardest, his mouth stretched too wide, revealing the sharp, yellowing teeth normally hidden by his tempered grin—a consequence, he had once confessed to Minnie, of too much coffee. Minnie had told him that it was fine, no one cared about yellow teeth, but watching him now, she finds that she does care—quite a lot, actually—not because of the discoloration, but because he has never been less appealing.

One of the girls gasps at her phone. "He's almost here!" The group titters, heads swiveling. Someone shuts the music off. "Hide!"

Bodies disperse. Nate grabs her and pulls her to the stairs, where others are crouched. The dread from earlier returns as she remembers, too late.

"Please, can we talk," she says.

"Shhh."

She hears them yell it: *SURPRISE!* Not a word, but a detonation. Beneath her feet the floor quakes, bearing the full weight of the party as it launches into celebration at Clark's arrival. Nate jumps up, pulling Minnie with him to the center of the flood, gunning to reach Clark first. The music turns back on and Lil Wayne's "A Milli" thunders in her ribcage. She tries to pry herself away from Nate's grip, but shoulders, hips, and elbows lock her in. Minnie has only been in one car accident in her life—her father driving down a one-way street and a car that pulled out without warning. When she saw the car, the only thing she could do was close her eyes. Closing her eyes meant that she did not have to see it happen, that maybe she could make it go away. This is what she does now, even knowing, through the forward momentum of her body, that she is being brought closer and closer to Clark—she closes her eyes, screws them up tight, hoping against hope that this will somehow make everything stop.

"You scoundrel!" Nate is saying gleefully. "You dog!"

Her eyes open. The time away was good for Clark, this much is clear. He has lost some weight and his skin is tanner. He wears the same wiry glasses he had on the night of the party, cheeks still that rushing shade of pink. The brown curls, now grown down to his ears. He is ever the picture of charming dorkiness, of harmless affability, but his eyes are viper green, just as she remembers. His eyes, hungrily scanning the crowd.

His eyes, boring down at her in the garish light of the bathroom. She goes limp, stops resisting the group that jostles around her, and feels herself being carried away, her body nothing more than air, until she washes up on the outskirts of the crowd, finally separated from Nate. He does not notice her absence. A platter of shots appears and he and Clark slam back three in a row, clapping each other on the shoulders as they finish.

What is she doing with Nate? How can he be friends with someone like Clark? How could he have written a story about her, about the boys? Why does she constantly feel like he speaks in a language she cannot understand?

She needs to calm down, to think clearly. More to stop her hands from shaking than anything, Minnie stumbles to the kitchen island and downs a can of beer, but she does not feel herself growing lighter or more courageous the way alcohol has made her feel before. Instead, she feels herself hardening, the anger flaring. A different kind of drunkenness, one that verges on blinding sobriety.

She looks around the kitchen. When she first met Nate, she thought it so admirable that he lived in a house, rather than an apartment like so many of his peers. But this house has cracks in the walls and oil stains around the stove. The counter is a graveyard of half-empty handles of vodka and rum, pitchers of souring Keystone and PBR. Nate's French press, turned on its side. The cake she bought—a purchase which had been too expensive for her—lies on the kitchen island, a jagged cliff on one side from whoever had pawed off a piece. But no one seems to care about artistic integrity and ethical consumption anymore. They all jump in the middle of the dance floor, screaming out every lyric of "Ignition."

They all think they are better, but the truth is that they are just as lost as she is.

It takes her a moment to notice Clark, who has ambled up to the kitchen island, red Solo cup in hand. Minnie can tell by the sway of his body that he is already inordinately drunk. She watches, frozen, as he grabs the nearest bottle of tequila and pours it into his cup. Only a little remains and most of it sloshes on the table. He eyes his cup with disappointment, but throws it back all the same. Then, he sees her.

"Hey. I'm Clark." He looks her up and down and then he steps closer. She can smell all of him—faint yogurt and that locker room body spray, now a suffocation. "You look really familiar. Have we met before?"

How could he forget, when all she could do was remember?

"I don't think so," she chokes out.

"I'd remember you," Clark says. "But maybe I'm confusing you with another Asian. Actually, I probably confused you with one of Nate's girls. She's Asian, too." He steadies himself against the kitchen island and takes another chug. "I hooked up with one of them once. Don't look so scandalized. Nate wouldn't care—he just cycles through them. It wasn't that memorable anyway; she was really boring."

"Oh," she says. She stands before Clark—drunk, sloppy Clark—and she hates herself because even this version of Clark, one who can barely see out of his fogged-up glasses, is still more powerful than she will ever be.

"Are you here with anyone?" He leans in closer. "I bet you're not boring."

Minnie knows that she should not leave the party without telling Nate. She knows how much he hates that. She knows that, in order to be a good potential *serious girlfriend*, she should withstand all the emotions that she is feeling, push against the darkness crowding the edges of her mind, and stay. But as she stands before Clark's leering face—disgusting in its confidence, its guiltlessness—she knows that she cannot stay. Not again.

She does not rage at him. She does not tell him who she really is. Instead, she sets down her drink and walks out the door. It is the middle of February and the nights in Texas are finally cold enough to be recognizable, wind shearing the trees and cutting through the sleeves of her shirt, but she does not shrink from it. Instead, she welcomes the chill, hoping it will numb her. She walks down the Drag, past the twenty-four-hour diner where she ate with Akash and Anna, up Whitis, and through the Honors Quad, until she is back at her dorm. The graduate student manning the front desk buzzes her in and as she watches them lazily press the button without so much as looking up, Minnie wants nothing more than to be just like the graduate student is now, sitting lopsided on the chair, one leg propped up, chewing on a pencil and bent over a textbook. She would give anything to be at peace.

She crawls into bed. Even in one of the worst moments of her life, Clark had found her boring. And then she hates herself for the thought. What had she wanted—for him to have found her exciting?

No, a voice whispers. It is meek, but it is there. *I wanted it to have mattered. For there to be a reason for why I feel the way I do.*

Or, another voice says. *You're disgusting and you deserve to feel this way.*

She closes her eyes and shrieks into the pillow. She wonders if the girls in the room next door hear her. Maybe not. Maybe they are at a party, just like everyone else in this empty hall. She pulls out her phone—of course, no text from Nate. Will he ever notice that she left the party? Probably not. Nate and Clark, they have each other. In the realm of their fixies and *New Yorker* subscriptions and infinite house parties, she will never really be more than just a girl. A girl who is obsessed with a boy band.

Ladybeth42: Are you okay?

MinnieTheGreat: i don't know

MinnieTheGreat: he's writing a short story about a girl who's obsessed with a boy band

MinnieTheGreat: he already told all of his friends. they knew and were laughing

MinnieTheGreat: at me. and the boys

MinnieTheGreat: that was the worst part. they were talking about the boys like they knew them, but they don't know anything. he never even took the time to talk to me about them, he's just assuming everything. maybe i wouldn't hate it as much if he had just talked to me about it, but he didn't, and now i feel like he's going to be making fun of me . . . and them. i've betrayed them.

Ladybeth42: He has no right to talk about the boys. At all.
MinnieTheGreat: it just feels so cruel

Anger is a strange emotion, one she is not used to hosting in her body. Sadness, yes. She has felt that many times. Confusion, even more so. But not the scald. Not red.

Ladybeth42: What are you going to do?
MinnieTheGreat: what can i do?
Ladybeth42: What about the essay you're writing for your zine?
Ladybeth42: Call him out on his bullshit. Get it out there before he does.
MinnieTheGreat: what if it just makes me sound more delusional?
Ladybeth42: It won't. And we're not delusional.
Ladybeth42: No one knows the boys better than us.
Ladybeth42: It's our duty to protect them. Because if we don't, who will?

A picture comes through the chat. At first, Minnie is not sure what she is seeing—it looks like the hallway of a hotel, the low lighting obscuring everything in shadow, but then she notices the outline of a figure on the left side of the photograph. She recognizes the delicate arrows of his elbows. It is Jelly, but Jelly as she has never seen him—back hunched over, shoulders skeletal through his shirt. The picture, rather than providing her comfort, disconcerts her.

MinnieTheGreat: what is this?
Ladybeth42: I thought you should see. Something's been going on with Halo and Jelly.
MinnieTheGreat: what do you mean?
Ladybeth42: This was taken outside Halo's hotel room. I'm sure they had an argument. You can see how bad Jelly looks.
MinnieTheGreat: but how did you get this?

Another picture loads. Minnie recognizes this one based off a series of photographs she had seen in *Pop Impulse*: shots of the boys as they exited their hotel the morning after the concert in Nashville. The photo Ladybeth sends her, however, had not appeared in the magazine or the website. This photo was taken inside the hotel lobby before Halo and Jelly emerged, but they are not alone—an ice-blond woman who Minnie recognizes as the boys' new manager stands next to them, her hand on Halo's back. Minnie does not recall ever seeing the boys interacting with their managers in this way before. The sight of the woman's talon on Halo's body makes her stomach shoot to the soles of her feet.

Ladybeth42: It's because of her.
Ladybeth42: Things haven't been the same since she became their manager. You've noticed it too, haven't you? The boys look really tense now. They're different.
MinnieTheGreat: you think she's the reason they're fighting?
Ladybeth42: Yes. We think she's in love with Halo and she's trying to steal him away. And Jelly knows it, too.

A third picture appears. This time, Halo and Jelly are in the back of an SUV, mid-conversation. Like the first photo Ladybeth sent her, this one is speckled with small grains, as if composed of sand, but Minnie can still make out their expressions. Jelly is speaking, his beautiful face contorted into a desperation she has never seen him wear before. Halo looks ahead, empty.

Ladybeth42: That's why they're fighting all the time.
Ladybeth42: It's slowly killing him. Do you see how tiny he looks?
MinnieTheGreat: he really is a lot skinnier :(
Ladybeth42: This is what I mean. We have to protect the boys when they can't protect themselves.
MinnieTheGreat: who is "we"?
Ladybeth42: What do you mean?
MinnieTheGreat: you keep saying "we." who is we?

It takes Ladybeth so long to respond that Minnie thinks that she must have logged off.

Ladybeth42: I could get in trouble for telling you this.
Ladybeth42: You have to promise me that you won't say anything to anyone else.
MinnieTheGreat: i promise
MinnieTheGreat: i don't have anyone to tell anyway
Ladybeth42: A few of us haven't been happy with The Heaven, so we created our own group.
Ladybeth42: We've been calling ourselves The Hellians.
MinnieTheGreat: why haven't you been happy?
Ladybeth42: Everything here is so superficial. None of these people actually care about Jelly and Halo. They're just here for the gossip.
Ladybeth42: It's The Hellians' responsibility to protect the boys, especially Jelly and Halo's relationship. Their bodyguards don't do shit. And this new blond bitch is only making things worse.
Ladybeth42: So we have been keeping an eye on the boys.
MinnieTheGreat: what does that mean?
Ladybeth42: We go where they go.

The pictures from Ladybeth. There was a reason they never appeared in *Pop Impulse* or anywhere else on The Heaven. They were not taken by paparazzi.

MinnieTheGreat: is that where those pictures you sent me came from? people in your group, following the boys?
Ladybeth42: You wouldn't believe the things we know.

She feels very far away from the person on the other side of the screen. She had thought of Ladybeth42 as her friend, a *real* friend, but Ladybeth42 is a part of something of her own, and once again, Minnie is on the outside. Even worse, that something is the boys—her boys.

MinnieTheGreat: can i join?
Ladybeth42: I'm sorry, but it's not possible.
MinnieTheGreat: but you know you can trust me
Ladybeth42: It's not a trust thing.
Ladybeth42: Everyone in The Hellians is there because they can provide something.
Ladybeth42: I work at the airline the boys use for their flights, so I know their flight numbers, when they're departing and landing, their seats, what they ordered for their meals, etc.

It is the first time Ladybeth42 has mentioned anything concrete about herself—their conversations had mainly focused on Minnie's problems, she now realizes with a pang of shame. She is not sure what to say back, so she types and deletes words into the chat box just to keep something alive between them. She knew that Ladybeth42 must have been older based on the way she spoke, but she assumed that it was by just a few years. Not by entire life experiences. The realization of this new gulf between her and Ladybeth42 engenders in her a sick sensation of betrayal. But it is not Ladybeth42's fault. It is her own fault, for once again wanting too much.

Ladybeth42: Listen, I'm sorry.
Ladybeth42: I shouldn't have said anything.
MinnieTheGreat: no, it's okay
MinnieTheGreat: i understand
Ladybeth42: Want to watch some videos of the boys together?
MinnieTheGreat: not today. i'll talk to you later, ok?

Nate's betrayal. Clark's triumph. The new revelation about the boys, the threat of this blond woman. And now, Ladybeth42's secret group. It is all too much. She feels the world spinning away from her, the boys edging further and further outside her reach. A surge of protectiveness rips through her as she remembers the jeers of Nate's friends, jeers that now seem inseparable from the picture of an emaciated and vulnerable Jelly. He should be floating across the stage, unencumbered. This defeated version of him she cannot accept. And as hurt as she is by Ladybeth42's rejection, she knows that she is right—the boys have done so much for her, for all of them. Is it not time for her to do something back?

POST #2011

Have you ever had your heart broken? Your muscles don't work and you can't get out of bed. Your mouth forgets how to smile and your stomach forgets to be hungry. Your eyes turn into dead black stones.

Trust me, I would know.

This is what's happening to Jelly. If you compare pictures of him now with pictures from just a month ago, you can see his wrists are thinner (I measured them—there's a 1.2 mm difference, which is significant). Those who have seen him up close can confirm that he looks even smaller in person. If we don't act soon, he's going to die from heartbreak.

EASON

He and Faye did what they could, all things considered. Secondhand thrifts, consignment shops, estate sales, everything-must-go closing blowouts. From a yard sale in Cinco Ranch, they picked up pacifiers and bottles; from a Goodwill off the Katy freeway, blousy tops and elastic-waist pants that could stretch around an oil barrel and still give space. Not that Faye needed much; as the months passed, her belly barely grew. It must have been all that running, Eason thought, not just on the track, but from their mother; the weight seemed repelled by her, intimidated by her ever-moving body and all the things it had to escape.

In the fourth month of the pregnancy, Henry's parents began inviting Faye and Eason over for Sunday family dinner, because that was what they were to be now, as decreed by the baby growing inside his sister's stomach: a family. The Ambroses were Christians, the type who were scandalized by their son's mistake (although they would never have called it that), but too God-fearing to do anything else about it. They lived in a house that looked like it had a bunch of other houses sprouting off it, making it impossible to tell how many stories there were. There was no sign of foliage in the yard; all the grass had been pulled up and replaced by small, smooth pebbles, so that the house looked naked and austere amid the cheerful lawns of its neighbors. His dad would have liked such a house, Eason thought as they pulled up to it. The Ambroses greeted Faye and Eason at the door, smiling at them with a resigned sort of wariness, as if he and his sister were wild animals that their son had picked up on the way home and was now demanding to keep.

Dinner was a multicourse affair. Chilled pea soup came first, then spinach salad served in a wooden bowl. For the main course, a spongy meatloaf accompanied by buttered rolls and dill-infused mashed potatoes. Key lime pie for dessert. Eason finished it all in a few inhales, but when asked if he would like a second helping, declined. He realized what it must have looked like to the Ambroses: a child who ate like a tornado because he was not getting enough at home. He did not want to make his sister feel bad about not being able to provide, for it was she who did the cooking whenever their mother disappeared into her room and spent days on the phone with the suanming xiansheng. But there it was, revealed in the span of a few quick bites: He had not felt full in a long time.

Mrs. Ambrose was gentle about it. "We'll never finish the leftovers," she told him. "You'll have to take some home."

She and her husband exchanged a knowing glance, which Eason read in an instant. A dreadful sense of betrayal struck him, dreadful because of how familiar it was beginning to feel.

The dinners continued. Every Sunday at four, Faye drove them over to the Ambroses' house with the naked lawn and they ate together. They told their mother it was extra tutoring for Eason, which she did not question. As uneventful as these dinners were, Eason could not help but feel guilty for attending them. He was not sure why—it was not as if he were rejecting his own family and accepting a new one. In fact, he suspected the Ambroses were only inviting him along because Faye had asked them to; once the baby was born, he would be nothing more than a distant memory, the little brother of the girl their son knocked up. He resented them for it, for how easily they could accommodate something so life-altering. But even so, he found himself looking forward to these Sunday dinners, to some sense of routine and normalcy, however fleeting. Perhaps that was what he felt most guilty about: that he missed a time when his home had been the same way. But asking for that, he reasoned, was also asking for his good-for-nothing father back, so he rejected this feeling of false family and security as best he could by maintaining a scowl during dinner and saying very little, even as he ate their food with zeal.

It was during one of these dinners that Mrs. Ambrose informed them that she had spoken to the family pastor earlier that day. "He gave a wonderful sermon about how even those beyond saving can still be saved." She hiccuped a nervous laugh. "And I—oh, I hope you won't be upset with me Faye, but I couldn't help but tell him about your situation."

"Mother," Henry said.

She swatted her hands at him. "I know, I know! I wasn't supposed to say anything. But Pastor Bryant is very supportive. He'd like to meet you, Faye. Maybe you could come to next week's service."

"But we're not Christians," Eason said. His voice, hoarse from disuse, startled everyone at the table. "We don't believe in that dumb stuff."

Mrs. Ambrose was clearly horrified, but she tried to hide it. He felt a small glimmer of satisfaction. This woman and her big mouth. What they were asking of his sister, who was practical and measured and did not believe in ghosts or gods or demons, was laughable—that was not her and it would never be her. If such a God existed, then explain their father's leaving. Explain the sunlight that always seemed to wilt and die just before reaching their house. Explain the two of them, sitting at this doily-ridden table eating food made by someone else's mother.

"I'm sorry," Faye said, to Eason's surprise. "What he meant to say was, we're not exactly religious people."

But that was not what he had meant to say, and Faye knew it.

"That's quite all right," Mrs. Ambrose said, resuscitating. "God welcomes all His children, even those who have not yet reached out to take His hand."

Faye smiled and nodded as if she agreed. Eason could not believe what he was seeing. He felt sickened by it.

"Just tell me you'll think about it," Mrs. Ambrose said, reaching across the table and grasping Faye's hand. "It would be a good thing to do before Chicago."

"What's Chicago?" Eason said.

"You haven't told him?" Mr. Ambrose said, looking surprised.

"What's Chicago?" he asked again. Nobody answered.

After dinner, Faye drove them home. Eason sat rigid in the seat with his feet outstretched before him, so that his back pushed against the cushion. He wanted to press himself through it. "Tell me what's in Chicago."

She sighed. It was a long sigh, one he had never heard from her before, and it scared him, for it was not the sigh of relief or settling in, but of exhaustion, the deep, dragging, to-the-bone kind. "Henry's aunt has a house there. She's a widower, so she has a ton of space. They think I should go stay with her and have the baby there. Away from—well, Mom."

"But you're going to Rice. That was always the plan."

"That *was* the plan," Faye said slowly. Carefully. "But once the baby's here, things will be a lot harder."

"I'll come live with you," Eason said defiantly. "I can help take care of it so you can go to school."

She patted his head. He hated it, but he craved it, too: the pressure of her hand soothed him, its weight pressing down the fear that churned up from the dark place within him. "You're just a kid, Eason. I can't ask you to do that."

"You're a kid, too."

She shook her head. "You have to finish school. Stay with Mom. She needs you right now. She loves you too much."

"I don't want it," he spat. "I don't want her love."

"Don't say that."

It was all happening too fast, this growing up business. He thought back to that night in Marfa, when he was certain he had seen the two shadows beside him melding into one. If only he had reached across to stop it. If only he had confronted Faye right then and there, and said, "Don't do this. Don't leave me all alone." But he had failed. Just as he failed, every time, to stop their mother from the possessions and his father from leaving. He was a failure through and through, and perhaps this was the consequence: He did not deserve to have Faye in his life anymore.

"So what," he said bitterly. "You're going to go to Chicago and have the baby there and somehow keep all of this from Mom?"

She nodded. "I'll leave right before the semester starts. She won't know the difference. She'll probably be glad I'm going away. Maybe she'll finally get better."

He stared straight ahead, refusing to respond to her, instead listening to the groans of the engine as it shifted gears between the on-ramp and the interstate. Now at five months, Faye's belly had only just begun growing, the top of it peeking out from under her T-shirt, a patch of skin that Eason was both fascinated and disgusted by, for what it reminded him of.

"Do you ever wonder why Baba didn't take anything with him?"

It was the first time she had brought up their father since he left, but this was not what jolted him. It was the name she used. *Dad* was easy to say. *Dad* meant nothing, because it was an abstraction for something that could never be captured with the English language. *Baba* was what they called him at three, at seven, at ten. *Baba* was who he was, tall and lanky with his socks in his sandals, his lopsided grin. Baba was the man who taught Eason how to throw a football; Baba was the laughter that bounced through their once-bright house. The language of home is the language that makes you feel like a child again, and this was what Eason could not stand, his back stuck to the car seat: hearing Faye use *Baba* to disarm him, to bring him back to that vulnerable place.

"Don't—"

"I always thought that was the worst part of it, him not taking a thing from the house. Not his books, not his magnets, not even a picture. Like it was all—the house, the stuff, *us*—disposable. Even after I forgave him for what he did, I kept wondering: Why didn't he take anything? Did he want to forget us that much?"

Eason couldn't speak. His head had started to burn. He wished his sister would stop talking.

"Mom thinks this family is haunted by a curse, but what she won't accept is that it's not true. It never was. That's why Baba left. All those superstitions and figurines and goddamn peach trees. He couldn't stand living with a woman who believes so hard in a ghost that she becomes a ghost, too. And you know what? I don't blame him."

"Stop," Eason said. He needed her to stop. What she was saying was ugly and terrible and, worst of all, true.

But she did not stop. "I don't want to be haunted by a ghost, real or not," she said. "And I don't want this baby to be haunted by it, either." Her right hand landed, reflexively, on the patch of her stomach that Eason could see. The sight of this simple action devastated him for how immediate and natural it was, how full of love. A love he would never come to understand or be expected to understand. The kind of love that could only exist in blood, one he thought existed between the two of them. Now, everything had changed.

It was not him and Faye anymore. It was Faye and her baby.

The car rolled to a light and stopped. She turned to look at him, but he refused her gaze. "The Ambroses have started putting money into a college fund for the baby. They'll continue supporting us as long as I continue making them think it's the godlike thing to do. I don't believe in God, Eason. But I do believe in making things right. I'm going to give this baby everything. I don't want him to hate me the way you hate Baba."

"Stop calling him that."

"Aren't you tired?" she said quietly. "Of hating him so much? Isn't that a curse, too?"

He was crying and he could not stop. How long until he could harden those tears into stone?

"I just don't get why you have to go," he said finally. It was the truth. He was talking about Chicago, but he was also talking about the long journey ahead, a journey that would leave him behind. Everything was going to change—why could she not see that?

"It's not forever," she said. The car turned onto their street, which looked gloomy and drab compared to the Ambroses' neighborhood. "Maybe just for a year or two. I'll come back for you. I promise."

It was a good plan, Eason thought. The Ambroses would be happy to continue supporting Faye. Hell, she and Henry would probably get married and they would pay for the wedding. Picture perfect, baby and all, in Chicago. Faye would still go on to have the life she always dreamed of, freed, finally, from their mother. Eason? He would be stuck here for another three years.

He thought again about what Faye said about their father. Why hadn't he taken Eason and Faye with him—were they too much of a burden? Did he see them as his curse? How could it be so easy for someone to throw away the very thing they had created and cared for? What was the point of trying so hard, he wondered as he looked at his sister, if everyone left you in the end anyway?

There was one way to make her stay. He had been thinking about it since the drive home. It was a betrayal of everything between them. But was it not Faye who betrayed them first? Had she not brought Henry and his parents into this mess and been the one to throw Eason aside?

She dropped him off at home before her shift at the sushi restaurant. When he walked inside, he was surprised to see his mother sitting in the living room, a book on her lap. Lately, she had been spending less time in her room, taking instead to strolling the length of their neighborhood twice a day. One evening, upon returning from one of these walks, she asked Eason if the house smelled bad and he said, yeah, it's the skunk vine. He expected her to shake her head and disappear back into her room, but she looked around said, "Yes, I suppose it is. Maybe we should get rid of it. What do you think?" It gave Eason hope, this new turn of his mother's. She was healing.

His mother heard him enter. She looked up from her book and her face broke into a smile at the sight of him. "You're finally home," she said. "How was tutoring?" Then, it quickly dipped into concern. "Hai zi de lian se bu hao," she said. "There are shadows all over your face." She closed the book and opened her arms. He remembered how he would hide in those arms as a child, how the nightmares that shook him turned to cloud dust against the shield of his mother's body. Her love, once the strongest thing in the world.

"I just need to sleep," he told her, hoping it would make it true.

But she knew. She always knew. "Lai lai lai. Gao su mama what's wrong."

Yes, there was one way to make Faye stay.

MINNIE

People ask me why HOURglass. Why this boy band? I'm almost nineteen and a freshman in college. Isn't it time I grow out of these things?

I understand their confusion. It's true, the idea of loving a boy band feels like a childish obsession that's meant for preteens. But if you were to ask me what I remember as a preteen, I would show you all my magazines. All the movies and shows I watched, the music I listened to, the CDs I had. I would point out who my favorite actors and musicians were. I stared at their faces and memorized the shape of their eyes. I knew their eyes better than I knew my own, but when I looked in the mirror, I didn't see those eyes.

I grew up in Colorado Springs. My parents and I were the only Asians in our neighborhood. It was okay, for the most part. I encountered racism, but back then, I didn't understand that that was what was happening. I just took it to mean that it was supposed to be this way. I thought, oh, I am supposed to feel ashamed, because I'm the problem. When we'd go to restaurants, people would stare as we walked by, and I remember thinking, it's our fault for making them look.

HOURglass is an American boy band modeled after a combination of Western boy bands and the K-pop groups of South Korea. There are four members: Minwoo, 23 (real name Hong Minwoo), Denim, 23 (Colt Fitch), Jelly, 22 (Julian Lý), and Halo, 21 (Eason Chen). Of those four members, three are Asian. That means three Asians standing on stage, singing and dancing in front of thousands of fans. Three Asians on your radio programs, your entertainment shows, your favorite gossip websites. Three Asians who are wanted.

I know it's not that simple and it's not the full answer. Three Asian singers doesn't solve racism. In fact, it solves very little. But I guess what I'm trying to say is, in the tiny world of my existence, they solve something for me.

When I look at them, they feel familiar. In their faces, I see something of myself for the first time: a self I am allowed to love. The boys have faced their fair share of racism, too—radio DJs will ask them ridiculous questions stereotyping Asians, and there are plenty of comments online that say they look too feminine, not manly enough. Some people have even said they look like robots. But the boys don't care. They're still out there, shining brighter than ever. Maybe that's what really appeals to me about them: Despite all the hardships, they're still there. And it makes me want to keep going, too, knowing that even after all they've faced, they're still trying. That kind of courage makes me want to keep trying, too.

Recently, I was at a party and the conversation turned to HOURglass. The people I was speaking to just couldn't understand why the boys were so popular. They chalked it up to girls being obsessed with them because of their good looks. I think there are several issues with this: For one, it totally ignores the months of training and sacrifices made by the boys. For some of them, it's been years. But there's also a larger issue that I'm beginning to sense: I think people just like to hate on the things that girls love.

The HOURglass fanbase is diverse, but there's no denying that it's mostly girls and women. But why should this be a bad thing? Why are people so quick to dismiss something, just because young women love it? Does it truly lack substance, or do we just not want girls to be happy?

Does it scare us that much to see a girl happy?

EASON

THE BOYS OF HOURGLASS, the magazine cover boasts, LIKE YOU'VE NEVER SEEN THEM BEFORE. The photos are accompanied by an interview explaining their departure from cotton-candy heartthrobs to serious musical artists. The next album, to be recorded in the fall, after the tour, will bring on Grammy Award–winning producers and respected hit-makers. "What, no break?" Colt had asked. Cecile simply stared back in imperious silence, and that was when they all knew: There would be no more breaks until they died, and even then, their images, their songs, the videos that captured them at their brightest would immortalize them, because this thing called celebrity would outlive them all.

"In the next era of HOURglass," the interviewer, a fearsome music journalist, had asked, "what can we expect?"

"We want to make songs that push the boundaries of where pop music is right now," Minwoo answered. "We want to show that boy bands are more than just love songs and catchy beats. Social issues, the realities of life, identity and justice—there's so much we want to explore with our art."

"And that's what you're working on now? Songs that push the boundary?"

They nodded. It was all part of the plan BabyGold Records laid out for them: The next big thing in pop music was not feel-good melodies and trite declarations of heartbreak and reconciliation—the next big thing was its stars becoming active citizens of the world. It was the perfect side dish to accompany the growing narrative that Halo and Jelly were in love—who better to speak on the injustice and crushing weight of the world than two young men forced to keep their relationship a secret?

"But since we are talking about pushing boundaries," the interviewer continued, directing the question to Eason and Julian. "There have been rumors that there's more to HOURglass than meets the eye. Some of your fans believe that to be the case, at least. How do you deal with rumors, especially in your love lives?"

"Our fans know our hearts," Eason said. "If any of us ever get into a relationship, they'd be the first to know." He placed a hand on Julian's knee then. The interviewer raised an eyebrow and began scribbling furiously. It was almost too easy, Eason thought. When the interviewer left, Julian stood up without looking at him, flinging off Eason's hand as if it burned.

"What's going on with you two?" Minwoo asked.

"It's nothing," Eason said. "We're fine."

"But it doesn't work if you're just *fine*. It has to be *perfect*."

The magazine spread includes three full-page photos: them in the sunflower field, dappled in fake sunlight; them mid-jump, bodies floating against the sky; them shirtless and laughing, piled on top of each other like newborn puppies, the football nestled somewhere at their nucleus. *Young gods*, the caption reads. In these photos, their faces are so free and blithe that Eason is almost jealous of whoever those boys might be.

There is a fourth photo in the spread, a shot of Eason and Julian facing each other, both bare-chested. *My baby looks so GOOD; I want to nuzzle your pecs; You're my baby boy I love you.* He reads the comments online and then he stops, because he can no longer tell the difference between the ones that come from the fans and the ones that come from *her*. Of all the photos taken of him as Halo, it is this photo where he looks most like himself, for his expression here is not one of boyishness, but wounded alarm, like a dog who has just been hit. He remembers how the assistant tore at his nipples—the very same nipples that now stand pert and at attention in the photo, betraying his discomfort—and how surprising the sensation of that violence was, because, he decided, it was indeed a sort of violence. He wishes he could go back to that moment and cover up, grab the assistant's hand before it ever touched him. Instead, he rips out the photo and crumples it in his fist.

POST #2480

Some of you don't deserve to be called an HOURglass fan.

If you were a real fan, you'd see that something is wrong with HOURglass and has been for the past few weeks. They're not the same anymore. If you disagree, you're blind or you just don't want to see the truth or you're homophobic and if that's the case, please stop calling yourself an HOURglass fan and consider killing yourself. The boys don't need you.

MINNIE

Nate sends her a text three days after the party. *Clark was asking about his bike. I guess you never apologized to him for losing it?*

No, she messages back. *And I don't plan to.*

He calls her. She lets the phone ring three times before answering.

"What's going on? You're being incredibly rude."

A week ago, such words would have hit her as a shattering indictment. Now, she feels nothing. What he did—using her and the boys—redrew all the things that previously made him so irresistible. In place of his brilliant intellect, she sees his arrogance; in place of his popularity, she sees a man who has no problems being friends with a predator like Clark. She cannot believe she did not see it before, actually. If she measured Nate up to the boys, to Halo, he would never stand a chance. Halo would never make fun of her. He would not scoff, nor deride, nor, most crucially, make her feel so unseen.

"I don't like the way you've been acting," Nate continues. "You left the party *again* without telling me. You know how annoying that is for me, but you still did it."

"I guess I don't really care what you find annoying anymore," Minnie says. It is a thrill to say these words.

"What the hell? Do you want to rephrase that, Min?"

"No. And I hate it when you call me Min."

"What?"

"My name isn't Min or whatever you feel like calling me. It's Minnie."

Her defiance is a new shock for Nate, she can tell: He had expected her to beg. To place him back on that pedestal he so enjoyed for the past few months. But she will not give it to him. Not anymore.

"You know what," Nate says finally. "I think this is as far as I want to go with you, Min—Minnie."

"That's fine with me," she says. "I'm sure it's not really a loss for you, seeing as how you've got a bunch of other girls on your roster. I just hope you got what you needed for your short story."

A pause. This time, the silence on his end is not one of punishment, but of his own unmooring. "I'm really disappointed this is how we're ending things."

She releases a bitter laugh. "Maybe you should ask your best friend about it."

"Clark? What does he have to do with anything?"

"I have to go," she says. "I'm pretty busy."

"Hold on—"

"Have a good life." She hangs up.

Ladybeth42: I can't believe you really did it.
Ladybeth42: He deserves to suffer.
MinnieTheGreat: i thought i would be sad, but all i feel is light
MinnieTheGreat: i feel so light
Ladybeth42: How is your essay going? Are you almost done?
MinnieTheGreat: i sent the rough draft to my editor this morning. keep your fingers crossed for me!!!
Ladybeth42: I'm proud of you, Minnie.
Ladybeth42: The boys would be proud, too.

"I could *hug* you."

Anna is waiting for her outside Parlin, the first English building in the Six-Pack, black combat boot tapping impatiently against a stone bench. "Actually, I'm going to hug you. Can I hug you?"

She allows herself to be enveloped by Anna's sharp arms. The chains on Anna's shirt are cold against Minnie's skin, but her body is surprisingly warm. "How did you know I would be here?"

"I keep track of everyone on my staff," Anna says, releasing her. "I just finished your piece. It's great, Minnie. Exactly what I was hoping for."

"You don't think it's too much?"

"Not at all. In fact, I think you could do even *more*—the part where you talk about grappling with your Asian American identity feels a bit superficial, for example, but I love how you conclude it—asking why we're so quick to judge and dismiss things that young women love. It's a feminist issue, don't you think?"

Minnie hesitates. She has never before associated herself with that word, finding it somewhat intimidating, but hearing it through Anna's lips, as a benediction, makes her want to nod vigorously, stand up, own the word for herself. Over Anna's shoulder, she sees Jillian and her two girlfriends emerge from the social sciences building and make their way to Parlin.

"That's what I want our readers to ask themselves, too," Anna continues. "But overall, I'm so happy with the way this piece is turning out. It's like I can finally see you on the page."

Yards away, Jillian and her friends come to a stop. Alice, the dark-haired one, lights a cigarillo and puffs from it with her trademark slinky confidence before passing it around to the rest of the group. Minnie watches Jillian receive the stick and wrap her lips around it, cheeks tightening as she sucks.

"Minnie? Are you still with me?"

"Yes," she hears herself saying.

"Good," Anna says. "Because I have more feedback. I think you need a quote from the band, for starters."

Her attention snaps back. "You mean find a quote from an interview they've done?"

"No, not like that. Like an actual interview between you and them."

Minnie laughs, then quickly stifles it, afraid that Anna will interpret it as disrespectful. "Yeah, that would be nice. But that's impossible."

"What if it's not?"

"What do you mean?"

A strange look passes over Anna's face. Minnie has trouble placing it, until Anna looks down at her boots, breaking eye contact for the first time. "My uncle's in architecture," Anna says to the ground, and Minnie realizes that the strange look is embarrassment. "His firm worked on the design for the NRG Arena in Houston. Your band is playing there in two weeks. Did you know?"

"The show has been sold out for months. No one can get tickets anymore."

Anna tugs on the ends of her hair. "Are you really going to make me say it? My uncle can get us backstage and put us in for the meet and greet after the show. If you want to go."

"What?" Her voice is forceful, strong, the loudest it has ever been. She feels Jillian's head swivel in her direction, but she cannot remember why those girls were so fascinating in the first place. "You would do that for me?"

"I'm not proud of asking for favors, all right? In fact, don't tell anyone. But this feels cosmically aligned and I'd like to believe that I'm doing this in the name of art and journalism and all good things—on one condition: If we meet them, I want you to interview them for your piece. It's good now. I think you can make it even better."

She is no longer listening. Instead, she sees before her Minwoo, Denim, Jelly, and Halo, and this time the lines of their bodies, lines that distinguish them from the rest of this ordinary world, are clearer than ever before. The distance between her and them, once incomprehensible, shrinks to a stepping stone in a small pond. Standing on the stone, one step away from the other side, she does not index happiness, nor excitement, nor ecstasy. There is no feeling in the world that existed before what she feels now, no word accurate enough to capture its magnitude.

"Okay," she breathes. "Yes."

Ladybeth42: I am screaming.

MinnieTheGreat: it's not a guarantee that we'll get to meet them!!! i'm sure there are more important people waiting for a meet & greet

Ladybeth42: It's going to happen.

Ladybeth42: You're going to meet them. I can just feel it.

MinnieTheGreat: i don't think i can handle seeing Halo up close. i might die if he looks at me
Ladybeth42: You have to tell me everything. You have to hug them and then tell me everything.
Ladybeth42: How hard Minwoo's sixpack is.
Ladybeth42: What Denim smells like.
Ladybeth42: How tall is Halo really.
Ladybeth42: If Jelly looks just as skinny in person.
MinnieTheGreat: okay!!! i'm taking notes
Ladybeth42: Good girl.
Ladybeth42: But in all seriousness, this is actually a great opportunity for you.
MinnieTheGreat: ?
Ladybeth42: Remember how I said everyone in The Hellians is able to contribute something of value? Some of us have the means to follow the boys wherever they go. Some have access to their personal information through our workplaces, like me. Others have enough money to get close to people on their staff and buy information.
MinnieTheGreat: right. and i don't have anything that i can contribute
Ladybeth42: Well, now you do.
MinnieTheGreat: how?
Ladybeth42: No one in The Hellians has actually been able to speak with the boys. You'd be the first one.
MinnieTheGreat: so i can join because i'll have talked to them?
Ladybeth42: Sort of.
Ladybeth42: We need you to deliver a message to Halo.
MinnieTheGreat: i don't know how much time i'll have with them. i need to make sure i get through my interview questions first . . .

For the first time, a video appears in the chat and begins to play automatically. She sees the interior of a hotel bathroom, which she deduces based on the small bottles of shampoo and conditioner left unused on the counter. The camera scans over the length of the bathroom, taking extra care to graze over the toiletries scattered on various surfaces; whoever filmed it had a nervous hand, but Minnie makes out a pouch full of skincare, a sleek razor along the bathtub, mussed-up towels strewn across the floor.

MinnieTheGreat: what is this?
Ladybeth42: Halo's bathroom.
MinnieTheGreat: WHAT?

She replays the video, this time looking for signs of Halo. Nothing about it is personalized to him, and yet. The turbulence of the room does somehow feel familiar.

MinnieTheGreat: omg
MinnieTheGreat: there's no way
MinnieTheGreat: how?!!!!
Ladybeth42: One of us paid housekeeping to let us in while the boys were away. You're looking at Halo's bathroom, Minnie.
MinnieTheGreat: but why were you in his bathroom?
MinnieTheGreat: isn't this kind of creepy?
Ladybeth42: Pause the video at :45 and you'll see why.

She does as Ladybeth commands. Forty-five seconds into the video, she hits the space bar and stares, searching until she sees it: an orange, cylindrical bottle nestled between a container of mouthwash and a tube of leave-in conditioner.

MinnieTheGreat: what is that?
Ladybeth42: Meds for anxiety. I recognized them immediately.
MinnieTheGreat: but why would he need them?
Ladybeth42: It's obvious, isn't it? It's because his relationship with Jelly is falling apart.
Ladybeth42: This is why you need to talk to him and give him our message. The Hellians have wanted to warn him about something for a

while, but there's no good way to do it. You know the boys are always talking to us, but there's no real way for us to talk to them.

Ladybeth42: This way, we can make sure he hears it, since it will come from you. You're one of us now.

Ladybeth42: He's not okay, Minnie. This is proof.

She plays the video again, straining her eyes to see. The thought of someone breaking into Halo's room makes her uncomfortable, but a larger, more vicious impulse overshadows the discomfort: envy, yet again, at the fact that someone could have been so close to the boys—her boys, her Halo—and that it had not been her. It could be her. It should be her.

And the bottle on the counter—that disturbs her more than the video itself. She thinks of the previous pictures Ladybeth had sent her depicting Jelly's physical deterioration and Halo and Jelly's open despondency in the car. The boys continued smiling for the cameras, but The Hellians have proof of the truth: The boys are no longer happy.

And if that is the case, is it not up to her to give them back some of the happiness that they have given her? *We are yours and you are ours.* To be *theirs* comes without consequences and hesitancies—she is theirs, she has been theirs from the moment she saw that video all those months ago. Now is her chance to prove it.

MinnieTheGreat: ok

MinnieTheGreat: what do you want me to tell him?

EASON

Houston is as he remembered, all pickup trucks and concrete and slab-flat land. Back before his father left and his mother went mad, his parents would take him and Faye into Houston proper on the weekends to visit the museums, because that was where they could lounge in the AC without getting dirty looks. While his parents sat on the benches, not really noticing the art, he and Faye wandered through the galleries of The Menil. That was when Faye first started loving art. He remembers.

He remembers, too, his eighth-grade graduation ceremony, when his mother holed herself in her room and refused to come out, even though he sat outside her door and begged for hours. Faye drove him instead and he tried not to notice the red marks on her arms, which she normally hid with long sleeves. But it was hot and humid that day, and she rolled them up, forgetting.

Eason had been looking forward to the ceremony all year—he was excited to finally escape his middle school, and the graduation marked that—but now he wanted nothing more than to just keep driving. His mother would not be there, and neither would his father, so what was the point? When they pulled into the parking lot, he told Faye to turn the car around and go home, but she refused, dragging him out of his seat, telling him that he would regret it if he did not attend.

Standing up on stage, all he could hope for was to vanish. The auditorium was packed with families and well-wishers for each graduating student, their cheers like taunts in his ears. He did not need to see just how loved and cared for his classmates were—how their families were normal, their mothers sane. He hated them all then, their tender smiles, the bouquets they held in their hands.

When his name was called, he walked across the stage, eyes burning.

The student before him had brought an extended family of cousins and godparents, and the auditorium rang with their applause. In contrast, his reception elicited a few polite claps from sympathetic parents who could see just how badly he wanted to fall into the center of the Earth. But when he reached the principal to accept his graduation scroll, he heard his name being chanted, loud and clear, soaring over the heads of everyone in the auditorium, so unwavering that a few people turned to look for the source of the sound. After that, everyone started joining in, even those who did not know him, because the first voice was simply too convincing, too indefatigable in its efforts to make sure everyone had his name on their lips. As he walked off stage to a militant *EASON! EASON! EASON!*, he could not help himself: He smiled.

"Quite a show," the principal told Faye, somewhat disapprovingly, during the reception afterward. "Your parents couldn't make it?"

Instantly, Eason felt his shame return.

"Our mom wasn't feeling well," Faye said, without missing a beat. "She wishes she could be here."

"I'm sorry to hear that," the principal said. "She must be so sad to miss out on her son's graduation."

Faye put her arm around Eason's shoulder and brought him in close. "We'll be fine."

That was what Eason admired most about his sister—that no matter how bad it got with their mother, Faye never made it seem like anything out of the ordinary. *Our mom has a cold*, she would tell people, or *I got this bruise during practice*. For Faye, the imperative was to maintain a sense of calm and normalcy for as long as possible, because how else could they go on? She would take as many bullets in her chest as possible, if only to make sure the two of them could get out of this unscathed.

After, they went out for ice cream and Faye encouraged him to get the largest cup size possible, paying for it with the cash she had earned in tips from the night before. He remembers, still: two scoops of green tea, one scoop of vanilla bean. They ate it in the store while Weezer's "Beverly Hills" played over the speakers, and he felt, in that moment at least, happy, for once not thinking about how they would have to return to the townhome and face their mother. Faye kept delaying it, too, suggesting that they go to a park and then a movie, which they did, and even though the movie was bad, Eason enjoyed himself because he had never felt more grateful for his sister.

By the time they returned home, it was nearly dinnertime and the house smelled like eggplant in garlic sauce, Eason's favorite dish. He and Faye were both shocked to see their mother in the kitchen. She had made a feast, but neither of them were hungry—the ice cream was still sitting firm in their bellies. *Please eat*, their mother said, shoving bowls into their hands. *If you eat, Er zi, I'll know you're not mad anymore.* So they ate, forcing down fried rice and caramelized potatoes and duck soup, until the worry on their mother's face became a smile, and it was, Eason supposed, despite everything, a perfect kind of day.

As the plane begins its descent into Hobby Airport, he gazes out over the tangled freeways of the city, feeling both removed and deeply embedded. Look, he wants to tell his bandmates—this is the hospital where I was born. And that's Kim Son, we used to eat there every Sunday. That park is where I first learned to ride a bike. This stadium is where I attended my first Astros game. How inanely human, he thinks, that even at the highest heights, we still search for evidence of ourselves down below.

"Do you miss it?" Minwoo asks from beside him.

"Some parts," he says, staying vague. There is something about returning to a place as a completely different person that forces you to face the version of yourself that left. He does not know if he likes that feeling.

"I could never live here," Colt remarks from the seat in front. "It's just so much driving. I don't know how you did it."

"I didn't drive that much," he says without thinking. "It was mostly my sis—"

He stops himself, hoping no one has noticed. Julian, who sits next to Colt, moves his head a little, but does not say anything. As much as

Eason is glad for it, he is also stung; the old Julian would have noticed Eason's lapse and asked him to finish his sentence, wanting him to be heard. But not this version of Julian, and certainly not this new normal of silence between them.

"Will your mom be coming to the show tonight?" Minwoo asks. This is as much as Eason has told his bandmates about his family—that his mother lives in Houston.

"It's not really her scene," he says. "Did you know that *Rushmore* was filmed here, in a neighborhood called Montrose?"

"Wow," Colt says. "Can we try to stop by before we leave? I love Wes Anderson."

The rest of them agree. Over the intercom, the captain announces their arrival. Eason sinks back into his seat, grateful for the distraction.

The Remoras are waiting for them at the gate. Eason clocks the regulars: the brunette with glasses and cat ears; the rail-thin man who has traded his usual point-and-shoot for a gigantic professional camera that sits against his face like a long snout; an older woman with curly gray hair, her arms and ankles covered in striped socks; a twitchy girl with straight-cut bangs and a splatter birthmark on her arm. These are just the ones he recognizes.

Eason exits the jet bridge with the others. Upon seeing them, the Remoras raise their cameras in unison and follow, as if magnetized. "Give me a break," Julian mutters. "Aren't they tired of doing this yet?"

Cecile forges ahead with the bodyguards, clearing a path. Together, they rush through the airport, heads down. The Remoras follow at a run, cameras pointed out in front of them like spears. On both sides of Eason, the bodyguards have their elbows out, forcing distance between him and the Remoras. "Get back, make space, MOVE," they keep saying. It is enough to keep the Remoras at bay, but barely—as they continue to speed through the airport, the space around them gets smaller, until Eason is nearly climbing on top of Colt to stay afloat.

At baggage claim, they quickly load their suitcases onto carts.

It is here that one of the Remoras tries to snatch a leather duffel—Minwoo's—off the carousel, but crumples under its weight. A bodyguard tears her away easily, as if her body is filled with straw, and she begins yelling about pressing charges. The distance to the exit, where the SUVs are waiting, is scant, easily a thirty-second walk, but with the Remoras, now agitated, and others who have joined the crowd out of curiosity, they can barely take a step forward without meeting resistance. "Get back, get *back*!" the bodyguards keep yelling, but they no longer have mass or power on their side. The swarm continues pushing against them from all around, until they move together as one toward the exit.

When the doors slide open, the surge of bodies spills out onto the curb. Eason cranes his neck to see even more fans waiting outside. He spots the ice blond shock of Cecile's hair bobbing ahead—and then she is lost, overwhelmed by the crowd. The bodyguards form a phalanx around the four of them, their huge arms outstretched like football players running down the field, but Eason counts the number of heads that press against them, and there are simply too many now for the bodyguards to hold.

"HALO!!" someone shrieks. "I LOVE YOU!!!!"

"MY HANDSOME BABY."

He jerks around, expecting—dreading—

"Jesus—" he hears Julian cry out. "There's too many—"

It happens fast. There is a group pushing to his left, threatening to break through, and another advancing from the front. Three bodyguards fight upstream to stop Cecile from being pulled under by the tow of arms. In their absence, the right side opens, completely unguarded.

By the time he sees the opening, it is already too late. In tumble the bodies. At first, all he hears is the rapture that descends upon them at the realization that they have finally broken through. Then someone is feeling his arms, someone is running their palms over his back, someone is digging under his shirt, trying to caress his stomach—there are hands all over him, and now they are rolling him, turning him into an edifice or a sacrifice, he is not sure. The delight in their screams morphs into something he does not recognize, but faintly, in the back of his mind, he does know what it is, for he has been waiting for it to catch up with him for the length of his hateful life. It is the sound of a demon, or a curse, or the heartbreak of a girl, a sister, a mother, who has been betrayed.

Looking up, he sees Minwoo reaching for the sky, letting himself be pulled this way and that like a toy held between the jaws of two monsters. He sees Colt lose his bag to one of the Remoras, who tears it from him as if it is the most important thing in the world. Julian just ahead of him, arms stuck to his body but elbows out, still attempting to move forward, not caring who he hurts or if he hurts. The air grows tight. Eason sucks at it in panicked gulps, but it does not feel like it will ever be enough and still, those hands are clutching every bit of him, and he is paralyzed by their precision, their multitude, by his own inability to be more than what he is. As he lets his eyes roll skyward, he wonders if this is it—if this is how he will pass from this life into the next—and would that be such a bad thing?

He hears a shriek. It takes a moment for him to recognize the sound as a whistle, announcing the arrival of the police. The crowd around him begins to loosen—the Remoras screech as they are pulled back, vultures picked off by a larger beast, and he feels his lungs replenish. The SUVs are just ahead of him. The door opens and Cecile clambers in, one of her shoes ripped at the heel, then Minwoo, who has been rescued by the police, then Colt and his bag, the strap torn, then Julian, still propelling himself forward, elbows out, smashing into dazed Remoras along the way, and finally Eason and every hand still clinging to him. For a second time, the impulse seizes him to let himself be pulled back into this squall—how pitiful a thought, how equally freeing—but then Julian reaches out for him from inside the car.

He grabs on.

The door closes. Instantly, the crowd descends upon the car, their bodies banging against it. From inside, they sound like a hailstorm. The driver slaps his hand against the horn, but the Remoras do not relent.

"Are you okay?" Julian asks, panting. It almost feels as if everything between them has gone back to normal.

Eason nods, but his skin crackles. Their nails had scratched him. He still feels their fingers everywhere—on the back of his neck, on his face, and yes, even the place between his legs, the most vulnerable part of him now red and tremulous in the aftermath. Shock gives way to shame, which rears into anger—the first time he has felt *anger* toward the fans. They had touched him everywhere, and even though they had not taken anything from him, hadn't they? Hadn't they?

Colt rubs the top of his head. "One of them ripped my hair out."

Minwoo checks the spot. "It's just a small patch," he says, as if it makes things better. "I'm sure the stylists can fix it."

"It's my *hair*—"

In the front seat, Cecile pats her hands down her body. At first, Eason thinks she must be feeling for bruises or broken bones, having been tossed through the crowd, but then he realizes that she is simply smoothing out the creases in her suit. Her fingers, Eason notices, are trembling.

"We need to refocus," she says when finished. She turns around to assess the four of them. Her own shirt has a button missing from the collar.

Julian looks incredulous. "We need to go to the hospital."

"We can get you checked after the interview."

Eason remembers: They are scheduled for an appearance at the local radio station.

"Colt's missing a chunk of his hair and Minwoo almost got pulled apart!" Julian's voice rises. "We're not doing the interview."

Cecile looks at him coolly. "The station head partners with one of the biggest music festivals in Texas. You don't seem to understand how big of a get this is for us."

"We'll do it," Minwoo says. "We're fine."

"What?" Julian says. "No, we're not. Look at us!"

"Minwoo is right," Eason says. "We have to do the interview."

He cannot stand the look of betrayal on Julian's face. As if he has any choice. As if any of them has ever had any choice.

"I can't believe you," Julian says. He turns to Colt, waiting.

"We can do it," Colt says, although he looks uncertain. He gingerly taps the top of his head, feeling for the missing chunk of hair. "Maybe if someone gets me a hat . . ."

Julian slumps back in his seat.

"Your first full-length album is in the works. Can you tell us more about that?"

"Yes, we can," Minwoo says. No one listening would know that only an hour ago, his limbs were being torn in four directions. "With our EP, we wanted people to have fun. We wanted to make music people could dance to. Now that we're working on our first *real* album, you could say we're finally getting to express our true selves as artists. We're interested in exploring the absolute limits of pop music—and pushing past them. We're collaborating with a lot of artists, bringing in new producers, and taking a bigger role in the writing of our songs. We're not interested in being one-hit wonders. We want to stay around for a while."

"And I think you will," the interviewer says. "Any last words for the fans or listeners of the show before you go, boys?"

"I have something," Julian says. This is not the smooth, angelic lilt of Jelly. This is Julian's real voice, a harder staccato that clips its vowels and rushes over consonants. The rest turn to him in surprise—the script had not called for this. "What happened this morning was unacceptable. We could have been killed. For those who call themselves 'fans' and mobbed us at the airport today, I want you to know that if you really were our fans, you would have stayed home. This kind of behavior is not okay anymore."

The interviewer does not know what to do with this. He glances at Cecile, who observes them through a glass to the studio, then over to Minwoo, who looks similarly unsure.

"We're just singers," Julian continues. "We're not your fucking toys. Please respect our space and our lives."

Almost instantly, Julian's mic goes dead. Minwoo puts his head in his hands. Outside, Cecile is livid.

"Sorry about the language, folks." The interviewer motions to the producer to cue in the commercial break. "We'll be right back and ah, my apologies, again."

Done. The interviewer stands and exits the studio without a word. Through the glass, Eason watches him yell at Cecile, spittle flying from his mouth, before charging off.

"We're banned from the station and all of its affiliates," she tells them as they walk back down the hallway, to the green room. "And they won't be considering us for the music festival anytime soon. Oh, and we'll also be fined for that f-bomb."

"Thanks, Julian," Colt says glumly.

"I don't understand you," Minwoo says. "Are you trying to sabotage us?"

The record label tries to suppress it, but it is too late—shortly after the interview, an audio clip of Julian's tirade spreads across the coasts of the internet, appearing on everything from gossip rags to CNN. "We're singers," the chopped-up clip says. "Respect our fucking space." At the same time, someone uploads a video from the airport, this time focusing on Julian as he elbows his way through the crowd. The video depicts him jabbing two girls in the face, and another in the arm, cutting off just before the airport security arrives. FRAGILE EGO? HOURGLASS' JELLY GETS VIOLENT WITH FANS AT AIRPORT one headline reads. Eason makes the mistake of looking at the comments:

Wow, this dude is asking people to respect his space but he can't even respect his fans? Trash.

Why is he complaining when he's the one who signed up for all of this?

Are we supposed to feel sorry for him?

If you can't handle the heat stay out of the kitchen ladyboy.

POST #2559

Jelly's outburst was his way of telling us that he needs HELP. If we don't do something, this could be the end of HOURglass as we know it.

He's scared, he's sick and tired, he needs us more than ever. He wants us to ACT. None of the boys can do anything because they're at the mercy of the record label and their contracts. Their careers are on the line. The blond bitch has her claws in deeper than ever. And we all know what that slimy CEO is trying to do to Halo . . .

But even if the boys can't do anything, WE CAN. HOURglass wouldn't exist if it weren't for the fans—the boys have told us this themselves. If we don't protect them, who will?

MINNIE

"I came because I know you've been worried," Halo says.

Tomorrow, she will see the boys in person. But tonight, all she can think of is that horrible footage from the airport, the now-viral video of Jelly shoving two girls, and the ensuing radio interview. It rocked her, seeing him move with such violent force and speak with equally violent language. His anger was an engine ripping down a quiet street.

There was an additional consequence to Jelly's outburst; hateful comments swilled at the bottom of their most recent pictures and videos: *FUCK U SISSIES; Hack band; bunch of girls fighting girls; I'd tell you you suck but I don't want to get karate chopped too; Honestly, die.* When she came upon those awful comments, it was as if they had been directed at her. In fact, she wished they had been, for at least then she could shield the boys.

Now Halo is here, addressing it all. Steadfast Halo. Even in the face of this hate, he heard her despair and returned to assure her—and the 150,000 others watching the livestream—that he is all right.

Halo runs his hands through his hair and looks off to the side. He sighs. "That audio of Jelly was altered, you know that, right? We would never talk to our fans that way. But I don't have to tell you. You already know our hearts."

Yes, she knows. She had heard the full radio interview as it aired, but it is easier, more convenient, for the public to believe in a narrative of spoiled pop boys throwing a fit. She thinks about Nate and his friends, how they would clap each other on the back for being so right. Perhaps Nate would even add the incident as a plot point to his short story.

Into the chat box, she writes her message to Halo, hoping that, once again, out of the hundreds of messages streaming through, he will see hers.

I hope you know how much I love you.

He smiles, but still, he looks sad. "Thank you for loving me. I don't know what I would do if I didn't have you."

She nods at him, knowing that he sees.

I'll be with you tomorrow. I can't wait.

"I know," he says. "I can't wait to be with you, too."

Ladybeth42: He looks awful. Like he's being eaten alive.

MinnieTheGreat: i feel so bad for him. for all of them

Ladybeth42: You know why this is all happening, right?

Ladybeth42: Halo is clearly in distress. Jelly, too. That's why he was acting out.

MinnieTheGreat: were the hellians there, at the airport?

Ladybeth42: Some of us. It was all so confusing. We were trying to protect the boys.

MinnieTheGreat: i wish i were there to protect them too

Ladybeth42: The record label wants to end their relationship. That's why they brought this blond vulture on—to seduce Halo away from Jelly. You see it too, don't you?

MinnieTheGreat: i just don't know anything anymore. i'm so confused by all of it

Ladybeth42: That's why we need you to give our message to Halo. We need to warn him and let him know we stand with him and Jelly.

Ladybeth42: You'll remember, right? You won't forget?

MinnieTheGreat: i won't forget

They set out early in the morning. Minnie waits for Anna on the sidewalk outside her dorm, repeating the words Ladybeth told her to say. She tests the weight and shape of every syllable, stomach in coils at the momentous task ahead of her.

Anna arrives in a yolk-yellow Volkswagen. Inside the car, Minnie competes with art and photography books, an easel lodged behind her seat, and several balls of yarn in varying stages of unravel. Accustomed to Nate's immaculate Jeep, a car he took great pride in paying a contractor to detail every two weeks, Minnie finds Anna's car charming in its disarray.

"Sorry," Anna says, balling up a pelt of black cardigans and throwing them behind her without looking. "I'm living between the studio and my apartment right now."

To Minnie, Anna is no less intimidating than her first day at the recruitment meeting. Still, the car ride is not unpleasant. Every time her mind wanders back to Ladybeth's request and flutters of panic threaten to take over, Anna, as if sensing Minnie's nerves, starts speaking. As they finally escape the traffic out of Austin, Anna suggests that Minnie put on some music by HOURglass so she can have an idea of what she is getting herself into. Minnie obeys, then watches Anna's reaction, the coil in her stomach easing as the boys' voices fill the car.

"It's definitely heavy on the pop production," Anna says halfway. "Not my taste, but I can see why people love it. It's very catchy and fun."

This is compliment enough. They stop for gas and lunch at a taco trailer near Bastrop, where Minnie offers to split the gas bill. ("Are you kidding? I'm invoicing everything—this a work trip.") Anna convinces her to try lengua for the first time, which she does. She is surprised by its slow, tender texture, how satisfying it is to mash the tiny organ against the roof of her mouth. Anna pays for the tacos ("Say it with me, Minnie: Invoicing!") and they are off again, sliding down 71, past Bastrop and small towns she has never heard of before—Smithville and Plum and La Grange—the kind of towns that someone made up just so they could put them in a story. This Texas is different from the one she knows or assumes, not the cheery city lights of Austin nor the cowboy on horseback, a myth and an exaggeration, she knows by now, but still a kind of Texas all the same. Here, the grass unfurls into a verdant carpet and the trees stretch like old men in the aftermath of waking. When, passing a pasture in Columbus, she spots a fold of black-and-white stripes, she cannot help exclaiming, "I didn't know there were zebras in Texas!" and Anna, laughing, replies, "There's *everything* in Texas."

The more time she shares with Anna, the more she likes her. Up close, she is not just dour, but surprisingly funny. There is also an air of frenzy to her that Minnie had never noticed before, as if she is constantly running out of time. She has a habit of biting her lips and blinking with her nose, and every ten miles or so, she rummages through the bag of Hi-Chews wide open on her lap and pops one into her mouth. When the truck behind them pulls up alongside their car, boxing them in against the highway barrier, Anna slams the horn with the heel of her palm confidently and glares at the other driver until he pulls past. It makes Minnie like her even more.

"Are you excited to graduate?" Minnie asks as they merge onto I-10. Their surroundings gray and flatten, giving way to miles of highway construction and agriculture warehouses and JESUS WILL SAVE YOU billboards.

"I don't have feelings about it either way," Anna says, popping another Hi-Chew. "My parents want me to go straight to grad school or get a job, but I applied to a residency in Mexico City."

"That's really cool."

"What about you? Looking forward to your sophomore year?"

"Kind of." Would sophomore year be more of eating early in the dining hall and watching Jillian and her friends laughing and avoiding Nate and shrinking from Clark? She wishes all of that could be erased and only she would remain, with the boys and Ladybeth and The Heaven.

"It gets better," Anna says, reading her silence. "My first year was rough. I was living in the dorms and my roommate was on the track team so she was never there, and everyone else on the floor thought I was weird."

"What did you do?"

"I just kept my head down and worked on my design projects. It's only three more years, I kept telling myself. Sophomore year, I moved out of the dorms and got my own place. I started making friends in my major, too. The point is, it takes time. And you know what? We're in a college bubble right now, but this isn't what the rest of life is like. Personally, I'm way more excited for everything that comes after this."

"Hm," Minnie says. Hearing Anna speak, she realizes that she never once contemplated what came after—and that there will be an after.

"You're seeing someone, right?" Anna asks, her voice inscrutable. "So at least you have a person to go through it with."

"Sort of," Minnie says, wincing at the memory of Nate. It has been two weeks since the party and their final phone call. "Not really. We broke up."

"I'm sorry."

"It's okay. I don't think it was ever going to work out. He's five years older than me."

"Ah," Anna says. "I had something like that once." A pause as she adjusts the rearview mirror. "The thing about dating someone who's way older is that you always feel like you should be grateful they chose you. They could be with anyone, but still, they chose you."

"Yeah," Minnie says, swallowing. "I felt like that."

"And you're not wrong. They *could* be with anyone. There are plenty of hot, intelligent, available girls his own age. So why did he choose you?" She glances at Minnie. "Sorry. I didn't mean that as in you're not good enough for him. I just meant—we're always worrying about whether or not we deserve them. We never ask ourselves how it's benefiting them, to be with *us*." She taps the steering wheel with her thumbs.

Minnie gazes out the window, more to avoid the directness of Anna's statement than anything. "I don't think it benefited him to be with me," she says quietly. With a squirm, she remembers his short story. "Well, maybe it did. He was writing a story about me and my 'obsession' with this band. Maybe that's why he stayed with me. Or maybe he just liked having another freshman to add to his collection."

Anna is quiet. "That's terrible."

"It's okay. It's just so silly, because this whole time I felt like I needed to catch up to him. He was so much smarter and cooler than me."

Anna snorts. "And yet, he felt like he needed to write about you. Sounds like you were the smart, cool one, not him. She pops another candy into her mouth. "You know, I've seen the two of you around."

"You have? Where?"

"I walked past you on campus once. But you didn't notice me."

"That doesn't sound like me. I'd notice you anywhere."

"Because I dress like this, right? You'd be surprised how many people look past me because I look the way I do. It's actually a great way to blend in. Anyway, your ex is pretty tall, right?"

She remembers, with a pang, the first time she met Nate. The allure of his athletic body pitched against the bookstore. Their first conversation and the thrilling play of flirtation. So much had changed since then. "Right."

"I realized he's the barista at JP's Java. I go every morning before Studio and he's always working the counter. He's really bad at making coffee."

Minnie cannot help herself—she laughs. She laughs and the sound is loud and robust, as if all of the laughter she has not been able to release since coming to college has been waiting for this moment.

"What?" Anna says, looking defensive. "It's true!"

"I'm not laughing at you," Minnie says. She cannot stop, nor does she want to. It is hilarious to her, the idea of Nate, who was always so pretentious about his coffee, being poor at making it himself.

"It's not like it was the worst coffee I've ever had," Anna concedes. "He just burns it. Every time I've gone in there the past few weeks, his dude friend is in there distracting him and I'm over here wondering if the guy can make a cup of coffee that doesn't taste like wet dirt. It's not that hard, you know?"

Minnie's laughter stops. "His friend. Does he have green eyes?"

"I don't know. I've never looked at his eyes."

"Curly brown hair? Glasses?"

"I think so." Anna scowls at the memory. "I don't like the way he looks at me, so I never acknowledge him."

"His name is Clark," Minnie says. It is the first time she has spoken his name out loud, and the feel of it escaping her mouth terrifies her. But there is also something freeing about being able to release his name, here in the safety of this car, and with Anna, someone who sees him not as the genial roommate or unassuming geology student, but for what he is. "He's . . . not a good person."

"Clark," Anna repeats. In her mouth, his name is small and unimpressive, nothing more than a bug to be squashed. "Sounds like a creep."

The concert does not start until seven thirty, so Anna drives to a neighborhood called Montrose, where the sidewalks are uneven and every house is painted a different color. "This is the real reason I agreed to come," she sings as they walk up to a brown, square building without windows. "I've been wanting to visit this place ever since I got into UT." It is called, Minnie learns, the Rothko Chapel.

Inside, there is only one room. It is shaped like an octagon, with black panels on each of the eight walls and benches facing them. There is one other person there, an elderly woman with her head bowed in meditation. Anna closes her eyes and breathes deeply, as if siphoning an invisible power from the room. It is quiet.

"Where's the art?" Minnie asks, glancing around.

Anna opens her eyes. "Minnie," she says, looking at her with a concerned expression. "This *is* the art." She motions to the black panels on the walls. Minnie turns to behold them.

"I'm not sure what I'm supposed to be seeing."

Anna points to a bench and the two of them sit in front of one of the panels. "You're supposed to see what you want to see."

Minnie leans forward, looking closer. At this distance, she can see that the panels are not black, but painted in shades of purple, perhaps even blue. She tries to trace a thread of violet in the canvas before her, seeking out its beginning and end, where it morphs into blueish black and gray, but she finds that the longer she follows it, the more it disappears. She does this again and again, reading the different hues as if tracking an animal's prints on a trail, but the color always dissolves into a new one before she can catch it. What is she looking for? In one moment, she sees a ball of scribbles, in another, a man with a crown. The truth: There is nothing to see. Or, everything to see. Underneath the octagonal skylight, where light pours down on her, she begins to sense that she is the one on display, and the longer she looks, the more naked she feels. In every direction a panel pushes back on her gaze, demanding from her some kind of answer. She shudders. *I have nothing*, she wants to tell the panels. But she knows that this would be a lie.

After the chapel, they grab a snack at the museum's café, a pricey chocolate croissant that dissolves into flakes under her fingers. The chapel and its panels left her feeling unsettled and raw, as if the mercurial colors seeped out from the paintings and into her skin during the hour she spent staring at them. For the first time, she lets that feeling wash over her. She sees herself then not as Minnie looking out at the world, but a world looking inside Minnie, and inside her it is long and deep, like a well that someone could drop a penny into and never know the fate of, until it finally hit the bottom of her, where all her hurt had lived for too long. But like the panels, the walls of her well are not just one shade—there is hope and light woven into the hues of her sadness, too, and maybe in time she can finally reach for it, draw it out of herself, rebuild it into something necessary and powerful and good.

Anna is quiet, too, her pencil moving back and forth over a page in her notebook. Minnie leans over—it is a sketch of the chapel's octagonal interior. "This is the kind of art I want to make," Anna says.

"What do you mean?"

"Art that finds you and not the other way around."

"I think that's amazing," Minnie tells her. "I'd like to come to your show one day. You know, when you're a famous artist and all."

Anna rolls her eyes. "Tell that to my parents." But still, she looks happy at the idea. "What about you? What do you want to do?"

Minnie hesitates. There is one thing she has loved all her life, but saying it out loud is both scary and inescapable She never liked asking for things when she was a child, never liked expressing hunger or desire or want of safety, because it was that desire, that unbridled need, that made her vulnerable. The moment she vocalizes her desire, it is in danger of being taken away. "I like to write," she says finally. "I'd like to be a journalist."

Anna nods. "I think it would suit you. You're so observant."

"But I feel like there's a lot I have to catch up on, especially when it comes to my place in the world. Growing up, I thought it was better to try to fit in. But now I wonder if fitting in is another way of disappearing. I want to know more about what it means to be Asian American. I want to know more about history. I want to know what my responsibility to the world is. You and Akash seem to have it so figured out."

"I promise you, we don't. We're barely getting started."

"It's more than me, anyway."

"It's not a race to see who knows more," Anna says gently. She closes her sketchbook. "There's a writer named Theresa Hak Kyung Cha that I like. She was really important to me when I started asking myself these questions. Can I lend you her book?"

"I would love that." Then, not looking Anna in the eyes, she speaks again. "I'm sorry I was phoning it in with the zine. I think I was afraid to try."

"I know," Anna says, patting her on the arm. "I'm just glad you're still here. We're all on our own journeys, you know. Any growth is always met with resistance first, from yourself most of all. Like I said: I was the same way."

She has never met anyone so sure of themself, so certain of their path in life. Anna is different from Nate, who seemed to do everything for the sake of how he would be perceived by others; Anna did things because she wanted to, because that was what was right for her.

"Did you like the chapel?"

"I did," Minnie says. It has been a long time, not since she discovered the boys, that something could stir her the way the panels had. For that, she is grateful.

"Good," Anna says. She cracks a proud smile and it makes Minnie feel proud, too. "Now let's go to the show."

EASON

The stop in Houston lasts three days. From the interview at the radio station, it's straight to rehearsal. Lunch. More rehearsal. The next day, he wakes and drags himself to the physical therapist, who elbows the knots in his lower back and the evergreen ache in his shoulder.

In Houston, he sees his mother in the face of everyone he comes across—the physical therapist who stretches him and the sandwich girl working lunch catering and every crew member he passes on the way to the stage, who smiles at him with big, bright eyes and whispers, "You got this." He sees her in every comment online, every time someone calls him *gorgeous* or *talented* or *baby*, and eventually there are no words in the English language he hates more.

Three hours before the concert, during soundcheck, a side door in the arena opens to let in one hundred fans. They are here because they have spent an additional $300 on a Platinum Member VIP package that comes with priority seating, limited-edition T-shirts, autographed posters, and these precious next fifteen minutes—now fourteen!, now thirteen!—during which time their idols will run through three songs and they, the luckiest hundred on the planet, get to bear witness.

Eason watches them enter one by one, each body bursting through the door and rushing to the stage. "PLEASE WALK! PLEASE DO NOT RUN!" the security guard shouts, already exhausted by the commotion. They obey, but when the security guard looks away, they gallop like wild horses to the lip of the stage, where they stand chests against backs, their screams whipping at him in a constant wind.

He scans them, these sunflowers. Looking for her. Is she here? If she could so easily give $300 to a hack fortune teller for all those years, what was another $300 to finally gain access to him here, now?

"Stand by," the voice in his ear says. "Sound team is ready."

The guitar of Song Ten plunks away and there's that string again, the one that holds him up. No time to think, it says. Just MOVE. So, he moves. His arms strike a diagonal, his feet stomp together, his head snaps right-left. *What're you doing, baby?* he hears himself singing.

Is she here? Is she watching him? But the string is there again, pulling him to center stage, and he's launching into the next part of the choreography, loose legs, chase, shuffle and dodge, and now he's feeling it, now his muscles have taken over, and he can crawl into the back, watch the trees zoom by, let the stone-cold body of him do what it does best, just let go, don't think, let someone else drive.

The sunflowers are chanting his name. They're chanting the others' names, too, but he hears it clear as day for the first time: His name is loudest. And this is when he realizes a new truth, breathing hard like a bull, body pearlescent from all its activity. It does not matter if she is here. It does not matter where she is. In this moment, he is Halo, not Eason, and Halo does not have a mother. Halo does not have a past. Halo exists in light and glory and the divinity of having been chosen. As long as he continues to be chosen, he will be protected. He, their idol. They, his absolution.

MINNIE

NRG Arena is as big as a planet. Not for its size, which reminds Minnie of several soccer fields stacked on top of one another, but for its gravitational pull, of which they are now at the mercy. As they leave the car and begin the long walk to the entrance, Minnie sees that they are not alone. All around them, girl bodies zoom to the venue, legs pumping fast, shrieks jetting them forward in excited bursts. Minnie hears snatches of their conversation as they flit past—girls squealing, girls holding hands and singing, girls adjusting skirts or hairpieces for other girls, girls tying each other's shoes, girls brushing an eyelash off a girl's cheek before whispering, *There, now you're perfect.* It is a girlhood that is magical and sweet, and she and Anna are a part of it, two of eight thousand. Anna shoots out her hand and Minnie, understanding, grabs it, the feel of Anna's palm suddenly securing her into place, even as her feet scurry faster, the two of them now in a silent race to outrun the crowd around them.

At the mouth of the arena, the venue staff point them to a separate security line for backstage ticketholders. They probe a flashlight into her purse, noting the extra tampons, her ratty wallet, the phone slowly draining of its battery. Anna, they let keep the hardware in her ears and around her neck, but take her pepper spray. A ticket scanner, then another staffer who checks their badges against a list, then an authoritative-looking manager who loops a neon-colored band around their wrists. And then, they are through.

It is deafening inside the venue. Girls exchanging crafts, girls passing out candy, girls making sure their friend gets to the bathroom. Anna grabs her hand again, tugging her to the escalators that lead to the backstage entrance. Minnie lets herself be pulled away from the current. It is finally beginning to hit: She is going to see the boys. It is as if every path she had walked, every hardship she endured, was placed before her as a test, as a certainty, just so she could reach this moment. All those days and nights funneling her love into the boys, playing their voices over and over again until she fell asleep and into their arms, taking the sadness inside her and brewing it into fake smiles and placid remarks—it was all for something, culminating in the magic at hand. Her and her boys, together at last. If this was what it had all been for, then it was worth it. It would always have been worth it.

At the backstage entrance, another staff member waits for them. He scans the tickets, the wrist bands, checks their names against a list one more time. "Okay, you're good to go through," he finally says, and Minnie could swear that those are the most beautiful words in the English language. The staff member opens the door as if unlocking a sacred chamber, and she and Anna walk through. Backstage is dark, not at all the magnificent kingdom of neon lights and pageantry she had imagined. Instead, she sees darting flashlights and the urgent scuttles of crew members as they complete their final checks. She looks around for the boys—she wonders from where they will enter the stage.

Another security guard appears, blocking them from going any farther. "This way, ladies," he tells them, using his body to herd them to a metal staircase on the side of the stage, and even though his voice is gruff, she swears, once again, that she is hearing music in his words. They climb the stairs, the security guard lighting the way for them with a little flashlight, and then they are hovering above the stage on a platform. There are ten other people there, dressed, Minnie notices, in expensive-looking clothing, but for the first time, she does not feel out of place. This is where she belongs.

"This is wild," Anna says, her eyes big and dazed as they stare out at the audience. With minutes to go, every seat is filled, the volume of voices so loud it almost sounds like quiet. But if everyone were to open their mouths and say *oh* at the same time, then it would no longer sound like *oh*; rather, it would sound like a great wave or the growl of a tiger or the aubade of the Earth as it left one century for the next.

Minnie turns to Anna. The boys would appear soon down on the stage below. Up here, high above, she feels like an angel watching over them, waiting for them to soar and join her. "I never thanked you," she says. "For doing all of this for me."

"Oh god, don't get all sentimental now," Anna says. Without warning, the stage goes yellow, every light in the building turned on. Minnie can see the whites of Anna's eyes. At the back of the stage, a large LED screen flickers on, turning silver, then gold, then HOURglass blue. *TEN*, it reads. *NINE*. The audience erupts into screams.

"I don't know what to do," Minnie hears herself saying over the crowd's roar. "I might die."

EIGHT

SEVEN

"You'll be fine," someone says. She sees Anna's mouth moving, but she cannot be sure if those words belonged to her, or if they came from the voice of the venue, the voice of all its inhabitants.

SIX

But would she be fine?

FIVE

Or would her heart, which was already the size of a galaxy, explode?

FOUR

Anna is fiddling with her nose piercing, catching the light.

THREE

Stop the concert, Minnie wants to say. I cannot bear it.

TWO

She is back in the bathroom in Nate's house, but the door is open. It has never been open before. Clark is not there with her, but he would be there, very soon. He would walk through that door and lock her in with him and then he would gaze down upon her the way he gazed at her that night and every night, and demand of her, not ask:

You don't want to go through college a virgin, do you?

ONE

Boom. Minnie screws her eyes shut, waiting for Clark to appear or her heart to burst or her entire being to evaporate, whichever one comes first does not matter—they would all feel the same. But someone has their fingers wrapped around her arm, someone is shaking her to and fro. "Minnie," she hears. "Minnie!" And she remembers that it is Anna, Anna who is standing next to her, not Clark or anyone else, rocking her gently back from whatever abyss awaited. "Look," Anna is saying. "They're here."

She hears it. The first few notes, major in key. Familiar. The guitar riff. Familiar. The synths that slide in, easy, like a breeze through an open window. Familiar.

I don't want to lose you baby

But I think I'm losing you baby

She opens her eyes and sees them. The boys are here. One, two, three, four, they emerge from somewhere underneath the stage, and of course it makes sense that this is where they come from, for who are they if not gods that levitate from the depths of the Earth? Tonight, they are wearing all-black suits, their silver, acorn, honey, and black hair slicked back and smooth. The audience erupts at the sight of them, every scream a kaleidoscope of love, death, awe, need, and Minnie swears she can feel each fiber of her being plucked out and cut clean by those screams. Even the bodyguards, who stand before the barricade at the front row, look stunned.

If we're not going to make it

Just tell me and I'll break it

The boys leap forward as sparklers explode behind them, violet and yellow and brilliant cherry red, and now the boom of the bass replaces the insistence of her heart, now she is sure that her body and her life are not dictated by her brain, nor the blood that pumps through her veins, but by the necessity of the boys. She howls, coming to, stomping up and down with the music, and never before has she felt so alive, awash in the song she has heard so many times, so many nights, under so many circumstances, but none of that matters now, because *now* is what matters, and she knows that the door she saw was open not because Clark would be entering through it; it was open because she could finally leave.

I've loved you since I saw you

Loved you since I lost you

From where she stands, high in the rafters, she can see the boys clearer than ever: the veins that surface in Minwoo's neck when he sings; Denim's teeth, reflecting a rainbow of stage lights; Jelly, slight and slender, recalling the essence of something otherworldly, something divine; and Halo, her Halo, shining stronger and brighter than them all. It does not matter anymore. Nate, Clark, the red boa feathers on the bathroom floor. Her loneliness and her longing. The sadness at the bottom of the well that she could not seem to stop falling down. She watches the boys and for the first time, she sees where her bright heart has gone—it left her long ago and settled in each of them. They are everything she wants to be, everything she used to be: untethered, open, and free.

She urges herself to remember: which songs they play and in what order; how handsome Denim looks when he spins; the illuminated topography of Halo's jaw and neck as he glances up, blinking the sweat from his eyes. Remember it all. But it is an impossible task. She forgets almost as soon as the moment passes, because she is overloaded and overrun. All she can do is receive, just as the panels in the chapel had asked her to. And so she does. She relinquishes control of her mind and memory, allowing herself to be empty, and the boys, recognizing her efforts, turn to her now, pouring themselves into her and filling her with their shine.

It ends too soon.

"Thank you for loving us," Minwoo calls into his microphone.

"We love you," Denim says.

"We'll be back," Jelly promises.

"Get home safe," Halo says. For him, the cheers are piercing.

They shout, together: "We are yours and you are?"

The audience, knowing only one immovable truth, roars back together, Minnie the loudest of all: "OURS!"

And then they are gone. In a splash of brilliant fireworks, they vanish from the stage, leaving behind a puddle of confetti and balloons, which look sad without the mighty presence of the idols who bequeathed them. Minnie stares at the spot where they stood and realizes that her face is wet; when she had started crying, she does not know, but this was a kind of ecstasy that deserved tears—she would bleed for them if they asked; salt was simply the beginning.

Anna tugs at her arm. "We need to go."

The boys are gone, but it is not the end; she remembers then, with a flash of panic, what they had come for. She follows Anna as they file down the metal stairs, descending from their lofty perch back down to Earth, but this time the Earth is just as good as the heavens, for it is also where the boys stood.

The security guard from before waits for them at the bottom. "We have passes for the meet and greet," Anna tells him. "I'm Daniel Wu's niece."

He presses his earpiece, speaking to the person inside it. "What did you say your name was?"

"Anna Peng. And this is my friend, Minnie."

He repeats the names. Then, he nods and turns, motioning for them to follow. "You'll have five minutes," he calls back. "They're on a tight schedule."

"That's more than enough time," Anna says.

They are walking forward now, deeper into the dark folds of the stage, treading the heavenly pathway to the boys. That is what Minnie should be focused on, preparing herself to be in the presence of her idols and the mission assigned by Ladybeth. But why, then, is she wrapped around what Anna had just called her: *friend*?

Down another set of stairs. This time, they emerge into a narrow hallway with mealy walls. It is hard to imagine that the boys could have been held in such an unremarkable container. From here, the audience sounds like a distant ocean. Minnie understands that she and Anna must be somewhere beneath the stage.

The security guard stops walking. Behind him, Minnie sees a black door. "Five minutes," he says again. Then, he opens the door.

EASON

When, in the future, he would be asked to reflect on his time as Halo and as a part of HOURglass, he would always begin with the same sentence: "Everything changed in Houston."

It is the best concert of their lives. Everything, from the loud chants of the fans, to the resonance of the live band, is sublime, so natural that it feels like he is a marble falling into its groove. His bandmates can feel it, too. Together, they flow through song after song, hitting every move with the strength of ten thousand men. The lights splatter across the audience, and Eason sees, one by one, their beatific smiles, their pure adoration. This is what carries him through.

"Was it just me," Colt says as they descend back into the fluorescent tunnels beneath the stage, the fans' screams still floating above them, "or was this our best one yet?"

"No, you're right, they were extra loud tonight."

"Maybe because it's Eason's hometown . . ."

Cecile waits for them in the green room. "Nice work," she says curtly. "We've got some meet and greets, then you can go back to the hotel."

"None of us have eaten yet," Julian says. "Can we get ten minutes?"

"This isn't for fun," Cecile barks back. "After your little tantrum on the radio, people think you've lost touch with the fans."

The first meet and greet is with a couple, rich with oil money, who donated a sizeable amount to the concert venue. "Listen, I like women, but you guys were *hot* out there," the husband tells them, shaking their hands one by one. The wife asks for a few dozen photos, perching herself in the middle, her gigantic Chanel bag swinging from her torso like a quilted brick. The second meet and greet is with a real estate tycoon and his three daughters, who dissolve into exalted giggles the moment they enter the room. They are named Ashley—Bailey—Chelsea—and isn't it just perfect, the real estate tycoon tells them, because he could always refer to them as ABC. Eason wants to have a real conversation with them, ask them who they are and why they love him, but Ashley keeps talking over Bailey, and Chelsea cannot make eye contact without hiding behind her hands. The third meet and greet is with a single mother from Lubbock and her seven-year-old daughter, who is dying. "She just loves you boys," the mother tells them tearfully. The daughter is not able to speak in complete sentences, but she keeps murmuring "Jelly," and Julian kneels down so that he is the same height as her and says, "I've got you." The mother cannot stop thanking them for how they have helped make the last months of her daughter's life some of her happiest. When the bodyguard returns to sweep them from the room, Eason has to look away.

"How many more?" Julian asks when the girl and her mother leave. His eyes are red.

"One," Cecile says, as the door opens.

The newcomer is a scowling girl in khakis and combat boots, a marked difference from the pastel-colored confections fans frequently wear to their shows. Behind her enters another girl, taller, but without the large, confident movements of the first. Eason stares at her, and when she notices him looking, her face reddens, as if something within her has burst.

"Uh, hi," the first girl says.

"Hey there," Minwoo says. His voice goes high and soft, reminding Eason of the tone one would take to talk to a child or a dog. "I'm Minwoo. Thanks for coming to the show."

"I'm just here for support," the scowling girl says, opening her body so that the second girl is in view. "This is Minnie. She's the real fan."

The four of them turn to the second girl, who still has not left her position by the door.

"Hi, Minnie?" Colt says, smiling at her.

"Minnie's writing an amazing piece for our zine," the scowling girl says. Eason can tell this is not the first time she has had to take the lead for them—a trait that reminds him of his sister. "It's about your band and how much it's helped her."

"That's really kind," Julian says.

"Do you want to join us over here, Minnie?" Minwoo offers.

The girl takes three steps forward. Her movements are unsure, as if compelled solely by Minwoo's invitation, rather than her own power. She keeps her limbs close to her body. A trait that reminds Eason of himself. "I was wondering," she says, "if I could ask you some questions for my article."

"You can ask us anything," Colt says kindly.

"Thank you," the girl says. She comes a few steps closer, but does not allow herself to be within arm's length of them, as if afraid of puncturing something only she can see. "What do you want your fans to take away from your songs?"

"That they're not alone," Minwoo says automatically, "and we're thinking of them all the time. Everything we do is for them."

The girl nods vigorously, drinking in his words. She pulls out a notebook and scratches into it Minwoo's well-practiced quote. Eason notices that her hands are shaking.

"Take this," he says, giving her a hot pack from his pocket. "It's cold in here, right?"

She stares at his hand as if it might be handing her a gun. Then, she reaches for the hot pack and grabs on with a surprisingly firm grip, squeezing it between her fingers as if distilling from it all the essence of the hand that gave it to her. *Relax*, Eason wants to tell her. *We're human, just like you.*

The questions continue. She asks how they collaborate on their songs, what it means to them that most of their fans are women, how they have dealt with discrimination during their journey. A true fan, Eason thinks, for there is an earnestness to her questions that other interviews have lacked. He can tell the others are surprised by her; each question draws from their brows a faint quirk of delight.

"What does it feel like to know that you've helped so many of your fans go through some of the hardest moments of their lives?"

Julian puts his hand on his heart. "I'd say they've done the same for me."

The girl Minnie nods vigorously. She is beginning to loosen up, Eason thinks. There is something about her that makes him both soft and bitter at the same time—he wants to protect her, but her timidity also makes him angry, as if to say: Why can't you be stronger, more outspoken? Why can't you look me in the eye?

Cecile steps in. "That's time," she tells the two girls. "We've got to get going now."

"Thank you for coming," Julian says. "Good luck with your zine." The four of them turn. Already, Eason is thinking about the hotel, a long shower, sleep.

"Wait," the girl says, stricken. "There's something I need to tell you."

Cecile gives her a tight smile, one that does not reach her eyes. "I'm afraid that's all the time we have." She motions to the bodyguard. "Can you make sure these two ladies find the exit?"

"No, wait," the girl says again, this time more forcefully. The strength of her voice startles Eason. *There you are*, he thinks.

Cecile whispers something to the bodyguard, who nods and mutters into his earpiece. Two additional bodyguards appear at the door. Cecile points them to the girls.

"I have to warn Halo," the girl says. He stops and turns. She stares at him, and her gaze is fierce, direct, so unlike the girl who first walked into the room. *There you are*, he thinks again.

"Halo has to be going now," Cecile says, eyes daggering the bodyguards, compelling them to move faster. But the girl slips through the first one's grip, her movements shockingly fast. She dodges the second one's outstretched arm and steps closer to Eason.

"It's about your sister," she says. "They've known about her from the start. You're being used."

The room is still. His bandmates stare from the girl to him. His body is aflame, hands shaking at a frequency that he can no longer subdue. This girl could not be a real fan of his. A real fan would never try to hurt him like this.

"What's she talking about?"

"Is this a joke?"

"Your sister, Faye," the girl says. "The record label knew about it from the beginning. They're trying to use her to keep you and Jelly apart. But it doesn't matter. We can protect you, Halo—I mean, I can protect you—"

"That's enough." He does not recognize the voice that comes from him, cold and distant and bitingly cruel. "I want her out of here."

"Wait—" the girl says, but the bodyguards grab her by the arms and pull her away from him, and even though Eason hates her false meekness and the poison of her words, he watches her go, watches her face drain of its blood as she realizes that she will likely never see him from this distance again. This is the only control he can regain, the only balm for her violation. He watches them throw her out the door and slam it in her face, and he feels glad.

Colt first. "What . . . was that?"

"She was talking about a sister," Minwoo says. "But Eason doesn't have a sister, do you?"

They look at him, but he is staring at Cecile.

"Must have been a hit job," she says. "I'll talk to The Duke about this and take care of it. Let's get out of here."

"Thank you," Eason murmurs, feeling grateful for her impassivity for the first time. They follow her out of the dressing room, Eason trailing behind. It is almost eleven and the arena lobby is quiet now, an emptiness that matches the pallor of the evening. His hands are still shaking, the wretched tremors crawling up his forearms and to his elbows. He reaches into his pocket, searching for a hot pack, but finds it empty—he had given it to the girl.

MINNIE

THE WORLD IS BURNING. This is all she can think as she is dragged away, torn from Halo's prismatic light. The bodyguards hook their arms under her armpits and throw her from the dressing room. She flies through the door easily, a bag of trash. Anna is a staccato step behind her, crowding the narrow hallway with her questions. *What was that, Minnie, what happened?* She does not answer. All she knows is that she must crawl, scrape, bite her way back so that she can be with Halo once more. Whatever magic had been broken, she can repair it, she is certain.

But the door slams shut, the sound of it terrible in its finality. She sits on the floor where she lands and stares up at the door. She imagines Halo and the boys on the other side—their confusion and Halo's fury, his handsome features morphing from polite intrigue to a snarl.

"Minnie," she hears Anna say from somewhere. "What the hell happened?"

EASON

When they finally get back to the hotel, it feels as if they have been driving for hours. A crowd is waiting when they pull in, but he has nothing left to give them. He and Julian descend from the car, both shielding their faces with their hands, and rush into the hotel lobby.

In the elevator, Cecile watches him. "We've been in touch with a few editors. They didn't send her. Either they're lying, or she really was some crazy fan."

He wishes she would stop calling the girl a fan when it was clear she was anything but. No energy left to spar, though. He leans on Julian without thinking, the warmth of his body providing a small reassurance. Julian does not pull away.

"We'll do some pap photos of you two in the morning," Cecile is saying. "A stopgap, in case this becomes a problem. But it's likely nothing."

"Sure," Eason murmurs. Next to him, Julian nods, compliant for once. The elevator stops at floor 26, and Eason gets out. He feels Julian grab his arm, hears the elevator ding as it closes and takes with it Cecile's expressionless face, and then he is being led down the quiet hallway, until the two of them reach the door at the end.

Inside, Eason crawls into bed without bothering to change. Julian sits by his feet. The weight of him is welcome, familiar, like a star or mountain when one is lost. "Do you want to talk about it?"

Eason shakes his head. His brain feels too big for his skull.

"Okay," Julian says, standing. "I hope you feel better, Eas."

He leaves. Without him, the room rotates. The memory of the girl's face swims before Eason and a shudder of nausea passes through him. He runs to the bathroom, feet freezing against the spotless tile. He stares into the toilet bowl. The porcelain rim twinkles back at him as if it were laughing. He laughs back at it, and then he hurls.

When he told his mother the truth about Faye, she did not believe him at first. *No daughter of mine could be so stupid*, she said. He remembered the stick that he had kept, waiting at the back of his desk drawer. He showed it to his mother. *It's true*, he said. *It's been true for months.*

She took the stick from him and turned it around like a piece of fine jewelry. Then, she set it down on the table. "You're a good boy," she said. But a shadow passed over her face, a season changed.

When did he know that he had made a grave mistake? Was it when she sat at the kitchen table staring at the stick, her silence draining the light from the sky? Was it when the front door swung open, signaling that his sister was home? Or was it when Faye walked into the kitchen and saw their mother sitting there, the stick a bomb between them?

Faye's eyes moved from Eason to the stick to their mother. Then back to Eason. He would always remember her eyes, how she looked so certain that it was not he who betrayed her. In that nanoscopic moment before everything erupted, she saw Eason's hurt and anger and shame, his childish hope and his selfish need, and only then did she understand. She gave him a sad smile, as if to tell him that it was all right. That was the worst part: She forgave him, even knowing what was coming.

Their mother stood. One hand went to a drawer where she kept the peach wood switch. He saw the danger then and perhaps that was why he said, weakly, "Stop." But what had he expected? His mother's life was founded on the belief of a curse, and now a hack made her believe that a demon was living inside her daughter. Maybe that was why he told his mother Faye's secret—because he was starting to believe it, too.

"I thought we had finally been spared," their mother said. "I was wrong."

He expected her to strike Faye with the switch, but for once, she did not. Instead, her body began to writhe and convulse, as if there was something in her chest trying to claw its way out. He heard the most horrible sound then, like a retch and a snarl all in one. His mother's mouth opened and her back arched and through her throat, she turned herself inside out.

Then, silence. His mother raised her hand to her mouth, the one that did not hold the switch, and into it she coughed a knot of phlegm. She held it out to Faye, who looked just as frozen and small as he felt.

Eat.

"Please," he heard himself saying. But it was no use. What good were his words when he himself could not act? All it would take was for him to wrestle the switch from her. But he could not move. He could hardly breathe.

Glass was shattering somewhere. He ducked and then he looked up. It wasn't glass. It was the switch, snapping through the air.

"Eat," his mother said again.

He ran. He ran from the kitchen, from his sister, from his mother, he ran tripping across the powder-blue carpet, he ran up the stairs and to his room, he ran until he collapsed, chest to his knees. Downstairs, in the kitchen, glass continued to shatter and he shattered with it.

That was the night of the storm. All week, the weatherman warned of high winds and promised rain that would descend like bullets from the sky. Have a plan, he had said with a somber face. Seek shelter. If you come across standing water, don't try to drive though. Turn around for your life. They gave the storm a name: Ike.

Ike made landfall at 2:10 A.M. Those who lived in Galveston experienced the worst of it, the coastline and its surrounding area ravaged by widespread flooding and winds that blew at 110 miles per hour. In downtown Houston, windows exploded into iridescent confetti. Roofs were torn away. Many in the city lost power.

In Eason's home, no power was lost, no windows broken. Instead, he woke just shortly after Ike arrived, not from the storm, but from a faint, animal cry that crept under his door. He lay in his bed, certain that he was hearing things in the rain. It was pouring down diagonally, bleating against his window as if asking to be let in. He wondered if their shitty townhome could survive the storm—a part of him hoped that it would not and that Ike would take with it this poor excuse for a house, their poor excuse for a family. All of their misery, washed away in an instant.

The animal sound came again. He slipped from his bed and opened the door.

He found her at the bottom of the stairs, bent over the banister, the skunk vine curling out from the crease her body made, like it was growing out of her. He ran to her, his clumsy feet tumbling down the steps, and turned on the lights.

"Hurts," she said.

He nodded, slinging her arm over his bony shoulder, and walked the two of them to the front door. At the entryway closet, he rifled through her purse, which held her ID and insurance cards. They stumbled out into the yard as a massive streak of lightning cracked open the sky, lifting the entire house from darkness, and for a brief moment, he could see all the good it once held—his father, helping him with math homework; his mother, happily chattering as she set dinner on the table; Faye, chasing him around the sofa—but then it was over and the house was dark again, and all he could see was his father, leaving; his mother, unspeaking; his sister, leaving, too; and him, the loneliest creature in the world.

He helped Faye into the car, trying and failing to shield her from the downpour. In moments like these, he could only think of the irrational superstitions their mother told them when he was young: how being wet in air conditioning would cause sickness and allow the demon to further infiltrate the body, and even though he knew that this was not how diseases worked, he kept the AC off so that Faye would be okay. He turned on the windshield wipers to maximum speed, but one of them kept getting stuck in the middle of the glass, making a sickening squelch as it dragged across and left rainwater in its wake.

Next to him, Faye groaned, clutching her belly. There was no time to think about the windshield wipers, nor the fact that he had only driven a few times before, around a Walmart parking lot while his dad supervised. He backed out of the driveway, nearly swerving into the trash can, and sped down the street, rain hounding them through the roof of the car. The main road to the hospital, which was only fifteen minutes away, had flooded, so he diverged and shot for 90. By now, rain overpowered the car, the one windshield wiper swiping madly without much effect. It was difficult to see. He hunched over the steering wheel. Faye's hands were balled up into fists, the strings in her neck tight and visible. He had never seen her like this before, not when their father left and not even when their mother's abuse started. But now, there was some insurmountable force tugging her down, to hell, and the worst part was that there was nothing he could do to stop it. He turned the radio on, hoping it would provide some relief, but every channel was glued to the storm.

"Is it bad?" he wanted to know. "Is it the baby?"

"I don't know," she said. She kept saying it, and every time it frightened him more.

There was a turn ahead. Eason knew the way from there, the local roads and neighborhoods that he could take to the hospital. He veered to the left at the last second and barreled into the turn, the rear of the car peeling out slightly as its tires, the old, useless things, hydroplaned along the surface of the road. But their grip stayed true and he managed to straighten the car out again.

"Almost there," he said, more to himself than Faye. The road ahead was empty. He bolted his foot to the accelerator pedal.

That was when, for the second time, he felt the tires slip out from underneath him. He feathered the brakes and guided the steering wheel to the right, then to the left, trying to correct as his father told him to, but there was too much water on the ground and those goddamn tires had not been changed since his father left and now the car was sliding and he was struggling to keep control and next to them a Chevy came out of nowhere, slamming into them, dragging them around and around until he saw the guardrail materialize and the airbags pop out like birthday balloons, the final and most important explosion in a lifetime of explosions, and then it was just the smell of engine fuel and smoke and the insistent drill of rain on the roof, the one windshield wiper still waving to and fro.

It took him a moment to come to. Then adrenaline kicked in, refueling his shocked muscles into action. They still needed to get to the hospital.

He turned to his sister. She leaned forward, held aloft by the seat belt. He wondered why her side of the car looked so different from his. Then, he realized: Her airbag had not deployed.

He said her name. Not the name their parents had given her, the name of the famous Cantopop singer she had been modeled after, but the name that only he could use for only her: *Jie*. He was five and running after her like a bum beetle—*Jie*—he was seven and searching for her hand, into which he needed to deposit newly found treasures—*Jie*—he was twelve and waiting for her car to pull up to the pickup at school, and he could not wait to tell her about the poem he had written in English class, an acrostic of her name.

Somewhere, a siren wailed. Other cars had stopped around them; a man was running over, drenched by the rain, his arms waving over his head. *Jie*. He was fifteen and trapped in a car, screaming her name over and over again, knowing that she could not answer to it anymore and maybe that was why he screamed her name so hard, for so long, even after they got the door open and pulled him out, because he knew that after that day, he would never have a reason to speak such a name again for as long as he lived.

MINNIE

According to Ladybeth42, The Hellians had recently been contacted by an anonymous source via email. The source claimed that they were a former employee of BabyGold Records, the label under which the boys were signed. They had something big—possibly career-ending—about the band and the BabyGold Records CEO, and would The Hellians like to know about it? If so, all the source required was a cool $50,000 and the information was theirs.

The money was raised in a matter of hours; $50,000 was nothing compared to the titanic responsibility they owed the boys, Ladybeth reiterated to Minnie. They did not want this information falling into the wrong hands. Better to keep it safe with those who loved the boys most. Plus, the source had sent undeniable proof that they were indeed a former employee—one who had resided in the record label's innermost circle. The Hellians wired the money and an hour later, they had their information.

According to the source, the CEO had planned to blackmail Halo with information that would destroy his career if ever made public. What that information was exactly, Ladybeth would not tell her. Not yet, at least. But it was clear: The boys had to be warned of the label's plan, and that was where Minnie came in.

MinnieTheGreat: but why are they blackmailing him?
Ladybeth42: Isn't it obvious? They don't want Halo and Jelly to be together. They need to control the narrative, and the only way they can do it is by using Halo's past against him.

Yes, it all made sense to Minnie. Or did it? She could not even be sure anymore—it was all so much, and so fast. But even so, she knew that Ladybeth was right: No matter the truth, the boys' safety would always have to come first.

At a twenty-four-hour diner two blocks from their hotel, she tells Anna everything. Anna, who does her best to maintain a neutral expression during the story. Anna, who places her head in her hands and shakes it back and forth when Minnie is finished. "You've been talking to a stranger online all this time?"

"Not a stranger," Minnie says, hurt by the implication. "Her name is Ladybeth and she's my friend."

"Oh, I'm sorry," Anna says. She does not hide her sarcasm, which stings even more. "Do you know anything else about Ladybeth? What's her age? Where does she live?"

Minnie does not have an answer for her. Such details had been trivial when it was just her and Ladybeth; their connection of loving the boys was deeper than age or location or the boring details of daily life. But Anna's questions plant a feeling Minnie has not yet allowed herself to entertain: doubt. What was real and what was not? This diner, its ripped leather booths, the caustic glare of the fluorescent lighting: real. Anna, Anna's frown, Anna's concerned eyes: real. She tries to conjure Ladybeth then and for once she cannot do it, cannot place her within this diner and its very real occupants. Instead, Ladybeth, formless, faceless, blows through her and before Minnie can reach out to stop her, begins to fade, growing more translucent with each second.

The waitress arrives with their food. Minnie stares at the cinnamon roll she ordered, dough sagging under the weight of the stale icing. Ten hours have passed since the chocolate croissant at the café across from the museum, but that memory feels like it no longer belongs to her.

"So this group—Ladybeth42 wanted you to warn him about the record label's plans to blackmail him—and it was something to do with his sister?"

"I guess." The shame of the encounter burns through her. She wishes the lights were not so bright. "I didn't think he would react like that. It just made him so angry, and sad."

Anna takes a bite of her huevos rancheros, leaving behind a stain of red oil on the plate. "I can't pretend to understand," she says, "but I do know that it doesn't help to dwell on it. He's not a real person that you personally know. He's a celebrity. They're used to this kind of stuff."

Minnie begins to cry. It is the last thing she wants to do—show weakness in front of Anna—but everything about the past few hours, from the rage in Halo's voice to the sad cinnamon roll before her, has made this day feel like the last of her life. Whatever special relationship she had with Halo is ruined, and it is all her fault.

"Hey," Anna says, looking both disarmed and concerned. Minnie can tell that people do not often cry in front of her. "It's okay, all right? I'm sure this is just another day on the job for them. And if you're worried about the interview for the zine, I actually think this was the best thing that could have happened. You can pivot to write about the online forum, the botched interview, all of it—"

"It's not that," Minnie wails. At the counter, their waitress raises her eyebrows. "I ruined everything. You don't understand. The boys will never love me again."

Anna stops chewing. She sets her fork down and reaches across the table for Minnie's hand. "I hate to break it to you," she says, her tone uncharacteristically soft. "They never loved you. I mean, they love you as a fan, sure, but even then, it's an illusion. They make you think they love you because that's what they're supposed to do. That's their job."

It is too much for her to hear. It is too close to what she knows is the truth—has been the truth—all along. Still, she refuses. "You're wrong," she says, her body shooting up. "You think you know everything just because you wear black and make art no one will ever look at, but you're just as clueless as the rest of us and you're not better than me or anyone else."

She storms out of the diner. The boys have been there for her through it all. They carried her past the horror of Clark, helped her see the reality of who Nate really was. They propelled her forward and brought her a community of new friends. And, they made her believe in herself again. If that is not love, then what is?

She stands outside the diner, watching eighteen-wheelers roll along on the interstate. The night is heavy with dew. She raises her wrist to her nose and inhales the perfume that Ladybeth42 gifted her, surrounding herself once again with Halo's scent. The strongest notes have faded by now; only a sickly peach lingers. *It does not smell like him anymore*, she thinks miserably. Nor does it smell like her.

The door dings. The perfume disappears, replaced by Anna's scent of hemp and spice. It is strong, freshly applied. She hears Anna clear her throat. The cautious weight of her, stepping forward to stand behind Minnie.

"I'm sorry," Anna says. Minnie hates the tenderness in her voice. She wants to turn around and scream in Anna's face, make her feel the despair that she feels, but all she can do is keep watching the interstate, wishing that she were a passenger on one of those eighteen-wheelers. "I know they make you happy. But you can't forget the real world. You're here, with me and Akash and everyone at the zine and your parents and even your shitty ex-boyfriend. You're here, with us. Not with them. They're not real. We're real. And so are you."

She wraps her arms around Minnie, who resists at first. She wants to hit Anna, to tear herself away, to dissolve into a million pieces and then, maybe then, she will find a way to repair all of this, to repair herself, to have never entered that bathroom with Clark or gone to Nate's party or said yes when he asked if she wanted to go on that date. She will simply float along in the atmosphere, and it will just be her and the boys, forever. But Anna squeezes her, those stringy arms shockingly strong, her smell working like a trance, until she cannot help but let herself go limp and be held.

"We're all here, Minnie," Anna is saying. "Be here, too."

Back at the hotel, the clock on the wall reads 3:50 A.M., which seems wrong; it would not surprise Minnie if centuries had flown by between the morning and now. In the lobby, she tells Anna to go up to the room without her—there is something she needs to do first.

"Are you sure?" Anna says. She looks reluctant to leave Minnie alone. "I'll wait for you."

"It's okay, really. I'm much better now. I'll be up in a bit."

Anna nods and steps inside the elevator. Minnie waits until the doors close. She then walks to the front desk, where she retrieves a keycard for the business center. She walks through the lobby, past the nook for the complimentary continental breakfast and the sad fitness room, with its broken treadmill and mismatched dumbbells, until she reaches the business center, where she swipes the card to unlock the door.

There is one computer inside. Minnie sits and logs on to the internet, typing the familiar address into the browser. The computer is slow, perhaps a thousand years old. Minnie watches as the loading bar crawls forward, every increment amplifying the drum of her heart.

The page finally loads. The layout of The Heaven, its tables and frames and the soft, comfortable palette of blue and white, is all there. And Ladybeth42 is there, too, just as she said she would be. What did she tell her family, on a night like tonight? Did she put her kids to bed, kiss her husband goodnight, then sit in front of the laptop waiting for Minnie to come? Of course, this is just the Ladybeth42 that Minnie has made up in her head—she does not know if the person on the other end of the screen has children or if she is married. She does not even know what the 42 in her name stands for. Everything they ever talked about was related to the boys or Minnie. She had thought this was a hallmark of Ladybeth42's friendship, a woman who was mature and patient and receptive to hearing the woes of an eighteen-year-old girl. But now Minnie cannot stop remembering the rage in Halo's face, and she also cannot stop placing Ladybeth42 in that very same roiling contempt. After all, if not for Ladybeth42, she would never have said what she said to Halo.

Ladybeth42: How did it go?!

MinnieTheGreat: It was amazing.

MinnieTheGreat: The concert was beyond anything I could have ever imagined. The boys were so REAL.

Ladybeth42: I'm so envious! I can't wait to see them live one day.

Ladybeth42: Did you get to meet them aftewards?!

MinnieTheGreat: I did.

Ladybeth42: Oh m goodness!

Ladybeth42: Tell me everything!

MinnieTheGreat: They're even more beautiful up close. Minwoo has the kindest eyes, and Denim is just as cute and funny as he comes across in interviews. Jelly was an angel, of course. And Halo . . . he was everything.

Ladybeth42: I can't believe it . . . I really cant believe it!

Ladybeth42: So?

Ladybeth42: Did you do it?! did you give Halo the message?

MinnieTheGreat: I did.

Ladybeth42: !!!

Ladybeth42: i knew you could, Minnie!

Ladybeth42: i wish you could see me right now i'm smiling so big! =D

Ladybeth42: What did he say?!

MinnieTheGreat: He shocked me. I don't think anyone would have expected his reaction.

Ladybeth42: What?! Really?!

Ladybeth42: The Hellians will be SO curious to hear about this!

Ladybeth42: I think this will fianlly get you in Minnie. Youve done us such a huge favor.

Ladybeth42: So what did he say?!

MinnieTheGreat: I'll tell you. But first you have to tell me which hotel the boys are at and when their flight is for Denver.

Ladybeth42: Why is that?

MinnieTheGreat: I know you know. Since you seem to know everything about the boys.

MinnieTheGreat: And it's only fair. It's not even a big deal, really. I could probably find it out myself, but I wanted to ask you first, since we're friends.

Ladybeth42: I'm really not supposed to be sharing this kind of information.

Ladybeth42: It's privileged for Hellians only.

MinnieTheGreat: But I'm a Hellian now, right?

Ladybeth42: Ha!

Ladybeth42: Okay, you got me!

Ladybeth42: =)

Ladybeth42: They're at Hotel Zaza.

Ladybeth42: A few Hellians have been staking it out. One of the valet drivers confirmed it with us last week.

MinnieTheGreat: And their flight?

Ladybeth42: Their taking a 9:42am to Denver. Flight number AA1035.

Ladybeth42: Happy?

MinnieTheGreat: Yes.

MinnieTheGreat: Thank you.

Ladybeth42: Now tell me what Halo said when you warned him!

Ladybeth42: Did he confirm that the information is true?!

Ladybeth42: Did he already know?!

Ladybeth42: i bet he was measured because he has to be but also devastated inside.

Ladybeth42: and I bet Jelly immediatly went to comfort him because that's just who Jelly is. Our sweet little prince!!!

Ladybeth42: So whatdid he say?!

Ladybeth42: Minnie?

Ladybeth42: Hello?

Ladybeth42: Are you there?

Ladybeth42: Minnie?

POST #2803

Why should I be satisfied with the people in my life when the boys are the epitome of life?

EASON

His jaw is sore by the time he wakes up, a sign that he must have been grinding his teeth in the night. The room is still dark, but he can see the glow of daybreak edging past the corners of the curtain. He remembers closing his eyes and falling asleep, and yet it feels as if he has not slept for a long time. His bones ache.

He looks down, taking stock of himself. Red dots trail the side of his T-shirt. So he had been scratching in his sleep, too. Both the grinding and pawing were things he had not done since he was a child. He is older now, but clearly no different.

A sharp knock at the door. He remembers then the source of his regression: the girl from the meet and greet. She had said something about the record label and warning him, but he cannot recall about what. It had all been thrown aside when she mentioned Faye.

Another knock. He rises and pads to the front door. Cecile is outside, fully dressed in a crisp gray pantsuit, every strand of her blond hair straightened into line. Through her carefully applied makeup, however, he spots the violet grooves under her eyes. So she had not slept much, either.

She steps inside. He closes the door behind her, self-conscious of the used underwear hanging from the bathroom doorknob, the bunched-up socks spilling from his overturned boots. "I've been on the phone with The Duke," she says. "Someone's been talking."

"That's not reassuring," Eason says flatly. He imagines the Remoras pouring into his childhood bedroom, their greedy fingers clawing through every inch of his life. A violent desire to protect his home surges through him. "How do we stop them?"

"For now, it's business as usual. As far as we know, *Pop Impulse* is still the only outlet that knows about your sister. But if someone is leaking information, we're going to have to move faster than we thought."

"What does that mean? How much faster?"

"We're going to turn up the heat on the Jelly-Halo relationship. Keep all eyes on that and divert attention away. In the meantime, we've got our lawyers on the situation with your sister. We'll find a way to nail the fuckers in court for meddling with the private lives of our artists. We just need a little more time."

The rest of the team is already downstairs in the lobby when he finally leaves his room, Cecile leading the way. His bandmates are speaking animatedly but stop when they see Eason.

"Good sleep?"

"You don't have to handle me with kid gloves."

Minwoo looks at the others and nods. "There's a crowd outside. We didn't know if you'd be okay."

Through the glass windows at the front of the lobby, he sees them: Remoras and fans alike. He cannot seem to tell the difference anymore.

Julian turns to Cecile. "Can we leave through the back? Just for today, considering what happened last night?"

She shakes her head. "We agreed with *Pop Impulse* to do a pap shoot while leaving the hotel. And we're finalizing a brand ambassadorship with Cartier, so wear these and make sure they're visible."

Julian grimaces, but does not argue further. Eason accepts the thin silver bracelet from Cecile and clasps it on his wrist. He can already see tomorrow's headline: BOY BAND ROMANCE HEATS UP WITH MATCHING BRACELETS.

"Let's go." Cecile says.

The morning is windy. Gusts billow through the crowd, blowing up their bedazzled shirts and making them look like birds ruffling their plumage.

Minwoo and Colt walk out first, delivering a few friendly waves before entering their SUV. The door closes. *Safe*, Eason thinks. Julian goes next. When he reaches the middle of the walkway, he runs his fingers through his hair and the silver bangle gleams on his wrist. Eason hears the flutter of the paparazzi.

"Go," Cecile commands from behind him.

He walks outside, but stops when their screams reach him, forming a barrier that makes the air suddenly impassable. Cecile gives him a shove and he breaks through, stumbling a little. He adjusts the strap on his duffel bag, which hangs off his shoulder, and the sleeve of his shirt falls, revealing just enough of the silver bracelet. Again, the hungry clicks of paparazzi. *Pop Impulse* would have their headline tomorrow indeed.

"HALO, MARRY ME!!!!"

"MEETING YOU IS MY ONE DYING WISH!!!!"

"I'M LITERALLY DYING!!!"

For once, their words do not charm him. Do they hear what they are saying? Do they know how ridiculous they sound, talking about death and dying, when they have no idea—no idea at all? He looks into the crowd, searching for the culprit, wanting to make them understand.

That's when he sees her, standing at the front of the crowd, staring at him.

The girl.

But is it her? Hair as black as a crow, expression inscrutable for all its knowing, legs long enough to run down cracked sidewalks and a beaten track and hills, dips, fields and yes, even long enough to traverse the distance between his memory and his believing. Standing there, unmoving, pitched so clearly against the horde of bodies behind her. She watches him with those glittering eyes and he gazes back, needing to know: Is it her? Is it her? Is it her?

Jie? he hears himself call.

It all falls away then, the growing crowd, his bandmates waiting in the SUVs, Cecile still behind him. Not the concept of distance, not even air. There is only her and all the things she took with her. Before he can control himself, he is storming toward her, and he does not know what he will do when he gets there, but only that he must get to her, touch her face to feel its aliveness, look her head-on and say, *I'm sorry, I miss you, I'm sorry.*

"No—" Cecile hisses, but he no longer hears. It is very clear to him what he must do. Cecile tries to grab his arm, but he jerks it away—again, the bracelet reveals itself and the paparazzi click frantically. He pushes past the bodyguards, who look at each other, unsure if they should guard him from the fans or the fans from him. Soon he will reach her—she still has not moved, because she knows that he will come.

For the second time, someone tries to grab him, but he dodges it again, moving with the same quickness that his body knows so well. Over a year of training and dancing and staying light on his feet, and now he finally has a use for it. He is almost there. Around him the fans scream their delight—they cannot believe that their idol is actually coming, descending, that he will be so near. This is their chance to touch him, to profess their dying and undying everything, but she is not like the rest of them: She is still frozen, and now he finds it strange, that he should be this close and still she stands there without so much as a flicker, unspeaking and morose and haunted just like a ghost or a demon or his mother—

It happens too fast. A flash, then a blur of bodies. Hair. Hands. The smear of flesh. Someone is screaming behind him and then there is screaming all around him, but these screams are different. He hears sizzling—someone must be cooking nearby. Acrid smoke.

He turns. Cecile is kneeling over a figure on the ground, their face obscured by their hands. He does not understand—was someone hurt? But the fans are swarming now and the bodyguards, weighed down by their slow muscles, are lost to the torrent flooding in past the flimsy rope barricade, and he, too, is lost and useless, his body overwhelmed, his ribs struggling to expand for breath, and that is when he thinks, again: *It would be nice to die right here, taken by this kind of wave.*

"Help—"

Silver flashes in his periphery. He turns back to the figure on the ground. Their hands are at their sides now, revealing their face, but that is not where his eyes land. He is looking at what he missed the first time: a bracelet, the slanted inscription *Cartier* on the band.

But Julian was already in the car. Eason had seen him climb in. And yet Julian is here, on the ground—it is his face that Eason sees, but it is not the face he knows, for now Eason realizes the real source of the sizzling and smoke. Julian's face is burning, melting, the skin sliding off, and his head looks as if it has been cased in lava, his face lit from within, but there is nothing glorious or beautiful about this kind of light—there is only blood and rot and the white bark of bone, and this is where Eason collapses, this is where he goes limp and lets the wave of bodies tumble over him, hoping they will bury him forever—

One of the bodyguards yanks him up. He feels himself being pulled away, in the direction of the car. Above, the sky has finally rid itself of night, shifting from violet to bluing white. *Those are our colors*, he thinks dumbly. He props his head up, searching for the girl, but she is gone.

HER

funny to think a man could abandon a woman funnier to imagine a woman abandoning a man a woman would never a woman knows her place a woman is good and isn't that what i said when i walked to that little house at the end of the dirt path clay walls two rooms i walked through his village like a ghost they came out to watch strange girl trembling eyes never able to stay in one place never able to steady they watched me walk to his house and their hands came to their mouths and their mouths moved behind those hands and did they already know i wonder did they know then

the chickens were purring in the yard when i came they dug their heads in their chests like they knew the gate moaned when i walked through i knocked on the door three times he opened it looked down at me like he had never seen me hadn't fed from my mouth or run a finger down my spine or touched me in my sweetest place i looked at him the way i did when he promised himself to me i said do you remember do you know it's your child do you remember the kiss we shared like a fruit remember what sugar tastes like

she was in there i heard her voice she said invite her inside give her a cup of tea and i wanted none of those things not her kindness nor pity i just wanted him the way he had been promised to me

he did not let me in never saw what she looked like i knew she was beautiful he spoke to me in the yard a threatening low that made the core of me numb with fear and longing oh i am ashamed to say even as he stood there telling me he wanted nothing to do with me my body still arched for him a treacherous thing

happy he said i am happy

the lake behind his house is nice and cool it is summer here but the water keeps its temperature i sit by the water and i can hear them inside they will have a baby soon i look at my own swollen belly it knows neither of us are wanted the rocks next to the lake are big but not too heavy that i might tie my arms to them my ankles bruised from all that walking so much walking to find him now i don't have to walk anymore i can sit in this lake and rest

Funny to think a husband could abandon his wife, funnier to imagine a wife abandoning her husband. A wife would never. A wife knows her place, a wife is good. Isn't that what I said when I drove to his office, that flat concrete monster on the outskirts of Houston with a ravine in the back? That's where he told me he saw two alligators after a rainstorm. Why didn't they come after you? I asked him. They know they could never get me, is what he said.

I walked through his office like a ghost. Everyone came out of their cubicles to watch me: this strange woman with eyes that had been crying for days. They watched me walk and their hands came to their mouths and their mouths moved behind those hands. I met you all I wanted to say. I met you at the potluck and the company offsite and when he won employee of the month you shook my hand. You said *What's Ed doing with a beautiful wife like you?* You clapped him on the back and we all laughed but none of you will look at me now because you know.

Where is she, I said.

Let's go outside, you said.

Where is she.

Now is not the time.

Was she the one in the red blouse at the potluck, too many buttons undone? Was she the one who embraced us both at the offsite but held on to you a little longer? Was she the one who sent you home with hand lotion saying *Your wife will like this?*

Where is she?

I still do not know. At least if I knew I could have something to hate, but I don't know what she looks like, the color of her hair, or how long her legs are or the shape of her mouth. All these things you do know.

You have come to know so well. I sit in the dark of what was once our bedroom. I imagine her face. Every day a new face, every day she is more beautiful, every day I grow uglier.

But the suanming xiansheng tells me I have a good face. Good, but troubled. He says I should not hate you or her. It is beyond any of our control. He tells me there is a way to bring you back and end the pain. He is a good man, the suanming xiansheng. I listen.

How weird to think a dad abandoning his family could cause a mom to abandon it, too. One year ago this was a happy home. Today when I step inside, I could whisper and my voice would travel out the back door in a second for all the emptiness here.

Sometimes I press my ear to her door and I listen. My cheek flush against the wood, I can't help but stare at the wall next to the door, the one marked up with our heights. Once, I was as tall as where my waist is now. My little brother's marks are less predictable; one year he was down by the doorknob, the next year he was at my chest. A few more years and his marks on the wall will pass mine, and then his marks will be the only things on this wall, because I'll have erased all of mine before I'm gone.

I hear her in there, her voice a low murmur. She's on the phone again and she's talking to a man, the scammer who takes all her money. I dig my ear into the wood and I swear I can make out the syllable of my name. I heard a story once, one of those old Chinese ghost stories. A man sleeps with a pretty girl, only to discover that the girl is a ghoul with painted skin. The ghoul tears his heart out. His poor wife does things, terrible, disgusting things, to save him, and in the end I think she succeeds. She puts his heart back inside and presses the wound together and he comes back to life.

I think this is the story that man has been telling her.

Once when I was at her door, she must have known, because she opened it as my ear was still pressed there. I almost fell, but I shot my arms out and steadied myself against her. I hadn't touched her for so long, I hadn't meant to. It was a reflex. We looked at each other, surprised. Me, by how delicate her shoulders felt in my hands, how I had forgotten that she was a small woman for the bigness of her rage. Her, by the fact that I dared touch her at all. She used to hug me every night before bed when I was a kid. I stopped letting her sometime in middle school, and I don't think either of us knew on that night that it would be the last time either of us touched and it didn't hurt. Except for this one time, when I stopped myself from falling by bracing against her body.

The world stopped. It's stupid to say, but it's true. We looked at each other, my hands on her shoulders, and it was like she knew that this was all bogus and the curse wasn't real and the demon comes from a stupid ghost story and she had to stop, all of this had to stop. If not for me, then for Eason.

But she shook me off and her eyes narrowed again.

Hello? I heard someone say from inside the room. I tried to see where the voice was coming from, but it was so dark. *Are you still there?*

MINNIE

When the police ask for witnesses, she is the first to volunteer. The boys leave in a whirl of ambulances and the hotel is roped off with yellow tape, pushing those who remain under a lone oak tree. It is here that they take her statement.

"What happened?" they ask. Mustachioed men, one through three. Their eyes follow her as if afraid she might change into a wolf. "What did you see?"

"I'm not sure," she says. She is surprised she can be so calm. "We were waiting for the boys. They took—"

"Hold on," mustache one says. "When you say *boys*, you mean the band?"

"The band, yes."

He scribbles in his notepad. He asks her to continue.

"It took them a while to come out, but then they did. And when Halo came—"

"That's Mister Chen?"

She falters. The name sounds ugly in this officer's mouth, turning Halo ordinary and earthbound when he is anything but. "Yes. He started walking this way and everyone went crazy. His manager tried to get him to go back, but he kept coming. And Jelly—"

"His bandmate, Mister Lý?"

"Yes," she says. "Please stop interrupting me. It's making it hard to remember."

"We have to make sure we get everything straight," the mustaches tell her.

"Jelly got out to help, but they were too close to us. When they were about an arm's length away, someone threw something and it hit Jelly in the face."

"Who was it? Did you see?"

"It was too fast. They ran away."

The mustaches jot her words down on their flimsy notepads. The pages rustle in the wind.

"That's all I saw," Minnie tells them. "But there's something else you should know."

Earlier that morning, Minnie's cell phone vibrated under her pillow, sending a rumble through her brain. She awoke, expecting an earthquake, but the room was dark and orderly, no sign of disruption but for her own pounding heart. She turned off the vibrating alarm and slipped out from beneath the covers, already dressed. In the other bed, Anna's sleeping figure rose and fell peacefully like a buoy in the ocean. Looking at her, Minnie wondered if she should stay. *Be here*, Anna had told her.

I will be, she thought as she watched Anna sleep. *But there's something I have to do first.*

During the car ride to the boys' hotel, it dawned on her that Ladybeth42 could have lied about where they were staying. It would be a shame if so—the cab fare had breached thirty dollars by mile four. But when they pulled up to Hotel Zaza, Minnie knew that Ladybeth42 had not lied: There was already a group of fans outside, waiting for the boys. Minnie paid for the ride with all the cash she had, minus fifty cents, which the driver begrudgingly waived, and joined the group. It was six o'clock, the sun just beginning its ascent. Soon, Minnie thought, she and the rest of the group would be baking on the asphalt. She hoped the boys would hurry.

She had gone with the intention of apologizing to Halo, but now that she was here, she did not know what she would say nor how she would get close to him again. Still, she had to try. It did not matter if there was a secret group with inner access to the boys; it did not matter if they hoarded pictures and traded information—her relationship with the boys, with Halo, had changed because of them, but it was not yet forfeit. She was there to recover the right to love the boys on her own terms.

It was nearly seven when the boys appeared. By then, the group outside had tripled in size. Minnie tried to place herself in a visible spot. Some in the group were aggressive, shoving their way to the front with cameras despite the protestations of those who had been waiting longer. It was a jarring difference from the energy of the fans at the concert—this group had come to feed at the feet of their idols, and they would resort to ugliness if it came to that. Somehow, Minnie managed to remain in place. She remembered a trick her father taught her when she was younger, about keeping her weight balanced between both feet and forming a small cage around her torso with her arms. Miraculously, it worked. For all the bucking and colliding, she held steady.

The bodyguards were the first to show. Then, a stream of the boys' entourage, the managers, stylists, choreographers, and others she recognized from paparazzi photos and behind-the-scenes videos. Minwoo emerged next, sporting a black leather bag and opaque sunglasses. The crowd surged forward, demanding acknowledgment; he gave them back a small wave. Second was Denim, who threw a thumbs-up before joining Minwoo in the first SUV. The group around Minnie began pushing again, incensed by the proximity of the boys. Minnie stayed in place, but only just.

Jelly came next. At the sight of him, the crowd lurched like a ship thrust by a big wave. Someone behind Minnie screamed his name in a bloodcurdling loop. He glanced up in the direction of the noise, and Minnie could see his face from beneath the hat he wore. He looked exhausted.

Her heart was beating hard now, for she knew what came next. So did everyone around her.

"Where's Halo?"

"Halo's next."

"Oh my god, I'm going to die when I see him."

The doors slid open again.

He was there, her Halo. As devastating and arresting as the first time she saw him in that grainy video all those months ago, when she understood: *This* is what love is. The very same Halo who had accompanied her, walked side by side with her throughout it all. After everything that happened, she felt it more than ever: She could not bear to live without his forgiveness.

He took a step forward, emerging from the sliding doors of the hotel lobby. Upon seeing him, the crowd began to thrash. Minnie forced her elbows out, dulled to hurting the people around her. She needed to stay here—she needed Halo to see her. He was moving toward the car now, the blond manager behind him urging him to go faster. Soon, very soon, he would disappear into the SUV to join Jelly and she would miss her chance.

She heard it then: a sound so strange and foreign that she could not be sure if it was she who produced it. It almost sounded like a song. But it was sharp enough, needling enough. A sound that originated from deep within, as if the being who produced it had been locked up, snuffed out and beaten down, until there was nothing left but this sound.

He looked over and froze, recognition passing over his face. She beheld his expression—there was anger there, but also confusion, and hurt. She tried to communicate to him, with her eyes, that she was here to say sorry.

It worked. He began walking to her. The fans dissolved into madness as he neared, yipping and clawing and crying, but Minnie barely registered them. He stopped in front of her. He was close enough to touch. She gazed into his eyes and she saw the truth of his existence, free from lights, from smoke, from camera filters and the magic of distance. It was him, just him in broad day, a foot away, face naked and bare with all its human features. She saw, for the first time, the reality: that there could be lines on such a face as his, that there could be small craters, veins like fine threads, shadows under the eyes and crepe-like creases in the brow. That he could be real, as real as she.

What she had always known was indeed true: He *had* been made for her. Made, crafted, and perfected into the idol of her dreams. All this time, she believed that she knew him, that she was close to him, but *this* was real closeness—his face in front of hers, the flare of his nostrils as he breathed in and out. His existence, which she could see etched along every curve of his tired face, was just as flawed and human as hers. He had been made for her, but he was not hers to keep. He never was.

What happened next was too fast for her to see, cascading in a series of events that would dog her for years. When she least expected it, she would be reminded of an image or a sound or a smell, and that was when she would remember: First, the blond manager reached out to yank Halo away. Second, the fans roared at her to stop. Third, Jelly's face appeared. Sweet, sylphlike Jelly. Then, just as quickly as he came, Jelly was on the ground. That was when the sounds overtook the rest of her memories: Jelly's screams, his once-silver voice cracking, as if someone were ripping him down the middle. The crowd was screaming, too, bodies toppling as the bodyguards razed those nearest. When Minnie looked up again, Halo was gone. He had never been so far away.

She does not tell the police officers all of this, of course. They do not need to know, for how could they understand? How could anyone?

Once back in the Austin city limits, Anna does not turn down Whitis Avenue to Minnie's dorm. Instead she drives east, away from campus, to a one-bedroom bungalow on the edge of Cherrywood. Akash waits at the front door, a paper bag of takeout in his hands. Minnie, who has not eaten since the diner, recognizes the scent of fish sauce and fried eggs, and suddenly the only thing she can feel is hunger.

On instinct, she reaches for Akash, who pulls her into a hug. His body is warm and solid, a stable frame against which she is not afraid to place all her weight. He will not disappear. It is only after they separate that she realizes this is the first time they have touched.

Anna unlocks the door. Her house is a surprise: cozy, with woven blankets tumbling over the sofa, pillows on the floor, and knitted coasters strewn across the coffee table. Small figurines of animals with cartoonishly big eyes line the bookshelf.

Anna shrugs, noticing Minnie's gaze. "I like cute things. Make yourselves at home."

She pads to the kitchen. Minnie sits down on a tartan pouf and grabs the nearest pillow, a large plush Totoro. She places it in her lap, feeling somewhat fortified by its presence. Akash lays the food out on the coffee table, then sits on the couch, facing her. She cannot look at him. Somehow, it had been easier to touch him than to let him read the shame in her eyes.

"Anna told me what happened. Are you okay?"

"I'm okay," she says. "Really."

Anna emerges from the kitchen with a teapot and three mismatched cups dangling from her pinky. Minnie takes hers, grateful for the interruption. They sip their tea but do not touch the food.

Anna and Akash look at Minnie. Minnie looks at the floor.

"It's been all over the news," Akash says finally. "They're still looking for the person who did it."

"That's good. I hope they find them."

"They will," Anna says. "I'm just glad you didn't get hurt."

Minnie remembers Jelly's screams. His body, writhing on the ground like a common animal that had been shot down from high above. Higher than any of them could ever fathom. She takes a big gulp of tea, trying to drown the memory. "I know you're both wondering why I was there in the first place. I didn't do it, if that's what you're thinking."

"We would never think that," Akash says, sounding horrified.

"But why *were* you there?"

She sets her cup down on the ground and watches the liquid tremble from the impact of the landing. Just a little more force and everything inside would have spilled over. She knows that feeling well. "I wanted to apologize to Halo."

"Oh, Minnie," Anna says, but she sounds more concerned than annoyed. "I told you it doesn't matter. They probably don't even remember."

"It matters to me." She looks up to see them both staring at her. "I know you don't understand. But I had to make things go back to the way they were before."

Anna leans forward, her eyes scanning Minnie's, refusing to let them go this time. "And how were things, before?"

Minnie opens her mouth. *Happy*, she wants to say, because that was what she had been before all of this, when it was just her and the boys and no one else. But that is not true, either. They made her happy, yes, but she had also been sad, so sad, and lonely, too, and silenced and shamed and tossed aside. The boys made her *happy* because she had to be, because otherwise it would just be her and the secret she was forced to bear: all those red boa feathers scattered across the tile floor; Clark, zipping his pants back up and washing his hands in the sink; her, untouched, but never quite the same.

"Minnie?"

"I lied," she says. She looks at Akash. "When you asked if I was okay. I'm not okay. I haven't been okay for a long time."

It is here that she finally gives way. Here that the tears come. She lets them fall until they collect at her jaw, dripping onto the Totoro in her lap.

"I'm not okay," she says again. Not to Anna and Akash, because she knows that they heard the first time. To herself.

The two of them kneel down on the floor, bracing her from both sides. "We know, Minnie," Akash is saying. His hands reach for hers, and she grabs on. "We're not going anywhere."

POST #1

****** MOD NOTE: PLEASE READ ******

Out of respect for the events of the past 24 hours, we will be locking and archiving all posts. There will be one main post that we will continuously update with news of the attack on the boys and Jelly's condition. Please leave all your comments in that post [linked here]. Any off-topic comments will be deleted and the commenter banned.

As there is still an active investigation going on, please do not engage in speculation of any kind.

We recognize that this is a deeply troubling time for many of our members, and we encourage you to step away if you need to. Go outside, take a walk, get some fresh air. Reach out to a family member or a friend if you have to. We know you're all waiting for news, but remember to live your lives too.

There will be a thread to organize gifts and donations for the boys in the coming days. In the meantime, take care of yourselves.

EASON

Cecile books them a suite at a hotel near the hospital, which they refuse. "He's going to be in surgery for the next few days," she tells them. "Waiting at the hospital won't change anything."

Minwoo wants to take her up on it—for him, the hospital brings back bad memories. Colt gets antsy; he doesn't like the food. But Eason stays glued to his chair in the waiting room like a dog at his post. They are still a team, aren't they? They spend the first night there, accompanied by a muted television. When the news replays the incident, this time supplemented by the commentary of police officers, forensic experts, and even one of their bodyguards, Minwoo changes the channel. By now, the media has compiled a decent timeline of everything that happened, pieced together from dozens of pictures and videos submitted by those in the crowd. The scene looks strange to Eason from these new perspectives: He is in these videos, but he does not recognize himself. He strains to find the girl, but she does not appear in a single one.

The authorities determine it was nitric acid. Fortunately, whoever threw it had done so without much aim, sparing most of Julian's face but catching his left eye and brow bone. The acid took his skin, his hair, and half his sight. But he will be whole, for the most part. One eye is better than none, Colt reminds them, and they all agree, although no one feels good about it.

They are still searching for the person behind the attack. Some retired nobody detective appears on an entertainment news spot and implies that there could even be multiple people involved. The perpetrator ran off that day, but it will not be long now—hours after the attack, the detectives assigned to their case found an online message board where users frequently referenced throwing acid on Cecile. They were convinced that she was in love with Eason—he almost wants to laugh for how ludicrous it is. It begins to make sense: Cecile was only a step behind him that day. Julian was a surprise. The attack had never been meant for him, but still he caught it.

For the emotional distress of the moment, BabyGold Records postpones their remaining concerts for a month.

By the second day, the three of them concede and spend the night at the hotel. It feels wrong, but Eason manages to eke out a few hours of sleep before daylight. When he makes his way down to the lobby, he sees The Duke in a large armchair next to the electric fireplace. It is strange to see him alone, no Cecile or bodyguards or assistants buzzing about. Just him and his loose hemp shirt, his tanned leather thongs.

"You're up." He motions to the armchair next to him. Today, his hair is tied into a small bun that buttons at the back of his head. "Join me for a coffee."

"I don't drink coffee."

"Tea, then." The Duke waves to a server and the tea arrives quickly. Eason accepts it, but does not drink. He needs to go to the hospital, not sit here taking tea in front of a fake fireplace. But The Duke gives no indication that he plans on moving, so Eason stays, too. When he next speaks, his voice is soft, which makes his question feel even worse. "Why couldn't you just go to the car?"

He had not told Cecile, nor Minwoo nor Colt what caused him to walk toward the fans: that he thought he saw the girl, Faye, his mother, the demon, or all of them, combined. But what use, hiding it after everything that happened? "I thought I saw someone," he says. "The girl at the meet and greet who knew about my sister."

"And was she the one who threw the acid?"

"No." Now that the stopper holding him has been removed, he wants to tell The Duke everything. "It was my mother. She did it all to punish me—she leaked the story to *Pop Impulse* and she threw the acid and she's been following me, she won't stop until I come home, she—"

"It wasn't your mother."

"You don't get it." His voice cracks, breaking from the need to make The Duke understand. "I see her in the comments of our videos all the time threatening to tell everyone about what happened—*what Eason did.*"

The Duke watches him, amused. "*I* told Brooks to leak the story. What I didn't expect is that he'd turn around and sell that information to some message board for a quick payday."

Eason stares at him, his brain slow and heavy. All he can say is "but" and "I don't." Futile words.

"And while we're on the subject of your mother, you should know that she had a stroke last fall and another one this year. I doubt she has the strength or mental faculties to do all the things you're saying she did."

"Stroke?" Eason says dumbly. And then, coming to, narrows his eyes. "How do you know?"

"Because we've been taking care of her as of a few months ago," The Duke says. "After the second stroke, she needed at-home care and a full-time, live-in nurse. Who do you think has been paying for that? Certainly not her, based on what I've seen of her finances. A very gullible, irresponsible woman, your mother."

"You've been—I don't—"

"In exchange," The Duke says, speaking over him, "she's agreed to leave you alone."

Eason gapes, mouth opening and closing like a stupid fish.

"Well?" The Duke's face stretches into a plastic smile. "I told you I would protect you."

It can't be real, Eason thinks. It can't be so easy. "And that's why you're here? To tell me this?"

The Duke picks up his coffee. He inspects the perimeter of the cup's mouth, then takes a long, slow sip from it, not for the coffee, but to hold Eason in abeyance. When he is finished, he sets the cup down before speaking. "I'm here because I want to know if you'd like to keep going."

"But we can't tour after this. Julian's in the hospital."

The Duke leans forward. He looks at Eason straight on, lashes the same yellow as his hair. "Julian won't be a part of HOURglass anymore. From now on, it will just be the three of you."

All those months spent training together, the ecstasy and the misery. They are a team. They have always been a team. "No, we can't. He'll get better."

The Duke laughs. "It'll take nearly a year for him to make a full recovery. We're already losing money just by postponing for a month. And even when he is *better*, do you think people will be comfortable seeing a mangled man performing and dancing in front of them? Don't you think it cruel?"

Eason is silent. No, he had not thought about it like that. "Have you talked to Minwoo and Colt about it?"

"They both agreed it was for the best."

Eason looks down at his feet. "It doesn't feel right. We need Julian."

"I'm going to let you in on a little secret," The Duke says, his eyes flashing. "This word you're using, *need*? We don't *need*. I've got a dozen boys in training who are willing to work harder and be hungrier than any of you, and they would trade places in an instant. They would kill to be where you are now. So no, we do not *need* Julian." He pauses, sitting back. "But we do need you."

"Me?"

"The nature of celebrity is changing," The Duke says. "People don't want their idols to feel like unreachable gods anymore. People want their idols to feel real. They want to feel close to them. And nothing is more real right now than you. No one has suffered and been more fallible than you."

Faye was pronounced dead at the scene.

"She's pregnant," he told the EMTs when they arrived. It was all he could say.

The paramedic had white hair and a kind face. He got the sense that she had been doing this her whole life, and it made him angry, how calm she was. For her, this was another day on the job. "Do you know how far along she was?"

"Five months," he said. "Is the baby—?"

"We're going to do everything we can," the paramedic assured him. She stood and mouthed something to her colleague, who unbuckled Faye and carried her from the car seat. Eason watched. He was certain that at any moment, his sister would come to and open her eyes, just as she did when they played the demon hunting game. He should have plucked a hair from her head. She would wink and laugh and say, "I'm fine," and then they would be on their way. But she did not move. She remained limp, eyes closed, the blood on her forehead now the color of dark rust.

"So that girl was right," he says now. "You've always known. You were using me."

"Like I told you back then," The Duke says. "You're only here because of me."

"But why leak it?"

"I knew you were hungry from that first day of auditions. What I didn't know was how far you were willing to go. Here's what you need to understand: It was never going to be the four of you. People don't want a band—they want a star. I thought it would be you or Julian, so I put it to the test. A shame about Julian, really. But it worked, didn't it? You're the hottest you've ever been."

He had been right about The Duke. Those eyes had followed him ever since that first day of practice and they had seen what he himself had tried to deny for so long: He had always been a selfish, desperate, angry thing. But The Duke was not rejecting him for it. No, this was different.

"You think people will still love me, knowing what I did?"

"They already love you the most," The Duke says. He almost sounds proud. "But I can make them love you even more. This thing with your sister? It's never going away. If it's not *Pop Impulse* now, it'll be someone else later. But as long as you're with me, I can protect you. We choose when and how we make it public. And I promise you, they will love you even more when we do."

He pulls out his cell phone, from which he begins responding to the myriad notifications that had arrived during their conversation. Eason understands that the negotiation—if there ever was one—is over.

His mother believed the curse only went after the women in the family and Faye did not believe it existed to begin with. Both of them were wrong. He can see it now. The curse was real and it had jumped and jumped and jumped, and when it had no one left, it chose him, living in his bones, cursing him with the anguish and vengefulness of a century's worth of tears. That was why he could never quite get it right, why he caused destruction wherever he went. His failure to protect Faye, his jealousy and indecision and betrayal. The utter need that coursed through him. What he feared all this time—and what he rejected—was not his mother. It was him. It had always been him.

"Is there someone we can call?" the paramedic had asked him.

Faye had been that someone, but they were putting her on a stretcher and wheeling her away. "There's no one at all."

But now The Duke is offering a way out. Protection and, one day, freedom. He allows himself to imagine it: The wretched truth of who he is would no longer be a secret, but a story that people could grow to understand, perhaps even love.

"At the end of this," he asks, "is there beauty?"

The Duke looks up from his phone and smiles.

"More than you can ever know."

MINNIE

Five days after the concert, she receives a call from one of the officers she spoke with. "Miss Minnie Yang?" he wants to know.

"Yes," she tells him. "That's me."

The officer is calling all witnesses who gave statements, closing out the case. He wants her to know that they have caught the person who threw the acid. It was a premeditated attack, he tells her, planned by a group of individuals from an online message board. "Without your statement, we wouldn't have found them so quickly. Thank you."

She hangs up and sits, thinking. Then, she reaches for her laptop, which she has not opened since before the concert. Her browser is still open to The Heaven, but she feels none of the happiness she once did upon seeing it, just cold guilt. The message board is quiet by the looks of it—no new posts for the past few days. A once-bustling town, now inhabited by ghosts.

In the notification bar, she sees the familiar red jewel announcing that she has 100+ unread messages. The guilt in her stomach tightens. She takes a deep breath. Then, she clicks to unravel the messages.

The majority of them—108, to be exact—are from Ladybeth42. Minnie's eyes pass over the most recent one—*die you fcuking bitch*—and presses X to delete the entire chat. *You'll lose 8,467 messages*, The Heaven warns her. *Are you sure?*

It is easy to be angry with Ladybeth42. The woman is older (or so Minnie thinks—she still does not know for sure), she had been the one fully involved in the secret group, and she had been the one to lure Minnie in and use her loneliness for her own machinations. Easy to imagine an evil witch hunched over the computer screen in some dark cave, feeding Minnie poison over the course of several months.

But Minnie had clicked, hadn't she? She had viewed the pictures

Ladybeth42 sent. She had participated and she had consumed. Every picture of the boys, every narrative, every prickling feeling of hatred and suspicion toward the blond manager, every delusion she allowed herself to believe. She had been there, too, just as eager to eat the poison herself.

"Didn't you think the posts in the message board were alarming when you saw them?" the officer had asked her.

"You don't understand," she told him. "That was just the way everyone talked about the boys. It sounds crazy, I know. But that's just how we talked. It was normal."

No, she is not entirely innocent, but it is easier to see that now, standing on the other side, having also seen the consequences of what such "normal" has wrought. This time, there is nothing for her to mask her pain with or run away to. She is a house without its walls, an island with no water surrounding it. Maybe that is what she deserves. She will simply have to live with it.

Delete all messages in this chat? The Heaven asks.

Yes, she clicks. Delete all.

The last two messages are from HannahIsOurs18. Minnie still remembers their conversation from her first day on The Heaven, when they had exchanged messages detailing the loneliness of being a freshman and how hard it was to make friends. The new messages were sent to her nearly three weeks ago, but Minnie had missed them in the whirlwind of notifications from her chats with Ladybeth42.

hey, miss seeing you around the board, the first message says. *things have been weird here and i havent been comfortable with some of the things people have been doing, so i decided to leave. but i had so much fun talking to you and would love to keep in touch! heres my email—maybe one day we can meet up, since were both in texas* :)

Minnie stares at the message, a spring of softness and gratitude welling up inside her. She writes down Hannah's email address. For her final act, she navigates to the Settings tab of The Heaven and clicks DELETE ACCOUNT.

Are you sure? The Heaven implores. *We're sad to see you go.*

Yes, she taps several times. The request takes a moment to process. Then, the screen refreshes, and when it finally loads again, she finds herself back on the home page for The Heaven, only now, her username is gone.

The next time she sees Nate, it is a surprise. She is walking to class via the West Mall and Anna has just sent her something funny. She laughs and begins typing out a response, and when she looks up again, Nate is walking her way with a girl. It is Jillian, and Minnie knows it is Jillian before she even sees her face, but she does not feel shock or sadness or envy. She feels, instead, acceptance. The two of them walk with carefree synchronicity, deep in conversation—maybe about his short story, which had not appeared in the school journal as Minnie had expected, but online, in a new literary journal that Nate started himself. They look good together, Minnie thinks. So much better than she and Nate ever did. They pass Minnie without seeing her, and in that moment, Minnie knows that their lives have forever diverged. She allows herself to feel a clutch of grief, slight but potent, mourning the sweetness of that first encounter at the bookstore. She hopes that he and Jillian will be happy.

She keeps walking. She messages Anna back with a huge *L O L* and when she enters her next class, Poetics in the 1960s, she realizes: *This* is what college is all about. Her first time feeling and unfeeling heartbreak.

"We have a problem," Anna tells her that night. "We still need a lead story for our summer issue."

After the events in Houston, Minnie had decided to scrap the essay on the boys. Anna was understanding, but that left them with a hole in place of her story.

"It's my fault. I'll come up with something else."

"Are you sure?" Anna says, looking uncertain. Lately, she has taken to speaking about anything related to the boys in a hushed voice, as if worried that loud noise might conjure memories of what happened. "I would need it by the end of next week for the printers."

"I'm sure," Minnie says. "I already know what I want to write about."

"It's not about them, is it?"

"No," she says. "It's something I've been meaning to talk about for a long time."

When she gets back to her dorm, she goes straight for her laptop. The boys have just been spotted at the hospital where Jelly is being treated, and videos documenting the tragedy have already begun sprouting up all over the internet. *BOY BAND MARCHES ON IN THE FACE OF ACID ATTACK; FANS PRAISE HOURGLASS FOR THEIR STRENGTH; HOURGLASS' HALO SHEDS TEARS AS HE ARRIVES AT HOSPITAL.* Minnie does not watch. There is a more pressing matter at hand, something she desperately needs to say. She opens up her word processor and begins to type:

The first thing I noticed about Clark, she writes, *were his eyes.*

EASON

Julian gets out of surgery on the third day. On the fifth, they are allowed to see him. They tiptoe into the hospital room with flowers and a pre-approved basket of gifts from the fans, which feels ridiculous given the circumstances. Julian is propped up on a pillow, his scalp mummified by thick white bandages. There is a gauzy patch covering the spot where his left eye should be. It makes Eason's stomach turn, imagining the emptiness underneath.

"Hey Jules," Minwoo whispers. "The doctor said we could come in."

Julian's right hand raises weakly, then flops back down on the bed.

"You don't have to talk," Colt says. "We just wanted to see you."

"I'm okay," Julian croaks.

Eason sets the basket—filled with stuffed animals, candy, homemade candles—on the nightstand next to the bed. He gives his full concentration to this action, staring intently at the basket as if it is the only thing in the room. He does this because he cannot bring himself to look at Julian.

"What?" Julian says, noticing. "Do I look ugly?"

Eason laughs, more to dispel his own discomfort than anything. The truth, they all know, is that he does. "How are you feeling?"

"Tired. My head's foggy and my face hurts and half my vision's gone. But at least I'm alive, I guess."

"It could be worse," Minwoo agrees. "We're just glad you're okay."

An awkward silence follows. Eason remembers that The Duke already spoke to the others about continuing without Julian and they had said yes. He wonders if that is why they hold themselves at a distance, why they refuse to get closer.

Colt tries again. "How's the food here?"

"I wouldn't know. They're feeding it to me through a tube because I can't keep anything down."

Colt chuckles, but the sound is forced. "We brought you some gifts from the fans. Letters and cards and stuff. This is just the first batch. There's a ton more downstairs, but we didn't know if you wanted it all or not."

"That would be nice."

"I'll get them," Minwoo says suddenly. He walks past Eason on his way to the door. "Sorry," he whispers. "It's just too much."

Colt stands with his hands on his hips, inspecting the room. "The cards will be a nice way to liven everything up. It's kind of depressing in here, isn't it?"

"I guess," Julian says. "I can't really tell."

"Oh, right," Colt says awkwardly. "Sorry." Then, looking around, he shrugs. "It really is a lot of stuff. I should go help him carry everything."

He walks out of the room, too, leaving Eason alone.

"Am I really that horrible to look at?"

"No," Eason lies. "They just don't know what to do now." He waits, unsure if he should continue. "It's nice that you get a window, at least."

"That's what the nurse said. Apparently, patients recover faster with a window in their room."

"Lucky you," Eason says. He knows that his words must sound stilted. He walks over to the window and looks down. There is not much to see, just rows and rows of cars lined up in the parking lot, their multicolored hoods livid with the reflection of the Texas sun. From Julian's vantage point on the bed, though, all there is to see is sky.

"The Duke came by," Eason says finally, turning back around.

"I know."

"Did he come see you?"

"He did, but I wasn't awake yet. Cecile told me."

Eason looks down. "He wants us to keep going without you."

"I know," Julian says. "They said they'd leak the coke stuff and my eating disorder if I don't step away. I can handle a lot, but I don't think

I can handle that yet. Didn't I tell you? They don't actually care about us. It's always been about the money."

"Yeah."

"Are you thinking about saying yes?"

"I don't know. I don't know anything anymore. It feels wrong, not having you. What would you do, if you were me?"

Julian shifts in his bed, groaning from the effort. "It was always my dream to perform, Minwoo's to sing, and Colt's to be famous. But what about you?"

Eason turns away, a rising tide of guilt in his throat. "I didn't have dreams before this. But now, it feels like all I have."

Julian does not answer at first. Eason knows that he must be staring at him. "This deal we made with *Pop Impulse* wasn't because of me, was it?" he says finally. "It was because of you and whatever happened with your sister."

"Yes."

"And those pictures of me—that was just a cover, wasn't it? Ronald's people took them. He was just using them as collateral, in case I walked away."

"He needed everyone to think there was a scandal worth fighting against together," Eason says.

"I figured. I guess you told him about my eating stuff, too. Help me sit up, would you?"

The last thing he wants to do is get close to Julian again, to face him after admitting his betrayal. But he turns and obeys. Julian grabs on to his arm and pulls himself up, propping his head on the baseboard behind him. "Thanks," he says. "That's better. It's nice to get a different view."

"Do you hate me?"

Julian makes a noise somewhere between a laugh and a sigh. "I could never hate you, Eas. I think you already hate yourself enough for the both of us."

"I just don't know who I would be if I didn't have this. I don't want to go back to being who I was."

It is Julian who looks away this time, his good eye drifting over to the window. Eason wonders what it must be like, having half of what you knew taken away from you. But then again, he does already know such a feeling. He has been feeling it since Faye died.

"You know," Julian says after a moment, "I still remember our first few practices. When they showed us the choreography for 'Dying for You,' you looked like someone just told you you had to go to war."

Eason laughs and the sound brightens the room. "I was a really bad dancer. Still am."

"Hey," Julian says sternly. "After all the work I did with you? That hurts."

Levity. Jokes. This is what he wants. What he has missed. Funny, how it takes a cataclysmic event to sew up the torn seams of the past few weeks. "I'm sorry, you're right. You're the best teacher I ever had. Turned me into a damn prodigy."

"You weren't as bad as you think you were," Julian says, serious now. "You were just too in your head about it. Everyone thinks dancing is about being able to reproduce the choreography, but it's so much more than that. It's the way the moves live in your body. Where the weight is. How you stop or start time. The textures, the momentum, the suspense. It's not something you can learn just by copying. It's something you become, only after doing it for a while. But I think you know what I mean by now. You've gotten so much better, like you're finally letting go."

"Sometimes it still feels hard," Eason says. He is not sure if he is talking about dancing anymore.

"Remember the string? The one that holds you up and leads you into every move. You have to follow the string."

"You make it sound like I'm a marionette," Eason says. "What if I want to cut the string?"

Julian pauses, and it feels like the opening has closed over them once more. The room is dark again. "I can't tell you what to do with your life, Eason," he says. "I only know that HOURglass, Halo, The Duke can't fix whatever it is that's haunting you. You know that, too, right? The fans and the fame—they can't replace the thing you're missing. Because one day, they'll all leave you. Just look at me."

"You'll be okay," Eason says, even though the words feel empty. He hates that he is crying when he is not the one in the hospital bed. How weak he is, how very childish. But he cannot stop, either. "You'll make it out of this alive."

"I know," Julian says softly. "But will you?"

They held Faye's funeral at a small church down the street. The Ambroses organized and paid for it. They held his mother's hands and told her how sorry they were. Mrs. Ambrose's eyes welled with tears. Henry did not cry, but his jaw remained taut. He left the ceremony early and that was the last Eason saw of him.

His father came, too. He had expected his mother to rage and cry and beat her fists against his chest, but she did none of those things. When his father pulled her into his arms, she simply dissolved and wept quietly into the crook of his elbow, and for a moment, Eason felt a flicker of longing for his mother and father both, to be their son again. But he pushed the feeling aside and walked away. He had nothing to say to his father, even though he knew that Faye would not have wanted it that way.

The local paper did a quick write-up of the accident on page nine, in three paragraphs squared off by a box and placed in the corner. *Pregnant teen killed in car accident during Hurricane Ike; younger brother driving.* The baby did not survive. It was determined during the autopsy that he—for it was a he—had died hours before the accident.

After the funeral, things quieted down again. His father flew back to his new family in Virginia and the Ambroses went back to their nice neighborhood and Eason went home, where his mother spent her days on the phone with the suanming xiansheng. Once, he picked up the phone to eavesdrop on their conversation. *I can't help but think*, he heard his mother say, *the curse finally died with my girl.* The fortune teller seemed to agree. Perhaps, he said, the demon has finally eaten its fill.

In the weeks that followed, his mother became a restored version of herself. She cooked the kitchen to warmth, she hummed as she did laundry, she started an herb garden in the window. *We should both live well in your sister's place*, she told Eason. And it was all he could do not to spit back in her face: Is that why you beat her, why you cut her, why you could not let her live in peace? But he always stopped himself, for if he accused his mother, then he might as well accuse himself. Instead, he put his head down and washed dishes at the sushi restaurant where Faye used to work. For the next three years, he did not speak to his mother. Then, the day he turned eighteen, he walked out of that townhome with a backpack and all the money he had saved from the restaurant, and he did not return. Just like his father.

On a bench outside the hospital, he allows himself to sit, taking it all in. Today is one of the few days when the humidity has retreated, leaving behind a dry, crackling heat. On days like this, Faye would take him to the swimming pool near their house, where they spent hours jumping off the kiddie springboard, making shapes in midair that the other called out.

To his left, a family of five pushes an old woman in a wheelchair through the parking lot. She looks close to dying, Eason thinks. Like her bones are made of candy floss. A nurse rushes out to receive the woman, wheeling her inside. The family follows. One of the adults is crying.

Eason watches them, remembering the concrete structures that he, Faye, and Henry visited when they went to the museum in Marfa. If he stepped through one now, he would be an Eason who, in a faraway future, would be wheeling his much older mother the way this family is. He would have cared for her up to this very moment, and he would have loved her, forgiven her, and forgiven himself. But it is a stupid thought. His sister had been the one to show him those stones, but his sister is gone and he is the reason why. He is here, the same Eason as he ever was, but there *is* an alternate version of him out there, one he can still step into. It has been there all this time, waiting for his answer.

"Eason?" He turns and sees Minwoo standing just inside the sliding doors. "Julian's going to sleep soon. If you want to say bye."

"I do," he says. "Give me a sec."

"Okay." There is more Minwoo wants to say to him, he can tell, but that will come later. "I'll let him know you're coming up."

He watches Minwoo disappear back into the lobby. Then, he takes out his phone and calls Cecile.

2018

Minnie stands in the middle of the festival, newly graduated, body thrumming with the sound of music. A crowd the size of a small city moves in currents around her, flowing from stage to stage. She remains still, searching for one person.

"Who should we check out next?" Akash asks from beside her, poring over the festival schedule.

"Let's get a little bit of everything," she says, still scanning the crowd.

"I like that plan," Akash says. He folds up the schedule.

When she spots Hannah, she runs to meet her. The two hug. It has been months since they have seen each other, for Hannah recently moved to Dallas, a three-hour drive from Austin.

"This is Akash," she says when they release each other. "Akash, this is my friend Hannah."

"From online, right?" Akash says, extending his hand. "I've heard so much about you."

"Same," Hannah says. Her nails are painted candy pink and she has aquamarine braided into her hair. "Shall we go?"

The three of them merge into the crowd that flows toward the west end of Zilker Park. The sun is on its last breath, an orb of fierce orange holding on to the skyline. Nervous excitement descends over the festival, nightfall promising the big musical acts that everyone came to see. The three of them veer to the right just before the soundstage at American Express and lean against the fence, watching as an old rock band begins their set.

Akash looks back and reaches for her, knowing that tight spaces and loud noises still have the power to startle her. She squeezes his hand and gives him a smile, then releases it. He turns and begins nodding in time with the music. She watches his head bob, then his body join in, and she does not know why, but the sight of it makes her feel so completely happy.

"I have to pee," Hannah shouts apologetically. "I'll come right back."

"I'll go with you," she says. "I should pee, too."

They leave Akash, who promises to hold their spots, and duck through the crowd, toward the porta-potties. She grabs on to Hannah's shoulders as they move through a large group of college-aged boys who are shouting and high-fiving drunkenly. Her grip tightens.

"I've got you," Hannah reminds her. "You're okay."

Just then, a flock of young women rushes past, their ponytails and backpacks banging the sides of her body. Another hurricane of preteens is hot behind them, leaving a trail of sticky breath and indistinguishable squeals. She watches their path and realizes that they are all angling for the Miller Lite stage, which has just erupted in brilliant white light.

"Whoa," Hannah says, noticing too. "Who's playing over there?"

A rapper, she thought. But the name that flashes on the big LED screens flanking the stage says otherwise.

"No way," Hannah says, halting. The imperative of peeing forgotten for both of them.

Later, they would learn that the rapper had pulled out last minute with laryngitis. *He* had been a surprise replacement, and what a surprise he is. He struts out onto the stage and the crowd, which has grown much bigger than all the others, ripples with screams and applause. Just a week ago, a documentary had been released about his life: the tragedy of his sister's death, the terrible acid attack that broke his band apart. More recently, the death of his mother, for which the CEO of his record label held a lovely funeral service. But he emerged victorious and beloved, and his upcoming album, which has already garnered a record number of presales following the release of the documentary, would be coming out in ten days.

She cannot take her eyes off him. He still carries the same power she remembers, but there is an ease and comfort to his movements now—something that only comes from doing the same thing over and over again. He has lost the nervous edge that he once possessed, replaced by a haughty kind of relaxation. He is, she notes, a professional. Watching him on stage, it is clear: This is where he belongs.

A whirlpool of bodies at the front of the crowd reaches out their hands to him, shrieking in drunk delight. He kneels down and lets one of them unbutton his shirt to the chest, revealing a tattoo of a meteor just under his collarbone. Someone proffers a beer—he downs it, then pours the remaining few drops over his head. The crowd goes wild.

"This one's for all the fans who have been with me since day one," he breathes into the mic. "You know who you are. I fucking love you!"

It is the first song she ever heard; the same song the boys performed in the video she saw online. Back then, the boys had been young and their voices reflected it, although at the time, she thought them the best singers in the world. Now, his is the only voice that remains and he takes the place of all four, his sensual croons reshaping the song. A bittersweet feeling builds within her as she remembers the magic of discovering them for the first time, the heady rush of first love and the sour regret for all the things done and undone. It is no longer the same song she remembers, but still, she recognizes it, just as she recognizes herself as she listens to it: the past her who needed them and the current her who stands here today, both of these selves activated by this song, the current self thanking the past self for surviving, for remaining open to love and light.

She sees the boys clearly, as they first appeared to her: the silver-haired sylph who moved in cursive; the honey-voiced alto with a chest as big as a drum; the laughing funny boy with a high school athlete's charm; and him, a menace and an intoxication. A home, if only for a short while. Listening to the song now, it sounds both familiar and entirely unknowable—the boys were beautiful and bright for all that they promised, but false, too. Back then, she had wanted to take a bit of the light that lived in them for herself. Now, she understands: Nothing so beautiful can also be real.

She turns to Hannah, who is also staring at the stage with a distant expression on her face. "Should we get closer? For old time's sake?"

"I think I'm okay," Hannah says. "I can see fine from here."

She smiles. "Me, too."

ACKNOWLEDGMENTS

Endless thanks to my editor Caroline Bleeke, whose perceptive guidance and care made this novel and its characters sing. It is a forever joy to work with you! My incredible agent, Stephanie Delman, who I am certain possesses actual superpowers. My wonderful UK editors, Lily Cooper and Nalisha Vansia, for your brilliant insights and collaboration, and everyone at Penguin Michael Joseph.

Allison Malecha, Elizabeth Pratt, Khalid McCalla, and the mighty team at Trellis Literary.

Megan Lynch, Mary Retta, Claire McLaughlin, Clay Smith, Laywan Kwan, Leah Carlson-Stanisic, Sydney Jeon, Emily Walters, Ryan T. Jenkins, Eva Diaz, Maris Tasaka, and everyone at Flatiron working on behalf of this book.

Yaddo, which served as a much-needed respite while I finished revisions.

The amazing dance instructors at Ballet Austin and Evenground Dance Studio for sharing their knowledge, vocabulary, and moves.

My friends near, far, wherever you are. Like Minnie, I tend to burrow deep into a hole during times of pain. Thank you for pulling me out of those many holes. For supporting me, challenging me, inspiring me, eating with me, hugging me. Extra thanks to Ryan and Mala for reading early drafts of this work and sharing their thoughts. Nancy, for reasons you know.

My mom and dad, of whom I am superfans. My family in China.

Joe, who turns up all the colors of my world to their brightest hues. Maebe, who we miss every day.

Finally, I would like to thank all the people I have met at concerts (most notably at Carly Rae Jepsen, where a group of sweet boys took me out dancing afterward)—the ones who belted out every word and danced with their whole souls, who gave me a reason to write this book. It has been an honor to scream, laugh, weep, and dissolve with you all.

LINER NOTES

The poem that Minnie recites on page 5 is "To the One Who is Reading Me" by Jorge Luis Borges.

The phrase "purple, lemon, baby blue, and gold" on page 8 comes from the song "Cave-o-sapien" by Wolf Parade.

Faye's joke about palm trees on page 46 is something I heard my friend Itzel Basualdo once say.

Minnie's message to Halo on page 92 is inspired by a comment I saw on a livestream by J-Hope of BTS.

The use of "Remoras" as a name for a group of parasitic fans comes from the *Johnny Depp v. Amber Heard* defamation trial, where a former friend of Depp's testified that the disgraced actor would insult his fans by comparing them to suckerfish. Ironically, it was those very fans who spearheaded much of the vilification and cyberbullying of Heard and shifted public sentiment in favor of Depp—even after learning of the actor's pejorative nickname for them.

The anecdote on page 98 is based on a real incident from 2019, in which a young Japanese pop star was followed to her home by a stalker who was able to identify a train station in her selfie.

The song Akash plays for Minnie on page 129 is "Dr Strangeluv" by Blonde Redhead.

The chapter "Her" was inspired by *Beloved* by Toni Morrison, which I truly believe is one of the best books ever written.

Faye's story on page 270 and the final confrontation with her mother is a reference to the short story "The Painted Skin" by Pu Songling. The epigraph in the beginning is a quote from him regarding this story.

Eason's last question to The Duke on page 285 was inspired by a question Yoon Jeonghan asks during episode 3, season 2, of *In the Soop: Seventeen*, translated into English: "At the end of waiting, is there beauty?"

ABOUT THE AUTHOR

Jenny Tinghui Zhang is the author of the novels *Superfan* and *Four Treasures of the Sky*, named an Idaho Book of the Year and short- and longlisted for the Chautauqua Prize, the Dublin Literary Award, the Carnegie Medal for Excellence in Fiction, and the VCU Cabell First Novelist Award. Her work has appeared in *The Cut, Foreign Policy, The New York Times, Texas Highways*, and elsewhere. She is a National Book Foundation 5 Under 35 honoree and has received support from Yaddo, Kundiman, VONA/Voices, Tin House, and the University of Wyoming, where she completed her MFA.